TRAITOR ANGELS

Also by Anne Blankman
Prisoner of Night and Fog
Conspiracy of Blood and Smoke

TRAITOR

ANGELS

ANNE BLANKMAN

BALZER + BRAY
An Imprint of HarperCollinsPublishers

Balzer + Bray is an imprint of HarperCollins Publishers.

Traitor Angels
Copyright © 2016 by Anne Blankman Cizenski
All rights reserved. Printed in the United States of America.
No part of this book may be used or reproduced in any manner whatsoever
without written permission except in the case of brief quotations embodied
in critical articles and reviews. For information address HarperCollins
Children's Books, a division of HarperCollins Publishers, 195 Broadway,
New York, NY 10007.
www.epicreads.com

MAY - 5 2016   ISBN 978-0-06-227887-6

Typography by Michelle Taormina
16 17 18 19 20   CG/RRDH   10 9 8 7 6 5 4 3 2 1

First Edition

To two of the "traitor angels" in my life—Lynn and Peter:
readers, writers, and beloved parents.
Thank you for my beautiful childhood.

Part

One

OUT OF THE DEEP

The mind is its own place, and in it self
Can make a Heav'n of Hell, a Hell of Heav'n.
—John Milton, Paradise Lost, Book I

One

"IN THIS EARTHLY LIFE," MY FATHER OFTEN SAID to me, "we move with real or willful blindness. But only one way leads to true darkness."

I puzzled over his words whenever I descended into the cellar. There the blackness was absolute, but I was accustomed to moving in the dark. That summer morning, I dipped a cup into a barrel of sand, listening to the grains sifting together against the vessel's earthenware sides. Soon it would be time to sprinkle the sand across the pages covered with my father's poetry, to prevent the ink from smearing, and thus to capture his words forever. As soon as I joined him upstairs, he would begin dictating to me, his story transporting my mind from myself into a strange and new world.

"Elizabeth!" our cook-maid, Luce, hollered down the cellar steps. "Your father's waiting for you!"

"I'm coming!" I clapped the lid onto the barrel. Somewhere above me church bells were ringing, the sunrise chimes summoning farmers to their fields. The mingled scents from bins of potatoes and damp stone walls wafted to my nose, and beneath the thin soles of my shoes I sensed the unevenness of the packed dirt floor.

Every morning I visited the cellar without a candle because I wanted to understand how it felt to be my father—locked in an endless darkness, dependent on his other senses to survive. Some of my sisters thought I was mad; Mary despised the dark, and once she fetched an apronful of potatoes, she always raced back toward the slivers of daylight shining around the edges of the door at the top of the steps. Not me. I was my father's daughter, after all, and night held no terror for us. Our fears were made of kings and nooses.

Stop it. I couldn't let my thoughts slither into that old, familiar pit again. Father was alive. As long as he did nothing to regain the king's attention, he would remain that way.

I went up the stairs, trailing my hand along the wall for balance. In the kitchen Luce was stirring a pot that hung over the fire. Beneath her white cap, her lined face was flushed from the heat of the flames. She sent me an annoyed look.

"Have you been rummaging about in the cellar again without a candle?" she asked. "You'll break your neck one of these days, Miss Elizabeth," she went on without waiting for my response. "You'd best see to your father; he's been asking for you."

"Yes, Luce."

Although my stomach rumbled, I hurried to Father's sitting room before breaking my fast. My shoes clacked on the bare floorboards—a poor man's sound, for we didn't have the money to buy rugs. Even the whitewashed plaster walls were a silent testament to the meager state of our family purse; they ought to have been covered with striped paper or the strips of fabric that the genteel poor used for decoration. Instead they were unadorned except for iron brackets holding cheap tallow candles.

Father sat by the window in his private sitting room, his chair turned so he could feel the first shafts of sunlight on his face. Silver strands glinted in his shoulder-length auburn hair and wrinkles scored his pale cheeks. He wore his usual clothes: doublet, breeches, stockings, and shoes with wide metal buckles, all in black, so unlike the greens, blues, and reds of the men who now sat on Parliament's benches.

Once my father's dress had been indistinguishable from that of the political leaders he used to work with. They had seemed so alike, these revolutionaries in their clothes of Puritan black, that my then-childish eyes couldn't always tell Father's colleagues apart.

But that was before the government collapsed and a king was placed again on England's throne. Before the new leaders had called Father a traitor.

"Ah, Elizabeth," Father said. "You have such a quick step, it must be you. Let me see you, daughter."

Obediently I crouched before him and did not move as he ran his hands over my face, tracing the swell of my cheek, the length of my nose. I gazed at his pale blue eyes filmed over with a thin layer of white. His eyes never met mine, of course. If only he could see me, even once—then maybe he'd tell me the reasons behind my unusual upbringing. As a child I'd sat beside him on hundreds of mornings, at first learning to read and write; later mastering Latin, Greek, Hebrew, and Italian; then studying the great philosophers such as Plato and Cicero. My education was a replica of the lessons Father had given his students when he was a young teacher. His *male* students, for he had taught me as though I were a boy.

But I doubted he'd ever tell me anything, for I must be frozen forever in his mind as a toddler, which was how old I had been when the last sliver of vision in his right eye had darkened to black. I swallowed down my disappointment.

He dropped his hands into his lap. "I've been composing lines in my head for hours. Elizabeth, I think I've done it at last. This poem will be my masterpiece."

I sighed. Not this impossible hope again. Father's writing might be beautiful, but the story's simplicity would surely prevent it from being well received, let alone considered a masterpiece.

I sat down at the writing table. "Of course your poem will be wonderful." I shifted uncomfortably.

Father's poem was a ten-book epic centered on the oldest tale of all: the origins of mankind. Satan and his band of angels attempt to overthrow God's rule and are cast out of Heaven, so Satan decides to infiltrate Earth and corrupt its only human inhabitants, Adam and Eve—which he does, ushering evil into our fallen world forever. A straightforward tale, written in the English tongue, and utterly unlike my father's earlier elegant Latin elegies and fiery political tracts.

"Let's get to work," Father said. "The minutes pass too quickly, and it won't be long before your stepmother and sisters are awake and we'll have no more peace for the rest of the day."

Smiling, I dipped my quill into a pot of ink. These early hours, when Father and I were closeted in his study with only words for companionship, felt like coins clenched in my fist: valuable and rare. Since we had fled last year to this village, Chalfont St. Giles, to escape the plague in London, he had altered his writing habits; he used to write only during the winter, saying the cold stirred his creativity. Of late, however, he had taken to writing year-round and seemed determined to work on *Paradise Lost* constantly, regardless of the weather.

"It isn't their fault they don't understand," I said. I sneaked a look at him, even though I knew he couldn't see me. "Sometimes I don't, either, Father—understand why you're educating me, I mean."

"Someday you'll learn my reasons," he said. "Until then, you must trust in me."

"My faith in you will never be shaken," I assured him, but he shook his head.

"Untested faith is not faith, but ignorance," he said. "I wouldn't wish such an easy but meaningless existence for you." He took a deep breath. "Now we must plunge into Satan's world."

Then he spoke in such a rush I couldn't think; could only cling to his words and scribble them down. "His ponderous shield / Ethereal temper, massy, large and round," he dictated in a breathless gasp, slicing the air with his hand to signal a line break. My fingers flew across the page. I recognized these verses; he was revising a section he had written last winter. By this point, Satan has escaped from the flaming lake and is moving toward the shore. The shield he wears on his back looks as big and bright as the moon a man would see when peering through a telescope at the night sky. Then Satan calls his band of rebel angels closer to hear his plans to invade God's newest creation, Earth.

My quill paused on its journey across a page. Whenever we worked on this section, I found myself wondering about the man looking through a telescope, whom my father called a "Tuscan artist." Why make this man a citizen of Tuscany when Father was writing in English for the English populace?

Before I could puzzle over it further, I realized my father had stopped speaking. As usual he had dictated about fifty lines in a thunderous cascade, then halted without warning. He sat with his head bowed, lost in thought.

I recognized the dismissal. It was time to fetch his morning meal. Hastily I sprinkled sand across the pages and left them to dry on the writing table before leaving the room. As I stepped into the kitchen, my sister Mary thrust a bowl of stew into my hands. "Eat up, for pity's sake!" She ran anxious fingers down the front of her bodice, smoothing imaginary wrinkles. "Betty said we could go into the village to buy bread, and if we time things properly, we may bump into Mr. Sutton. He usually goes for a walk in the early morning."

I groaned and dropped onto a stool. Francis Sutton was the squire's son and, for reasons I couldn't understand, he seemed to think he was irresistible to all the females in the village. "Then I'll tarry, so we can avoid him."

"Elizabeth!" Mary flung herself down beside me. Our sisters, Anne and Deborah, watched wide-eyed from their stools next to the hearth. "Don't be so heartless! You know I can't go alone, and Deborah has to finish mending the table linens."

She didn't say why Anne couldn't accompany her—she didn't

have to. Unbidden, my gaze slid over to my eldest sister. She had stood, and one hand gripped the seat of her stool for support, the whiteness of her knuckles betraying the effort it cost her to remain upright. Every evening when I helped Anne change into her nightdress, I saw the uneven lengths of her legs, the muscles wasted and spindly, the flesh ghost white. As always, I had to look away, my eyes stinging.

"How can you be so cruel about Mr. Sutton?" Mary wailed.

"I was teasing." Partly. "I can't go anyway—I have to bring Father his food."

"I'll do it," our stepmother said in her quiet voice that always reminded me of water running in a creek bed, clear and clean but icy cold. Betty brushed past me to pick up Father's tray from the table in the middle of the room, where Luce was chopping vegetables.

Saying nothing, I studied my stepmother from the corner of my eye. A white cap covered the red hair she had scraped into a bun. Her thin face was set in the habitual expression of distaste it assumed whenever she dealt with me.

Quickly I turned my attention to my stew, trying to ignore the bitter taste rising in the back of my throat. As soon as the door closed behind Betty, Mary grumbled, "You know she'll take credit for the stew, Luce, although you cooked it."

"Hush." Luce wiped her hands on her apron. "There may be bad blood between you girls and your stepmother, but you still ought to show her respect." She trudged to the back door, stopping to glance at me. "I'm checking the pennyroyal in the garden. I don't want you saying nasty things about Mistress Milton while I'm gone, do you understand?"

I hitched a shoulder in halfhearted acquiescence, pushing around the carrot slices in my bowl with my spoon. Fine. I wouldn't utter a word about Betty. But I *would* think about her. Her narrowed eyes watching me slip from the house once darkness descended, dressed in boys' clothes, a sword gleaming silver at my side. As soon as she had married Father three years ago, she'd learned that I practiced sword fighting every night, and had since I was a small child, at Father's command. What she didn't know was why. In fact, none of us did but Father. When I pressed him once for an explanation, he squeezed my hand. *Elizabeth, a veil covers the world, obscuring our sight,* he replied. *I'm training you to keep it safe or to cut it—only time will determine which you must do.* All I could think was that his plans must involve his political past—and whatever he intended me to do sounded terribly important. And this had made my heart swell with pride.

Mary's plaintive voice interrupted my memories. "Elizabeth, I have to find opportunities to see Mr. Sutton. You know how Father says he hasn't any money for our dowries, even though he keeps dozens of expensive books. It's up to *us* to secure our futures."

Suppressing a sigh, I surveyed my sisters. It was like looking at reflections of myself: chestnut-brown hair that peeked out from beneath white caps, freckles sprinkled across their noses like spices in milk, identical blue eyes. Only a couple of years apiece separated the four of us—Anne was twenty, Mary nearly eighteen, I sixteen, and Deborah fourteen—and between our similar appearances and our Puritan garb of cheap linsey-woolsey, we were often lumped together as "the Milton daughters." I was all too aware, however, how different I was from my sisters. Just because I had no inclination for romance, though, didn't mean my sisters should be denied.

Besides, eventually we would all have to be married off—or we'd be dependent on our relatives or the almshouse to survive. Each option turned my stomach, which was why I rarely let myself think about the future. I set my bowl down with a clatter. I wasn't hungry anymore.

"Very well," I said. "I'll accompany you."

Mary squealed and flung her arms around my neck. "You're a darling! Let's be off at once. Deborah doesn't mind doing the washing up—do you, Deborah?"

"Actually—" Deborah began, but Mary had already seized my hand and pulled me from the house. I couldn't help laughing as we practically flew through the gardens, the strings of our caps fluttering behind us. Mary jerked open the gate and we started down the dirt road. I glanced over my shoulder. The sun had risen behind our small brick cottage, turning the structure into a black mass rimmed with gold. I could faintly make out the white oval of Anne's face; she had managed to hobble to the door to wave farewell. I waved back and caught the gleam of her smile before Mary tugged on my hand again, forcing me to follow her.

"Let's head for the woods," she said. "He often walks there." She aimed a warning look at me. "And do keep a civil tongue in your head, won't you?"

"That won't be easy," I said, and then laughed when she looked horrified. "Mary, I spoke in jest! Naturally I'll be polite to him!"

"One never knows with you," she muttered, then smiled and slipped her arm through mine. "He's so charming, isn't he? And such a learned gentleman—he just finished his university studies at Oxford, and I daresay his father will give him his own estate when he gets married."

Inwardly rolling my eyes, I listened to Mary chatter as we walked along the road. Fields feathered out on either side of us. Among the sheaves of wheat I glimpsed the white flashes of the farmers' shirts as they moved among the rows of crops, which looked straggly and withered even to my citified eyes. Our steps kicked up clouds of dust. I coughed, trying to ignore the burning in my throat. This so-called Year of the Devil, 1666, was certainly living up to its name. So far we'd suffered through a virulent plague that had spread through London like wildfire, and a year-long drought, which had desiccated the countryside until the leaves and grass were as brittle as parchment.

"This dust is unbearable!" I sputtered.

Mary grabbed my arm. "Don't complain!" She cast a nervous look at the sky, still flooded with pink and yellow at this early hour. "We don't know what else could happen if . . ."

She let the words trail off, but she didn't need to complete her thought. I understood. If we angered God, he might have another disaster in store for us: a new wave of the plague, perhaps, or repetitions of the comets that had blazed across the skies two years ago and frightened so many Londoners half out of their wits—for some believed that falling stars were evidence of God's displeasure with us.

I shivered. "I won't say anything else."

As we neared the woods, I breathed in the rich, loamy scent of soil.

"I wonder if it's possible to calculate the age of these trees," I said. "They must be very old to have grown so tall."

Mary made an impatient sound in her throat. "What does that matter—there he is!" she interrupted herself, pinching her cheeks to force color into them. "How do I look? I ought to have changed clothes!"

"Why?" I asked, peering through the interlocking tree branches. Francis Sutton was striding across the field toward us, whistling a jaunty tune I didn't recognize. Like most of the well-to-do gentlemen in Chalfont, he wore sober clothes of black wool. Despite myself, I had to admit he was handsome, with his fair hair and wide-set eyes. "Mary, all of our gowns are brown or green! Mr. Sutton is hardly likely to be more smitten with you if you wear one color instead of the other."

"Hush. No! Laugh as though I've said something amusing."

Dutifully, I burst into gales of laughter. Mary threw me an exasperated look. "Try not to sound as though you've lost your reason. Oh, he's coming! Be quiet."

"With pleasure," I said, and subsided into silence.

Francis wove between the trees toward us. His teeth flashed white in a broad grin. "Miss Mary, what a lovely surprise. They say there are no rays more brilliant than the sun's, but truly, your smile puts the sun to shame."

Was he really so addle-brained that he believed such ridiculous compliments would capture a girl's heart? I glanced at Mary, who had blushed to the roots of her hair and was giggling as Francis leaned over her proffered hand to kiss it. Hmm. Apparently these sorts of pretty words did work.

Francis straightened and nodded briskly in my direction. "Miss Elizabeth." His tone was flat.

I jerked my head in the barest suggestion of a nod. "Mr. Sutton."

He turned to Mary. "And what delightful set of circumstances has placed us in each other's path on this fine morning?"

I tried to hold in my laugh, but this made the trapped air burn in my chest and set off a coughing fit. As I doubled over, wheezing, tears smarting in my eyes, I heard Mary saying, "You must excuse my sister. She's . . . er . . . not accustomed to polite company."

"So it would seem," Francis murmured. "Speaking of company, that reminds me of interesting news I just heard in the village—your family should expect company of your own today."

"What do you mean?" Mary asked. "We haven't received word of any visitors."

"Nevertheless, you have one. A man—he's a foreigner, so I don't presume to call him a gentleman—this man, as I say, arrived at the Rose Inn last night. He said he planned to rest so he could present himself favorably to your father when he calls upon him this morning."

"What could a foreigner want with our father?" Mary asked. "He's merely a poet."

"He didn't use to be," Francis said gently, and heat rushed into my cheeks. He was right, of course. Once Father had been the most important political writer in the land. His revolutionary tracts had made him both reviled and adored throughout Europe. He believed that countries should be ruled by the people, not monarchs, and that religion had no place in government. Some seventeen years ago, after civil war had swept across our country and Mr. Oliver Cromwell had assembled a new government,

14

Father had been a logical choice for Latin secretary, the official in charge of diplomatic correspondence with other countries. After the government had crumbled, though, Father was branded a traitor to the nation. Only his frail health and the intervention of several of his friends kept his neck out of the hangman's noose.

I looked at Francis. "Are you certain this foreigner came here to see our father?"

Francis nodded. "He said he wished to visit upon the man they call 'the notorious John Milton.'"

I stiffened. "The notorious Milton" was the name by which my father was known throughout Europe to his political detractors, those who decried his ideals of revolution and parliamentary government.

So this foreigner was an enemy.

Mary's eyes met mine. In the green-tinted shadows cast by the trees, I could see she had gone pale. "Elizabeth—" she started to say, but I was already moving. The trees whipped past, slender black lines that I had to weave around until I reached the fields. The rippling golden grasses slapped my skirts, and a few farmers turned to call a greeting to me as I rushed by them. I didn't stop to answer.

By the time I reached the road, I was running.

Two

THE ROSE INN WAS A RAMSHACKLE WOODEN structure that stood in the middle of the village. From the front steps, I cast a wary glance over my shoulder. The dusty lane seemed deserted; the sprinkling of wooden houses were quiet, their shutters open in a futile attempt to catch a soothing breeze. No servants foraged in the gardens for salad greens; no children played jacks in the road. The villagers must still be breaking their fast before beginning their day's work. Thank goodness we Miltons and Francis were early risers; there'd be fewer people to witness what I was about to do. I couldn't have gone home to warn Father, of course—given his weak health, I wasn't sure what this piece of news might do to him. No, dealing with the stranger would have to be up to me.

Taking a steadying breath, I pushed the door open and stepped inside. The dining room was empty, the scarred wooden tables cleared from last night's supper. Tobacco smoke still laced the air, pungent and sickly sweet. The candles in their wall brackets were unlit, leaving the weak beams of sunlight straggling through the windows as the sole source of illumination.

For a moment, I stood still. Once I confronted this foreigner, there could be no turning back. I would have gone to a man's inn chamber, unchaperoned, and that alone was enough to blacken my reputation forever, if anyone learned of it. Through the walls, I heard men's laughter. Old Tom, the proprietor, and his cook, no doubt, chuckling over a shared joke as they carried bottles of sack up from the cellar.

The sound pulled me back to myself. I had to get out of there before someone saw me. I crept up the winding stairs, wincing when they creaked. The men's laughter seemed to reach up the steps after me. I quickened my pace until I was nearly running.

Along the second-floor corridor, the doors to each of the four rooms were closed. I pushed the nearest one open. The curtains hadn't been drawn, and enough light flowed through the window for me to see the neatly made bed. No bags, no spare boots lying on the floor, no water gleaming in the basin on a side table. Nobody was staying in this room.

The next chamber was empty, too. Sunlight pushed through the closed curtains, leaving the room in half darkness. Someone had draped two brown leather bags across the foot of the bed, and a black velvet doublet, the cuffs trimmed in lace, lay on top of the wooden clothespress. My heart beat faster. This must be the foreigner's room—I couldn't imagine the Rose had any other guests; visitors rarely came to our small village, and those who did tended to be fellow Puritans, who wouldn't have dared to wear lace.

I slipped into the room, pulling the door closed behind me. Where could this foreigner be? I had to figure it out, and fast, before he had a chance to go to my family's home and trouble Father. After all these years of political exile and creeping poverty, my father deserved to live out his final years in peace. And I'd be cursed before I let anyone bother him.

Maybe the foreigner's possessions would give me a clue as to where he'd gone. I rifled through his bags. Inside the first one was a peculiar-looking cylinder. It was about a foot long, its worn leather surface stamped with a gold filigree design. One end was capped with a curved piece of thick glass. What sort of instrument was this? I'd never seen anything like it.

Sounds of footsteps wafted from the stairs—someone was coming.

I shoved the instrument into the bag, then spun around to survey the room, checking one final time to make certain everything was in place.

I ran my hands up my arms. Through the woolen fabric, I could feel the hard length of the knives I strapped to my forearms every morning, a practice my father had insisted on years ago, although he'd never told me the reason. Now I was glad for his caution. No matter how the foreigner reacted when he found me in his room, I'd be ready for him.

The footsteps stopped outside the chamber door.

I darted to the wall, to a spot where I'd be concealed once the door swung open. Better see if he was unarmed before I announced my presence.

My pulse thundered in my ears as I watched the doorknob turn. A shadowy figure entered the room, the door whispering shut behind him. He carried a candle, its flame licking gold fingers across his face. In the muted dimness, I caught the impression of a dark eye and the smooth curve of a cheek. I didn't recognize him—it had to be the foreigner. He set the candle into a holder on the table beside the bed.

Then he straightened and stood with his back to me, his head cocked to the side, as if listening. He wore no hat. His hair fell to his shoulders; it was raven black and straight, too real looking to be anything but his own. Strange. I would expect any man wealthy enough to travel to another country would sport a shorn head covered with a wig of flowing curls, like a nobleman. Perhaps foreign fashions differed from ours. His midnight-blue doublet didn't look foreign, though, merely rich, for it glittered with an intricately stitched pattern in silver and red threads. When he raised his hand to brush his hair out of his eyes, a gold band inlaid with a red stone on his index finger winked at me.

"I can hear you breathing," he said.

He knew I was in here!

"You can help yourself to anything you like, of course," he continued, keeping his back to me. He sounded pleasant, as if he were discussing nothing more troubling than our recent drought. "But I feel compelled to warn you that I'll hunt you down and retrieve what belongs to me. It's a matter of pride, you see. I don't mind your robbing me when I can't reach my sword"—he nodded at his bag, and I spied the tip of something silver gleaming from beneath it—"but I can't permit you to hold on to my possessions."

Either he was out of his wits to make such lighthearted comments when he believed he was being robbed—or he relished the prospect of tangling with a criminal.

"Why would I want to steal from you?" I asked quietly.

He heaved a sigh, as if he found all of this tiresome. "I may be unversed in English social customs, but surely I haven't been such a boorish guest that the innkeeper sent an assassin to my room to dispatch me. Therefore, you must be a thief. Take what you please, but remember I'll find you by nightfall."

The man was brave, I had to concede that much. I wrapped my hand around my wrist, in case I needed to unbutton my cuff and pull my knife free.

"I'm not here to rob you," I said.

He turned around. I started in surprise. He was younger than I had thought, perhaps seventeen or eighteen. His skin had been painted olive by a stronger sun than ours, and his brows were black slashes. His face was handsome enough, I supposed, and it was made up of strong angles and lines; there was no softness to him. He wore no powder on his cheeks; no cerise tinted his lips. Despite the finery of his clothes, this was no harmless fop.

My fingers tightened on my cuff. A twist of the fabric and the knife would be in my hand. "Why do you seek Mr. Milton?"

His expression remained impassive. "I've come here at his command."

Impossible. These days, my father had no dealings with foreigners. I glared at the boy.

"You're a liar."

He rolled his eyes. "You're a trusting sort of person, aren't you." Turning away from me, he busied himself at the clothespress, removing clothes and tossing them onto the bed.

With one smooth movement, I unbuttoned my cuff and slid my knife free from its bindings. Its wooden handle, reassuring and familiar, dug into my palm.

"No," I said slowly. "I'm not a trusting sort of person."

Something in my voice must have alerted him, for he swung around, his gaze falling to the blade in my grasp. His face tightened, but he didn't say a word.

"My father has endured hell," I said. "After the king was crowned, my father spent months in prison and was threatened with execution. He's an old man of seven and fifty years, and he's been stone-blind for the last fourteen of them. He has *nothing* left but his writing and his family. Whatever business you have with him, you'll tell me first, because I won't permit anyone to trouble him."

He murmured something under his breath, then shook his head as if to clear it. "Your father . . . Then you must be Miss Elizabeth Milton."

How had he guessed which of Father's daughters I was? A chill skittered down my spine. I opened my mouth, to protest or confess I don't know which, but the answer must have been etched on my face because the boy continued, looking deadly serious, "Your father sent my master a letter. Mr. Milton's mixed up in a dangerous scheme, and he intends to drag both of us into it with him."

I fought the urge to laugh. My father would never involve me in something that could harm me. "You sound as confused about the English tongue as you are about our social customs. It's true my father once wrote revolutionary political tracts, but these days he focuses on classical poetry. He isn't part of some sort of scheme."

The boy glanced again at my knife. "Your father's letter is in my pocket. May I retrieve it for you or will you slash me to ribbons first?"

Wonderful, I'd been saddled with a jester. Silently I hitched a shoulder in permission. He reached into his breeches pocket, and I stepped closer. His expression gentled as he looked at me. "I'm not reaching for a weapon. I'd never hurt a lady."

A *lady*. This boy must have thought I was an idiot, if he believed I would swallow such ridiculous flattery.

He slipped a piece of paper from his pocket. "It's in Italian. Shall I read it to you or do you want to take it to your father for translation?"

"*I* can read it." I snatched the paper from him. By the glow of the candle, I was just able to make out the words.

The letter was dated 10 April 1666, some four months ago. The addressee was Signor Vincenzo Viviani of the Via Sant'Antonino in Florence. I recognized the careful handwriting as Deborah's, but the missive must have come from Father, for none of my sisters knew Italian. Both Mary and Deborah had been trained to read aloud to our father in different languages by sounding out the words but without any understanding of them. Father must have spelled out every letter for Deborah to copy. The paper shook in my hands. He hadn't trusted me enough to dictate the letter to me, although I spoke Italian fluently. For some reason, he had kept this correspondence a secret from me.

There *must* be a good explanation for Father's actions. I knew it in my bones.

But my chest still felt tight as I began reading.

Most illustrious and excellent Signor Viviani—

The time has come at last to immortalize our portentous secret. Years ago, I toiled to hide our clues in such a way that they would not disappear as a result of the ravages of time but could remain concealed forever. As you know, we cannot destroy the object that has brought us so much despair and heartbreak, but also the everlasting joy that comes with intellectual exploration.

For reasons you know all too well, I believe that the world isn't ready for the knowledge we would impart to it. Do not fear that our secret will slip into the hands of those who would destroy it—only learned men who are familiar with the intricacies of my life (and thus, who must be lovers of liberty, as we are, my dear Signor Viviani) will be capable of stringing together the clues.

To that end, I must ask that you send your young man to England posthaste. He and my daughter Elizabeth shall become guardians of our secret, as we always intended, and they must understand the grave task with which we entrust them before the Good Lord summons me from my earthly home.

I am your most humble and grateful servant,

John Milton

My head whipped up. *What?* Deborah must have been mistaken in her dictation . . . or perhaps my father was sliding into senility. Maybe the years of blindness and pounding headaches had finally eroded his grasp on his wits. My throat tightened. *Poor Father.* It was a wretched end for the man whom many had heralded as the greatest political writer of our age.

"Are you convinced?" the boy asked.

I started. I'd forgotten he was there. He was leaning against the wall, his posture relaxed, but the tightness around his eyes betrayed him. He was as anxious as I was.

"Yes, you've come at my father's invitation." The words felt sharp as knives as they traveled up my throat. Why hadn't Father told me of this stranger's impending arrival? And why had he summoned him in the first place? There was no "portentous secret," and even if there was, my father wouldn't have joined forces with an enemy to protect it.

Unless my father had been lying to me for months.

Three

I LOOKED AT THE FOREIGNER. IN THE HALF DARK-
ness, his eyes gleamed, catlike. I knew nothing about him, not
even his name. But I had to respect my father's wishes, even if I
didn't understand them.

"You're welcome to visit our house, sir," I said. "I can bring
you to my father now."

"Then we can leave straightaway—I've just come from settling my account with the innkeeper." Fleetingly I remembered
the men's laughter through the walls. So that had been this boy
and Old Tom, chuckling while they exchanged coins.

The boy bowed slightly from the waist. "I'm Antonio Viviani,
assistant to Signor Vincenzo Viviani, court mathematician to the
Grand Duke of Tuscany. My master and I are cousins—distant
cousins. I need to gather my things," he added, glancing at the
bags on his bed.

Tuscany. Was this Viviani related to the Tuscan Artist in *Paradise Lost*? Oh, who cared anyway? Father had deceived me. His stupid poem could molder into dust, as far as I was concerned.

In silence I waited while Viviani threw his clothes into his bags. Together we crept outside. Early-morning sunlight had burnished the dirt road with gold. In silence we trudged along its edge. Maybe the letter had been a mistake, written during one of Father's hideous headaches when pain blunted his reason. This Viviani could leave England on the next boat bound for Calais. And my father could continue to survive, forgotten.

"Your desire to protect your father is admirable," Viviani said, breaking into my thoughts. "Although I"—he hesitated—"I don't understand your . . ."

He trailed off, but I knew what he was trying to say. No doubt he thought I had reacted to his arrival with unwarranted vehemence. If we'd been an ordinary family, I would have agreed with him.

"You know about the recent war in my country?" I asked.

He nodded, his expression remote. I could imagine what he was thinking—the same thing that so many foreigners had thought when England descended into war some twenty years ago. They had called us barbaric, for we had done what few nations had dared to do: we had beheaded King Charles the First for dissolving Parliament and unleashing a civil war on us.

"My father's voice was one of the loudest supporting the king's execution. He even wrote about it in *The Tenure of Kings and Magistrates*, a month after the king was beheaded, trying to persuade others that the execution had been just." I kept my gaze trained on the fields, unable to look at this stranger and the condemnation I would surely see on his face. "That was seventeen years ago, and by then he had become the most celebrated political writer in the land. After the king was killed, Mr. Cromwell asked my father to serve in the new government."

From the corner of my eye, I saw Viviani nod. "I've heard of England's rebellion."

"The new government lasted only a decade before it fell apart," I said. "Then Parliament invited the dead king's son to return from exile in Europe. And my father was condemned as a regicide. Parliament meant him to be the twentieth and final man to be hanged for the crime of killing a king."

"Yet he still lives."

For a moment, I couldn't speak. The memories were too sharp. All at once I was a girl of ten again, terrified and bewildered, living with my maternal grandmother and wondering what had become of my father. He'd gone into hiding right before the old king's son had returned to our shores in 1660, and for months we'd awaited the dread news that he had been found and arrested.

When King Charles the Second rode triumphantly into London, my sisters and I stood in the street while the crowds cheered and threw flowers onto the cobblestones. Never had I seen such a man: a giant at six feet tall, about thirty years of age, with black hair curling to his shoulders and skin as dark as a Spaniard's. His silver garments dazzled my eyes, which were accustomed to years of Puritan black and brown.

Behind him rode another man in sumptuous garb, his long face framed by light brown hair. He blew me a kiss. I raised my hand to wave at him, but my grandmother's fierce whisper stopped me. The man was the second Duke of Buckingham, the king's dearest friend since childhood, she told me, and if I valued my father's life I would do well not to catch his attention, even if it was with something as innocent as responding to a blown kiss in the street.

Blinking hard, I forced the images back. Those chaotic days were long past, the regicides and suspected traitors dead or gone, except for my father, escaped to new lives on the Continent or in the New World. All I could let myself care about was the fact that we were alive. As long as we remained anonymous, we would stay that way.

"Yet he still lives," I repeated at last. "He had influential friends who lobbied for leniency, arguing that a blind poet posed no threat to our new king. After his name was removed from the death list, he returned to me and my sisters from wherever he'd been hiding in the city. He never told us where he'd gone. Soon after, the king's men came for him. He was imprisoned for three months."

I tensed, waiting for the inevitable comments—*Your father deserves his blindness, for that is God's punishment for his revolutionary past. His antimonarchy stance might be pardonable, but his approval of the king's execution is not.* They were remarks I'd heard countless times before.

But Viviani said nothing. His hat's brim shadowed his face, so I couldn't see his expression, but I heard the thoughtfulness in his tone when he finally spoke. "Your father has suffered greatly. I understand why you'd wish to protect him from anyone whose intentions you don't know."

"Th-thank you," I stammered.

We'd reached my family's cottage. Without a word, I ushered Viviani into the hall. The whitewashed plaster walls and bare floorboards must have told him we were poor, but his lip didn't curl in derision. Instead he stood by the door, waiting.

"My father's probably in his sitting room," I told him. "I'll take you—"

Footsteps clicked in the corridor. "Elizabeth? Who is this man?"

Recognizing the sharpness of Betty's voice, I stifled a sigh and turned. Betty stood in the doorway, her arms crossed over her chest. "This is Signor Antonio Viviani," I told her. "He's the assistant to the mathematician of the Grand Duke of Tuscany. Father has invited him here as our guest. Signor Viviani, this is my father's wife, Mrs. Milton."

Viviani's arm brushed mine as he swept off his hat and bowed to my stepmother. Her eyes flickered over him, widening as she took in his fine clothes.

"I apologize for the simplicity of our home," she murmured. "We weren't expecting you, Mr. Viviani."

He straightened. "Mrs. Milton, I realize my appearance must be a surprise. As I wasn't certain of the reception I'd receive when I arrived last night, I sought lodging at the village inn, but now I see my fears were unwarranted, as you've welcomed me so graciously."

I had to bite the inside of my cheek to keep from laughing. How cleverly he had forestalled my stepmother's protests over his arrival! I couldn't figure him out, for each moment seemed to draw forth a different part of his character, as though he were made of many shifting parts—like the interior of the newfangled clocks I'd seen once, orderly on the outside, a mass of whirring gears and pieces within.

"I'm afraid you'll find your accommodations somewhat rough," Betty said, "but you're most welcome to them. Elizabeth, he'll take your room and you may share with Anne. Get him settled."

"I must bring him to Father first." And clear up this matter before it went much further. I jerked my head at Viviani, signaling for him to follow me. With each step I took, I felt his eyes boring into the space between my shoulder blades. Could he tell how unaccustomed my family was to visitors? How unsophisticated we were? And why did I care what he thought anyway?

In the sitting room, my father was perched in his usual chair, a brazier of burning coals at his feet to warm his aching joints. Behind him stood his most prized possession—a glass-fronted bookcase, its shelves crammed with leather-bound volumes. The books were a terrible extravagance, but one both Father and I had thought was necessary. They were like air to us.

"Elizabeth?" Father's head turned in my direction. "Who's with you? Those aren't footsteps I know." His voice held a note of fear, and I hastened to his chair, taking his cold hands in mine.

"A young man called Antonio Viviani is here," I whispered. "He says you summoned him to England."

Father's weathered face split into a smile. "Viviani," he said under his breath. "Thanks be to God."

My mind whirled. "But . . . you always warned me not to enter into dealings with Catholics! Don't you remember? You said their nations have grown too powerful and pose a terrible danger to England's security. You told me their faith is the only one we mustn't tolerate."

"Don't question me, daughter." A dull red crept up Father's neck. "This young man's master and I have never met, but our task has tied us together for nearly thirty years."

"But, Father—"

"You're my child." He gritted the words out, as though they were bits of gravel trapped in his mouth. He leaned forward, a signal that I was supposed to come closer. I brought my face so near to his I could see the tiny lines radiating from the corners of his eyes. "It's your duty to obey me without dissent. To have you question me again in front of a stranger would grieve my heart."

I reared back as though he had slapped my face. "Father, I beg your forgiveness," I murmured.

He ignored me. "Sit down, Signor Viviani," he said in Italian, "and tell me about your life in Florence. I'm most eager to learn about your experiments. Elizabeth," he added, frowning, "surely your stepmother has need of your strong arms to stoke the kitchen fire."

The dismissal was so clear I couldn't pretend to mistake his meaning. Yet I remained kneeling at his feet and unable to move. This was horribly wrong. Not once had he shut me out. Until now. When he'd returned from prison, thin and exhausted, I'd sat with him in the evenings long after the supper dishes had been washed and while the candles burned low in their holders. I'd traced the shapes of the Hebrew letters his faltering fingers had written, and I'd parroted the Italian phrases he had taught me. *I* had been his special companion. No one else. And now he spoke to me as though I were no more than a serving girl.

Behind me, someone cleared his throat. From my crouched position, I whirled, nearly falling backward in my haste. Viviani stood by the window. There was something in his face I couldn't make out; it might have been pity.

Shame burned my cheeks. "Very well, Father. I'll leave you to your discussion."

I rushed from the room, ignoring Viviani's bow. Father's voice floated through the open door after me.

"When I was a bachelor, I visited the Italian city-states myself," he said in his impeccable Italian. He would share those stories with a stranger, when I ought to have been the one listening to his tales? "They are full of many wonders. Of all the cities I saw, I admired Florence the most for its elegance, not only the elegance of its language, but of its inhabitants' wit."

"It's a most learned city," Viviani agreed, but I barely heard him. A lever seemed to snap in my mind. *Florence.* Where this Antonio Viviani and his master resided and my father had stayed during the autumn of 1638—eight and twenty years ago. He'd said that a shared responsibility had bound him and Vincenzo Viviani for nearly thirty years. Did the origins of the supposed "portentous secret" date from this long-ago trip to Florence? And how, when my father seemed determined to keep his own counsel for now, could I convince him to tell me?

Four

AT THE END OF THE CORRIDOR, A LADDER
stretched up to two loft bedchambers. Clutching Viviani's bags,
I climbed it one-handed. Well, there was one bright piece to the
fact that my father and Viviani were closeted in his study, discussing whatever had been deemed too important for my ears: if
Viviani had been following me, I would have given him quite an
educational view up my skirts. Small favors, I supposed.

On the landing, both doors were closed. I slipped into my
room, on the right. Even in the faded sunlight, it was obvious the
room was a shabby box: the walls bare of decoration; the bed the
old-fashioned sort with a wooden frame and a poor man's mattress of straw, instead of wool or feathers.

I loved every inch of it.

This was the first place where I'd slept alone. Where I could
fling open my shutters and stare at the stars pinning back the vast

canopy of the heavens and wonder what secrets they concealed. Why did each constellation move around its center, but the stars within the grouping never rearranged themselves in a new order? And why couldn't I see the golden chain from which our earthly home dangled, like a pendant on a necklace? The world was clothed in mysteries.

And I, as a mere girl, had no right to yearn to decipher them. Celestial matters belonged squarely in the realm delegated to men. Father had told me so, when I'd been a child and he'd regaled me with tales about his month in Florence and the time he'd met the infamous man called Galileo, who'd been under house arrest for thinking differently about the motions of the heavenly bodies than the Inquisitors in Rome permitted. If I'd been a boy, perhaps I could have become a natural philosopher, someone who studies the workings of the world and designs experiments. As things were, I had to content myself with gazing at the stars.

But I knew, deep down, it would never be enough.

"Enough of this maudlin thinking," I muttered. I grabbed my spare shift, gown, and nightdress from the clothespress, then hesitated over the stack of pages I'd hidden beneath them. The pages were covered with my drawings of the constellations. I couldn't take the chance that Viviani would go through my things. Holding the stack of papers to my chest, I went to my sister's room next door and knocked.

Anne's dragging footsteps sounded from within her chamber. She opened the door, peering at me. "Wh-what—you—doing?" she asked, nodding at the clothing and papers cradled in my arms.

"Staying with you, but only temporarily," I said. "May I come in?"

"Y-yes. B-b-b . . ." Her voice faded, the muscles in her throat working as she struggled to push the words out. They wouldn't emerge, we knew, or if they did, they'd stream forth in an unintelligible garble. Frustration flickered across her face. She smacked the side of her head, and I caught her hand, my garments and pages falling to the floor.

"Don't!" I said in a fierce whisper. "Don't you dare hurt yourself! It's all right," I added as she started to cry. I grabbed her in a tight embrace, pressing our faces so close together I could feel the wetness of her tears on my cheek. "I understand you, Anne," I managed to say despite the lump in my throat. "Please don't be upset. I can understand what you're saying, I promise."

She made a low, distressed sound. As always, I wondered if her life would have been different if our mother hadn't died after Deborah's birth. Maybe our mother would have known how to help Anne learn to talk clearly or to read—at the least, she probably would have known how to comfort her. Our father didn't seem to, but then again, we'd suffered so many losses after Mother's death that he must have been overwhelmed. Six weeks after Mother died, our toddler brother, John, passed away from a fever, and only a few years later our father's second wife and their baby daughter died, too.

I pulled back in Anne's arms, forcing a smile. "I'm sorry to trespass on your privacy, but I could hardly stay in my bed when there's a man in it, could I?"

She gaped at me. "Ex-explain!"

"If you require explanation of why a man might be in a woman's bed, then perhaps you should ask Betty for another lecture on how it is between a man and a woman."

Anne looked horrified. Laughing, I wrapped my arm around

her shoulders and helped her hobble to the bed. She started laughing, too. After I'd guided her onto the edge of the mattress, I picked up my clothes and papers.

"We have a houseguest," I told her. "He's come from Florence at Father's invitation. And yes, he's handsome," I said quickly, knowing Anne would want to know. Her face brightened. "Probably, like most good-looking fellows, he knows it and is therefore insufferable." I held up the stack of papers. "May I hide these in your clothespress?"

She nodded. "Y-y-you show."

"You know I can't show these to anyone but you. Everyone else would mock me."

"We—we best."

I kissed her cheek so she wouldn't see the tears gathering in my eyes. "Yes, because we're best friends. Forever, Anne."

From the village the church tolled the hour, twelve slow notes that hovered in the air, each trembling before being swallowed by the next. It was time to fix the midday meal. I groaned, realizing I'd forgotten to buy bread from the baker. Betty would box my ears, no doubt.

"We'd better get to the kitchen," I said.

As always, when Anne clambered down the ladder after me her uneven legs buckled. From a few rungs below, I kept a steadying hand on her backside.

In the kitchen, Luce stood at the table, slicing a loaf of bread—someone, probably Mary, had remembered to go to the bakery—and Deborah was arranging sliced beef and sweetmeats on platters. Mary was fussing with a bowl of salad greens. Betty was nowhere to be seen.

"There you are!" Mary exclaimed. "I was wild with worry when you went racing off. This foreigner doesn't appear to be a bad sort, does he." She tugged on my cap strings, which had come undone. "I went outside and peeked at him and Father through the window. He's rather handsome."

"I suppose," I muttered. "Did you hear what he and Father were discussing—"

A sudden wild pummeling shook the back door in its frame. A man's voice shouted, "By God's grace, let me in!"

"Merciful heavens!" Mary flung the door open. Francis Sutton staggered into the kitchen. He wore no hat, and his blond hair streamed loose to his shoulders. Through the tangled strands, his face looked pale, his eyes frantic.

"You all must flee at once!" He whirled to Mary. "The king's men were just at my home, asking for directions to your cottage. Whatever they want with your family, it has to be for a grave offense, for their party numbered at least a dozen, and they must have ridden all night to arrive here so early. I beg of you, begone from here before it's too late."

Five

SHOCK BLEACHED THE INSIDE OF MY MIND BONE white. I stared at Francis, silently entreating him to repeat what he had said, as if hearing his announcement a second time would bring clarity.

The kitchen erupted in screams. Mary threw herself at Francis, shouting, "What's happening? I don't understand!" Deborah dropped the platter she'd been arranging. It shattered on the floor, flinging pottery shards and slices of beef everywhere. From her stool, Anne burst into tears. Luce stopped chopping vegetables, her knife raised in midstrike.

I stood stock-still. My thoughts were encased in ice, frozen on Francis's earlier words. They didn't make sense. The king's men would hardly travel eight leagues from London merely to come to our cottage. Father no longer mattered to them; he was a grain of sand in a shoe, an irritant easily ignored. Unless the king had finally changed his mind—

Something seemed to burst within the left side of my rib cage, and I let out a choked gasp. It must have happened at last—what we had feared and half expected for years. The king had decided to execute Father for his revolutionary past. There could be no other reason for his men to travel such a distance.

I ran to the back door. Nothing but banks of pennyroyal and chamomile, shriveling in the heat, and Francis's horse, gleaming with sweat and nosing at the grass. If the king's men were coming from Francis's estate, they would ride east across the countryside. Anxiety coiled in my stomach. We probably had minutes at the most before the king's men were upon us.

My sisters were still screaming, such a cacophony of sound I could scarcely think. "Be quiet, all of you!" I shouted.

At once the room froze into silence. Everyone stared at me— each face a mask of terror. I shook my head, trying to still the panicked thoughts rising in my mind like swarms of gnats. *Father will die. Father will die. Father will die.* How could I protect him? I had to do something.

In the sudden hush, I could hear Anne rasping for air. "Deborah, see to our sister," I ordered. "I must get Father away from here at once."

"I should return home." Francis tried to disentangle himself from Mary, but she clung to him, sobbing.

"Unhand him, Mary!" I snapped. "He needs to get out of here before the king's men arrive."

Mary released Francis as though he had turned to flame. I clasped his hand. "Thank you. I can never repay the debt my family owes you."

Without waiting for his response, I raced down the corridor toward the sitting rooms. In vain, I fumbled at my long sleeves, desperate to get at my knives, but the fabric fit too snugly. I tore at the shoulder laces until they broke. Then I yanked the sleeves from my arms, flinging them to the floor.

I barreled into my father's sitting room. Father and Viviani sat at the writing table, their heads close together. Betty, who had been pouring drinks, set the pitcher down with a thump. She and Viviani stared at me, while my father craned his neck, seeking the source of the racket.

"Elizabeth, what's the meaning of this interruption?" Betty demanded. Before I could respond, she turned to Viviani, saying, "I hope you'll forgive my stepdaughter's behavior. She isn't accustomed to visitors—"

"The king's men are on their way here," I interrupted. Viviani glanced at the knives strapped with leather bindings to my arms, and he half rose, his hand drifting to his waist, where his sword hung. "Francis Sutton said they stopped at his home, seeking directions," I added.

The color drained from my father's face. "Did they say why they were coming?"

"No." I dashed to the window. Beyond the glass, the fields looked ordinary: golden-toned sheaves of wheat, white flutters from the farmers' shirts as they moved among them. No sign of the king's men, but it couldn't be long now. What should I do? With shaking hands, I drew the curtains closed, the rattling of the rings on the rods loud in the quiet room.

"Father, we must get you away from here." I tugged on his hands, trying to get him to his feet. He staggered up, his hands gripping mine for guidance.

"Elizabeth," he said urgently, "you must promise to protect my poem. Keep it safe, or its secret will be lost forever—"

The distant thunder of horses' hooves interrupted him. Viviani and I shared a grim look.

"Let me help," he said. "I can carry your father to the woods."

"No!" Father shouted. "My future is of little consequence. It's the two of you who must survive at all costs. Signor Viviani, run to the woods and remain there until one of my daughters fetches you. Trust no one else."

A muscle clenched in Viviani's jaw. "I can't leave you in danger—"

"Remain and you have assured yourself of a painful death and no means for me and your master to carry out our mission," Father growled. *"Get out."*

Viviani sent me an agonized look. I nodded, sliding my knives from their straps and handing him one. "This will serve you better in the close quarters the woods afford," I said. "But let's pray you don't need it. Make for the copse of elms we passed on our way here. As soon as I can, I'll come to you."

"I won't leave a group of females and an elderly man alone," he whispered to me. "I promised my master I would help—"

"We have to follow my father's directions," I interrupted. *"Please,"* I added when Viviani remained motionless.

The word had a galvanizing effect; Viviani's head snapped up, his eyes focusing on mine. He nodded once, hard, then rushed from the room. I whirled on my father, who was already issuing more instructions.

"Betty, hide Signor Viviani's belongings," he was saying.

"The king's men mustn't suspect he's been here. We'll lie—all of us. We'll say he may have stopped in the village, but he never came here. We haven't seen him. Is that understood?" His expression was so fierce I didn't dare argue. I murmured my assent.

As my stepmother hurried from the room, my sisters dashed in, pale faced and crying. The thud of horses' hooves pounding on a dirt road was coming closer. From outside, a man shouted something unintelligible. We were almost out of time.

"Father, they can't take you from us!" Deborah cried.

An emotion I couldn't identify rippled across my father's face; it might have been regret.

"I have been preparing for this day for several years," he said. "There's no shame in death, daughter, only shame in fearing God's final judgment. I can meet mine with a clear conscience. Elizabeth, what are you wearing?" he asked abruptly.

I looked down at my clothes. "A brown dress, Father, but I don't—"

"Then you can masquerade as a servant," he interrupted. "A village girl, mind, not a member of our household. Such subterfuge might keep you safe. If we're fortunate, they don't know how many daughters I have."

My mind barely grasped his words. Outside, several men shouted to one another, their words muffled by the walls separating us. I dashed to the window again and peered through the gap between the curtains.

In the front garden a dozen men were sliding off their horses. The men's faces were flushed from exertion. None wore the soldiers' redcoat uniform I had expected. Instead, the men were dressed in fine riding clothes: leather boots, doublets and breeches in a dazzling array of colors—peach, pale blue, grass green. Each man carried a sword at his waist.

I saw at once how Francis had known they were king's men: beneath their broad-brimmed hats they sported the shaven heads of noblemen, having foregone their usual wigs for the journey. Everyone knew the aristocrats were loyal to the king; these men were our enemies. As one, they crossed the yard, their strides quick with purpose.

"Merciful Lord," I breathed. "They're here."

The wind kicked up, knocking one man's hat away. As he walked closer, my heart surged into my throat. I knew this man's long, slender face, even though it wasn't framed by its usual wig of light brown curls. I had seen him often enough when he played ninepins in Hyde Park while my sisters and I huddled under the trees, watching the fine people all around us. Even if I hadn't seen him occasionally during the past six years, though, I would have recognized him as the man who had ridden behind the king on his triumphant return to London—the man in beautiful garments of silver and lace who had blown me a kiss.

It was George Villiers, the second Duke of Buckingham, one of the best-known men in the country. And the dearest friend of the king.

Six

I JUMPED AWAY FROM THE CURTAINS. "IT'S BUCK—"

The front door burst open. I sprang in front of my father, gripping his shoulder and trying to hold him in place. "Let me protect you," I said. With my free hand, I clutched my knife. A single sickening slice and one of our enemies would be dead. But there would still be eleven remaining, and I couldn't possibly fight them all. Dear God, what was going to happen to us?

Father pushed me away, his action startling me so much that the knife skittered out of my grasp. It hit the floor with a clang. I dropped to my hands and knees to retrieve it, but Father grunted, "Leave it. You can't pretend to be a servant if you carry a knife and touch me with such familiarity."

"I won't masquerade as someone else!" I hissed. "I want to stay with you—"

"Do as I tell you!" he snapped.

I stared at him. His face had contorted into a scowl, transforming him from the gentle father I'd known. My mouth opened and closed, but I could think of nothing to say.

From the hallway came the ringing of boots on floorboards. Barely daring to breathe, I listened to the men draw closer. Another instant and they would be upon us.

I dove for the knife. My fingers were closing around the handle when Mary kicked it under the table. "Listen to Father," she whispered. "And get rid of your armbands!"

With trembling hands, I unbuckled the leather straps. Footsteps tramped down the corridor, growing louder and louder. A low voice muttered something. I tossed the straps under the table.

The sitting room door was flung open with such force that it banged into the wall. Buckingham stood in the entryway. He was a handsome man of about five and thirty. In the curtained dimness, his shorn head shone white. Beneath the curve of his brows, his dark eyes darted around the room, then settled on my father.

"Mr. Milton," he said in a crisp voice, "I have it on good authority that a Florentine was recently seen at your home in London, seeking your company. A foolish mistake. The king and I know you are in league with some Italians, and a few days ago I planted a spy among your neighbors."

He half smiled when my father started.

"A grave mistake has been made," Father said in a ragged voice. "I bear the king no ill will. I am only a simple poet."

"A pretty hearth tale, Mr. Milton." Buckingham prowled the room's perimeter, studying the plain walls and the bookcase. "Four of you, search the house," he ordered without turning around, continuing to stare at the bookshelves. Pursing his lips, he reached for a volume and flipped through its pages. "Look for any sign of the Florentine's presence." He replaced the book and turned to gaze at my father. "The literary circles in London speak much of you, Mr. Milton," he said. "There is talk that you've been working on a new poem for the last few years. I hope you've abandoned the political writings that convinced so many citizens to take the life of our beloved king's father."

Four men slipped out the door. Twining my hands together to disguise their trembling, I listened to their footsteps separate as some headed to the kitchen, others to the bedrooms at the opposite end of the house. I prayed Betty had been quick enough to conceal Viviani's possessions—and that the men wouldn't be able to find them.

"My new poem is an epic on classical themes," Father said in a firm voice. "It can hold no interest for our king." A surge of pride flooded my heart. This was the father I knew so well—the patriot who bowed to no one.

"*I* will determine what interests our king," Buckingham barked. He snapped his fingers at the remaining men. "The poem's probably in this room. Tear this place apart until you find it."

I sagged with relief. We were saved. Buckingham would need to read only a few pages before he realized my father spoke truthfully. As long as Betty had hidden the evidence of Viviani's arrival, the king's men could have no reason to harass us further.

The men grabbed books off the shelves, thumbing through them before throwing them to the floor. I risked a look at my father, expecting to see a relaxed figure. Instead he sat hunched over, his hands knotting and unknotting in his lap. I remembered his warning to me and Viviani a few minutes ago: the poem must be safe or the secret would be lost. What the devil had he meant? *Paradise Lost* was an ancient religious story; there was nothing revelatory in its lines. And yet I heard the breath hitching in Father's chest.

Two men returned to the room, marching Betty between them. Her face had gone sheet white and she moved jerkily, tripping over the threshold.

"There's no indication any visitor has been here, Your Grace," the taller man said. "We found this woman in one of the bedchambers. She says she's Mr. Milton's wife."

Buckingham's eyebrows rose. "Good God, Mr. Milton, she looks young enough to be one of your daughters. What a rascal you are—I never would have dreamed it of you!"

"Your Grace," one of the men said. He held up a sheaf of papers covered with my handwriting. "I have found it."

The room seemed to hold its breath as Buckingham reached for the papers. A few minutes of reading and he would realize it was an innocent poem.

Without even looking at the manuscript, he flung it into the brazier of hot coals at Father's feet. At once the papers began to smoke. A hole, rimmed with orange, appeared in the top sheet. Even as I watched, the hole spread and the papers curled up, crumbling to black ash.

"No!" I screamed, falling to my knees. I reached for the burning papers, the tips of my fingers brushing the edge of the brazier. White-hot pain lanced my finger pads and raced toward my shoulder. Arms wrapped around me and dragged me back.

"Foolish child," a man grunted in my ear. "It's only a poem."

But it wasn't; Father believed it was his masterpiece. Through the sheen of my tears, my father wavered, like an image caught on the surface of a swiftly flowing river. He had dropped his head into his hands.

"My greatest work," he said in a choked voice. "I can never hope to replace it."

"Then I've accomplished my task." Buckingham leaned over Father. The room was so quiet, I caught his whisper: "Do you know what your enemies say about you? That your blindness is a punishment from God for your past sins. Truly, sir, you have earned your life of miserable darkness."

Father raised his chin in open defiance. Tears glimmered in his eyes, but didn't fall. Behind him, my sisters held hands, weeping.

"To be blind is not to be miserable," Father said slowly. "True misery is not to be able to bear blindness. My affliction is physical, and I'm certain I can meet my Lord with an unstained soul. Can Your Grace say the same?"

For a breathless instant, no one moved. Then Buckingham's face twisted. "Take him away," he growled at his men.

My heart squeezed. Where were they taking my father? What punishment did they have in store for him?

Nothing less than his death would satisfy the king. In the six years since he had returned to England, perhaps he had often thought of my father, and had been biding his time and waiting for the right moment to strike.

My father was going to die.

Unmoving, I watched as several men dragged him to his feet. I wanted to grab my knife and fling it at these men, but I shouldn't disobey Father—should I? Or was this how I could best aid him—by doing nothing and remaining silent? All of my body shook from the effort of staying still.

Betty plucked at Buckingham's sleeve. "Your Grace, I beg of you," she said, sinking into a deep curtsy when he turned to glare at her. "My husband's a good, God-fearing man. If he has done wrong by writing this poem, then I promise he won't write another. He's an old man of frail health. Surely he can be allowed to live out his remaining days in peace at home?"

Buckingham bent down until his face was inches from my stepmother's. "I'm most aggrieved to leave his wife and daughters without a man in the household to care for them." His tone was surprisingly gentle. "Sadly, I have no choice. If Mr. Milton tells the king the secret of his poem, then no harm will come to him, you have my word."

"How can you make such a promise?" The words burst from me before I could snatch them back. As Buckingham's gaze settled on me, I shifted nervously but continued, needing to know for certain what fate awaited my father. "You plan to have him executed, Your Grace, don't you?"

Buckingham looked startled, no doubt at having a "servant" speak so boldly to him. Then his expression hardened. "Oh, yes," he said, his tone so calm that the hairs on the back of my neck rose. "If Mr. Milton refuses to cooperate, then he'll swing from old Jack's noose."

My mouth went dry. I knew what Buckingham meant: on the next Hanging Day, Father would be crammed into a cart with the other condemned and rolled through the streets, to be strung up from the executioner's tree on Tyburn Hill, where crowds would pay a shilling for the right to watch him die.

I had to clear my throat twice before I could speak. "When?"

"The next Hanging Day is September fourth," Buckingham said quietly.

Today was the twenty-second of August. Unless my father cooperated, he'd be dead within a fortnight.

"Please," I whispered. "Your Grace, spare him, I beg you."

"Mr. Milton's destiny is in his hands." Buckingham tossed an amused look at my father. "The king tells me he cannot pardon a regicide, but he's had enough of death. It's his preference, Mr. Milton, that you share your poem's secrets with him. What do you say?"

Father raised his head. The misty film covering his eyes looked thicker, obscuring the pale sheen of blue beneath. "No," he growled.

"Oh, I wouldn't be so quick to refuse the king's generous offer." Buckingham's tone was as thin and hard as a blade. "The truth or your life: it's an easy choice. Give yourself more time to reflect upon the matter. As for your family," he went on, nodding at Betty and my sisters, "they will journey to London without delay. You'll settle in your house on Artillery Walk," he added to Betty, who nodded, her face slack with bewilderment.

"If your neighbors ask about your husband," Buckingham continued, "you will explain that his poor health has necessitated his stay in St. Bartholomew's Hospital. Do you promise to be faithful to this story?"

Questions swirled in my head as Betty murmured, "Yes, Your Grace." Pink had stained her cheeks, and I understood why: only the destitute stayed in hospitals, while doctors attended to the rich in their homes. By ordering us to tell others that Father was a patient in St. Bartholomew's, Buckingham shamed my family.

Social slights aside, though, nothing made sense. Why would

the king wish to conceal Father's arrest? There was something I was missing.

Buckingham looked at Betty, who sank into a hasty curtsy. "Who are your servants? Are they local girls?"

"We have our cook-maid, Luce." Betty's hands gripped her skirts so tightly, her knuckles had turned white. "She came with us from London—"

"I'm a village girl, Your Grace," I interrupted, recalling Father's instructions. Betty sent me a sharp look, a silent warning that a "maid" like me wouldn't dare cut short her mistress's speech. My father stood with his head bowed, his hair falling forward to curtain his face. With his expression hidden, I couldn't tell if he was pleased with me or if I had done wrong.

Buckingham circled me, the creak of the floorboards under his feet sounding as loud as the gunshots I had heard the townsmen fire when they were hunting birds—hard and final. I lowered my eyes. Beneath the writing table, my knife glinted in the shadows. Should I seize it and stab Buckingham?

"What a peculiar dress," he said. "Is it your habit not to wear your sleeves, miss?"

"I—" Dear God, what to say? "I was getting dressed when Your Grace arrived."

"I see. You aren't very well behaved for a serving girl. Perhaps Mr. Milton permits your boldness because he likes"—his eyes slid over to where my stepmother stood—"young women."

My face turned to flame. "I beg your pardon, Your Grace?"

"She has a saucy tongue," my father said quickly, "but we excuse it because she has a clever hand with a needle. My three daughters have been teaching her better manners."

Buckingham brought his face so close to mine I could smell the musk of his perfume. "You haven't paid enough attention to those lessons, miss, but you'd best listen to mine if you want to remain free. Tell no one what happened at your master's house today. My spies are everywhere, so don't think I won't find out if you've disobeyed me. Do you understand?"

My head jerked back and forth like that of a puppet on a string. He laughed, patting my cheek, then turned to his men and pointed at a few of them. "Mrs. Milton will direct you in packing up her household. The rest of you, with me." He snapped his fingers, then strode from the room.

Six men surrounded my father, forming a colorful circle around him. In the spaces between their bodies, I could barely glimpse the plain black of Father's clothes. His head was bowed. "Please," he said in a timid voice I hadn't heard before, "may I be permitted to say good-bye to my family?"

Tears burned my eyes as the men nodded and stepped back. My sisters and stepmother, murmuring and sobbing, crowded around Father. I stood to the side, irresolute. Everything within me longed to go to him, to feel his hands tracing my face one last time. But was it seemly for a "servant" to bid her master farewell? Indecision trapped me in place.

Betty and my sisters fell back. Father reached out his hand, waving it through the air as though seeking something. "And my serving girl," he said. "I must say farewell to her."

Somehow I pushed one foot forward, then another. I took Father's hand and pressed it to my cheek, trapping my tears between the flesh of his palm and my face. He smiled slightly.

"You've been a loyal servant to me." He leaned closer. I could not breathe. This was the moment. He would tell me what I needed to do in order to save him, and I would move Heaven and Hell until I released him from whatever place they were taking him—

"*L'avezza giovinetta pastorella*," he murmured.

A familiar young shepherdess? *This* was what Father had chosen to say to me at our parting—a nonsensical phrase in Italian? There must be something else he was trying to tell me, some secret woven into the Italian words.

He opened his mouth to speak again, but men seized his arms. "That's quite enough," one of them said, and they marched him from the room.

While my sisters whispered to one another, I ran after Father. In the garden, men were lashing him onto a horse. Even as I raced toward them, a man mounted my father's horse, then reached around Father's waist to grasp the reins.

"Wait! Please!" I shouted.

Father turned in the direction of my voice, mouthing my name. *Elizabeth.* My heart twisted. How could I stand by while he was ripped out of his life? How could I say good-bye to the person who meant more to me than anyone else in the world?

In the dirt road waited a wooden cart pulled by two horses. It was clearly intended to carry us and our possessions to London. Buckingham had come prepared to bring my entire family to the capital, I realized, a chill racing down my spine. Before seeing *Paradise Lost*, he had already made his decision. Why? And what did that mean for my father's fate?

"Remember," Father called, still turned in my direction, "the mind is its own place!"

Tears filled my eyes. Father had often said those words to me.

Your mind can become your heaven or your hell, he had counseled in his gentle way. *Only you determine what it shall be, Elizabeth. But you must build it carefully. Leave no holes or there's no telling what may slither inside.*

In a flash, I understood what he was telling me now: I must build the walls so fear could not come in.

The man he rode with kicked the horse's flanks, and they were gone, racing along the dirt road. The other horses in the party thundered past me, their hooves kicking up clouds of dust, choking my vision until I had to cover my face with my hands. Blinded, I listened to the hoofbeats grow fainter and fainter, carrying my father away from me.

When the air had cleared, I squinted into the distance, searching for the moving black dots formed by Father and the riders. But they had already rounded the curve in the road and disappeared from sight.

Numbness spread through my body. He was gone. Moving like an automaton, I trudged across the yard into the cottage. I had failed Father. I should have disobeyed him and attacked those men or begged to be taken with him. I never should have let him leave alone with them.

The door banged shut behind me. I stood in the hall, frozen. Somehow the effort to walk even a few more steps seemed insurmountable. My ears strained to pick up the murmurs of my sisters' voices and the thumps of trunks being opened. Soon my family, too, would be gone.

Act ordinary, I ordered myself. As far as the king's men were concerned, I was a serving girl, who would hardly be overly saddened by the departure of her employer's family. Setting my shoulders, I wiped at the dampness under my eyes.

I climbed the ladder to my bedchamber. Everything in here could remain—the furniture had come with the rented cottage, and my meager possessions should stay with me—so I went into Anne's room, where we gathered her clothes in silence under the watchful eyes of one of the king's men.

By the time the house was packed up, the afternoon sun had begun sliding down the sky in its daily, arcing journey. My stepmother, sisters, and Luce clambered into the cart. I stood on tiptoe to kiss them good-bye.

"D-do not stay," Anne stammered.

"I must." I blinked away tears. There was so much I wanted to explain to her—that I remained here at our father's command, not because I no longer wished her company; that I loved her with the fierceness and purity of a river's current, running cease-lessly without end. But the king's men who were standing nearby hampered my tongue. Instead I kissed her cheek, whispering, "You're my dearest friend, and no distance between us will ever change that."

Her face creased into a delighted smile. Swallowing hard, I raised my hand in farewell. The cart rumbled over the rutted road, my sisters turning to wave to me and crying.

I stared after them until my eyes ached. At last, when the cart was gone, I turned to the empty cottage. As I gazed at the blank windows, I realized that for the first time in my life I was truly alone. The only person I could go to for help was a stranger, whose loyalties I did not know.

I was on my own.

Seven

THE WOODS SEEMED DESERTED. OVERHEAD THE tree branches clustered so tightly together they blocked out the sun, enclosing me in a well of green-black shadows. As I moved deeper into the forest, dried elm leaves crunched underfoot, betraying my presence to anyone who might be near. Up ahead, Viviani's outline showed between the trees—a dark figure with a knife glinting in his hand.

He rushed toward me. "What happened? Is your family safe?"

His words brought the pain flooding back. I had to close my eyes against the image of my father being led from the cottage, his shoulders sagging in defeat, his steps unsteady.

"Elizabeth?" Viviani's hand brushed my arm. "You look ill. You should sit down."

Elizabeth? My eyes flew open. In the shadowed dimness, Viviani's face seemed different: softer, perhaps, the sharp line of his jaw gentled. "I'm well enough," I said, shrugging off his hand. "And it isn't proper for you to address me with such familiarity."

"I beg your pardon, Miss Milton." He smiled slightly, as if he found me amusing. I glared at him. "Please tell me what happened," he said.

"First tell me why you called my father 'notorious,'" I demanded.

"Isn't that how he is known?" The shadows hid Viviani's face from me, but I heard the surprise in his voice. "I meant no disrespect. In Florence, everyone calls him by this name."

Hmm. That made sense. The Italian city-states were populated by Catholics, who would be disposed to dislike my father's admittedly pro-Protestant religious tracts—particularly his documents advocating the practice of divorce if the man and woman were incompatible. Embarrassment heated my face. If I hadn't been so upset earlier, perhaps I would have figured this out on my own.

"Very well." I waved an impatient hand at Viviani. "Forget the matter."

Together we walked through the fields toward the cottage as I recounted the story to him. By the time I had finished, we'd reached the door. He opened it for me.

"As you can see, there's no reason for you to remain in England." I stepped into the hall. Somehow I had to convince him to leave so I could seek my father unimpeded. "With my father gone—" I started to say, then had to stop because my chest burned so badly I couldn't speak. Taking a deep breath, I tried again. "With my father gone, we can learn nothing about this secret he wanted us to guard. You're free, Signor Viviani."

He closed the door behind us, his expression unreadable. "I'm not leaving. When I make a promise to my master, I keep it. As Vincenzo bade me to help your father and I swore to do so, I must make good on my oath."

He slipped past me down the corridor, calling over his shoulder, "We have a day at the most before Buckingham reaches London. It's possible someone will tell him that Mr. Milton has *four* daughters and he'll return looking for you. We must flee this place by morning."

"You speak as if we'll be traveling together." Couldn't he understand that I didn't want his aid? I hurried after him. "I'm perfectly capable of tracking down my father by myself."

Viviani walked into the sitting room. In silence, he surveyed the smoldering brazier, the books knocked from their shelves, my leather straps lying under the table. "Yes, I see you handled matters perfectly on your own."

As though he could have done a better job than I had at protecting my father. I gritted my teeth. Viviani went on, "Your father has powerful enemies. You'd be wise to accept any help that's offered to you."

Not from someone I neither knew nor trusted. "*I* will find my father. You may return to Florence."

"Going after him is folly."

"I don't care. I'll track him down and free him from whatever place they're keeping him."

"And what then? You can't hide him forever."

"I'll take him to another country." Ideas tumbled in my head like a handful of jacks tossed by a child's hand. "To the Netherlands, perhaps. They're battling with England over a sea trade disagreement," I explained when Viviani looked blank. "Hollanders would be loath to help the king by returning a fugitive to him. In Rotterdam, my father and I could live without fear."

"Stop!" Viviani gripped my shoulders, holding me in place so I had no choice but to look at his face. It had hardened to rock. "Your father didn't ask you to go after him. He spoke instead about a young shepherdess."

My father's words rushed back to me: *L'avezza giovinetta pastorella.* Something rustled in my mind. The phrase seemed familiar. I could remember repeating it when I was a small child, sitting in Father's study, surrounded by books.

"It's a line from one of his early sonnets," I said slowly. "Sometimes he used his own poetry to teach me foreign tongues. Perhaps when he said it today, he was trying to remind me of happier times."

Viviani's hands fell from my shoulders. "Your father's a poet—words are his weapons. And he said to keep the secret in his poem safe. Do you have any idea what it could be?"

My hands fisted in my skirts. Secrets. Buried within poetry. Was *that* why Father had referenced one of his Italian sonnets— had he been trying to tell me of a message concealed within its lines?

I raced to the bookcase. Most of the shelves now stood empty, but one still contained a dozen volumes. Thank heavens Betty hadn't bothered to pack my father's entire book collection! My fingers flew across the leather spines, searching for a handful of pages bound together with black thread.

I found the booklet on the second shelf. As I flipped through the pages, Viviani leaned over my shoulder. "What are you doing?"

"This is a catalog I made of all of my father's works." I pointed to a page, which was divided into three columns. "Here's the title, and then the year in which the work was written, and then the form in which it was published. See, here's his poem 'The Nativity Ode.'"

"As fascinating as your father's writings are, this may not be the best time to review them." Viviani sounded sarcastic.

I ignored him, instead skimming the next page. "My father was alluding to one of his Italian sonnets when he mentioned the shepherdess, I'm certain of it. Here it is!" I pointed to the relevant entry. "Sonnet Three. He wrote it in 1628. Hmm, there's a notation that he revised it in 1644 and it was published in his book of poems the following year. That seems odd. He didn't revise any of his other Italian sonnets."

"Perhaps Sonnet Three was the only one that needed improvement."

Shaking my head, I continued staring at the sheet, as if it would somehow surrender its secrets if I gazed at it long enough. "They *all* needed improvement. My father thought they were poor imitations of the love poems written by native speakers of Italian."

My younger self had recorded additional information: Mr. John Rouse, then the librarian at the Bodleian Library, in Oxford, had purchased a copy of Father's first book of poems in the 1640s. My father must have seen his inclusion in the Bodleian Library's collection as a literary stamp of approval, or he wouldn't have bothered to have me write down the information. Quickly I scanned the bookshelf, but all of the works my father had written were gone. Betty must have taken them to London.

I could hardly go after her and demand to see the book, not when the king's men were keeping an eye on her and the rest of my family. And the places where I could find this volume of poetry were likely few, seeing as many of Father's works had been banned or burned after the king's return. But the Bodleian had probably kept its copy—Father had often praised the library, saying that although it was a new institution it was already the finest in England, with books from all over the world and a librarian who was committed to preserving knowledge for the generations of students to come. High praise from a Cambridge graduate, I used to think, but now I wondered if he had emphasized the Bodleian Library for another reason.

So I would remember it.

Although Viviani leaned against the wall, his arms crossed over his chest and his expression bored, I saw the way the muscles in his shoulders pushed against the velvet of his doublet. He was tense, ready to spring into action at an instant's notice. He could be a valuable ally—if he was trustworthy.

Father summoned him here, I reminded myself. *And your options are distressingly few.*

I shoved the booklet onto a shelf. "Do you still want to help, Signor Viviani?"

"It isn't a question of wanting to—I must, for my master's sake."

I took a deep breath. "Then we must prepare ourselves for a long journey. We leave for Oxford as soon as we can."

Gathering our supplies took several hours. Viviani returned to the village inn to hire two horses, and I crept alone through the fields, weaving between the lines of crops and praying no one would see me making my way to the Sutton estate. The fewer people who knew of my plans, the safer I would be.

I found Francis walking the edge of his property, white faced and shaking. After I promised him that my family was fine—the truth was too dangerous to share—I asked him for directions to Oxford, as he had recently completed his university studies there. Once he'd agreed to tell no one about my intended journey, he drew a crude map of the route we should take and advised me on the best times to visit the Bodleian Library. Students woke at five in the morning for prayers, he said, then broke their fast at six and worked in study halls for four hours, then for two more hours after the midday meal. Therefore the Bodleian would be emptiest in the later afternoon. We would visit the library then.

Back at the cottage, I fixed a simple supper of bread and the soup that Luce had left cooking in the hearth. In the dining room, Viviani sat across the table from me. The candlelight threw lines of gold all over him. Under the steadiness of his gaze, I found myself flushing like a child. I let my own gaze fall to the pewter dishes.

"When should we leave?" His voice broke the silence and I nearly jumped in my chair.

"Tomorrow morning at first light. In my country, highwaymen roam the roads at night. We'll be safer if we set off at dawn."

He shrugged. "As you wish."

"What do you think the secret is?" I asked, eager to change the subject.

He sipped wine. "I don't know. According to your father, he never met my master and they have little in common."

"I can't understand why the king would imprison my father now, after ignoring him for the past six years. What if . . . ?" My spoon clattered into my empty bowl, forgotten. "What if whatever my father hid in his poetry threatens the king's grip on the crown? That would explain why he's so desperate to silence my father and spirit him away."

Viviani raised his eyebrows, clearly unimpressed. "Your father uncovered sensitive information about the king thirty years ago? That's when this partnership with my master started, and your king would have been in swaddling clothes."

"Then not the current king." My mind spun. "The king's father, Charles the First, who was beheaded after the civil war. Thirty years ago, he sat on the throne. Suppose my father found out something about him—something that convinced him to oppose the royalists during the war? Something that could disqualify the entire line of Stuarts—which would include the current king—from the throne?"

For a moment, Viviani was silent. "It would explain the king's determination to hide your father—and why Buckingham burned the poem."

"We have to find the Italian sonnet as quickly as we can. If we can figure out what my father concealed within it, then we may have a bargaining tool to use to secure his freedom."

"He didn't ask you to arrange for his release." Viviani set his wineglass down. "You would defy him, Miss Milton?"

I looked at him steadily. "To save him, I would defy God himself."

His laugh rolled out. "I didn't think Puritans were a bold people. You're nothing like what I imagined."

"Aren't you the lucky one," I retorted, picking up the soup bowls.

When I'd finished the washing up, I led him to the loft bedrooms, insisting he climb the ladder first, remembering that otherwise he'd be able to glimpse up my skirts. As we clambered into the darkness, I could hear the silk and velvet of his clothes rustling together. Somehow the sound seemed terribly intimate. As though it served only to remind me that those same fabrics touched his bare skin. *Be quiet*, I ordered my brain.

On the landing, I opened Anne's door, gesturing for Viviani to go in. I felt him watching me, but I couldn't bring myself to look at him.

"There's fresh water in the basin," I said.

From the edge of my vision, I caught a blur of movement—he was bowing to me. "Thank you. Good night."

"Good night." I rushed into my chamber next door. Leaning against the bedroom wall, I exhaled a shaky breath. Somewhere on the other side of the wall I rested against was Viviani. Mere feet from me. I heard the splash of water in the basin as he washed his face, then the whisper of straw as he lay down. Lying on the same mattress where I had lain when the agony in Anne's legs chased sleep away and I rested next to her, rubbing her back in slow circles.

Heat rushed into my cheeks. What a child I was, every particle of my being attuned to the stranger in the room next door.

Determinedly shoving thoughts of him out of my head, I opened the window shutters. The black sky unfurled above me. There was Cassiopeia, easily recognizable from the W it formed from the points of five stars. They pulsed with a steady brilliance, as beautiful as they were undecipherable. I wondered how far away they were from England. A hundred leagues? More? And how they could shine so brightly when they hung in the heavens at such a great distance from my planet? Perhaps these were the same sorts of questions the Tuscan Artist in Father's poem is asking himself when he peers through his telescope.

Again I frowned at the bizarre image. Why had Father alluded to an Italian natural philosopher in a poem whose only characters should have been biblical? Maybe it had been a mistake, a slip he eventually would have caught on one of the mornings I read his verses back to him.

Or maybe it had been another hidden message.

Stupid, I decided, resting my arms on the windowsill and filling my eyes with the sight of the stars. Father's final words had been about a familiar young shepherdess, and I should follow his instructions and find the poem containing this character. Not concentrate on *Paradise Lost*.

Nodding hard, I left the shutters open and readied myself for bed: rubbing rosemary blossoms over my teeth to clean them, washing my face, tying my nightcap strings under my chin. Studying the sky had scrubbed the inside of my mind, leaving it resolute and determined.

I had always understood how Father had maintained his reason when darkness encroached on his sight; why he had dared to remain in England when his old colleagues were beheaded or had managed to flee to Europe or the colonies in the New World. It was for love of something greater than himself. Writing sustained him, feeding his thoughts and cheering his heart. He could live through any tragedy, for tragedy only deepened his understanding of the human soul and turned him into a better writer.

But I couldn't understand his decision to stay silent today.

By refusing to tell his secret to Buckingham, he had chosen death. He would disapprove of my plan to save him by bargaining with the king, I knew, but I didn't care. As long as I managed to keep him alive, it didn't matter if I flouted his wishes.

And if he died . . . I bit back a sob. His death would rip out all the stars in the sky, leaving me in darkness. There would be no more poetry, no more shared laughter in the early morning. Just endless black.

What would happen to us if he died? Mary, Deborah, and I could read and write—hardly useful talents for girls who hadn't been trained for a trade and had no dowries. We might be able to find work as scullery maids—but what about Anne? I thought of her twisted legs and childish grin, and my heart squeezed painfully in my chest. It'd be the almshouse for her, where she'd be forced to live off others' charity. She would hate feeling like a burden.

Or . . . there was one more possibility. One other option for females without dowries or useful skills: we'd end up walking the streets.

No. I pressed my hand to my mouth so Viviani wouldn't hear me moan. I wouldn't let that happen. No matter what, I'd keep my sisters safe from such an awful fate. I had to save Father, not only for his sake but for all of ours.

Viviani and I departed the next morning. Night still covered the land when we emerged from the cottage and saddled the horses. Even darkness couldn't lessen the heat pulsing from the ground in waves, drawing a line of sweat along my spine.

Our provisions were simple: full water skins, dried fruit,

bread, and cheese; spare clothes (we had found Viviani's stuffed inside Mary and Deborah's mattress); and sacks of oats for the horses. I opened my sumpters, the bags behind the saddles, checking to make sure I had packed everything I needed. Inside them there was food and water, and also a stack of clean pages, a bottle of ink, and two fresh quills. Father's poem might have been burned, but that didn't mean it couldn't be rewritten. Every time I had a chance, I would copy out as much of *Paradise Lost* as I could remember. With luck, I might save his masterpiece.

While I buckled the straps, I let the first lines rush into my mind: *Of Mans First Disobedience, and the Fruit / Of that Forbidden Tree, whose mortal tast / Brought Death into the World* . . . Tears blurred my sight. I could almost hear Father's gentle voice reciting the words and imagine he was with me again—not tied to a horse, galloping through the countryside toward his death.

Viviani swung onto his saddle. "Are you ready?"

I looked at the cottage, an irregular black hump in the predawn darkness. Its interior was still crowded with rented furniture, its bookcase still holding remnants of Father's cherished collection. But there was nothing in there for me anymore. Not with my family ripped apart.

"I'm ready," I said.

I climbed onto my saddle, my movements unencumbered by my usual skirts. Today I had donned black breeches, a shirt of white linen, a doublet of black wool, and riding boots. The clothes had belonged to one of Father's students, from the time when he was a tutor and boarded pupils in his home, before my sisters and I were born. With my braid coiled beneath a broad-brimmed felt hat and the flowing lines of the shirt concealing the swell of my bosom, I made a passable impression of a boy. I hoped.

This was the first time I would test my disguise by daylight. For years I had crept at night from our row house in London, praying no one would see me as I darted across the road into Bunhill Fields to meet with Mr. Hade, one of Father's former students and my fencing instructor. As far as I knew, no one ever had.

During the year we had lived in Chalfont, I had continued my weapons training, slipping into the thicket of trees along the village outskirts where I strung sacks of straw from the branches and then attacked them. A pitiful substitute for combat with a flesh-and-blood person, but it couldn't be helped; there was no one in Chalfont whom I trusted to fight me and maintain his silence, and Father insisted on absolute secrecy.

"Lead the way," Viviani said, taking his horse's reins. "You said Oxford was a distance of fourteen leagues?"

"Yes, a day's hard riding at least, but since we'll have to travel across the open countryside, the trip will probably take two days." I had never been to Oxford, although my mother's family hailed from the area. Indeed, I wouldn't have ventured there of my own volition. During the civil war, Oxford had been a royalist stronghold, and my father's name was one that its residents had cursed.

"Come," I said to him, pulling on the reins so my horse turned west. As our animals galloped across the fields, we left the rising sun behind us and raced toward a sky still black with night. I didn't look back.

Part

wo

THE TYRANNY OF HEAVEN

Better to reign in Hell, then serve in Heav'n.
—John Milton, Paradise Lost, Book I

Eight

OUR ROUTE WAS ROUGH AND MONOTONOUS, TAK-ing us across fields enclosed by hedges or avenues of trees. Of other travelers, we saw few: a handful of men on horseback, a couple of farmers driving a cart packed with chickens, and a stage-wagon crammed with poor riders who couldn't afford their own carriages.

When the noon sun beat mercilessly on our heads, we stopped in the shade of a tree to eat. Viviani fed the horses. Sitting cross-legged, I watched him through eyes slitted against the sun's glare, puzzling over this stranger whom I had tied myself to.

"Tell me about yourself." The words whipped out like a com-mand, and I blushed at how hard I sounded. How the devil was I supposed to talk to a boy? Mary would have known how, but I couldn't stomach the thought of copying the way she laughed behind her hand or looked through her eyelashes.

Viviani sat down beside me. "And what would you like to know, my lady?"

"I'm not a lady." Surely he was mocking me. I looked up, expecting to see a teasing smirk on his lips. But his face was calm as he picked up a linen-wrapped package of bread and cheese. "Tell me about your life in Florence."

"It's a city that inflames your mind and bombards your senses as soon as you enter it." Half-smiling, he rested his back against the tree. "Noise everywhere: street vendors shouting their wares of fruit and fish, carriage wheels rattling over paving stones, bells ringing from the dozens of churches. Wherever you look, there is bright color—red-tile roofs, olive-green shutters, the sumptuous clothing of fine ladies and gentlemen strolling past. I like to walk the Corso dei Tintori—the avenue of the cloth dyers," he clarified, evidently forgetting I was well versed in his tongue. "They hang lengths of wool and silk from their windows, and when you walk beneath them, you can see them snapping in the breeze above your head, such an array of colors that your eyes are dazzled. And the smells! A combination of rich scents you can find nowhere else: cinnamon and clove, ginger and pepper, goat, pork, poultry and fish, the beeswax of candles."

Despite myself, I inched closer to him, eager to learn more about the city my father had said was the most learned he had ever seen. "But isn't it such a large and magnificent city that you find yourself overwhelmed?"

He laughed. "Of course! That's the best part of Florence. Regardless of how long I live there, I'll never feel as though I've unlocked all of her secrets. But it's impossible to get overwhelmed to the point that you become lost," he added. "Florence has three tall landmarks that act as guideposts—the dome of Santa Maria del Fiore, Giotto's bell tower, and the tower of the Palazzo Vecchio, which can be seen from any point in the city. When I was a small boy and came to Florence, my master often sent me on errands throughout the city, and I was always able to trace my route home by looking for the Palazzo Vecchio tower. I was seven when I joined my master, more than half of my life ago, as I'm now eighteen, and I still feel as though I'm getting to know Florence."

"A city of wonders," I murmured to myself, recalling London's twisting alleys and narrow wooden houses, its aristocrats in bold colors and its religious freethinkers in black. His Florence sounded like an oil painting, pulsing with reds and golds, while my London was a charcoal sketch, plain and dark.

At my traitorous thoughts, warmth flooded my cheeks. Like all good Puritans, I had been raised to distrust color and pageantry . . . and yet a part of me yearned to see this city that Viviani spoke of with such love.

His voice broke into my thoughts. "My master's a good man." In between words, he munched, and I had to smother a smile: He had already eaten all of his bread and cheese and started on another packet. Mary often accused me of having an unladylike appetite, but this boy could eat as much as two of me could. "Vincenzo's both brilliant and kind," he continued. "He lets me assist him in many of his experiments—but those wouldn't interest you," he interrupted himself.

"I'd like to hear about your experiments." Even to my own ears, I sounded breathless.

So as we sat in the slanting shade, he told me about the experiments he and his master carried out. Their geometrical equations to demonstrate that an earlier natural philosopher had been correct when he hypothesized that the motion of light occurs in time, not instantaneously. At that, I set the bread in my lap again, my food forgotten. I listened to Viviani talk about his master's tests on the newest theory of water motion, which postulated that flowing water presses downward on a riverbed, not outward against its banks, and I could barely breathe. He and Signor Vincenzo Viviani had studied the tiny discs on the side of Jupiter, too, watching as they changed position relative to one another during the course of an evening—proof they weren't stars but moons, as the same natural philosopher had discovered fifty years ago.

Viviani's existence sounded like a hearth tale. A life colored silver by stars and black with ink: beautiful and useful. Listening to it had frozen me in place, as though his words had cast a spell on me. I found I didn't want to move, didn't want to take a deep breath, as if the slightest movement would break this magical feeling.

He grinned at me. "You woke with shadows under your eyes, but they're gone now. It's good to see you smile, Miss Milton. Joy sits easily on your face, and you ought to wear it more often. Now I think we've given the horses a long-enough rest, don't you?"

He had brushed the crumbs from his breeches and swung himself onto his saddle before I had time to form a proper response. Even if he had waited, I doubted I could have strung a sentence together; his fine words had pushed all my wits out of my head, leaving me with only a warm flicker beneath my breastbone.

Foolishness, I decided, climbing onto my horse. Joy as an

ornament for my face, indeed! But I couldn't banish the smile that insisted on remaining on my lips.

At dusk we made camp beneath a string of trees. Viviani was incredulous. "*This* is where you propose spending the night?"

I unbuckled the sumpters. Though I chafed at the prospect of halting our journey, we had to conceal ourselves for the night or risk being found by wandering highwaymen, and we would exhaust the horses if we didn't let them rest. As for myself, my legs ached from riding and pain stabbed behind my eyes, thanks to squinting in harsh sunlight for hours.

"Did you see any inns today?" I snapped. "Or perhaps any homes whose owners would be willing to take in a foreigner and a peculiar-looking boy?" I threw two bedrolls onto the ground. "This is the best we can manage."

Viviani, looking thoughtful, rubbed his horse's sweaty flanks. "A strange country, your England. No highways, no inns set up at regular intervals along the road, and no color. Everything here is brown and gray." He brushed down the horse, his movements unhurried and methodical. With his back to me, he added, "You shouldn't call yourself peculiar."

"Indeed? And what would you call a girl dressed as a boy?" I snorted. "Handsome?"

Viviani glanced over his shoulder at me. "Brave, to conceal her identity so she can help her father. Handsome, no—you're too pretty to be described as such."

Surprise stole my voice. *Pretty.* No one had called me that before.

"This sort of talk is nonsense," I muttered. I handed him the water skin, taking care our fingers did not touch.

His now-familiar laugh rolled out, but he said nothing more. As darkness closed in, we ate our simple supper in silence. When we had put away the remaining food, Viviani picked up one of his bags and ambled into the passage formed by the two rows of poplar trees. At our campsite I took out paper and ink and set to work copying the opening of *Paradise Lost*'s Book One from memory. Father had revised the beginning so many times that the words felt as though they had been embroidered on my brain, but eventually I would venture into less-traveled territory, and I knew I'd make mistakes and unwittingly substitute my own phrases for Father's. Still, it was better than leaving his masterpiece in ashes. At the story's start, Satan and his band of rebel angels have already staged a revolt against God in the Kingdom of Heaven and have been cast down to Hell, where Satan lies chained on a lake of fire.

For a short time, the only sounds were the whickers of our horses and the scratch of my quill on paper. Then I heard footsteps shuffling in dirt. Viviani dropped down next to me.

"What is it you do with such deep concentration?" he asked.

"I'm copying *Paradise Lost*."

He stretched out his legs, crossing them at the ankle. "Perhaps," he said, "since this poem figures in our mission, I ought to know more about its contents."

I hesitated. He was right, of course. But . . . these were my father's words, labored over for years, meant to be the culmination of his career. Sharing them with someone I barely knew felt wrong.

Still, I could hear Father's voice in my head, begging me not to let his poem vanish forever. He had intended it to be read by the people, and Viviani certainly numbered among them.

"Very well," I said at last. "It's a ten-book poem in blank verse, detailing the story of Adam and Eve and their expulsion from Eden, but from a different perspective—in many of the scenes, Satan's the central character. The story begins after he has already fought God and lost. While he's in the depths of Hell, he consults with his army of angels about how to recapture Heaven and overthrow the Lord once and for all. He decides to journey to Earth and poison it with evil by tempting its two humans to disobey God's commands."

Viviani held out his hand. "May I see it?"

"Be careful. The pages are still wet." I gave him the stack, and he began to read.

Overhead, the heavens were painted blue and purple, permitting just enough illumination to write by, but it wouldn't be long before the sky surrendered to night and I would have to put away my work. I increased my pace, working now on Book Two. I was remembering the words wrongly: even in my head, I could hear how awkward the lines sounded. But the plot, at least, was the same; that I recalled with absolute clarity.

At this point, Satan gathers his followers for "the great consult" and they debate whether or not they should fight another battle to gain control of Heaven. Finally Satan suggests they should go to Earth. When none of the angels volunteer for the task, Satan decides to make the journey on his own. It was odd, I thought as I scribbled the lines as best as I could remember them, but my father's Satan was almost always alone. Perhaps Father was saying something significant about evil—that it divides us from our souls, keeping us eternally distant from ourselves and one another. As though Hell was solitude itself.

"Your father's poetry is beautiful," Viviani said at last. "I've never read anything like it. His version of Satan . . ." He trailed off, giving me a wary look.

I took pity on him and decided to say what he clearly was reluctant to, out of respect for my feelings. "My father's Satan appears blasphemous," I said, wiping my ink-stained quill on a spare scrap of linen. "He's brave and charismatic; he rails against what he sees as God's tyrannical rule in Heaven. He's a leader," I added, "exhorting his followers to rebellion. A revolutionary, you could even say."

I looked up from my task to find Viviani watching me carefully. "It's a trick," I explained. "My father presents Satan in such a manner so readers will fall with him—they know he's the villain and yet he appears so heroic that they can't help rooting for him, at least in the beginning."

"Then your father's epic is meant to manipulate its readers." He sounded impressed. "It's a game played on our minds."

"Precisely." Mysterious or not, at least this boy was clever—he had latched onto my father's intentions immediately. "From the start, we know the story's outcome, and yet we still succumb to temptation and find Satan the most admirable character. Everything he says has multiple meanings, but we don't understand what he's truly saying until the story's end, when he tempts Eve."

For a moment, Viviani was silent. "It sounds like a literary marvel," he finally said. "But nothing you've told me explains why your father summoned me to England."

He jumped to his feet, then picked up an object from the ground on the other side of him. Gold flashed on its surface and my thoughts about Father's secrets scattered like leaves in a windstorm. The object was the mysterious instrument I had seen in Viviani's chamber at the inn.

"What is that?" I asked.

"A telescope. I was using it earlier." He opened his hands to let me see it more clearly: it was a cylindrical device, its leather covering stamped with a design in gold filigree. My heart beat faster. I had heard the term "telescope" before but until yesterday I had never seen one. I had imagined them to be massive, bulky contraptions made out of wood and brass, not like this slender instrument fashioned out of leather.

"These are used to study the stars, aren't they?" My hand itched to grab it, but I forced myself to speak calmly. I couldn't let anyone guess how fascinated I was by astronomy or I'd be branded as an aberration. "May I try it?"

He looked surprised. "Yes, of course."

We walked into the clearing. He stood behind me, reaching around my body to place his hands over mine on the telescope and direct its lenses at the full moon hanging low in the sky.

"There will be some discoloration around the edges of the moon," he said, sounding calm, as though he held girls' hands every day. Maybe he did. "I suspect this telescope's concave lenses gather and diffuse light improperly. Longer telescopes lessen the distortion. Someday I hope to build a telescope that permits us to see the heavens plainly."

I glanced over my shoulder at him. His face was inches from mine, so close I could smell his scent of spiced wine and sandalwood. In the silvery darkness, I saw a vein pulsing in his throat, where he had undone his cravat. Hastily, I looked into the telescope, fumbling for something to say. "I thought you were a mathematician, not an astronomer."

"I am, but the natural world fascinates me, too." His tone was easy. Obviously, our proximity wasn't affecting *him*. At least only one of us was addle-brained tonight.

Irritated with myself, I peered through the eyepiece. Then I gasped aloud. The moon looked as white and lustrous as a pearl, its curved shape blurred as though it were wrapped in fog. Dark shadows dotted its surface.

"What are those specks on the moon?" I asked.

"Valleys and craters. The moon's surface isn't smooth, as many believe, but pockmarked with valleys and mountains. By daylight I can show you something even more shocking. Have you heard of the phenomenon of sunspots?"

I shook my head and, loath to blink, I continued staring at the moon. The dark specks were tinged with blue. From this distance, I couldn't discern which were valleys and which mountains. It little mattered—this was still the most beautiful, awe-inspiring vision I'd ever beheld.

"Sunspots are dark fumes or vapors that travel across the sun's surface." Viviani's breath fluttered warmly on my neck. "They are proof that the sun rotates, stationary, on its axis."

I pulled away from the telescope so I could turn to look at him. "If the sun is stationary, how can it rise and set?"

Viviani's eyes held mine. There was something in his face I couldn't make out—it might have been a challenge. "Because the earth moves around the sun."

I stared at him, my heart throbbing against my ribs. "That's blasphemy! The Bible says all heavenly bodies revolve around the earth."

"You are holding the telescope of the man who discovered the sun's true movements," Viviani said fiercely. "Fifty years ago he published the work *Letters on Sunspots*, and instead of being hailed as the visionary he truly was, he was accused of heresy by the Inquisitors in Rome. We should be brave enough to seek the truth, even when it contradicts our beliefs! Yet everywhere I look, I see people wrapping themselves in darkness because they'd rather not upset the balance of their lives."

I hesitated, unsure what to say. Willful blindness was something I was all too familiar with. For years, I had heard others hurl insults at Father and Anne, saying their physical afflictions were God's punishment for their sins. Deep in my bones, I had known they were wrong—I'd known that Father was a good person and Anne was the best, kindest girl I would ever meet. His blindness and her deformed limbs and simple mind must spring from another source, I was convinced. Yet Psalm 104 stated that the earth stands still and the Book of Joshua told us that the sun revolved around our motionless planet, unless it was paused in its journey by God's hand. And I'd always been taught that the Bible contained unassailable truths.

"You must be mistaken," I said at last.

"I'm not." Viviani took the telescope from my limp fingers. "Some truths are inescapable, Miss Milton, whether or not you choose to believe them. Every night the stars will shine and rotate in their constellations, and continually our planet will revolve in its journey around the sun."

Pointedly, I looked at the ground. "The earth seems motionless to me."

"It's an illusion. Our planet is in perpetual motion, and other forces keep us anchored to the ground." Viviani stalked to our campsite. "The earth turns toward the east at a high rate of speed."

That was impossible! I raced after him.

"If Earth moves in such a fashion, then wouldn't falling leaves scatter to the west of trees?" I demanded. "And birds lose their way in midair?"

Viviani spun around and stared at me. "How do you know to ask such questions? You're a girl—"

"Yes, and therefore I ought to be sitting at home, embroidering and pining for a husband," I retorted. "Tell me how such things are possible!"

He didn't take his eyes from my face. "Because the earth imparts motion to all objects. Therefore, we don't fight the movement but become part of it. Like people walking along the deck of a ship at sea."

I thought of the times I had ridden on the small, flat-bottomed boats that traveled up and down the Thames, ferrying passengers who didn't want to traverse the clogged London streets. If I closed my eyes, I could still feel my body rocking with the motion of the current and hear the water slapping the sides of the boat. Viviani was correct: I had absorbed the boat's movement, rather than struggling against it.

Then . . . what he had said was possible. The earth *could* rotate on its axis. And we could move with it, unaware that at every single instant we were in motion.

I dropped my head into my hands. If Viviani was right, then the Bible was wrong. And the ground was no longer hard and strong but made of shifting sand.

"Many are afraid of the laws of nature because they seem to contradict divine scripture," Viviani said quietly. "My master, like his master before him, thinks the universe is a giant puzzle, laid out by God, and it's our task to assemble the pieces and make sense of them."

"I don't want to believe that," I said in a choked voice.

"No matter what you want to believe, the truth remains the same." His hand brushed my shoulder—a touch as soft as gossamer. "But my master's master dared to write what he saw in the stars. He recanted before the Inquisitors during his trial; this kept him alive, but he was sentenced to house arrest for the remainder of his life. If I'm ever called upon to defend my beliefs, I hope I can suffer the consequences as unflinchingly as Galileo Galilei did."

At the name, my head snapped up.

"You speak of Galileo," I breathed.

"Galileo?" Viviani's forehead wrinkled. "Maybe that's how he's known in your country, but that's his Christian name, and we refer to him as Signor Galilei."

I barely heard him. "My father met him nearly thirty years ago. He visited him secretly when Galileo was under house arrest."

In two quick strides, Viviani had closed the distance between us and gripped my hands in his. The telescope was pressed between our palms, the leather rod keeping our fingers from tangling together. "My master became apprenticed to Signor Galilei when he was seventeen and lived with him during the last years of his life, from sixteen thirty-nine to forty-two. Could he have met your father?"

I shook my head. "He visited Galileo in thirty-eight."

Viviani released me and paced around the campsite, his boots kicking up eddies of dust from the water-hungry ground. "Nevertheless, *something* must have happened all those years ago to link the three men together. The secret could be rooted in politics, as you thought. Before he was arrested, Signor Galilei was friends with the pope and dozens of important people. He could have learned something incriminating about the king's father—something the king is frantic to hide—and told your father about it."

I held myself still, trying to quiet my whirling thoughts and arrange them in some semblance of order. Shortly after my father had met Galileo, my country plunged into civil war, and Father revised his Italian third sonnet. In 1649, King Charles the First was executed, his family banished, and my father was invited to join the fledgling revolutionary government. Sometime after my birth the next year, when I was so young I can't now remember the beginning of my training, my father gave me my first dagger. Within ten years, the government had fallen, and by 1660 the beheaded king's son had been crowned and my family had begun our new life of quiet poverty. And now, in 1666, according to Father's letter, his increasingly frail health had prompted him to send for Viviani. Were all these events links in the same chain? And how could we possibly find out?

"The timeline fits our political secret theory," I said. "But why did Buckingham plant a spy among our London neighbors in the first place? And why was he so worried by news of your arrival in London that he sent men to our cottage in Chalfont? No," I corrected myself. "He wasn't worried about *your* arrival, but about the fact that you're a Florentine. Somehow he must have known that Italians were involved with my father's secret."

"And now we're left chasing after an old sonnet." Viviani sounded frustrated. He dropped down onto his bedroll.

For a long time, we didn't talk. I lay on my back, gazing at the sky, trying to empty my mind so answers could stream in. The stars looked like a scattering of coins tossed by a reckless hand—yet I knew they rotated with clockwork regularity. Overhead, the moon once again looked like its usual blank self, its mysteries of mountains and valleys concealed from me.

But I remembered what I had seen through the telescope's glass. My eyes hadn't lied to me.

Perhaps, said a small voice in my mind, *he's right, and we should be brave enough to look for the truth, even when it goes against what we've been taught.*

I shied away from the thought like a skittish horse. This was heresy, and people had been burned for less.

I turned my head a fraction, just enough so I could see Viviani's profile. He was staring at the stars, his jaw set, his eyes unblinking. His hands were crossed over his chest, rising and falling with the steadiness of his breaths. How strange the stars must look to him, hanging in different locations in the sky than he was accustomed to. Yet he remained here, in this foreign place, because he wanted to keep his word to his master. And he had told me what he believed to be the truth about the earth's movements, when it would have been easier to lie.

My mouth opened. "Signor Viviani," I heard myself saying, "you may call me Elizabeth. If you like."

Heat flooded my cheeks. From the corner of my eye, I saw him smile.

"Then you must call me Antonio," he said.

Antonio. I repeated the name silently, listening to the way its syllables rose and fell before stretching out. Such a foreign-sounding name, strange to my ears, but pleasing.

"Good night, Antonio." I rolled onto my side, away from him.

There was a pause. "Good night, Elizabeth."

He said nothing else. We lay in silence, silvered by starlight, surrounded by darkness.

Nine

IN THE MORNING WE WASHED IN A NEARBY
stream before breaking our fast. I plunged my hands into the
icy water, letting it sluice down my arms. Antonio had removed
his doublet, and he cupped water in his hands, then combed it
through his hair. Water splashed the front of his shirt, turning
the fabric translucent and plastering it to his skin. Through the
thin silk, I could see the muscles of his chest.

The sight should have been indecent—it was too much like
seeing someone straight from the bath—but I couldn't rip my
gaze away. What a marvel the human form was: a frame made of
bone, covered by flesh, and a thousand mysteries in between. As
I watched Antonio wash his face, I wondered for the hundredth
time how our bodies responded to the commands our minds
uttered. How did Antonio's hands know to cup themselves into
a bowl and capture the stream's water? How did my eyes know

to redirect their gaze because I wanted to look at him? Truly, our bodies and brains contained so many secrets. And I yearned to find out all of them.

"If you keep looking at me in that manner, my virtue may be in danger," Antonio said.

My face went hot. "You're an idiot," I muttered, busying myself with setting out bread and cheese. Whether I spoke to him or to myself, I couldn't be sure.

He laughed. Was there *nothing* that shook this boy's composure?

I stuffed a wad of bread into my mouth so I wouldn't be tempted to speak. But I couldn't help remembering Antonio's allusion to his virtue—which, judging by what he had said, was untouched. There might not be a girl in Florence holding a string to his heart.

I hated myself for the warmth that filled my chest at the thought. Truly, who was the idiot now?

Still, he's a decent sort, I told myself, chewing and studiously not looking at him. He could have mocked my father for his blindness or my sister for her mismade legs. Perhaps he'd been raised not to assume that physical ailments had been caused by God's wrath, for his master had served a blind man.

The bread turned to ash in my mouth. Galileo had been blind. *Like my father.*

I jumped to my feet. "Galileo was definitely blind, wasn't he?"

Antonio's forehead creased in surprise. "Yes. He slowly went blind in one eye, then the other. Why?"

I could barely breathe. Father had lost his vision in his left eye, then his right.

"When did he lose his sight?"

"I think he was completely blind by sixteen thirty-six or thirty-seven," Antonio said, "so he was sightless for the last five or six years of his life. My master said Signor Galilei damaged his eyes by looking through telescopes so often, but of course many said it was God's punishment for his heretical beliefs about the planets' movements. What does it matter?"

Knives of worry stabbed my stomach. Both men gradually going blind, one eye at a time, ostracized, then imprisoned for their political or philosophical beliefs. They had lost their vision for different reasons: Father for reading so much by candlelight, Galileo for using his telescopes—

I gasped aloud. Galileo had used *telescopes*. And he had been living in Tuscany when my father met him. In some respects, he could be considered an "artist," for he had used his creativity and imagination to attempt to solve the riddles of the skies.

In my mind, I saw lines from Father's poem, the ones we had been working on during our last session together: *Through Optic Glass the Tuscan Artist views / At Ev'ning from the top of Fesole . . .*

Galileo was the Tuscan Artist! I knew my father too well to pretend Galileo's inclusion in his masterpiece was a twist of chance or an homage to a natural philosopher he admired.

It was a clue.

"Elizabeth?" Antonio tapped my knee. "What's wrong?"

I shook my head, as if to clear it. "My father turned Galileo into a character in *Paradise Lost*. He's the only contemporary person in the entire poem. It's a message, I'm sure of it!"

Antonio's eyebrows rose. "What happens in *Paradise Lost* when Signor Galilei appears?"

"Galileo is mentioned just as Satan escapes from a lake of

fire," I said. "It's the moment when evil frees itself from a prison and prepares to unleash itself onto the world. The timing can't be a coincidence."

"Perhaps Galileo accomplished something that, like Satan, could change Earth forever."

Wordlessly, we stared at each other. How could we ever piece together all these separate pieces so they made one cohesive picture? And if Galileo *had* committed a momentous act years ago in his native Tuscany, then what bearing could that possibly have on the king now, decades later, in another part of the world? It made no sense.

"The answers must be waiting for us in Oxford," I said urgently.

Without speaking again, we packed the remaining food and swung ourselves onto our horses. Antonio took off at once. I slouched low in my saddle and followed.

We pushed our horses to the limit. By the time the sun had reached its noonday zenith, all of us, humans and beasts alike, were hot and flushed. On the edge of a wooded thicket, we sat with our backs braced against the trees, eating a simple meal of bread and dried fruit. When we had finished, I excused myself. Upon returning to our temporary camp, I found Antonio had gone, presumably to complete the same errand, and I took advantage of the momentary break to lie on the ground. I closed my throbbing eyes.

Pine needles sighed under approaching feet. "I beg your pardon," said a boy's voice that was definitely not Antonio's, "but have you seen a boy of about eighteen or nineteen, black-haired, who speaks with a foreign accent, and a girl of the same age, dressed in Puritan clothes? They should have passed this way recently."

My insides hardened to ice. Someone was already after us. My eyes flew open and I found myself staring into a stranger's face. His was so close to mine our noses nearly touched. He crouched next to my supine body, leaning over me. In the shadows cast by the trees, he was made up of white and dark: pale cheeks, the twin orbs of his eyes, a tumble of brown hair.

"No," I said slowly. "I haven't seen them."

"A pity." He said the words lightly, but I saw the way his mouth twisted: he was disappointed. "I would have paid you handsomely for any information you could have given me. Oh, well. Here's a guinea for your trouble."

He sat back on his haunches, digging through a small leather pouch strung onto his belt. Eyes narrowed, I pushed myself to a sitting position. My braid coiled heavily on my neck; my hat lay a few feet away. Apparently this stranger hadn't noticed my hair yet, but it couldn't be long before he did. I rotated my wrists, feeling my knives' leather bindings bite into my forearms. An instant's work and my blade could be at this stranger's throat. But there was no need to attack him and arouse his suspicions. Not yet.

I darted a glance behind me. The horses stood near the stream, but Antonio was still gone.

"You have my apologies for waking you," the stranger said. He spoke with a highborn London accent, his syllables crisp and precise.

He had gotten to his feet, and he flicked a guinea in my direction. It hit the dirt next to me, but I made no move to pick it up, watching him instead. This boy looked to be about my age, and his brown hair fell to his shoulders in curling waves. He was uncommonly tall, at least six feet, and wore a doublet and breeches of yellow silk.

"Who are you?" I asked, taking care to pitch my voice low.

He didn't seem to hear me; he was staring at some point on my chest. I followed the line of his gaze: my braid had slipped over my shoulder and hung over my bust.

"A girl—" he started to gasp, but I didn't give him the chance to finish. I pulled a knife free from its sheath, then launched myself at him. He fell hard, landing on his back in the dirt. Before he could even blink, I had my weapon at his throat.

"Who are you?" I snapped.

He hissed out an impatient breath. "It's clear who *you* are. Miss Milton, correct?"

"Your name or you'll feel the point of my blade."

"Robert Crofts!" he shouted. "I've come from London—"

"Elizabeth!" Antonio's voice cracked through the air like a rifle shot. I looked up to see him running toward me, weaving through the fringe of trees—a blur of black and white. He drew his sword free from its scabbard, the blade flashing silver with reflected sunlight.

"This boy has been looking for us," I called to him. "He says he goes by the name Robert Crofts."

Antonio dropped to his knees beside me. "Are you all right?" he asked in a low voice. "This fellow didn't hurt you?"

Why did boys always imagine they had to play the savior? I rolled my eyes. "I'm well enough, but I can't guarantee how much longer Mr. Crofts can say the same—unless he answers my questions."

"I mean neither of you harm, I swear it," Crofts said. All the color had leached from his face, leaving it deathly pale. "I've been seeking both of you to warn you that you're in terrible danger."

"An aristocrat like you wants to help the daughter of a supposed regicide like me?" I asked. "If you think I'll believe this hearth tale, then either you have too high an opinion of your storytelling abilities or too low an opinion of my intellect."

Beside me, Antonio snorted out a laugh. Crofts shot him a startled look. "Is she always this bold?"

Antonio grinned. "I only made her acquaintance two days ago, but based on what I've seen so far—yes."

"Instead of discussing my character, perhaps we could return to more important matters." I moved back slightly, keeping my weapon a few inches distant from Crofts's neck. "How do you know about us?"

He sat up. "A few days ago at court, we received word that a Florentine had come to London seeking John Milton. Buckingham left at once for Chalfont St. Giles, and I followed on my own. Unfortunately, by the time I arrived Mr. Milton's household had disappeared. The villagers thought they had tired of country life and returned to London."

Crofts hesitated. "They all seemed so inclined to believe the lie, I myself was tempted to. Until I spoke to Mr. Francis Sutton. Once I parted with some coins, he was happy to tell me your destination, and to draw me a map of the route he had advised you to take."

"A pretty story," Antonio said. "You still haven't told us why the king would care that I came to London in search of Mr. Milton."

"I don't know."

Antonio and I looked at each other. As one, we moved closer to Crofts, our faces hard. His eyes darted back and forth between the two of us, and he held up his hands in surrender.

"I swear it, I don't know!" A faint sheen of sweat gleamed on Crofts's forehead. "The king became wild with fear when we were told a Florentine had been looking for Mr. Milton."

The skin on the back of my neck prickled. The king's fear had to be tied into the secret my father had hidden thirty years ago. But how had the king found out about it in the first place? And how had he learned of my father's connection to any Italians?

"So why did *you* journey to Chalfont?" Antonio asked, touching the hilt of his sword, his ring clinking against the metal.

"After the old king was executed, the present king languished in exile for eleven years. Ever since he claimed the throne, he's been desperate to keep it." Crofts's face was grim, his voice steady. "Such men are too dangerous. Only a few slippery steps and they become tyrants. It wasn't too long ago that the king's dead father tried to assume absolute control over England, and all we got was a civil war and thousands of dead. I care too much about this country to let our rulers bully their subjects again. Even though I don't know you, I'll help you, if it means stopping the king. England can't survive another despot."

He held out his hands in a placating gesture. "As you see, I came alone at considerable expense and trouble to myself. Let me help you."

"Just a moment." I jerked my head at Antonio, then walked a short distance away. Even with my back turned to Crofts, I felt his eyes digging into my spine. "What do you think?" I whispered.

Antonio, looking thoughtful, rubbed the back of his neck. "If

Crofts was on the king's side, he would have ridden to Chalfont with Buckingham. As he's come all this way on his own, he must believe the king's intentions are wrong."

I glanced over my shoulder at Crofts. He had gotten to his feet. Even as I watched, he rested his hand on the hilt of his sword.

"His weapon!" I whispered.

But he didn't draw it. He stood waiting, his head bowed. Antonio and I exchanged a swift look.

"He easily could have crept up behind us and stabbed us," I said.

Antonio nodded, laying a hand on my shoulder. "I think he's just proved his trustworthiness."

I nodded. Dropping his hand from my shoulder, Antonio walked back to where Crofts stood. As I followed him, I could have sworn I still felt the weight of his hand and the heat of his skin burning through the thin fabric of my shirt.

Ten

WE RODE HARD ACROSS THE FIELDS, THE SUN BEAT-
ing down on our heads. When we stopped to sip from our water
skins, I explained to Crofts why we were journeying to Oxford—
that we believed my father had concealed a political secret in one
of his Italian sonnets, and the Bodleian was one of the last places
in the country where we could be assured of finding my father's
old books.

We reached the outskirts of Oxford by midafternoon. The
streets were long and straight. The farther we rode, the more I
was struck by the tidiness of the city's stone buildings and the
cleanliness of its gutters. This city, with its coffeehouses and tav-
erns and inns siting sedately next to one another, seemed another
world from London's jumble of buildings crammed higgledy-
piggledy together or Chalfont's cottages and farm fields. The
people weren't the tangle of vendors, merchants, tradesmen, and

aristocrats I was accustomed to seeing in London's narrow streets or the soberly dressed religious freethinkers and farmers of Chalfont. Here I saw university tutors in long black robes, their arms bent around bundles of books, and fine men and ladies in carriages, their clothes of midnight blue, green, or peach showing through the open windows as they rumbled past.

Crofts led the way. He said that he knew the city well, for he'd stayed here last autumn with his family to escape the plague that was then sweeping through London. The Bodleian was housed in a large building of pale stone that formed a quadrangle. The massive dragon of a structure was several stories tall, its walls pitted with dozens of windows.

We tied our horses to hitching posts. On the library's front steps stood a couple of students talking with one another, dressed in their required long black gowns. They stepped to the side, allowing us to pass.

Inside we found ourselves in a deserted corridor lined with windows. In the sun-flooded warmth, dust motes spun like dots of gold in the air.

Without looking at us to see if we followed, Crofts strode down the corridor. He led us through a series of long passageways, one of which was lined with numerous gilt-framed paintings. At last he brought us into a large, high-ceilinged room crowded with stalls, which were similar to what I'd seen in markets. All of them were lined on both sides with shelves of books. A few dozen students sat at wooden tables, studying or scribbling notes. The place was silent as a tomb, except for the scratch of quills on paper and an occasional cough. No one looked up as we entered.

A middle-aged man with shoulder-length dark hair hurried

toward us, his black robes fluttering about his ankles. "Your Grace," he whispered, bowing to Crofts, "I'm honored by your presence. If I had known you were in town, I would have arranged for you to have private use of the Bodleian. How may I be of help today?"

Something cold settled in the pit of my stomach. *Your Grace.* What had the librarian meant by addressing Mr. Crofts with such an illustrious title? Unless our new companion wasn't a mere gentleman, as his name implied . . .

Crofts gave him a polite smile. "How delightful to see you again. I didn't think you would remember me." He glanced at us. "This is the Bodleian librarian, Mr. Thomas Hyde." He turned back to the gentleman. "We need to see Mr. John Milton's 1645 book of poems."

"This way, if you please." Hyde ushered the three of us into an alcove. When he picked up a book, I saw it had been attached to its shelf by a long chain. As I ran my gaze down the stalls, I realized all of the folios had been chained to their shelves, no doubt to prevent students from stealing the library's many rare or valuable books.

"Here it is," Hyde said, setting the chained book on a nearby table. Sunlight pouring through the window cast a pool of dusty yellow on the leather-bound volume. Hyde flipped to the title page, and I read the irregular print: *Poems of Mr. John Milton, Both English and Latin*, and then the place of publication and the date, *London, 1645*. My heart painfully skipped a beat. This was it. I would find out what my father had been trying to tell me.

The librarian cast an anxious look at Crofts. "I hope you will pardon my predecessor's actions, Your Grace."

There was that troubling salutation again. What did the librarian mean by addressing Crofts so formally? I was missing something, but what?

When Crofts raised his eyebrows, Hyde said hastily, "Six years ago, when the warrant for Mr. Milton's arrest was written, all of his books were supposed to have been removed from the library."

Images of the bonfires I had seen throughout London during the summer of 1660—the summer of the king's return from exile—flickered through my mind. The flames had been stoked by the words of men who had once been leaders or visionaries, but who were viewed as traitors after the dead king's son returned. Father's pamphlets had disintegrated into smoke as my sisters and I watched from the steps of St. Paul's Cathedral, the acrid scent weaving into our hair and skin so we could smell it everywhere we went. I hadn't realized Father's books had been banned from the Bodleian as well. Yet here this volume sat on a table.

"They were taken out of the collection," Hyde said. "But Mr. Rouse, my predecessor, was a great admirer of Mr. Milton's poetry and couldn't bear to destroy any of his books. When I took over last year, I thought perhaps enough time had passed to put his works on our shelves again."

"Set your mind at ease, Mr. Hyde." Crofts clapped the man on the back. "You won't be punished for Mr. Rouse's actions. We require no more of your help."

The dismissal was obvious. The librarian bowed again, then backed away, keeping his front turned to us. Another block of ice dropped into my stomach. Although we didn't speak of the court in my home, I was familiar with the custom of never turning your back on a member of the royal family. Yet Crofts was too young to be the king, who was six and thirty years of age. And the king and his Portuguese queen had no children.

Which meant Crofts could be only one of two people. And they were equally dangerous.

I grabbed Antonio's wrist. "We must go at once," I whispered.

But Antonio had found the sonnet and was skimming it, his forehead furrowed in concentration. "'*Qual in colle aspro, al imbrunir di sera . . . ,*'" he read aloud quietly.

Crofts leaned across the table toward us, a shaft of sunlight laying itself on his face—a slash of yellow stretching from his left temple to the right side of his jaw. "What's wrong? You look scared of me."

"No, of course not." We had to get out of here right now. I knew who Crofts had to be—there was always so much gossip swirling about him, and the members of his family, in London, that I was sure I couldn't be mistaken. Even my father, who rarely mentioned the royal household, had talked about the twin brothers, so handsome and young, accomplished fighters who had grown up with almost nothing and who now had more riches than they could ever have dreamed of. But which twin stood before me?

"There's only one reason you would suddenly be scared of me," Crofts whispered, keeping his eyes locked on mine, "and that's if you've figured out who I am."

To my astonishment, he smiled—such a clear, relieved smile it transformed his face, changing him from forbidding to handsome.

"Masquerades are a burden," he whispered, "and I've labored

under their weight too many times."

"You didn't masquerade," I hissed. "Crofts is the name that you and your brother go by, isn't it?"

"Yes. One of our earliest guardians was called Crofts, and when we lived in France it seemed safer to adopt his surname than to use our true one." His eyes flicked over to Antonio, who was now watching us warily. "You're a foreigner, so I don't expect you to understand what we're speaking about."

He paused, as if bracing himself for what he had to say. "Seventeen years ago, my twin brother and I were born in the Netherlands to our father and his mistress. We would have been born in England if Fortune's wheel had spun in a different direction—or perhaps we wouldn't have been born at all. We spent our first dozen years in exile, slinking from one country to the next. When our father finally returned to these shores, we followed him."

He gave us a thin-lipped smile. "My brother James and I have been granted impressive titles—he's the Duke of Monmouth and I'm the Duke of Lockton—but the circumstances of our birth ensure that we will never truly belong in our family."

He took a deep breath, like a swimmer preparing to plunge into icy waters. "We're the king's eldest illegitimate children. All my life I've grown up beneath his hand. For this reason I slipped away and traveled to Mr. Milton's home as quickly as I could when Buckingham left London in search of him. I understand, better than anyone, what my father's capable of. He's a tyrant."

Crofts paused, the muscles in his throat rippling as he swallowed hard. "I hate to think what terrible secret must be buried in my family's past, but it is only right and just that the public should know what it is. Kings are permitted no secrets. If my father tries to deceive his people, then he no longer deserves to wear the crown. When we learned about the Florentine's arrival, my father swore he would stop at nothing to silence Mr. Milton. We must do everything in our power to learn why."

Eleven

IN THE END, THE LIBRARIAN PERMITTED US TO unchain the book and bring it to an empty room nearby. It was a small, plain chamber, unfurnished except for a table and a handful of chairs. Its long windows overlooked a courtyard that was slowly turning gold in the afternoon sunlight. The sudden privacy was a relief: our whispered conversations in the library had caught several students' attention, and they had glared at us, irritation plain in their features. I had feared it wouldn't be long before some of the highborn students recognized the king's son.

Antonio placed the book on a table. Crofts leaned against the door, watching us with agonized eyes. "I—I didn't know if I should tell you the truth earlier, when I met you in the woods," he faltered. "I was afraid you wouldn't trust me if you knew who I really am."

"And why should we trust you now?" Antonio shot back. "So far, all you've proven to us is you're a liar."

"Antonio!" I grabbed his sleeve, tugging on it until he reluctantly followed me to the far side of the room. "You can't speak so boldly to the king's son," I said in Italian, hoping Crofts was unversed in the language. "He may have been born out of wedlock, but it's well known that the king dearly loves him and his brother. The duke is one of the most powerful people in my country—no doors are barred to him; he can go wherever he wishes, do whatever he wants."

"He can lay no claim to me," Antonio muttered. "*I* have no king."

This, I knew, was true. Tuscany was ruled by dukes, and Antonio's master served the grand duke, the most elevated personage in his city-state. If Antonio ran afoul of our king's son, it was possible Grand Duke Ferdinand would intercede on his behalf. But it was a risk we couldn't take.

Crofts's boots rang on the floor as he walked toward us. His face was pale and strained. "I see I must speak plainly with you. Then perhaps you'll understand why I wish to help." For a moment, he was silent, a muscle twitching in his cheek. "Kings must uphold the laws of their land. If they don't, anarchy ensues. We only have to look back twenty years to see the proof—my grandfather dissolved Parliament and attempted to assume absolute power, and all he got for his troubles was a bloody war and his head severed from his neck."

He rubbed his own, shivering slightly, as if he could feel the steel of the executioner's ax. "I may be an illegitimate duke, but I consider the English to be my people, and I would battle my father to protect them. My coming after you may have been easy—I told my servants I was joining friends on a hunting excursion to Yorkshire—but if my involvement became known, I would be seen as a traitor. Nothing would keep me alive."

Emotion cracked his final word in two. Antonio and I looked at each other and nodded in silent agreement.

I turned to Crofts, who was staring at the floor. His breath shuddered between his lips.

"Let's read the sonnet," I said. "Together."

Crofts's head snapped up. "Then you're willing to let me join you?" At my nod, he clasped my hand, the leather of his gloves warm on my skin. "Thank you," he said softly.

We returned to the table. Crofts sank into a chair, resting his chin on his hand. "I don't know a word of Italian. Can you translate it for me?"

I bent over the volume, its scent of old paper and ink assailing my nose. The edges of the pages had already begun to yellow with age, and some of the words had faded to gray. "It's a sonnet written from the perspective of an Englishman spying on a young shepherdess at twilight. The plant she's watering isn't native to the area but flourishes under her touch, just as the writer says his love for her makes his tongue 'flower.'"

Crofts raised his eyebrows. "Begging your pardon, Miss Milton, but this poem hardly sounds like the great literature I expect from your father."

I frowned. Crofts was correct: the subject matter was unusual for my father, who often focused on weighty topics like politics or biblical stories. This flimsy love poem sounded utterly unlike him.

Antonio looked up. "It's clearly not written by a native speaker. Mr. Milton's grasp of Italian is admirable, but several of his phrases sound discordant to my ear. The last two lines are particularly awkward." He translated aloud. "'Ah! I wish my heart was slow and my chest hard toward she who sows such fertile terrain from the heavens.' 'Heavens' could also mean 'from above,'" he added.

"That's a strange image," I said. "What exactly is this 'fertile terrain from the heavens'? And what is this familiar young shepherdess planting? It must be important, since my father focuses on it for three whole lines."

"I would interpret *avezza* as 'expert,' not as 'familiar,'" Antonio said. "Someone who is experienced in her tasks."

"So we have an expert shepherdess tending a non-native flowering plant at twilight." Crofts heaved a sigh. "Miss Milton, are you certain your father was referring to this poem when you were bidding farewell to each other?"

I barely heard him, but latched onto the sonnet instead. A shepherdess watering a non-native plant—the sonnet began with this picture, and therefore I knew my father must have considered it important, for he had always told me that a writer's most crucial line was his first one.

"What's significant about this plant or the ground she tends?" I wondered aloud. "Why did my father identify this terrain as coming from the heavens?"

Antonio glanced at me, his face suddenly tense. "Signor Galilei's area of knowledge was the heavens—the skies, that is—"

"Who's Signor Galilei?" Crofts looked from Antonio to me. Before either of us could reply, he continued, "You needn't seek any heavenly ground in Oxford. The only special land around here is the Physic Garden."

I whirled on Crofts. "A garden?"

Beside me, Antonio sucked in a deep breath. He must have made the same leap I had: in *Paradise Lost*, as in the Bible, the Garden of Eden contains a multitude of plants and flowers— and the Tree of Knowledge. Beneath its apples' shiny red skin lie the intertwined blessing and curse of illumination and death. A single taste will make you wise, but mortal.

Crofts looked startled. "Yes, a garden. Why does that matter?"

"Something's hidden there." My pulse threaded unevenly with excitement. "Just like the Tree of Knowledge in the Garden of Eden."

Crofts tilted his head to the side, considering. "It's a clever hiding place. Gardeners tend it, so anything your father concealed there won't have been lost to lands turning wild."

"We have to find it immediately!"

Crofts shoved his chair back from the table and surged to his feet. "We can't risk others seeing us poking around in the garden—they'll be sure to ask questions or send a message to my father about my behavior. We should wait until night has fallen. There's an inn nearby with decent beds and a discreet proprietor. Once the sun has set, we can return."

He hurried from the room.

Although my legs burned to run to the Physic Garden, I knew Crofts was right. Father's secret had remained buried for who knew how many years, and a few hours more wouldn't make a difference. I made to follow him but Antonio caught my wrist.

"What do you think about him?" he whispered in Italian, nodding at the door through which Crofts had gone. "He's put himself in grave danger by helping us. My master would say he's proved himself to be a true nobleman, by showing us his noble heart."

I snorted. "An elevated lineage is no guarantee of a noble heart. Most nobles are immoral charlatans."

Antonio winced. "That seems unfair. I've known many good-hearted aristocrats. Florence's grand duke has always treated me and my master well and supported our experiments."

"You haven't had cause to hate nobles as I have." I thought of how Father had looked when he'd returned from prison six years ago: painfully thin, his chest and arms stringy, his hands shaking so uncontrollably that I had had to spoon soup into his mouth. Bitterness made my tone hard. "They presume to rule because of their lineage, not because they wish to take care of their country-men. They punished my father because he wanted to build a land in which men are equal. So if you find me unfair to them, I don't care. I'll never regret my feelings."

I ripped myself out of his grasp and stalked from the room. Without a word, Antonio followed me. His face was as dark as a storm cloud, and he kept his gaze trained straight ahead. The only sound was the tramping of our boots on the floor.

At the end of the corridor, Crofts waited. If he noticed the fury seething between us, he ignored it, saying, "Come, let's go to the inn."

Wordlessly we fell in step alongside him and walked outside into the oppressive heat of another afternoon unrelieved by rain.

The inn that Crofts had chosen for us to stay at was a short, squat building of yellow stone. As I had no money to pay for my lodgings, I offered to stay in a room on the ground level, where servants and travelers too poor to afford a bed paid for the privilege of slumping over a rope to keep themselves off the floor. Crofts smiled at my suggestion, saying we couldn't take the chance of one of my room companions noticing the ladylike way I used a chamber pot. With flaming cheeks, I stammered out my agreement—which was how I'd found myself ensconced in a fine chamber on the second story, paid for with Crofts's coins.

Crofts had ordered baths drawn for three of us—a dreadful extravagance in this drought, but his sack of guineas silenced the innkeeper's protests. Maidservants had hauled a wooden tub to my room and filled it from ewers of fragrant, steaming water. After I had washed, I dressed again in my travel-stained clothes. They were the only boy's garments I had, so it couldn't be helped.

The gleam of silver on the wall caught my attention. Rising, I felt as drawn to it as a river's current to its banks, moved by forces greater than itself.

I had never seen myself in a glass. The ministers of my faith said true value came from within, which was why we wore no color next to our skin and hung no mirrors in our houses. When I was a child, I'd often wondered what I looked like, and had tried to catch my reflection in shop windows or the reflecting pools in city parks, but all I'd been able to see was a pale oval framed with dark hair. I had reasoned I must resemble my sisters, for they looked remarkably like one another, but I didn't *know*.

Barely daring to breathe, I raised my head and stared at

myself in the mirror. A stranger looked back.

My face was long and narrow, ending in the strong curve of my jaw. The eyes I had always assumed I'd inherited from my father were his shade of pale blue, but clearer, unmarked by whitish film. Chestnut-brown hair cascaded down my back—the replica of my sisters' tresses. My skin wasn't the plain white I had expected but tinged with gold, doubtless colored by the last few days spent riding in the sun.

Suddenly I was smiling at my reflection. Looking at myself in the glass hadn't felt wrong or wicked. It had felt . . . right, I decided.

A knock sounded on the chamber door. Clapping on my hat and stuffing my hair under it, I hurried to open the door.

Antonio stood in the corridor. His face was scrubbed clean, his cheeks flushed pink. The tips of his hair were still wet from his bath. Even from a few feet away, I could smell lavender soap on his skin. He held a serving tray. Pewter domes covered the plates.

"I took the liberty of bringing you supper," he said. "I hope that's all right."

"Yes. Please. Bring it in." I was so startled to see him at my door that I stumbled over the words. Waving him inside, I slipped off my hat. I closed the door behind him and leaned against it, watching him set the tray on the writing table by the window. Beyond the glass, the sky blazed with its final strains of sunlight, rimming Antonio's form with gold.

He bowed. "Enjoy your meal, Elizabeth. I'll call for you again at dusk."

"Stay." The word was out of my mouth before I could snatch it back.

He froze. "You would invite me to remain when I wronged you in the library?" he asked quietly. "Your heart is more forgiving than I deserve."

"It's how I was taught by my faith," I said.

For a heartbeat, he was silent. "Then perhaps religion isn't as useless as I thought. Thank you for the invitation," he added, drawing a chair back from the table and looking at me, clearly waiting for me to sit.

"Not yet," I said. "You haven't apologized."

He threw his head back and laughed. "You're right, I haven't." Closing the distance between us, he took my hands in his. In the growing darkness, his eyes held a liquid sheen, as though they were made of brown glass. "I shouldn't have accused you of being unfair. Your feelings about the nobility are understandable. I ask your forgiveness, Elizabeth."

I smiled. "You have it." Together we sat down.

"I have four brothers," Antonio said. He removed the domes covering the plates, revealing dishes piled with mutton and potatoes. Although his tone was casual, the look he sent me was hesitant, as though he were forcing himself to speak when he would rather not. "I haven't seen them in years. They work with my parents in vineyards and olive orchards outside Florence."

I cut a slice of mutton. "Their profession sounds quite different from yours."

"I hear the question in your voice, although you're too polite to ask it." He didn't look at me but gazed instead at his plate. "I'm lowborn. By all rights, I should still be working in the vineyards with my brothers."

His tone became brisk. "Vincenzo Viviani isn't my cousin— that's a story he made up to explain my sudden appearance in his home. My true name is Antonio Galletti. When I was seven, I was traveling with my family, seeking new work, at the end of the harvest season. We came to a village inn. In these places, everyone sits at the same table, and I wound up next to a gentleman who was entertaining others by doing sums in his head with lightning speed. It was like magic.

"I begged him to teach me. By the time the dishes were cleared, I had mastered the two times table. He asked me my name and age, and then he said if my parents gave their consent I could become his apprentice. They were grieved to give me up, but they knew we couldn't refuse such an opportunity. I haven't seen them since. But I'm afraid if we met again, they wouldn't know me because I'm so greatly changed from the farmhand they knew. Or they would feel ashamed," he added, his voice cracking, "and imagine I no longer care for them because of the differences in our stations. And that is my secret, Elizabeth."

At once I understood what he had done: he'd given me a piece of himself, the part he hid from everyone else, because I had shown him my private pain about the nobility.

"You've given me a gift," I said. "Thank you."

He made a restless gesture with his hand. "I think it's time we left for the garden, don't you?" He strode to the door, then turned to look back at me, the white of his teeth flashing in an unexpected grin. "Why are you still sitting? Come! Where's your sense of adventure?"

Perhaps this was how he could push away fear and sadness so easily. He treated life as an adventure. This wasn't foolishness, then, as I would have thought only a few days ago. This was bravery.

I unbuttoned my cuffs and raised my arms, letting the fabric fall from my wrists to reveal my strapped knives. "I'm ready."

He laughed again. And I couldn't help wondering why he had sounded so bitter when he'd mentioned religion—and wishing I had the courage to ask him.

Twelve

THE PHYSIC GARDEN HAD BEEN BUILT ON TOP OF the old Jewish cemetery, Crofts told us as we slipped, as quiet as wraiths, through Oxford's dusk-painted streets. The sun was setting behind the stone houses, burnishing their roofs orange-red. Lanterns hanging beside front doors swung in the breeze, throwing alternating lines of black and gold across the cobblestones. Except for the creaking of lantern chains or the occasional rattle of carriage wheels, a blanket of silence seemed to have laid itself across the city in preparation for the coming night.

"Didn't the Jews object to the desecration of their burial ground?" Antonio asked Crofts. I kept my hand at my side, my fingers curled tight around the wooden handle of a spade. Antonio carried another. We had borrowed the tools from the innkeeper, who had hastily proffered them when Crofts asked if he had any shovels he could spare.

"There weren't any Jews to protest," Crofts told Antonio. "They were expelled from England hundreds of years ago. Only in the last few years have they begun trickling back in."

He didn't say why, but I knew: Mr. Cromwell had offered Jews the right to practice trade, provided they bothered no one. Crofts's father, the king, however, had done even more for the Jews: he had promised them religious tolerance. Maybe, I thought with an uncomfortable twinge, even the king carried some kindness in his heart.

At dusk the Physic Garden's imposing stone archway looked bluish white. As one, the three of us hurried beneath it. Orderly rows of plants, much shriveled by the drought, stretched out before us. Some rows had blank spaces where plants should have been, reminding me of a mouth with missing teeth. The scent of herbs I couldn't identify carried on the breeze. Except for a university don walking with a couple of students, all of them easily identifiable by their long black robes, the gardens were deserted.

"Rosemary is good for treating nausea," the tutor was saying in a broad Yorkshire accent. "And rue can be added to wine to ease a headache."

We slipped past them. In the gathering dimness, the gardens feathered out as far as I could see in all directions.

"Where do we go?" Crofts asked. "The Physic Garden covers several acres, so our search must be methodical."

"I was thinking on the walk here—does the garden contain any apple trees?" Antonio asked.

I gasped. *Apple trees—of course!*

"I know where they're planted," Crofts said. "My family and

I have toured the garden many times. Come!"

We dashed down the long paths between the plant beds. Crofts took several turns, stopping finally at a long line of medium-sized trees. There had to be at least twenty of them, spindly black silhouettes, their branches laden with dry-looking leaves.

But what now? My father couldn't have concealed something *within* a tree. He must have buried an object at its base. The question was, How could we guess which one?

In silence we walked the lines of trees. Judging by their middling height, they were about twenty years old. Perhaps they had been planted at around the time my father had revised the sonnet. Frustrated, I gritted my teeth. How could he have brought us this far and then deserted us without more answers?

"There must be additional clues in the sonnet," I said. Frowning, I ran my father's poem through my head again. An expert shepherdess tends a non-native plant while an Englishman watches her. . . . I spun around and stared at the trees. A non-native plant. At least one of these trees must have been grown from foreign seeds.

"I know," I breathed. "We seek an apple tree that isn't indigenous."

Crofts nodded. "That must be it! But . . . the university uses this garden as a teaching tool for its botany students, and they probably gather seedlings from all over the world. We have no way of knowing which— I have an idea," he interrupted himself.

He sprinted in the direction from which we had come, blending into the shadows until I could no longer see him. Each beat of my heart felt like the tick of a clock, counting away precious time we might not have. Antonio and I looked at each other grimly.

Just then Crofts returned, his face creased in a grin. "I spoke to the university tutor we saw when we came in. He said the third and twelfth trees in this row came from seedlings transported from the New World."

A gear seemed to move within my mind. "The number three is significant in *Paradise Lost*. The divine trinity of God, Christ, and the Holy Spirit is juxtaposed with the wicked threesome of Satan, Sin, and Death. Galileo is mentioned three times. And the sonnet that led us here was the third one in my father's book."

"It must be the third tree." Antonio and I rushed forward and dropped to our knees on either side of the tree's base. I pushed my spade into the ground, expecting it to give easily. But it had been baked solid by the drought: the dirt was hard and unyielding. To be so close to my father's secret and unable to reach it! I let out a growl of frustration and hacked at the earth, sending clumps of dirt flying through the air. I was dimly aware of Crofts standing behind us, waiting.

The ringing of metal on metal stilled my hands. I jerked my head up to look at Antonio. He was staring at the ground in front of him, his face tight with concentration.

"I've hit something!" he whispered.

A chill crawled up my spine. A small hole, no more than two feet deep, yawned in the ground at Antonio's feet. Inside it sat a small box. Metal gleamed through the layer of dirt covering it. With shaking hands, Crofts picked it up and brushed it clean. Then he held it out to me.

"The honor should be yours," he said. "You're his daughter, after all."

"Thank you, Your Grace."

The box felt cool, its surface gritty with dried dirt. I pried open the lid, its hinges protesting with a metallic shriek. The inside was lined with green velvet, so worn in places that it had been rubbed smooth. Nestled in the velvet were a rolled-up strip of vellum and a silver tube. The latter felt cold and was capped at one end. When I shook it, I heard liquid sloshing inside. I ran my fingers over the cap, wondering if I ought to pull it off. I hesitated. Father was a cautious man; he would have left instructions for handling such a peculiar object.

Crofts laid out the vellum on his lap, then shook his head. "There's writing here, but it's too dark to read it."

My heart was slamming so hard against my breastbone that it was difficult to breathe. "We must find light."

"Wait." Antonio scooped the mound of dirt back into the hole, then patted the ground with the flat of his spade, trying to conceal the evidence that anyone had been here. I watched him with mounting impatience.

Once Antonio was done, we raced out of the garden, making for the university building, where a couple of ground-floor windows glowed gold with candlelight. Their soft illumination was all I needed to see the letters scrawled across the piece of vellum. The vellum itself was a piece of animal hide, probably calf's hide, and was soft and butter yellow. I recognized the small, careful handwriting as my father's. This must have been penned before he lost his sight and had to rely on others as his scribes. He had written in Latin—the universal language, known by all learned men. He must have wanted anyone to be able to read this page, then, not only Englishmen.

The vellum was dated *Junius MDCXLII*—June 1642 in Latin. My throat tightened. I knew why that period of time was significant. "My father must have written and buried this when he came to Oxfordshire to meet and marry my mother," I said. By then he had already traveled to Florence and met Galileo and was working as a tutor and writing poetry while all around him England slowly descended into civil war.

"Tell us what it says," Crofts urged.

I looked at him in surprise. Surely a king's son, even one born on the wrong side of the blanket, was versed in Latin.

"My upbringing in exile hardly provided an atmosphere conducive to education." He sounded embarrassed.

Not wishing to cause him further shame, I hurriedly translated as I read aloud: *"In the month of June in the year of our Lord 1642, I, John Milton, poet, vow that the following story is true and witnessed by my own eyes. Four years ago, while journeying through the Italian city-states, I was introduced to the son of the natural philosopher Galileo. He arranged for me to meet his father at his villa outside Florence in Arcetri, where he lived under house arrest for thinking differently upon the motions of the heavenly bodies than the tyrants in the Church in Rome did. There I found an elderly man, much pained in his body but still brilliant in his mind. As the skies turned black and glittered with stars, we walked in the olive orchards outside his home toward the hill from which one can see Fiesole on one side and the plains stretching toward Pistoia on the other—*

"Fiesole!" I interrupted myself. In *Paradise Lost*, the Tuscan Artist who sees Satan through his telescope is mentioned as living near Fiesole. If I needed further evidence that my father had intended this literary figure to represent Galileo, then surely this was it. With a guilty twinge, I realized I had misspelled the place name in Father's poem.

Crofts made an impatient gesture, and I picked up the thread of what I had been reading: *"When the night had grown cold and the stars had hardened to balls of ice, Galileo said we had kindred minds, and therefore he knew he could trust me. We walked to his laboratory, where he showed me a small quantity of a silver liquid he kept hidden in a bottle covered with black paint. The substance was so bright it dazzled my eyes and left a stabbing ache in my head for hours afterward. It lies in the tube which you have found, and which I beg you not to open yet. You may disregard my warning, of course, but if you do I swear you will endure nothing but endless torment. If you wish to know how to keep yourselves safe, there is much you must learn about this liquid first—why it has the power to topple kings from thrones and why Galileo and I could not destroy it, although we longed to with every beat of our hearts. You will only have proved your right to know these truths by assembling every piece of the puzzle that Galileo and I have created for you."*

There the missive ended. For a long moment, the only sounds were our ragged breathing and the far-off chiming of church bells, marking the hour of ten o'clock. Slowly, like a sleeper trapped in a dream, I lifted my gaze from the vellum. Antonio's dark eyes burned into mine.

"There isn't anything else?" he asked hoarsely.

I shook my head. "I don't understand. How can this liquid destroy kings? Is this substance what the king is so desperate to conceal?"

Antonio reached for the vial.

"*Don't*," Crofts said sharply. "Mr. Milton complained of a headache after viewing its contents, and we mustn't forget both he and Galileo went blind. Perhaps that is the 'endless torment' Mr. Milton meant. And— What's that?" he interrupted himself. He pointed to a line of squiggles running along the bottom of the strip of vellum. "They look like drawings of some sort."

I peered at the tiny, twisted shapes: בחול ביתי. The hairs on the back of my neck rose. I recognized those markings. "They're words, not drawings—my father is fluent in biblical Hebrew, and he taught me. You would pronounce it as *bekhol bethi*. It means 'in the sand of my house.'"

"'In the sand of my house?'" Crofts repeated. "What the devil does that mean?"

"I haven't the slightest idea. It sounds like a line from the Bible, but I don't recognize it." I stared at the vellum, the letters stark and black against the yellowed animal hide. "My father seems to have put together a treasure hunt," I said slowly, thinking. "And designed it in such a manner that only those he deems worthy can solve it."

Antonio touched my hand. "In the letter your father sent to my master," he said urgently, "he wrote that the only people who could put together the clues would be those who were well educated *and* knew the details of his life—because he hoped that men who knew about him would agree with his political beliefs. Your father might be referring to *his* house, Elizabeth. Where was he living in 1642?"

I couldn't snatch hold of my whirling thoughts. "He—he was living in London, but he moved frequently. And I can't imagine he would have left the next clue at one of his previous lodgings, out of fear that the next occupants might happen across it. He would have taken it with him—*he would have taken it with him*," I repeated as my words' full significance hit me. "This clue must be hidden in my family's home!"

"But which one?" Crofts demanded. "Your lodgings in London or Chalfont?"

I didn't even need to reason that through. "London. My father has never considered any other place his home—he's a London man through and through. But the sand—I don't understand it . . ."

In my mind's eye I saw myself descending the cellar steps, as I had done most mornings, and dipping a cup into a barrel to get sand, which I would use to blot the pages I would cover with my father's dictation. I gasped. "The next clue is in the sand barrels in the cellar of our London house!"

Antonio grabbed the vellum and vial, dropping them into the box and shutting it with a clang. "Come on," he said, and the three of us took off running.

Thirteen

EXCITEMENT LENT WINGS TO OUR FEET AS WE slipped through the quiet streets. With each step I took, I imagined I felt eyes boring holes into my back, but when I looked behind us there was no one. In the wind, the lanterns swung wildly, throwing arcs of light across the roads.

At the inn, I crept upstairs while Antonio and Crofts saddled the horses. None of us had unpacked our things, and I made quick work of grabbing our bags and tiptoeing outside, where I found the boys waiting in the stables. Crofts had raided the inn's kitchens for provisions, leaving behind a handful of guineas as compensation.

Wordlessly we strapped our bags to the horses. Every flutter of the breeze made me start, but the night was quiet, the courtyard deserted except for us.

We led the horses to the street. As we swung ourselves onto

the saddles, Crofts said, "Go slowly. We don't want our speed to attract anyone's attention. Once we reach the countryside, though, ride as hard as you can."

Although I longed to urge my horse to go faster, I kept my hands easy on the reins. The horses picked their way over the cobblestones, their hooves ringing.

When we reached the city outskirts, we kicked our spurs and sprinted toward the fields. I kept my eyes trained on the jagged line of trees on the horizon. We plunged into the fields, the long grasses slapping our horses' legs. Beneath the crashing of my breath in my ears, I caught something else: the faint thud of hoofbeats on packed earth.

I twisted around in my saddle, straining to see in the darkness. Already the lanterns of Oxford were some distance behind us. The stars had begun to come out, raining silver on the fields. By their faint illumination I could just pick out three black silhouettes—the curved shapes of men hunched low on their horses' backs. They were racing directly toward us. One of them shouted, "Faster! Don't let them get away!"

They were after us.

Shock stole my breath. Were they highwaymen? Or Buckingham's spies? They must have concealed themselves in the fields, lying in wait for us until we passed—but how had they known where to find us?

For a horrible instant, my eyes met Antonio's. His were wide, and his lips were set in a grim line.

There was no time, though, to think. I kicked my heels against my horse's sides, urging him onward. We thundered across the fields so fast that the grasses became an endless blur.

My heart was slamming so hard into my breastbone I could scarcely breathe. With one hand I clutched the reins; with the other I reached for my sword, my fingers closing around the hilt just as a speck of black appeared on the periphery of my vision. It was one of our pursuers racing ahead of me, but he was still little more than a dark streak under the star-dotted sky.

Then he wheeled around to face me, pulling so hard on his reins that his beast shrieked and reared back on its hind legs. Its front legs kicked, narrowly missing my horse's head. I let out a harsh cry and yanked on my reins, trying to force my horse to move back. It staggered to the side, whinnying in terror. The other rider's horse kicked again, its hooves coming within a hair-breadth of my arm.

"Elizabeth!" Antonio shouted from somewhere.

My horse reeled and I nearly lost my seating. *Don't fall, don't fall.* Digging my knees harder into the horse's flanks, I drew on the reins once more, yelling, "Stay!" With my right hand I pulled my smallsword free from its sheath with a rattle of metal. From behind me I heard the sounds of fighting—clanging steel, panting breaths, muffled shouts.

The other rider's agitated horse danced from side to side. In the silver-spangled darkness, its owner looked ghostly, all traces of color washed from his face. With a jolt, I realized I recognized him as one of the students from the Bodleian Library this afternoon; he had been sitting at a table, darting irritated looks at us until we retired to another room. He had to be one of Buckingham's men—but how had he known how to hunt us down? Now he held a sword aloft.

Without warning he charged at me, his weapon descending

through the air toward me like a silver line. At once I whipped my sword into a protective blocking position above my head. Steel sang as his blade hit mine. A tremor shot up my arm. I didn't let my arm fall, but pressed with all my might, trying to force his sword away from mine. We remained seated on our horses, our faces inches from each other's. I could see the brown dots along his jawline where his barber hadn't shaved closely enough and the shadows beneath his eyes that spoke of sleepless nights. The scent of rose water clung to his skin—a rich man's perfume.

"What do you want?" I yelled. My arm trembled from the effort of blocking his sword.

The man glared at me, his face a mask of rage. "To stop your father! May God curse him and his traitor angels!"

"What—"

But I never had the chance to finish the question. With a bellow of rage, the man lifted his sword higher, as if he was preparing to lop off my head with one blow. He had left his chest exposed, though, and I saw my chance. I slashed at his side—two quick lines that formed an X. I took care not to make the cuts too deep, using just a shallow swipe of my sword to stop him in his tracks.

He let out a horrible cry and sagged forward. His sword fell, landing in the grass with a soft thump. He clutched his side, gasping. Lines of blood trickled between his fingers. In the night, the blood looked black.

"Come!" a man shouted from behind me. "We have it!"

My assailant streaked past me, clutching the reins one-handed, the other hand still holding his side.

"After him!" I shouted at my horse, digging my heels into his flanks. The terrified animal merely turned in a circle, whimpering. As we wheeled around, I caught sight of a crumpled form on the ground, a tangle of arms and legs surrounded by tufts of grass. It lay unmoving.

All the air seemed to rush from my chest. *Antonio.*

I pulled on the reins as hard as I could. A jumble of thoughts streamed through my head: *No, please.* I slid off the saddle. My legs were shaking so badly I didn't think they would support me, but somehow I was running across the field, the long grasses slapping at my chest. Dimly I heard our pursuers riding away.

Antonio lay motionless, his face pressed into the dirt. He still wore his broad-brimmed hat, which hid the condition of his head from me. I prayed a horse hadn't kicked him there, for I had never heard of a man recovering from such an injury. My hands grasped Antonio's shoulders, preparing to turn him over, and his hair brushed my fingers. The strands were stiff and curled.

It was a wig. No human hair felt like that.

"Crofts," I whispered. Not Antonio. A small pocket of warmth bloomed in my heart, but I couldn't let myself reflect upon my relief now. I rolled Crofts onto his back.

He was conscious, but barely. His eyes fluttered open and closed. Moonlight touched his face, showing the damage his assailant had wrought. His lips were swollen and split. A bruise already stretched along his jaw. When he coughed, flecks of blood flew from his mouth. A few drops landed on his cheek, the little circles marring his pale flesh. He kept his arms curled over his chest, making me wonder if any of his ribs had been broken.

Antonio dropped down next to me, sliding his sword into its sheath with a whine of metal. He was breathing hard. There was a shallow cut on his forehead, and his doublet had been torn, revealing his white shirt beneath.

"Are you all right?" he asked hoarsely.

"I'm well enough. We must look after the duke."

"I have failed in my duty." Crofts's voice was weak. His eyes snapped open, moving wildly until they focused on me. "My attacker dragged me from my horse. I tried to stop him, but he got the box."

I closed my eyes, enfolding myself in darkness. So these enemies of ours had gotten my father's clues. *Oh, Father*, I thought despairingly, *how on earth can we help you now?*

"Can you get up?" Antonio asked Crofts.

I opened my eyes to see Antonio with his arm around Crofts's back, struggling to help him sit upright. Something in my chest twisted at the sight. This Crofts didn't know Antonio or me, and by all rights he should have hated my father for encouraging his grandfather's execution. Yet he helped us, simply because he didn't want kings to transform into tyrants—even though it meant opposing his own father.

He ground out a curse between clenched teeth. "I should have stopped them from getting the box—"

"It wasn't your fault," I interrupted, brushing a stray curl from his jaw, which had already begun to swell.

"We'll take you back to the inn," Antonio said. "Then Elizabeth and I must go on ahead to London without you. As long as we can reach her family's home first, it doesn't matter that those men got the box." He sent me a grim look. "I hope the horses aren't already tired. We're about to embark on the race of our lives."

✼

Crofts insisted on going with us, though, saying his position of privilege would open doors that would otherwise remain closed to us. Rather than waste time arguing, we hurriedly bound his ribs—he swore none were broken, although I wasn't certain I believed him—and helped him onto his horse.

The position of the constellations told us in which direction the east lay, and we directed our horses toward the horizon where the sun would appear—toward London. We didn't dare stay on the roads, so we raced across the open countryside. I kept wondering if we would overtake our pursuers, and what we would do if we did, but I didn't see a soul. Who were those men, though? And how had they known where to find us?

Time ceased to exist. Fields stretched on and on, etched with silver from the moon. At last the stars gasped and died. There was only the black weight of the sky, and in the east, a pale swath of gray.

Crofts's horse slowed to a shuffle. Crofts sat slumped in his saddle, his head lolling on his neck. Was he ill? Or had his injuries grown too painful? Antonio and I pulled up alongside him.

"We shouldn't stop," Crofts mumbled.

I started to reach for him, then hesitated. *He's a king's son and you're the daughter of a suspected regicide*, I reminded myself. Then I saw how his fingers dug into his ribs, as if he were trying to hold them together, and every wall separating us seemed to crumble. I pressed my hand to the exposed flesh of his neck. It was burning hot and damp with sweat.

"He's ill," I said sharply to Antonio. "Get him down, and quickly. We must break his fever."

"I'm well," Crofts protested as Antonio and I scrambled off our horses. Antonio laid him on the ground while I searched the sumpters for the water skins. By the time I had returned with them, Antonio had removed Crofts's shirt. I wet a strip of linen and wiped Croft's chest and face with it, praying its cool touch would bring him some relief.

"We may have to bleed him," Antonio said. "Part of his blood could be poisoned from the fever. We must find the warmest place on his body, then cut there, before the polluted blood can circulate."

My hand paused in the act of drawing forth my knife. "Circulate? What do you mean?"

"The heart pumps blood and moves it throughout the body." Crofts's voice was a shaky whisper. "My grandfather's physician discovered it years ago, but few people believe in the theory." He coughed. "Don't bleed me. Please. When I was fighting the Hollanders, I saw so many men on my ship die from their injuries."

As Crofts paused for breath, Antonio sent me a questioning look. "Do you remember I told you about England being at war with the Netherlands over our sea trade routes?" I asked quietly. "The king's brother, the Duke of York, and the king's twin sons have fought in some of the battles at sea."

"I watched as cannonballs blew them apart," Crofts murmured, "and as blood poured from their wounds. It made me wonder if we must keep the blood in our bodies or die without it." He coughed again, laying a dirty, bloodstained hand on his ribs. "I beg you not to bleed me, Elizabeth."

My name sounded so strange coming from his lips—he had addressed me as a friend. If anyone had told me a few hours ago that the king's son would call me by my first name, I would have thought he'd lost his wits. Now I knew I would do anything, fight anyone, to keep this boy safe, for he could have died while trying to help my family. I rested a gentle hand on his brow.

"I promise I won't, Your Grace," I said.

"You're kind." His eyes drifted closed. "You remind me of my mother."

He said nothing more, his breathing shifting into the shallow rhythm of the slumbering.

"We should rest," Antonio said. "I know you must be desperate to continue to London, but we can't maintain this pace without killing the horses or ourselves. We'll have to hope those thieves won't notice the notation in Hebrew or that they won't be able to translate it."

I let out a shuddering breath. He was right. "Yes, we should sleep."

Neither of us, however, made a move to unpack the bedrolls. Instead we sat side by side on the hard ground. My skin prickled. I looked behind us, but there was nothing except for the unending fields. No attackers, no one at all. They must be far ahead of us by now. Helplessness and fury crested within me like a wave. If only we hadn't brought Crofts with us—maybe we could have caught up to our assailants and retrieved the box.

It was no use mourning what could have happened. Sighing, I hugged my knees to my chest. I could smell blood and leather on Antonio's skin. He looked into the distance, frowning as if deep in thought, his tired face framed by the tangle of his hair.

"Who's the duke's mother?" he asked.

"Lucy Barlow—she was a Welsh gentlewoman who died

several years ago. There are rumors the king secretly married her, which would make the dukes of Lockton and Monmouth legitimate and the rightful heirs to the throne."

Antonio's eyebrows rose, but I said hastily, "I can't imagine the king would have been so foolish. When Crofts and his brother were born, the king was still a young man living in exile. His father had recently been executed, but the stories go that the son never gave up hope of reclaiming the crown someday as Charles the Second. I doubt he would have jeopardized his future by making a disadvantageous match."

For a moment, we sat quietly, listening to the wind rustle through the fields. My thoughts turned to the men who had overtaken us outside Oxford. "The man who attacked me said something very strange—he asked God to curse my father and his 'traitor angels.'" I hesitated. "It reminds me of the way my father described Satan and his followers in *Paradise Lost* as an army of rebel angels. Do you think he was saying that my father is like the devil?"

Antonio shook his head. "Maybe . . . But how could he know about *Paradise Lost* in the first place? You told me that your father has kept his poem secret from everyone except for you and a few trusted friends."

That was true, and I knew those friends well—none of them would have told anyone about Father's poem except in vague terms. So what had the man meant? That my father and his allies were fallen men who were somehow betraying God? I shook my head in frustration. There was so much we didn't understand. "Who do you think are the other angels he mentioned?"

"Maybe Signor Galilei and my master—after all, it does seem

as though the three of them entered into some sort of arrangement thirty years ago. But why would they be called 'traitor angels'?" He frowned, looking frustrated. "And who were those men after us anyway?"

"The king's men," I guessed. "They could have forced our location out of Francis Sutton, like Crofts did." My stomach twisted at the thought. "I hope they didn't hurt him."

Antonio sighed. "I hope so, too. We should sleep." He got up and took a step away, then spun back to me, his expression fierce. "When I saw that man riding toward you with his sword outstretched, I thought—" He broke off, the muscles working in his throat as he swallowed. "I'm glad you're safe."

Without another word, he strode to where the horses stood and began rubbing them down, speaking to them in a low, comforting voice and leaving me alone to stare after him, wondering what he had meant to say and listening to my heart beat madly in my chest.

Fourteen

BY THE TIME WE HAD WOKEN AND EATEN A HASTY meal of bread and dried fruit, the sun was crawling to its noonday zenith. Crofts's fever had broken; his skin was no longer streaked pink, and though he kept a careful hand on his ribs, he spoke without his breath catching in his throat. While we saddled the horses, he insisted that there should be no ceremony between us and that we call him by his Christian name. Addressing a king's son so intimately was such a shocking breach of etiquette I could barely push "Robert" out of my mouth. When I said it, though, he smiled and looked pleased.

We raced across the countryside, pushing the horses until their mouths frothed and their flanks grew slick with sweat. The sun pounded mercilessly on our heads. Every time I closed my eyes against its glare, its yellow spark burned against my lids. A few times, we glimpsed travelers on the road—farmers riding a cart piled high with vegetables, nobles rolling along in a carriage. No trio of men on horseback. My heart sank in disappointment. We'd lost them—and maybe the race to my family's home as well.

When the sun began dropping in the sky, we stopped on the outskirts of a forest. The horses were stumbling from exhaustion, and we didn't dare continue for fear of roaming highwaymen. We led the horses between the trees, plunging deeper into the welcoming cloak of the woods. At last we found a stream to wash in. Antonio grinned at me as he stripped off his ripped doublet, and I wondered if he was remembering how I had stared at him yesterday when we cleaned ourselves in another stream. Flushing, I looked away.

"This drought has been unbearable," Robert muttered. He had rolled up his shirtsleeves and was scrubbing dirt and blood from his forearms.

"Except for the weather, your country seems like a good land." Antonio grinned. "Well, that and the food."

A reluctant smile tugged on Robert's cracked lips. "The food *is* poor, I'll grant you that. My brother James and I lived in France when we were children, and we feasted on delicacies unlike anything I've tasted here."

Antonio strung feed bags over the horses' mouths, saying, "Yes, I doubt most Englishmen have even heard of macaroni."

"What's that?" I asked.

They both laughed. "My point exactly," Antonio said.

We sat in a circle, leaning our aching backs against tree trunks. The trees crowded so close to us that I felt as though we had been enclosed in a pocket made of shifting green and black shadows. As we ate, the boys told me of wondrous foods: frogs' legs; fried zucchini flowers; roasted pigeons wrapped in bacon and figs stuffed with black grapes; and macaroni, a substance Antonio struggled to explain, likening its consistency to tender, pliant string, then laughing uproariously at my revolted expression.

"What do you think the liquid in the vial is?" Robert asked abruptly.

It was as though a lever had been thrown. My laughter died on my lips. All day I had been trying not to think about the box's contents, for fear my questions and my inability to answer them would drive me mad.

"It must be the result of one of Signor Galilei's experiments," Antonio said. "He worked in many areas—astronomy, mathematics, physics, the motion of the tides. It could be anything." He paused. "Whatever it is, though, it must be dangerous, or Mr. Milton wouldn't have warned us not to open it. I've been wondering . . . Mr. Milton suffered a terrible headache after viewing Signor Galilei's liquid. Is it possible that looking at the liquid could have affected both mens' vision? Signor Galilei might have been working on it for years, and that could have resulted in his going blind before he met Mr. Milton."

A knot that had been tied tight in my chest seemed to loosen. "Then you don't believe their blindness was caused by sin."

"Of course not." Antonio looked surprised. "All the time we are discovering new truths about the nature of the universe— why shouldn't we also be learning more about the God who made it? Perhaps he's nothing like previous generations have thought, and the more we uncover about the ways our world is made the better we'll come to know him."

"Men have been burned to death for speaking as you do," Robert warned. "You're walking on treacherous ground, Antonio, and so was Mr. Milton—if the contents of the vial can snatch crowns away from kings, as he claimed. But how can this substance possibly have such far-reaching political consequences?"

"It seems impossible," I said. "But if this liquid *can* somehow destroy a monarch's power, it makes sense that our king wants to suppress it." I stared at the ground turning black in the dusk; I was unable to face either boy. "If the king wants the vial in exchange for my father's life, I must give it to him. And whatever we find in the sand barrel, I'll give that to him, too."

"Is that truly what you think your father wants you to do?" Antonio's voice was low. "He said his life didn't matter—that we needed to survive and protect his poem at all costs."

"I know what he said," I snapped. "But I can't accept his instructions! I have to save him—not only for his sake, but for my sisters and stepmother, too. They can't support themselves, and without him, I don't know what will become of them."

At last I looked up. Antonio was watching me with a mixture of pity and sorrow. Robert's face was contorted in an angry scowl.

"Then you'll be giving my father what he wants!" Robert jumped up and paced, his boots kicking up eddies of dust from the parched ground. "Don't you understand that whatever reason my father has for hunting down the vial can't be honest? Not if he's hunting for the vial in such secrecy! Maybe he wants it not only to protect his throne but also to push other kings from theirs! He could become a tyrant if we let him. My love for my people won't let me stand idly by while you give in to his demands."

"Then we stand on opposing sides," I shot back.

His eyes, dark and furious, locked onto mine. I couldn't look at him for one more instant. I had to get away. I raced between the trees, the skinny black trunks blurring on either side of me. When I reached the edge of a clearing, I stopped, my heartbeat thudding in my ears.

Dimly I heard someone walking behind me, but I didn't bother turning around. Robert could yell at me until he grew hoarse, for all I cared. I'd never change my mind. No matter what sacrifices I had to make, I would save my father. Once the king released him, I would take him and my family to another country, where we could live in safe anonymity, far from our monarch's grasp. And if the prospect of bidding farewell to Antonio tugged on the strings of my heart, I ignored it.

"My master often told me how the Inquisitors broke Signor Galilei," Antonio said quietly from behind me. "He had been friendly with the pope and some of the cardinals on his examining team, but they abandoned him. He had to make a terrible choice—insist his discoveries were correct and endure torture and imprisonment, or renounce his findings and publicly confess he was a heretic." Antonio touched my shoulder, the weight of his hand comforting. "He chose life. Like you. I'll stand by your decision, Elizabeth. Let Robert think that we've discussed the matter and we agree with him."

I whirled around. My eyes traced Antonio's silhouette, dark against the filigree of the trees. He had removed his doublet when we washed in the stream, and his white shirt was the only part of him easily discernible, a faded gray in the dimness cast by the thickly clustered elms.

"You think we should lie to him?" My voice was a hoarse whisper. "That . . . that's a sin."

"Who says a lie is a sin when it's told for the right reason?"

"Then we'd be helping the king—letting him become a tyrant."

Antonio sighed. "I know. But you have to decide—your father's life or the king's crown."

Tears burned my eyes. It was a terrible choice, like Galileo's had been. And then I thought of my father sitting in his chair by the window, smiling gently and turning in my direction when he heard my footsteps.

It wasn't a choice at all.

Slowly I took the hand Antonio offered me. "Then we must smile in the aristocrat's face and plot behind his back."

"We should pretend to work alongside him for as long as possible." Antonio's expression was solemn. "As the king's son, he can probably help us in all sorts of ways. And at some point . . ."

Our eyes met, saying what we could not bring ourselves to speak aloud. At some point we would trick Robert and bring my father's secrets to the king.

"Let the game of deception begin," I said grimly.

By the time we returned to the campsite, Robert had fallen asleep, no doubt exhausted by his injuries. I glanced at the bags on the ground next to our bedrolls. Antonio's telescope was in one of them, and I might not have this chance again after we reached London.

"I love astronomy," I said to Antonio, my tone stiff, daring him to laugh. "For as long as I can remember, I've yearned to unlock the secrets of the stars. If you'll teach me everything you know about them, I'll be grateful forever."

He blinked in surprise, but he didn't laugh or smile. He merely fetched his telescope from his bag and handed it to me. "It would be my honor."

Was he teasing me? I sent him a searching look, but his face was calm, not twisted in mirth. He meant what he said. Something inside me softened, and I smiled at him as my fingers closed around the telescope, its worn brown leather covering still warm from his hands. Through its thick glass lenses, a string of stars looked like silver nails that had been hammered through the sky to keep it from collapsing onto the earth.

"It's called the Milky Way," Antonio said. "Before Signor Galilei studied it, people believed it was one mass, like a large mist. When he published *Sidereus nuncius*, he revealed how the Milky Way is actually made up of hundreds of stars invisible to the naked eye. It was an astounding discovery."

"Could his work in astronomy have to do with the vial?" I asked. "After all, it was his theory on the motions of the planets that brought him to trial in Rome."

"Maybe. But then your father would have buried calculations, drawings of the constellations, things of that sort—not a tube of liquid. Those Inquisitors," he spat. "They hounded Signor Galilei because they couldn't understand it's possible to disprove the workings of the natural world as the Bible presents them *and* still hold God in your heart."

I pulled back from the telescope to peer at Antonio. "Then Galileo wasn't a heretic?"

"No. That's what everyone thinks, but Signor Galilei loved

his Christian faith, even though the Inquisitors took everything from him—his work, his reputation, even his freedom, because he had to spend the rest of his life under house arrest."

I rolled the telescope between my palms, thinking. In 1633, Galileo had been sentenced by the Inquisitors. Five years later, my father visited him, and Galileo confided something to him. Shortly afterward, England descended into civil war and my father began hiding clues about Galileo's secret. Did the links in this deadly chain stretch even further back than we had thought—perhaps all the way to the beginning of this century, when Galileo had undertaken the experiments that would eventually incur the Church's wrath? Or was I merely seeing connections that weren't truly there?

Antonio cut into my thoughts. "For Signor Galilei's sake, I'll always despise the machinery of religion."

I nearly dropped the telescope. "You despise God?"

He let out a pent-up breath. "I hate when people twist religion to suit their own purposes or force others to believe what they do. I believe in the eternity of the soul and the beauty of Jesus's teachings. But I won't believe in the tyrannical Heaven that the Church wants us to worship. Why would God curse babies with ill health for their parents' deeds? Or send a child to Hell if he dies before he's baptized?"

I stared at him, unable to tear my gaze from his agonized expression. These were the same questions I had asked myself countless times because of my family. Why God had warped Anne's legs and mangled her speech as punishment for our parents' supposed sins. Why Father's sight had faded to black as payment for his revolutionary ideas.

"Have I horrified you?" Antonio whispered.

I stepped closer to him so I could hear the gentle inhalation of his breath and see the silvery sheen of moonlight on his face. He didn't smile, as I had half expected, but kept his eyes intent on mine.

"No," I said. "I've struggled with the same ideas. Perhaps your master and Galileo were correct—the universe is a giant puzzle and the discoveries we make about its workings don't need to erode our faith." I hesitated. "Maybe God is the greatest natural philosopher of us all."

At dawn's first light we prepared to set out again. While I washed in the stream, Antonio told Robert we had come around to his way of thinking and had decided to assemble everything my father had concealed and to protect those things from the king. I didn't even feel a guilty twinge when I returned to the campsite and Robert clasped my hand, thanking me for seeing the situation his way. Father's life was worth endless lies.

It was the Lord's Day, so by all rights we should have spent the day at services, but we couldn't spare the time even to kneel at our campsite. There were only ten days left until the next Hanging Day. Ten days before my father died, unless I saved him.

Don't think about it, I told myself fiercely. Thinking would bring pain and fear, and I could afford neither now.

We spoke little and stopped only for a hurried midday meal from the supplies we had packed. When night turned the sky black, we set up camp beneath a fringe of trees. Antonio tended the horses while I laid out our simple supper. By my calculations, we ought to arrive in London sometime tomorrow. I prayed we would be fast enough to get there before our assailants.

"Any idea who those men were who attacked us?" I asked Robert. "Did you recognize them from your father's court?"

He was whittling a piece of wood, his knife flashing in his hands. "No. But it was too dark to see them clearly. I only hope, if they're on their way to London, too, they've taken a different route. I suspect they must have, for I've seen no sign that anyone's on our trail." He hesitated. "I've been thinking about where we should stay when we reach London. I have my own lodgings at Whitehall—in a building separate from the palace, but it's so close I fear my father and his men would be bound to notice if I had any unexpected guests."

Lodge together in London? Clearly he'd believed Antonio's assurances that we were now working in tandem to prevent the king from gaining possession of my father's secrets. I shifted uncomfortably. If Antonio and I succeeded, my family and I would soon be living in a foreign land and he would be on his way home to Florence . . . and Robert would never forgive us for betraying him.

My face went hot. I glanced at Robert. He was sitting cross-legged on Antonio's bedroll. His face was still bruised, but the swelling in his lips had gone down enough so he could speak without slurring his words like a drunkard. Despite our horses' quick pace, he'd continued wearing his wig, keeping it clapped to his head by securing the ties of his hat tightly beneath his chin.

"I thought we would go directly to my family's home." Even to my ears, my voice sounded unnaturally high. "We need to retrieve what my father hid in the sand barrel."

"Yes, of course, but afterward we might need a place to hide while we figure out how to help your father," Robert said. "We should stay with my intended—she has a large estate and a mostly absent chaperone."

"You're engaged to be married?"

"Yes." Robert forced a smile. "My betrothed is Lady Katherine Daly of Ireland. My father hopes to curry the favor of his Irish and Scottish subjects by tying his sons to their country-women. I'm lucky, though," he said hastily, "for Lady Katherine's a beautiful maiden of sixteen. I easily could have been saddled with someone dull-witted and old. And she's devoted to me—we can trust her discretion if we lodge with her."

"Don't you wish to marry for love?" The words tumbled out of my mouth before I could stop them. *Odd's fish, how could I have spoken so boldly?* Without daring to look at Robert, I busied myself setting out the packets of bread and cheese.

"No," Robert said quietly. "I haven't let myself reflect upon such things. Even when we lived in poverty in exile, I knew my life was not my own, whether I had been born out of wedlock or not. I belong to England before I belong to anyone else, and I'll do anything to help my country. Even if it means marrying a stranger or fighting my father."

If only we could work on the same side. I had to let him know how much I admired him. Maybe someday the memory would make my deception taste less bitter in his mouth. Impulsively I grabbed his hand. "You must know I'd prefer a government ruled by the people, but . . . if I had to choose between you and your father as a ruler, I'd choose you."

This time, his smile didn't look forced.

❧

After supper Antonio built a small fire for me to work by, and I continued copying out *Paradise Lost*. There must be additional clues concealed in the poem, the three of us had agreed while we ate. Unfortunately, I knew I would only be able to capture some of my father's original words. At best, most of the verses would be paraphrases; at worst they'd be my own inventions.

Antonio and Robert paced nearby, talking in low voices. At last I stopped and read what I had written. I had reached the section in which Adam speaks with Raphael, an angel who is visiting Eden from Heaven. Satan is creeping through Eden like a low-hanging black mist, and the two humans are still safe—the temptation hasn't yet occurred.

I skimmed the passage in which Adam asks Raphael about the workings of the universe:

When I behold this goodly Frame, this World
Of Heav'n and Earth consisting, and compute
Thir magnitudes, this Earth a spot, a graine
An Atom, with the Firmament compar'd
And all her numbered Starrs, that seem to rowle
Spaces incomprehensible . . .

In this section Adam sounded as though he was an astronomer. An odd image—I'd always pictured him as a farmer.

My hand hovered over the paper. *Adam is an astronomer*, I repeated, my heart thudding in my chest. *He wishes to count the stars, to number the constellations turning in the heavens; he wants to understand the rules of our galaxy.*

Slowly I raised my head to stare at the two boys walking

145

beneath the trees, their outlines red from the firelight.

"I think I've found one of my father's clues!" I called.

As one, they raced to me. "What is it?" Antonio asked.

"There is astronomy in my father's poem," I said, shoving the page at them to read. "In this passage, he portrays Adam as a budding natural philosopher."

They scanned my scrawled lines. Then Antonio's head snapped up.

"These are the sorts of questions I asked my master when I was a boy," he said. "How could your father know I said such things?"

"I don't know. I . . ." I flailed, searching for an answer. "Your master must have told him. Perhaps he and my father have written each other letters for years. How else would my father have known your master's street address?" I asked as the image of my father's letter to Signor Viviani appeared in my mind's eye, the addressee's name and street written in Deborah's handwriting.

"Then if this character says your words," Robert said, darting a look at Antonio, "maybe he's meant to represent you."

A tingle raced along my spine. Father did often weave real-life figures into his poetry. Hastily I flipped to a fresh sheet and scrawled: *Adam. Antonio.* Both began with the letter *A.* Both referred to young men—natural philosophers who study the stars and the makings of the world around them.

As though my fingers moved of their own volition, they tightened on the quill and wrote two more names: *Eve. Elizabeth.*

"My father made *us* into the characters!" I breathed. "The entire story—good and evil, different sides battling one another, two young people seeking something that will give them knowledge, like Adam and Eve and the apple and us and whatever it is that my father hid—it's all a reflection of our quest!"

"By God, I think you must be right!" Robert edged closer to me, his eyes intent on the papers in my lap. "What about the other characters—could they be real people, too?"

I scribbled several angels' names.

"It's an alliterative scheme," I said at once. "My father's fond of such literary tricks. See—there's Michael, an angel, and Milton. The archangel Gabriel and Galileo—he must appear twice, both as himself, 'the Tuscan Artist,' and disguised as an angel to show he's doubly important to the story. There must be a third angel named for Signor Viviani—Uriel!" I concluded triumphantly. "The *U* and *V* letters are so similar, my father would have forced the pattern to fit. These three men represent God's angels, who've fought Satan and his army in Heaven and are determined to keep God's kingdom protected from evil."

"Just as Mr. Milton, Signor Galilei, and my master wanted to keep Signor Galilei's discovery secret but safe," Antonio said. "They appointed themselves its guardians."

"Then why," Robert said urgently, "did that man who attacked Elizabeth refer to those three men as 'traitor angels'? He made them sound wicked, as though they were on the side of Satan and his rebel army."

"Sometimes evil depends on your perspective," Antonio said. I knew by the pained expression on his face he must be thinking of his revered Galileo. "Our assailants probably think Mr. Milton, Signor Galilei, and my master are the wicked ones."

"Evil is eternal and unchanging," Robert disagreed. The boys started arguing as I skimmed through the stack of papers, trying to find more clues. Now I saw my father's poem with new eyes. Eve, whom I had never paid much attention to, fairly leaped off the pages at me: beautiful and sweet, with blond hair curling down her back. She's ruled by what Father refers to as "fancy," but which I knew meant her imagination. Several lines caught my eye:

My Author and Disposer, Eve says to Adam, *what thou bidst, / Unargu'd I Obey; so God ordains, / God is thy Law, thou mine: to know no more / Is womans happiest knowledge and her praise.*

Something icy jabbed my heart. Father was saying Eve not only was inferior to Adam, but rejoiced in her lower status, believing it was the lot of females. I hadn't misremembered those lines; when Father had originally dictated them to me, I'd found them so irritating they'd burrowed into my brain like burrs, difficult to shake loose.

Was this Eve who my father had wanted me to be? This golden-haired, empty-headed beauty? She was nothing like me. I must be missing something—a vital clue hidden somewhere in the story that would tell me why my father had chosen to portray me as a character wholly unlike myself. I flipped through the pages again, but I could find nothing. Well, I hadn't copied out the poem's final three books yet. There might be answers at the story's end—

"We haven't considered one question." Robert's voice interrupted my thoughts. His eyes were wide and frightened. "If many of the characters in *Paradise Lost* are meant to have counterparts in real life, then there's one person whom we must identify as quickly as we can."

My stomach dropped. I knew who he meant.

"Satan," I whispered.

Antonio released a heavy breath. Wordlessly he began kicking dirt onto the fire, smothering the flames. I watched the burning twigs vanish beneath a layer of dark earth, and I couldn't stop shivering, even though the night was warm.

Fifteen

ALL THE NEXT DAY WE RODE. AS WE CANTERED, WE took turns tossing out names to one another as possibilities for my father's Satan. Buckingham? Impossible; his name was George Villiers. The king? The only *s* in his name came at the end of "Charles," and it was apparent from my father's literary scheme that he selected names that began with the relevant letter.

Frustrated, we raced across the parched fields. Whoever my father had selected as his version of the devil, it had to be someone powerful, and the aristocracy presented us with dozens of options. Robert called out suggestions until he suddenly drew hard on his reins. Antonio and I jerked our horses to a halt, then wheeled them around to look at Robert. He sat motionless, his chest rising and falling with labored breaths. When his eyes met mine, they looked dark.

"I know who it is," he said hoarsely. "I don't want to believe it but . . . it has to be my father."

"We've already rejected him," Antonio objected. "There's no *s* in his name—"

"Yes," Robert broke in desperately, "there is. My father belongs to the house of Stuart."

A chill shivered along my spine. *Of course.* English monarchs had always been descended from particular lines—the Plantagenets, the Lancastrians, the Tudors, and now the Stuarts. In my mind, I ran through the catalog of my father's literary version of Satan. An enormous creature. A leader. Charismatic, seemingly brave. Powerful. And so seductive that a reader doesn't realize she has fallen alongside him until he tempts Eve and his true nature is revealed.

The king was also massive—six feet tall. So charming that he had romanced dozens of women and even persuaded his wife to permit his illegitimate babies to be brought up in the nursery at Whitehall. The man who held the most powerful position in the land.

It had to be. I almost let out a whoop of satisfaction; then I spied Robert's agonized expression and the sound died in my throat. No one would want to believe his father was capable of being termed a devil—even if it was only a literary allusion.

I reached out to grab Robert's bridle, my bare fingers brushing his gloved ones. "I'm sorry. This must be hard for you."

His smile quirked up the corners of his mouth but didn't change anything else in his face. A false smile. "It's fine," he said quickly. "I've always known he wasn't angelic. Kings can't be. They don't have the luxury of kindness, not when so many lives depend on them. It's fine," he said again when Antonio clapped his shoulder in solidarity. "Let's ride, can't we?"

I wanted to press the issue, but the misery on his face kept me quiet. We spurred our horses onward without another word.

Just as the sun had begun to dip beneath the horizon—a blazing red ball sending its last fiery rays across the sky—we spied the irregular wooden houses and crooked lanes of Southwark. London lay across the river. My heart kicked in my chest. We were so close.

We clattered through the narrow streets. Tradespeople wended their way home after a long day's work: milkmaids carrying jugs on their heads, butchers whose leather aprons were stained with animals' blood, and cobblers who stank of lye. Market vendors led their horse-drawn carts, laden with empty baskets that had once contained cloth and buttons, strawberries, fish, onions, potatoes, and grain, sold and gone now.

London Bridge loomed ahead of us. It was the only crossing that spanned the Thames, and this ensured both of its ends were usually crowded with travelers waiting to make the trip to the other side. Today was no exception: coaches, carts, and people on horseback or on foot stood in a long queue. We joined the back of the line. No one gave Robert a second look; he wore his hat low, obscuring his face. In everyone I looked at, I imagined I saw my Oxford attacker's face, but when I looked again, he wasn't there. Even so, the back of my neck prickled. He and his companions might have made it to London ahead of us. They could be anywhere. I swallowed hard, realizing I had been staring at one of the men waiting in line. Hastily I looked away.

Beneath the bridge, massive waterwheels groaned in their slow revolutions. The river's surface bristled with a variety of craft: grain and timber ships, oyster-, dung-, and eel-boats, coasters, merchantmen, and wherries, the cheap, low-bottomed boats that had helped me understand Galileo's theory of constant motion. On the opposite bank, the Thames lapped at the water gates of the Tower, whose lower walls were dotted black with cannons. The White Tower speared toward the sky, a vast column of pale stone, the original part of the fortress and prison that had been built some six hundred years ago. A massive wall wrapped itself around the Tower and the vast complex of buildings surrounding it.

As we inched forward on the bridge, I saw the city spreading out in all directions before us: a mix of workshops, warehouses, tenements, and slums alongside mansions, guildhalls, and churches. Lines of shadows snaked between the buildings, marking the streets, alleys, and lanes that made up the confused jumble of London's system of roads. Earthenware roofs glowed orange in the light of the setting sun, and above them, kites flew back and forth, searching the streets for carrion.

A portion of the bridge was lined with grand timber-framed houses with elaborately carved and gilded facades. I saw the house belonging to my weapons instructor, Mr. Hade, whose success as a merchant had enabled him to rent a place in such a coveted area. I wondered how he had fared during the plague—he and my father hadn't written each other letters, fearing the disease could live in the paper.

Robert leaned across his horse, murmuring, "What are you looking at so intently?"

I nodded at the five-story wooden house we were passing. "The man who trained me in sword fighting, Mr. Hade, lives there."

Robert glanced at the house. "He's a lucky man, to live surrounded by water."

"A hard taskmaster, too. I used to hate how he'd strike my hands with the flat of his sword if I let them drift out of position." I shivered, remembering the man in the fields outside Oxford, the lines of blood trickling between his fingers. "I'm grateful now for his high standards."

We reached the stone keep of Bridge Gate, the last impediment before we could move onto land again. A score of criminals' heads had been left impaled on the battlements. Ravens had picked out most of their eyes and eaten the flesh off the skulls, leaving behind only sun-bleached bone. Shuddering, I looked away.

Our horses stepped off the bridge. Side by side we plodded down the street. At the corner I grabbed Robert's bridle, forcing him to come to a halt. He looked at me questioningly.

"I must go to my family's home alone," I told him, as Antonio and I had earlier agreed. His mouth dropped open in astonishment—I doubted anyone had spoken to him so firmly before—but I didn't back down. "My sisters and I are the daughters of one of the most notorious political traitors in the country," I reminded him. "If they see a king's son at their door, they'll be terrified."

"Very well," Robert muttered, but he didn't look pleased. "Where should we meet you?"

"At the edge of Bunhill Fields. It's close to my family's house on Artillery Walk." I slid off my horse, holding out the reins to Antonio. "I can't ride home. I live on a poor street, and a boy on a horse would attract attention."

He took the reins, his gloved hands brushing my bare ones. "Keep yourself safe." There was something in his tone I couldn't identify.

"And you, as well."

His gaze weighed heavily on my shoulders as I walked away. Every beat of my heart seemed to scream *hurry, hurry*, and I quickened my pace. By the time I rounded the corner, I was running.

The farther north I went, the more twisted and narrow the streets became, a sign I was entering a poor section. Here the wooden houses sagged against one another, their additions jutting out so far that the houses on opposite sides of the street almost touched, blotting out the last strains of daylight. Some of their doors still bore the faint impression of an X, indicating that the people who had lived there had fallen ill from the plague.

The sounds of the city rose up all around me: dogs and cats screeching from alleys, wooden signs creaking overhead, carriage wheels rattling over pavers, and everywhere, everywhere the voices of dozens of people, calling, shouting, laughing. I had forgotten what an *alive* city London was—how it wrapped itself around you like a cloak, surrounding you with colors and sights and smells until your senses were overcome.

All at once Artillery Walk opened up before me—a slender lane lined with shabby row houses. My family's home was a plain brick building fronted with a couple of steps where my father used to sit on summer evenings, strumming his mandolin and chatting with neighborhood men as they returned home from their work.

The steps were empty now. In the lane a handful of dirty-faced children were playing jacks, and several men walked together, their steps slow and tired after a day spent baking bread, sewing clothes, or toiling in the tanneries that lined the river. I recognized some of them and ducked my head, pulling my hat lower over my face. I hoped my boy's clothes provided enough of a disguise to trick their eyes.

I jogged up the steps, then hesitated. What if our attackers had already reached London—and were inside with my family right now? Fear swirled in my stomach. All I had were my knives; they would have to be enough.

Setting my shoulders, I reached for the door. The handle turned easily in my hand. I stepped inside, then stood still, listening with all of my might. The low murmur of female voices. No males. Either our assailants had already been here and left, or they hadn't reached London yet. Either way, I'd better be fast.

Although it had been well over a year since I had last seen the parlor, it looked just as I remembered: a small, plain chamber containing a few wooden chairs and a single table, the whitewashed plaster walls devoid of decoration. Mary, Deborah, and Betty sat perched on the chairs, their heads bent over the samplers in their hands. As in the old days, Anne sat on a stool by the hearth, humming under her breath. When they caught sight of me, their faces slackened in shock.

"E-E-Eliz," Anne gasped out. Hearing her familiar voice brought tears to my eyes. She jumped to her feet and managed a few unsteady steps before tripping and landing hard on her knees. I ran to her, dropping down beside her and pulling her into my arms. The bones in her back felt as delicate as a bird's. Only days had passed since we had seen each other, but she already seemed thinner. I hoped the strain of Father's imprisonment hadn't been too much for her. *Save her and all your sisters*, whispered a voice in my mind. It was up to me to secure Father's release, I knew, or he would die, leaving us to face an uncertain future. The pressure built up in my chest until I could scarcely breathe.

I looked at Betty.

"Have any men come here since you returned?" I demanded.

"No. The king's men escorted us here, but they've left us alone ever since."

I sagged with relief. Thank God, I had arrived in time. Arms encircled my waist from behind, and another pair twined around my neck. Mary and Deborah—I recognized their scent of flour and chamomile.

"There's been no word of Father," Mary said in a strangled-sounding voice. "Oh, Elizabeth, we've been so frightened for you! Where have you been all this time?"

"I wish I could tell you everything, but I must hurry." Gently I released Anne, who regarded me with tear-filled eyes. "I want to stay with you, more than I can say, but I need to help Father. There's something hidden in the cellar that might free him."

As my sisters murmured in surprise, I turned to the table where my stepmother kept our supply of tallow candles and was startled to see her holding out a lit taper.

"You'll need this." There was a catch in her voice.

It was the first time I could remember her helping me. "I— thank you," I stammered.

With the candle clutched in my hand, I hurried to the back of the house, where a set of steps in the kitchen led to the cellar. The smell of damp earth assailed my nose as I crept down the stairs, the candle's flame splashing gold on the dirt walls and floor. Wooden bins and barrels lined the edges of the room.

The creak of decaying wood told me my sisters were descending the steps. Without turning, I said, "Father hid something in one of the barrels of sand. Please, I'm begging you, help me find it—"

"What are you talking about?" Mary interrupted. "You're scaring us, Elizabeth!"

I whirled around. Mary and Deborah stood a few feet away, their faces slack with confusion. Anne watched us from the top of the stairs, her hands braced on the wall for support. Even in the golden-lit darkness, she looked pale.

"I'm sorry," I said quickly. "There's no time to explain. The king's men desperately want whatever it is that Father has hidden down here. If I find it first, I can use it in exchange for Father's release."

Anne cried out something unintelligible, and Mary and Deborah gasped.

"You might be able to free Father?" Mary raced down the steps. "How? The king will never let him go!"

"If we have something he wants, he will." I flew to the opposite wall, where the barrels of sand stood. One-handed, I ripped the lid off the nearest one. The candle I held showed me its interior: layers upon layers of pale yellow sand, which we'd used for years to scour the kitchen dishes clean and to blot my father's writings. I plunged my hand down as deep as it would go. Stiff granules pressed against my skin. I felt around, my fingers raking through the sand from one side of the barrel to the other. Nothing.

Mary and Deborah, white faced, appeared on either side of me.

"Tell us what we're seeking," Deborah said.

"I don't know, not exactly." I dropped the lid into place. "A box, maybe, or papers."

The next barrel had been shoved in the corner, behind the vegetable bins. Again I tore off the lid, letting it land on the dirt floor with a soft thump. I reached inside. More granules of sand, cold and minuscule. I pushed my hand deeper. The tip of my index finger brushed something hard. My heart knocked against my breastbone. Could this be it?

My fingers wrapped around the object. It was no bigger than my hand. With a gasp of triumph, I pulled it out, sending a shower of sand raining down on the floor.

What I held was a small metal box. Its hinged top looked as though it had rusted shut. Probably it had lain in this barrel for years, the cool, damp sand slowly warping the metal and stretching reddish streaks across its surface.

Mary and Deborah rushed to my side. "What is it? Open it!"

My fingers tightened on the box. I *could* try to open it right now. A few minutes' work and I should be able to pry the top off. And then I could know the secrets behind the vial—the secrets that might cost my father his life if I wasn't careful.

Overhead a floorboard creaked. My head snapped up. I peered into the darkness, holding my breath, trying to trace the source of the sound. Was it Betty, pacing impatiently in the sitting room? Or were the king's men entering our house even now?

There was no time to waste. I had to get out of there before they arrived. With shaking hands, I slipped the box inside my shirt, where it nestled against the warmth of my belly. "I must go," I said in answer to my sisters' bewildered expressions. "Men might come here looking for this box. If they do, you know nothing of it. You haven't seen me, you haven't searched the cellar—do you understand? Your answers could mean your lives."

"But Elizabeth, you haven't explained anything—" Mary started to protest.

"I can't right now! I must get away." I clasped Mary's hand, squeezing hard. "You have to trust me."

Her eyes, shining with tears, met mine. "I would trust you with my life."

Emotion welled in my throat. Despite all the differences between us, she still trusted me. It was the best thing she ever could have said.

"Good-bye, I pray only temporarily," I said. Then I dashed up the stairs, pausing at the landing next to Anne. She looked up at me, her lower lip quivering.

"E-E—no go," she said.

"I have to." Blinking away tears, I kissed her cheek, murmuring, "I'll save Father. I swear it."

She nodded hard, choking back a sob. I turned from her quickly, before I could think myself out of leaving. Father needed me; there was no other choice I could make.

I raced through the hall and out the front door. Down the front steps into the road, where children played jacks and shrieked with laughter. I barely heard them. Sunset had pressed a heavy hand onto the earth, staining the row houses bloodred. I held the treasure to my stomach and took off at a run, making for the fields beyond the houses on the opposite side of the street. As I raced up the hill, my eyes seeking the dark shapes of Antonio and Robert, I allowed myself a grim smile. I had done it.

Sixteen

"I THINK," ROBERT SAID, "YOUR FATHER MAY HAVE
been too clever for his own good."

The three of us looked glumly at the piece of vellum in my
hand. We were alone, the fields deserted at this early evening
hour. I glanced over my shoulder, wondering if our Oxford
assailants were out there somewhere, but I saw no one. Our only
companions were the bones of the dead, for the fields had been
turned into a burial ground during the plague. From where we
stood beneath the shelter of a group of trees, I could see the
dark outline of a brick wall, presumably erected to encircle the
new graves.

I turned away from the depressing sight to study the vellum
strip again. After I'd found the boys waiting for me at the edge
of the fields, we had led our horses to this wooded thicket, where
we had pried the lid off the box and peered inside. As before,

my father had inscribed a message on a piece of animal hide. Unfortunately, this time he had written a poem that seemed incomprehensible.

"I know little about poetry," Antonio said. "Is this typical of your father's style, Elizabeth?"

"He experiments with different literary forms," I replied. "He has little interest in natural philosophy, so the subject matter is unusual for him, although it does link the poem to Galileo."

Silently I reread it, hoping a previously unnoticed word or phrase would leap out at me:

The stars hide their mysteries from our eyes,
Keeping us foolish when we would be wise.
From naught to silver to gray, thence again,
Dazzling our sight and confounding men.
We chart their progress across the dark skies,
Seeking their movements, misled by old lies.
Who among us watches as master of all,
A human fail or then an angel fall,
Without a flicker of pain in his heart,
And lets the new world end instead of start?

"Who is this master he writes about?" Robert asked. "Could he be Galileo?"

"I think the 'master of all' must refer to God," I said. "My father is saying it's impossible to imagine the Father of the Universe as uncaring—as someone who isn't grieved when he sees someone sin. As for this final line, I think it means God isn't narrow-minded, that he's willing to usher in a new age of understanding. By phrasing this passage as a question, my father is forcing his readers to consider the true nature of God."

"This poem may provide fodder for a fascinating discussion, but it doesn't help us." Antonio had taken off his hat, and his hair tumbled loose to his shoulders, framing a face tight with impatience. "There *must* be something more."

We all looked at the vellum again. The imagery was unlike Father's, but what else? I tried to imagine him writing this as a young man, before his eyes were misted white or his hair streaked with silver. A slender figure in black, hunched over a desk as his quill moved across the vellum, swooping higher to form a capital letter before dipping lower into its lowercase follower—

Capital and lowercase letters. I reread the poem, my heart beating faster. The punctuation was utterly unlike my father's usual patterns.

"The grammar is peculiar," I said. "And ordinarily my father would have capitalized nouns such as 'master' or 'angel,' and the uppercase verbs ought to be lowercase."

I looked up from the sheet of vellum to find both boys staring at me.

"It must be a message!" Robert said. "Quick, string together the capitalized words. What do they say?"

"The stars their keeping from dazzling we progress across seeking who us a without and lets start," Antonio said haltingly. Then he groaned. "Unless my understanding of the English tongue is worse than I thought, surely that can't be correct."

"Let's try ignoring the first word in each line and take only the other capitalized words," I suggested. "Stars their progress across us lets start. Hmm. That isn't much better."

For several moments we stared at the vellum, as if by gazing at it long enough we could convince it to surrender its secrets to us. Again and again I tried different combinations: starting with the final capitalized word and collecting them backward, stringing together the lowercase words. Nothing. All I got for my efforts was nonsense.

Robert swore under his breath. "It's no use. I can't make head or tail of this message." He glanced around the boneyard, his eyes narrowed. The sun had almost disappeared, a giant red ball limning the horizon with fire. We had been immersed in my father's clues for longer than I had realized. "We shouldn't remain out in the open like this. There's no telling when we'll come across someone who recognizes one of us. Come." He strode toward the horses, tossing over his shoulder, "My lady will let us stay with her. Once we get to her house, we can talk more in private—and I pray we'll get to the bottom of things. Or else I fear the answers may be irretrievably lost to us."

Which would mean my father was lost, too. Even as I gasped in horror, Robert wheeled his horse around and took off across the fields, leaving me and Antonio to race after him just as the last vestiges of light faded from the sky and the city spread out below us, a shifting mass of shadows painted blue and black by the deepening twilight.

Once the most prized lands in London had lined the Strand, but the street had become clogged with massive homes. After the king's triumphant return to the capital, scores of nobles had flooded back to our island after a decade of exile on the Continent, and the most fashionable place to live became Piccadilly. Lady Katherine Daly, I realized as I followed Robert through the thickening night, may have been an Irishwoman, but she was well informed about London's most desirable address, for this was where she kept a home.

The road was quiet except for the rumble of carriages. Although Antonio, Robert, and I rode side by side, we said nothing—indeed, there was nothing to say.

Sorrow and fury pressed down on me, bowing my shoulders and tightening my fingers on the reins. We had failed. We had no ideas, no bargaining tool to secure my father's release, nothing that the king could possibly want. Father would remain hidden until his execution.

Up and down Piccadilly, homes were tucked away behind elaborate gateways, set so far back from the street they were wrapped in black. I saw them with dull eyes, catching only the impression of hulking blocks of stone and brick.

We turned under a large archway. Lady Katherine's estate rose before us: a massive brick box of a house flanked by two wings and topped by a cupola whose gold-covered dome glittered in the darkness. Flaming torches lined the courtyard.

As we dismounted, a couple of passing grooms came over to relieve us of our horses. I pulled my hat's brim lower over my face, thankful the light the torches provided was faint. The grooms bowed and murmured "Your Grace," to Robert, who acknowledged them with a brisk nod.

"You must forgive my bruised face; I had a fall from my horse," he said smoothly. I wondered why he bothered explaining himself to the servants, then realized he probably wanted to prevent their gossiping about his appearance. "Is your lady at home?" he asked.

"Yes, Your Grace," a groomsman answered, then whispered

to a boy behind him, "Find one of Lady Katherine's servants and tell her the Duke of Lockton has arrived." The boy nodded and scampered away, silent as a ghost.

"Come," Robert said. He led me and Antonio up a row of steps topped by a set of double doors that sprang open at our approach. I could see the glimmer of candlelight from within, flickering like liquid gold.

We entered the hall. The sound of our riding boots clicking on the stone floor seemed loud in the cavernous space. The servant who had opened the door, dressed soberly in black, bowed as we passed him. Automatically I started to bow in return, but Robert caught my eye and shook his head. Hastily I straightened.

At the room's far end a girl of about my own age stood at the base of a staircase that rose high and split in two, each end spreading off to a different wing of the house. This must be Lady Katherine. I had assumed Robert had called her beautiful because he was expected to, but I saw now he had simply been telling the truth—she was the prettiest girl I'd ever seen, with a delicate heart-shaped face. Her pale pink gown skimmed her bodice before flaring into full skirts. The front half of her dark, curly hair was drawn into a bun, the rest tumbling in waves almost to her waist.

"Your Grace, you do me great honor by visiting my home." Lady Katherine's Irish accent lent a soft lilt to her words, turning them into music. Smiling slightly, she glided across the room. Robert dropped into a bow, kissing the hand she offered him.

"My lady, you're more beautiful than ever," he said.

"And I see you continue to hold your own appearance in low regard." She giggled. "I hope you got the best of whoever it was you fought. What was it about this time? A dice game? An insult to your honor?"

"Your good humor does you credit." Robert rose. "Unfortunately, my lady, we've come here with a desperate purpose, and we beg to become your guests. My father has imprisoned hers," he added, jerking his head in my direction.

Lady Katherine peered at me in my boy's clothes, her eyebrows rising. "That is a girl?" she whispered.

"Yes, and I fear we have more distressing news," Robert said. "We suspect my father possesses something that has the power to push kings off their thrones."

There was a long beat of silence. Lady Katherine's face had gone blank. At last she opened her mouth. "Well," she said, "I suppose you had best stay for supper, then."

Antonio and I were given rooms on the same corridor. Alone, I stood at the window, studying the countryside behind Lady Katherine's estate, a rectangle of black in the deepening darkness.

My father was out there somewhere. Perhaps even in Newgate. One of Father's friends been jailed there for his Quaker beliefs, and many times I'd heard his tales of unlighted dungeons where lice crawled so thickly on the floor that when one walked, one heard them crunching underfoot. Prisoners waiting to be hanged were kept in cellars underground, where they could watch the jailers boiling the heads of the recently executed in massive kettles, to keep the flesh from putrefying so the heads could be displayed on poles throughout the city.

I sank to my knees. *Please, Lord, don't let this be Father's fate. Don't let him tremble in his own darkness while all around him the air fills with prisoners' lamentable cries and the stink of blood.*

Eight days. That was all that was left between tonight and the next Hanging Day. We were running out of time. I would go to Whitehall and throw myself on the king's mercy. Offer myself in my father's place. Anything. I would save him. I had to.

A knock sounded on the door. I swiped at the tears on my cheeks. "Enter," I called.

The door swung open to reveal Antonio. He wore only dark breeches and a white shirt. The half smile I was accustomed to seeing on his lips was gone. He looked wild, his jaw clenched, his hair raining to his shoulders as though he had been running his hands through it.

He stepped into the room, closing the door behind him.

"I swear to you," he said, "I won't rest until your father is free."

"Why do you care?" My voice cracked. "You should return to Florence and your master and the work you love so much."

I covered my face with my hands, unable to look at him. My tears trickled down my palms, hot and fast.

"Elizabeth." He said my name like a breath. His clothes rustled as he sank to his knees beside me on the floor, silk and velvet rubbing together. I kept my hands clapped to my face, shielding me in my own private world.

"I can't go on like this," I choked out. "Wondering all the time if he's still alive or already dead."

I broke into sobs. Rough and hard, they tore up my throat, and I had to gasp to get them out. Antonio's hand fell to my shoulder, his touch gentle.

"I'm sorry," he said quietly. "No matter what happens, your

father's a good man—let that thought comfort you."

"A good man!" My voice lashed out, bitter and ragged. "He's chosen death, even when he knows he'll leave behind three daughters and a wife who can't support themselves! They'll have to depend on our relatives' charity or go to the almshouse." *Or the street, to work as doxies*, I thought, but couldn't bring myself to say the words aloud.

For a moment, Antonio didn't say anything. "You didn't include yourself. Won't your father be leaving you, too, if he dies?"

I swiped at my eyes, still not looking at him. "I can take care of myself. And I'll do my best to help my sisters—and what does it matter to you anyway?" I interrupted myself. "You should return to Florence."

"I care because you love your father," he said. "That's reason enough for me to stay."

"You're remaining here for my sake?"

He didn't answer, and I dropped my hands from my face.

The guttering candlelight illuminated Antonio's face, brushing it with gold one instant and shadow the next, flickering him in and out of focus. He was studying me closely, in a way I couldn't remember anyone looking at me before—as though he wanted to commit each of my features to memory so that years from now he could unwrap my image from the farthest recesses of his mind and be able to recall me in exact detail. I shivered under the intensity of his gaze.

"Are you cold?" he asked. Lacing our fingers together, he squeezed my hand. The heat of his skin nearly made me jump. I knew I should move away to a proper distance. I *must*.

But I stayed where I was, now cross-legged on the marble floor, so close to Antonio our knees touched. With his thumb he traced circles in my palm, sending sparks shooting up my arm. My voice shook when I spoke. "Wh-what are you doing?"

He made a strangled noise that might have been partly a laugh. "If you have to ask, then . . . Never mind, Elizabeth. I will see you at supper."

He turned my hand over in his, then bent his head over them. He kissed the inside of my wrist. His lips felt impossibly soft and warm. I sucked in a breath, staring down at his head bowed over our joined hands, candlelight glinting gold in the black strands of his hair. The blood that he and Robert had said circulated in our veins seemed to turn to honey in mine, traveling from my wrist up my arm to my chest, melting me from within.

Then he lifted his head. I couldn't speak as he smiled at me. The lines of his face were tired, and there was a smudge of dirt on his temple—he had come to my room without bothering to wash first. Because he hadn't wanted to wait to comfort me.

He's beautiful, I realized with a jolt of shock. The hands that held telescopes and scribbled long mathematical equations; the eyes that peered at the stars night after night. The slim line of a cut on his forehead from our fight in the fields outside Oxford. The way the fabric of his shirt stilled, as if he were holding his breath while he looked at me.

The fabric rose and fell; he had released his breath. "I had better dress for supper," he said quietly.

Dress. For supper. Which meant in a few minutes he would be in his own room, taking off his shirt and breeches. I could almost imagine the ridged muscles of his chest, which I had seen through his water-soaked shirt.

My face turned to flame. Antonio laughed and sent me a wicked grin, as if he knew precisely what I was thinking. Odd's fish! Couldn't I just melt into the floor and be put out of my humiliation?

Jumping to his feet, he said, "I'll see you in the dining room."

I couldn't say a word. I stared at the black and white marble squares of the floor, watching Antonio's shadow cross them. The door opened and closed; he was gone.

I laid a hand on my overheated cheek. What on earth was wrong with me? Betty would tan my hide for having such impure thoughts.

Like someone in a trance, I went to the door. When I pressed my hand against it, I imagined I felt the vibrations of Antonio's footsteps traveling along the corridor and up the wooden door into the tips of my fingers. Linking me to him. And I couldn't help wondering if my thoughts truly were impure . . . or if maybe I was just beginning to see the world with different eyes.

Seventeen

THE DOOR BURST OPEN, NEARLY WHACKING ME IN the face. I jumped back just in time. Robert came inside, grinning and waving my father's strip of vellum in the air.

"The entire word isn't capitalized," he said.

Antonio appeared over Robert's shoulder, buttoning his travel-worn shirt one-handed, as if he had been in the middle of undressing when he'd heard the commotion and rushed out. I could see the lines of his collarbones. Quickly I averted my gaze.

"You'd better come in before you attract the servants' attention," I said, ushering the boys into my room. "What exactly are you talking about, Robert?"

"Only the first letter is capitalized." He looked expectantly at Antonio and me, but we stared at him blankly. "Don't you see? If only the first letter is capitalized, then perhaps only the first letter is significant! We should put together only the capitalized first letters and see if they spell out a secret message."

I shrugged; it was as good a suggestion as any. "We can try that."

Antonio closed the door and leaned against it, raising his eyebrows. It was clear he didn't think much of Robert's idea. I took the proffered vellum and scanned it again. The first capitalized word within a line was "Stars." "S," I said aloud, privately wondering if there was another layer of meaning behind my father's poem—for stars, after all, had been the focus of many of Galileo's investigations, and it had been his findings about the skies that had raised the Church's ire and nearly cost him his life.

I skimmed the rest of the line. "Their—*T. S* and *T* so far." Oddly enough, there weren't more relevant capitalized letters in the next three lines, and then there were two in adjacent words. "*P* and *A*."

"*S-T-P-A*," Robert recited, and frowned. "It doesn't sound like a real word yet."

"Let me finish." Father wouldn't have made a mistake; I was sure of it. Thus far he'd shown himself to be a canny word magician, imbuing his writings with multiple meanings. I skimmed the rest of the poem. There were three more words we could use—"Us," "Lets," and "Start." "*U, L,* and *S*. The entire message reads, '*S-T-P-A-U-L-S*.'"

My heart raced. *St. Paul's!* I knew it well; there probably wasn't a soul in London who didn't. It was the largest church in the city, perhaps the largest church in the world. And the place held a tender place in my father's heart—as a boy, he'd attended St. Paul's school, which was affiliated with the church, and as a young man he had mourned when Cromwell allowed his troops to use the church as a barracks and the building fell into terrible disrepair.

"St. Paul's?" Antonio asked. "I thought you Protestants didn't worship saints."

"It's a church." A wide grin crossed Robert's face, and he clapped me on the back, laughing. "Your father must have hidden this treasure in St. Paul's!"

My heart sank. "The place is enormous," I said. "St. Paul's must have hundreds of possible hiding places. How can we ever hope to find them all? And how can we even look? The ministers and worshipers would certainly notice us tearing apart the walls and floor!"

"Confound it!" Robert aimed a vicious kick at the wall, then hopped around in agony, clutching the toe of his shoe and uttering a string of curses.

"When you've finished dancing, you might want to take a look at this," Antonio said dryly. He had bent to study the vellum in my hand, coming so close that his hair brushed my fingers. I jolted. Antonio glanced over his shoulder at me, grinning as if he knew exactly why I had started. I scowled at him. Never mind that the dusting of his hair on my fingers *had* made my pulse leap; he didn't need to know that.

Robert limped over to us. "What is it?"

"The ink has faded in an odd pattern," Antonio said. He pointed to the words "our" and "would." "Do you see how the letters *r* in 'our' and *d* in 'would' are gray, while the other letters are still black? I can't think why only some letters should have faded unless"—he regarded me, all trace of merriment gone—"unless your father used two bottles of ink."

"A second secret message," I breathed. "What do the gray letters spell?"

I held the vellum while Antonio rattled them off: "*U-n-d-e-r-t-h-e-f-o-n-t.*"

Under the font. The baptismal font, it had to be! Most likely it was a small piece of furniture made of wood or carved from stone, kept near St. Paul's altar to be used in infants' baptisms.

I seized Antonio's hand, tugging him after me toward the door. "Come! There's no time to lose!"

We shot into the corridor. As we raced headlong down the passage, the stones in the walls flashing past us, Robert grabbed my wrist, jerking me to a stop.

"How long has it been since your father hid this treasure?"

"I don't know." I tried to shake his hand off; I was desperate to keep going. "Years, I suppose. The box in Oxford was buried in 1642, and this poem is in my father's handwriting, so he must have penned it before he went blind."

"Then let's pray the church hasn't replaced its font anytime in the past twenty years," Robert said grimly.

St. Paul's Cathedral was a massive building clad in white stone, which gleamed ghostly in the darkness. A series of lean-to shops huddled against one wall; they were little more than shacks. By day the stalls did a bustling business, selling books and pamphlets. Many times I had strolled among them, looking for yet another book my father had requested. Now their flaps were tied closed for the night, and the air was quiet except for the clatter of our horses' hooves on the courtyard pavers.

We left our horses at the church's western end, in front of a series of black marble steps leading up to a portico. I had feared the doors would be locked, but Robert pushed them open and strode into the place. Antonio and I hurried after him.

The sanctuary smelled of candles and stone. It was dark, its long rows of pews empty. The interior was fashioned like a cross, with the sanctuary forming one long line intersected by the north and south transepts. The only light came from a patch of evening sky showing through a jagged hole in the roof. Bluish lines appeared elsewhere in the vaulted ceiling—the sky peeking through the cracks, I realized. Instinctively I looked at the walls. Even in the dimness I could see how they bulged outward, clearly buckling from the tremendous pressure of supporting the damaged roof. It was a wonder the building didn't fall down on our heads at that very moment.

Pieces of the floor were broken or missing entirely. The lack of light forced us to adopt a shuffling gait, stepping carefully over missing stones in the floor. As we reached the spot where the transepts met the sanctuary, footsteps sounded in the distance. The guttering yellow circle of a candle's flame appeared ahead of us—coming from the altar, I guessed.

"Who goes there?" called a man's pleasant voice. "Have you come to worship?"

Antonio and I looked at each other, and he shrugged. Playing the part of a late-night pilgrim was far better than admitting the true reason for our visit.

"Yes—" I started to reply, but Robert interrupted me with a harsh whisper: "It's no use pretending—I recognize the man's voice. He's one of the ministers, and he knows me.

"It's I, the Duke of Lockton," he went on, more loudly. "We've come to pray in solitude."

The minister hurried toward us, the candle flame bobbing beside him. By its weak illumination I could see the man's weathered, friendly face and shoulder-length gray hair. He wore a white clerical collar and long black robes.

"Your Grace," he said, beaming, and bowed. "You are most welcome in the Lord's House, as indeed are all those who praise his name. If you wish to worship in private, then by all means I will remove myself from your presence."

He backed away, but Robert stayed his progress with a raised hand. "Wait. Where's the font? I—I wish to see it, for I've heard it's in poor condition. Perhaps I could replace it."

"Your Grace is most generous," the minister said, bowing again. "Have you come on behalf of the commission?"

Robert's forehead wrinkled. "The what?"

"A commission has been formed to oversee the possible renovation of our beloved church." The minister's words tumbled out in excitement, one after the other. "It's a group of respectable gentlemen—John Evelyn, Hugh May, Roger Pratt, and Christopher Wren. They began inspecting our church earlier this month."

My eyes darted to the front of the sanctuary, which was draped in shadows, so I couldn't see anything, not even the small half-pillar shape of a baptismal font.

"Oh. Yes. We're new members of the commission," Robert said hastily. "We've come to look at the font."

"Follow me, Your Grace." The minister walked backward to the altar, keeping his body half bent in a perpetual bow. It took all of my self-discipline not to snap at him to go faster. At last, we were so close! He bumped into the altar rail and stopped, waving toward a shadowy object to his right. "The baptismal font is here, Your Grace."

"Thank you. You're dismissed." Without another word, Robert took the candle the minister held out to him and clambered over the altar rail, with Antonio and me right behind him. My hands shook with excitement. We were almost to the answers now. I glanced over my shoulder at the minister. He was shuffling backward down the center aisle between the rows of pews. Soon enough he'd be gone, and even if he found our behavior strange, he wouldn't dare complain about it to anyone.

The font was carved from dark wood. We ran our hands over its sides. In some places the wood was warped, its surface bulging out like miniature bubbles. When I pressed my fingers into the protuberances, though, the wood gave easily. It was rotted, probably from decades of water damage. There was nothing hidden inside.

"Roll it onto its side," Antonio ordered. "Maybe there's something under it."

Quickly we levered the heavy font to the floor. By the light from Robert's candle, we peered at the bottom. The octagonal panel of wood was still pale, untouched by water or sunlight. Two tiny nail holes marred its otherwise smooth surface. Nothing else.

Robert vaulted over the rail. "What are those holes on the bottom of the font?" he called after the minister.

The elderly man rushed up the aisle toward us. "An object was nailed there, Your Grace. The commission found it when they came a fortnight ago, for I told them it's cracked and leaks holy water onto the floor—clearly an intolerable situation."

My heart dropped. We were too late.

"What was it?" Robert demanded.

"Your Grace, it was nothing important, I assure you—"

In a few strides, Robert had reached the minister and grabbed the man's hands. "What," he said through gritted teeth, "was it?"

The minister opened and closed his mouth a few times. I gripped the altar rail so tightly wood splinters dug into my palms. Beside me, I heard Antonio's ragged breathing.

"It was a piece of vellum," the minister said shakily. "Inside it was rolled a piece of paper covered with drawings and writings in a tongue that looked remarkably like Latin, but which one of the commission gentlemen said was Italian." He drew himself to his full height, his mouth settling into a disapproving frown. "To my eyes, it looked like witchcraft, and I was relieved when they took it with them. Only the Lord knows how long the paper's impure presence has polluted our house of worship."

I couldn't move, could barely breathe as I listened.

"Where's the paper now?" Robert demanded.

The minister glanced at his hands gripped in Robert's and cleared his throat, looking nervous. "In a place most easy for you to reach, Your Grace. Mr. Wren is an accomplished astronomy tutor at the University of Oxford, you see, and he grew nearly wild with excitement when he saw the paper. He said he knew well of the king's interest in natural philosophy, and he insisted on bringing the discovery to him immediately." The minister attempted a placating smile. "For the past fortnight, the vellum has been in your father's possession. I daresay if you told him of your interest, he would be happy to share it with you."

Eighteen

BACK AT LADY KATHERINE'S ESTATE, A FAIR-haired serving girl in a plain gray gown helped me prepare for supper. She chattered while she washed the dust of travel from my limbs with a dampened strip of linen, saying her name was Thomasine Adams and she had been hired as Lady Katherine's maid when the Irish girl had been invited to London by the king himself. I couldn't bring myself to say a word to her. I didn't want to talk ever again.

Our ride from St. Paul's had been silent. Not even Antonio had spoken or made a jest. Sometimes I felt the weight of his eyes bearing down on me, but I didn't lift my hanging head to look at him. I wished a curtain could drop around me, surrounding me on all sides, hiding me from the world outside, so I wouldn't have to see the sun rise and set and know another day had passed without my father in it. And more days would pass without him, I knew. Because we had failed.

The king had the next clue. The *king*.

My throat tightened until I could scarcely breathe. My father was as good as dead, and there was nothing I could do to save him. Either the king now had all the information he needed to solve the treasure hunt, or my father would never tell him the rest. All because of his lofty ideals.

Tears spurted into my eyes. *How could you do this to us, Father? You abandoned your daughters and your wife, all for the sake of an old secret. Don't you care about us? How could anything be more important to you than your children?* Despair sealed off my throat. For the first time since he had been arrested, I wondered if I would be able to forgive Father.

"His Majesty has been seeking a wife for the Duke of Lockton," Thomasine said, "and I daresay he wanted to see if Lady Katherine would suffice."

I nodded absently, choking back a sob and staring at my hands. The same hands Father had wrapped around a quill and moved across a page when he had first taught me to write. Even blinded, he had known the letters well enough to teach me how to form them. Because he was brilliant and he was tough. And soon he would be nothing more than dust. Tears swam in my eyes, blurring my hands.

I couldn't help it—I still loved him, even though a part of me resented him for maintaining his silence. How could I go on without him? All of my life, I had been at his side, taking down his dictation, letting my mind open and swell from his teachings. We were so alike, feathers from the same bird. Who was I without him? And would I even want to be whoever that person was?

Thomasine's voice was akin to a droning bumblebee, echoing in my ears as she helped me into garments lent by Lady Katherine. The snowy white shift and dark blue gown were finer than anything I had put on before. Another time, I would have been secretly thrilled to put on something so fancy, to wear colors other than green or brown.

If it would bring Father back, I would gladly wear my Puritan garb for the rest of my life. Gowns made of hissing snakes that bit me, like in the stories Father told me when I was a child. *Anything.*

"You're ready, miss," Thomasine said brightly.

I raised my head. In the large, gilt-framed mirror, a girl stared at me. She barely resembled the person I had seen in the glass at the inn in Oxford; this girl was dressed as an aristocrat, with the front of her hair drawn into a bun, the rest left to flow down her back. A pearl necklace had been strung around her neck. I hadn't noticed its weight until now, its cold spheres slowly being warmed by the heat of my skin. As for the gown, it was unlike anything I had worn before: silk dyed to match the sky at twilight, and cut low to expose the swell of my breasts. The bodice was so tight I could manage only sips of air, and the enormous skirts rustled when I rose from my chair.

"Are you pleased, miss?" Thomasine asked.

It almost hurt to open my mouth, as though I were a machine long gone rusty. *Say something or you'll hurt her feelings.* "I'm more than pleased. You've made me pretty."

"If I may be bold enough to say so, you already are, miss." Thomasine bobbed in a curtsy, then ushered me into a hallway lit by candelabra. We walked a series of long, straight corridors until we came to the dining room—a massive, high-ceilinged space where dozens of white candles glowed on the table, casting gold on the plates and the silver tableware. Ancient-looking tapestries covered the stone walls.

The others were already seated. Lady Katherine remained in her chair, inclining her head in acknowledgment when I entered the chamber. The three boys lounging about the table stood and bowed to me. Antonio had changed into a clean doublet and breeches of sky blue. They hadn't been among his possessions when I had gone through his room at the Rose Inn, and I supposed Robert must have lent him the clothes. The sleeves were too long, the cuffs extending over his wrists.

Robert stood at the head of the table, opposite Lady Katherine. Once again he was dressed in yellow silk, but these clothes were fresh. "Elizabeth, may I present my brother, the Duke of Monmouth? I went home to Whitehall while you were dressing and convinced him to return with me. You needn't worry," he added, correctly interpreting my startled expression. "There's no one else in the world whom I would trust with my life other than my brother. We may speak freely in front of him."

"Ah, Miss Milton, the daughter of the Puritan regicide." Monmouth's tone was light. He looked so much like Robert I would have known at a glance they were brothers—they had the same clear hazel eyes and impressive height. He gave me a lazy smile, then turned my hand over in his and kissed my palm. Unbidden, my eyes darted to Antonio. He was watching us without expression. Apparently hand kisses were commonplace among aristocrats and their friends. So it hadn't meant a thing when he had pressed his lips to the inside of my wrist. What a child I was!

"I hope the food's decent," Lady Katherine said. "Since my brother is away for the evening, I hadn't ordered a proper meal prepared, so I sent for fare from a cookshop."

She snapped her fingers. Several servers who had been standing against the wall came to the table, bearing bowls of rose-scented water. Once we had washed our hands, a seemingly endless stream of servants flowed into the room bearing platters of food: a brace of stewed carps, six roasted chickens, a jowl of salmon. It was more food than I'd ever seen on one table.

"You are dismissed," Robert said to the servants. "We'll ring for you when we want you again."

"Very good, Your Grace," they murmured, bowing before they backed out of the room.

Monmouth opened his mouth to speak, but Robert stopped him with a raised hand. He crept to the door and looked out into the corridor. Nodding as if satisfied, he closed the door and returned to the table. "I thought some of the servants might remain in the corridor to spy on us." He sent Monmouth a grim look. "You can never be too careful. Father taught us that."

"Yes, and now you plan to go against him." Monmouth shook his head, looking suddenly tired. "This is treason, Robert. If Father finds out, he'll have no choice but to order you executed."

"I know." Robert's fingers tightened on his table knife, the knuckles whitening.

"Where you go, I cannot follow," Monmouth said softly. "I'll help you concoct a plan, for you begged me, and then wash my hands of this business. You said earlier that this valuable paper is in Father's possession, and though I have wracked my brain, I can't think of how you could retrieve it."

Robert glanced at me. "Doubtless the paper is at Whitehall. Our father's an amateur natural philosopher, and he keeps his personal notes in his laboratory at the palace."

The king was interested in natural philosophy? I froze. Was this a coincidence—or yet one more link in a tightening chain?

"Even if you find the paper from St. Paul's, what good will it do?" Lady Katherine toyed with her wineglass. "His Grace explained the circumstances to me while we were waiting for you to arrive for supper," she said when I looked at her in surprise. "Anyway, it sounds to me as if the king and his men already have Mr. Milton's secrets in their possession." She ticked off items on her fingers. "The piece of paper from St. Paul's, which they found a few weeks ago and which probably started this hunt in the first place. The vial and vellum from the Physic Garden in Oxford. You may have the box from Miss Milton's cellar, but since that directed you to St. Paul's, I'd say you have—"

"Nothing," Robert interrupted, and slumped in his chair.

"Maybe not." Antonio leaned forward, his eyes bright. "Mr. Milton's Italian sonnet sent us to the Physic Garden. And it stands to reason that the paper in St. Paul's would have had a different message, correct, Elizabeth? Would your father have planted two clues pointing to the same location?"

I fiddled with a piece of cheese, unable to bring myself to eat. "I doubt it. That would have been out of character for him. He would have wanted each clue to direct its seekers to a new place."

"So presumably the message in St. Paul's alerted the king's men to the possibility that there were dealings between Mr. Milton and some Italians—which was why they were on the lookout for any Italian visitors to his London home and why they sent men to the cottage in Chalfont as soon as they heard about my arrival." Antonio held up his hand for silence as we started to interrupt. "That partly explains why they went to Chalfont. But how did they know to go to Oxford? Robert found out our destination from Elizabeth's neighbor. Perhaps the king's men did the same. Or maybe there was another reason—such as a clue nailed to the font in St. Paul's."

"There are too many pieces to this puzzle, and we only have a handful of them." Robert groaned.

Lady Katherine gazed at Antonio, realization dawning on her face. "But what Mr. Viviani is saying is, maybe the king and his men have only a handful of them, too. You *need* to find out what is written in that paper from St. Paul's. Maybe you'll glean clues from it that the king's men haven't. It's the only road left open to you now."

My heart lifted. Could she possibly be right—was there still a chance we could outwit the king and save my father?

Robert nodded hard. "I agree. But when my brother and I are at Whitehall, we can't move about unobserved—there are always dozens of eyes watching us. So I can't sneak into my father's laboratory, and there's no way either Elizabeth or Antonio can get onto the palace grounds. The whole thing seems impossible."

I sagged with disappointment. He was right. The palace gates were heavily guarded.

"Maybe not," Lady Katherine said quickly. "The Touching for the King's Evil ceremony is scheduled for tomorrow, isn't it?"

"Yes, but what does that matter . . . ?" Robert trailed off, his eyes widening.

Antonio looked up from his plate. "What's the Touching for the King's Evil?"

"It's a very old ceremony," I replied, my mind leaping ahead of my words as I realized what Lady Katherine was suggesting. My heart began to beat with a rapid, steady sharpness. "The city's ill and infirm gather at the Banqueting House at Whitehall. The king blesses them, and his benediction is thought to heal them. Everyone who attends is permitted inside the palace grounds."

"*Everyone*," Robert repeated. "Elizabeth and Antonio will disguise themselves as sick beggars. As soon as the rites are over, they can steal away from the Banqueting House and into the palace." He jumped to his feet, his grin quick and fierce. "Elizabeth, I'd say it's finally time you returned to your birthplace, wouldn't you?"

Whitehall was hardly a sumptuous palace that befitted the city many called the greatest in the world. Instead it was an undistinguished heap of houses, interconnected by cramped courtyards and crumbling passageways. As Antonio and I joined the throngs lining up outside the Banqueting House on the following morning, I glanced at the jumble of stone buildings, searching for a flicker of a memory, anything that would tell me this was where I had spent the first few years of my life when my father served as the Latin Secretary.

There was nothing. I didn't know if I should be grateful for the void or angry on my family's behalf that we had lost so much and didn't even have recollections of my father's former greatness to comfort us. Only a week until his execution. I swallowed hard. It might not be enough time.

Don't think, I ordered myself. The thought of Father would make me come apart, and then I would be no good to him or anyone else.

The line trudged forward, a dismal collection of people dressed in threadbare clothes. Some were covered in oozing sores, others breathed with the air rattling in their chests. A few were little more than skeletons and so weak they had to clutch the walls for support. The air reeked with the stench of unwashed bodies. I held my sleeve over my nose to block out the stink.

At my side, Antonio remained silent. Today he looked like a stranger—like me, he had smudged his face with charcoal to dirty his skin and disguise his features, and he had donned a hooded cloak.

"It feels wrong to deceive Robert when he's been so kind to us," I whispered to Antonio. We planned to retrieve the paper and follow its clues until we learned the truth about Galileo's secret, which we would share with the king in exchange for my father's release.

He brought his lips close to my ear, murmuring, "I don't like it, either. But what choice do we have if we want to save your father?"

I nodded reluctantly. Part of me hoped he would whisper something else, just for the chance to remain near to him, but he straightened and looked around, obviously studying the surroundings.

As we waited, I tilted my head back to get a proper look at the Banqueting House. The building, a massive structure of pale stone, was separate from the main palace. Its ground-floor windows were walled up. Robert had said the bottom story was divided into compartments for storage, but I wondered if he was only repeating what he had been told. Was it possible my father was hidden behind those shuttered windows? Alone except for crates as companions?

No, surely not. The Banqueting House also contained the Great Hall, which included a large theater that catered to London's elite. My father's jailers would hardly risk the possibility of their captive's shouting for help to entertainment seekers. So where *was* he?

The long queue shuffled forward. Inside the Banqueting House, sunlight struggled to shine through dusty windows. Some hundred people crowded the vast hall. The walls were made of white marble, the ceiling painted with vivid murals. I remembered my father telling me that Charles the First had been executed directly outside this building. The blood-splattered scaffold may have been dismantled years ago, but our current king still had to live in its imagined shadow. I wondered if the constant reminder of his father's execution was a sort of long torture for him, or if he had managed to banish the matter from his mind.

Antonio nudged my shoulder. "He's here," he murmured.

My head snapped around. At the hall's far end, the king sat on a throne. I had forgotten how big he was, a giant at over six feet. He wore ceremonial red robes trimmed in ermine and a long, curly black wig.

Something inside me started to shake. This was the man who controlled my father's fate. I flexed my arms, feeling my knife straps dig into my muscles. As long as I had my knives, I wouldn't let myself descend into fear.

A man in the first row was led forward by the king's physicians. They helped him into a kneeling position on the floor before the king. The king leaned forward, stroking the man's face with his hands while a chaplain standing next to him announced,

"He put his hands upon them and he healed them."

My heart dropped. I had thought we would remain in an anonymous crowd while the king blessed us all. Apparently we would be presented individually to him so he could draw the evil scourge of illness from our bodies with the power of his touch.

I whipped around to look at the doors. They were closed. Guards stood on either side of them, their hands clasped on their sword hilts. There was no way we could slip out unnoticed.

Antonio glanced at me. Even with his face half hidden by his hood, the wariness in his eyes was unmistakable.

The king doesn't know what we look like, I tried to reassure myself. Maybe if we didn't attract anyone's notice we could make it through the king's rites.

My pulse pounded in my temples as Antonio and I moved with the long line snaking toward the king. Over and over the chaplain intoned, "He put his hands upon them and he healed them," and the sick knelt and received the laying-on of hands before shuffling to the rear of the hall, where they waited for the next part of the ceremony to begin.

"And he healed them," the chaplain recited as the elderly woman in front of me struggled to get to her feet. It was my turn. I stood motionless, ordering myself to move. My feet felt nailed to the floor. The chaplain beckoned to me.

The sounds of the room receded until all I was aware of was the king's face, his brows raised as if he wondered why I hesitated. *Go, you simpleton*, I scolded myself. My legs awakened, and I trudged forward a few steps before sinking to my knees at the king's feet.

Nineteen

THE KING PRESSED HIS HANDS TO MY CHEEKS. HIS palms were warm and soft. The corners of his eyes crinkled when he smiled at me, as if he sensed my unease and wished to reassure me. Kindness from *him*. It seemed like a mangled daydream.

With the pads of his fingers, he touched my forehead, then my cheeks again, ending at my chin. Beside us the chaplain recited, "He put his hands upon them. . . ." I got to my feet, fighting a wave of dizziness. The king was already looking past me at the next sick penitent. Antonio. *Don't speak*, I silently begged him. As soon as any words left his mouth, even if they were only a murmured "Thank you," the king would hear his foreign accent.

Hunching my shoulders beneath my cloak, I made my way to the back of the hall. With my heart in my throat, I watched as the king ran his hands over Antonio's face. Only when the chaplain had spoken and Antonio had begun walking toward me did I take a full breath.

The rest of the ceremony sped past in a blur. When everyone had been touched, we all filed in the same order to the throne, where a second chaplain passed white ribbons knotted around gold coins to the king. One by one, the king placed the ribbons around our necks while the first chaplain said, "That is the true light who came into the world."

Once everyone had received a ribbon, the chaplain read an epistle. I turned the coin over in my hand. It had been engraved with the figure of angel.

Two sumptuously attired men brought the king a basin, ewer, and towel. When he had finished washing and drying his hands, he rose. As one, the crowd bowed to him. Somehow I forced my back to bend. By the time I had straightened, the king and his attendants were gone.

The crowd shuffled outside. Antonio and I let ourselves be swept along by its slow-moving tide. A handful of guards, armed with halberds, watched the crowd. As Antonio and I had planned, as soon as we stepped into the weak sunshine I pretended to have a coughing fit—which was hardly unusual, given the pitiful state of the people surrounding us. I sagged against Antonio. He laid his arm across my shoulders, leading me around the edge of the Banqueting House toward the court gate. From the direction of the Banqueting House I heard a halberd ringing on pavers—at least one guard was coming after us.

Antonio and I glanced at each other. We would have to move fast. Across the courtyard a handful of beautifully dressed court-iers strolled out of the jumble of buildings. My stomach twisted in distress. Although they were several yards distant, we couldn't chance their looking in our direction when we shed our cloaks—but the guard was coming; I could hear the *clink* of his halberd getting louder.

The courtiers formed a circle, laughing and chattering with one another. Quickly we threw off our hooded cloaks, revealing the fine clothes we had worn under them. With the cloaks, we wiped the charcoal from our faces as fast as we could. I unwound my hair, letting it fall loose. In his sky-blue breeches and matching doublet, Antonio looked every inch an aristocrat who belonged on these grounds—provided he didn't speak. If anyone stopped us, I would have to talk. I prayed my wits would be quick enough to keep us safe.

We dropped the cloaks at the base of a tree outside the court gate, kicking at the carpet of drought-deadened leaves to cover them. Just as we finished, a guard rounded the wall. He peered around the courtyard, his eyes lighting on us for an instant before moving on. I let out a breath of relief.

We had to keep moving. Together we rounded the Banqueting House again. Before us rose the Tiltyard and the Porter's Lodge. To their side stood a gateway, which led to the Tiltyard Gallery with its two flanking towers. According to Robert's directions, behind the gallery lay the old battlemented tennis court, which both his and his brother's lodgings overlooked. When we had retired last night, he had left for Whitehall, saying he would tell his father he had returned from his hunting excursion in York-shire. Staying at court would permit him to keep a close eye on his father, he had explained when I protested he might put himself in greater danger by returning.

Heads down, Antonio and I hurried through a series of small courtyards. With every few paces we took, we passed more people: finely dressed courtiers, servants in livery, a group of ladies in riding costumes whose like I hadn't seen before, with doublets splitting into wide skirts, like men's. The air filled with a cacophony of sounds and scents: the bright laughter of the queen's attendants, the yeasty smell of baking bread from the kitchens, the clatter of horse hooves across cobblestones in a nearby courtyard. And laced with the mix of flowery perfume, horse dung, and pastries, discernible no matter where you walked, was the dark, rank scent of the Thames.

Finally we found the exterior staircase Robert had told us of and climbed it, emerging into a musty-smelling corridor. We rushed down a series of passageways, occasionally coming across a group of courtiers whom we acknowledged with a brief nod.

In one corridor, two guards, carrying halberds, stalked toward us, their expressions grim. My heart thudded in my chest. Someone must have realized we didn't belong here and alerted them about the palace intruders. My pace slowed. I scanned the passageway—it was lined with closed doors. What if we darted inside the nearest one?

"Keep walking," Antonio whispered.

I shot him a disbelieving look. He held his head high, moving without a hitch in his stride. I hurried to stay beside him. *We have to get away*, I silently told him, wishing he could magically hear my words in his mind. He didn't look at me.

The king's guards were growing closer. Ten paces distant. Now five. Their eyes swept us up and down. I stiffened. Any instant now they would rush at us, their weapons drawn, and we would be forced to fight and eventually be overpowered when more guards flooded in from other areas of the palace—

The two guards stepped aside, pressing their backs against the wall. They bowed.

I exhaled hard. They thought we were courtiers.

Antonio strode past the guards without sparing them a glance. I followed his example. Our shoes rustled on the rushes-strewn floor, our footsteps muffled. Anyone could be coming up behind us and I would barely hear him. What if the guards had merely pretended to be taken in by our disguises and were even now sneaking up on us? I glanced over my shoulder.

No one. The guards were walking away, talking to each other in low voices, laughing over a shared joke.

"How did you know how to act?" My voice came out in a whisper.

Now Antonio did look at me. "My master and I spend much of our time among aristocrats, presenting our experiments to them. They always ignore those whose social stations are lower than their own. I figured if we paid no attention to the guards, they would assume we were aristocrats and belonged here."

"Thank you."

We were passing a window, and I looked out at the garden below us. Dozens of birds swooped across browned grass as several spaniels chased them and yipped. This must be the king's aviary. We had to be close to his personal apartments now.

An empty corridor stretched before us. We counted doors until we reached the one Robert had said led to his father's laboratory. I glanced over my shoulder. No one in sight.

"Go," I said, and Antonio pushed the door open. We stepped inside, letting the door fall closed behind us.

The laboratory was a large, airy room. Notebooks, bottles of ink, and a pot of quills covered a wooden table; diagrams of the constellations and the human form had been tacked to the wainscoted walls; and glass-fronted cabinets housed bottles filled with various-colored liquids or tiny preserved animals. On a table running alongside a wall stood a white ball, which I now recognized thanks to Antonio's teachings as a pasteboard model of a lunar globe. According to its inscription, it had been presented to the king as a gift from Mr. Christopher Wren.

Wren! He was the member of the St. Paul's commission who'd given the king the paper found under the baptismal font. Perhaps these men had been acquaintances for some time. It would certainly explain why Mr. Wren had been so eager to hand over my father's paper to him.

I scanned the notebooks on the closest table for my father's name or Galileo's. At another table, Antonio did the same. The only sounds were our uneven breathing and the pages crinkling in our hands.

The notebooks were filled with the king's musings on matters pertaining to natural philosophy. I could scarcely believe the king was so fascinated by the subject. Was it merely a hobby for him—or something else?

With a lurch of my stomach, I thought of Father's Italian natural philosopher colleagues, Galileo Galilei and Vincenzo Viviani. What if I was wrong and politics weren't at the heart of the secret? Maybe it was natural philosophy instead.

Stop guessing, I ordered myself. There would be time enough to think over the matter after we got out of this place. I turned back to the notebooks, skimming over diagrams of the human skeleton; lists of questions, such as whether flakes of snow were bigger or smaller in Tenerife than in England and why it was hotter in summer than in winter (the king had no answers, but wrote he had heard a number of theories); and an account of the time his friend Buckingham had brought what he promised was a unicorn's horn to the Royal Society for inspection.

An organization of which I am proud to be patron and founder, the king had written in flowing script.

> *Legend has it that a circle drawn with a unicorn's horn will keep a spider within it until it dies. The Society men tried the experiment, drawing a circle with powder from the horn and placing a spider inside it. At once, however, it ran out. Although they attempted the experiment several more times, it did not succeed, and so I wonder if the tales about the powers of unicorns' horns are false.*

"Antonio, listen to this," I hissed. "The king and the Duke of Buckingham are both members of the Royal Society. It's a group of natural philosophers that meets weekly in London," I explained in response to his blank expression. If he wondered why I had heard of the organization, he didn't ask, and I didn't tell him that in my more foolish moments I had daydreamed about attending their meetings and becoming a member myself—an impossibility, of course, because of my gender. "Buckingham even brought a unicorn's horn to show to the Society."

Antonio frowned. "Anyone who believes in unicorns' horns either is a fool or wants to find magical cures—unicorn horns are said to heal all illnesses." He returned to his book, and I skimmed through the next entry in mine, about a recent experiment the Royal Society had conducted on the effects of viper bites on dogs and cats.

"Look at this," Antonio said abruptly, crossing the room to place a leather-bound volume in my hands. A piece of paper, yellowed with age, had been tucked between the pages. The handwriting was small and cramped, the words slanting stiffly down the page. The passage had been written in Italian. In the top corner someone had sketched a figure of a man bending over a pool of water.

"This is in Signor Galilei's hand!" Antonio said. "He must have written it toward the end of his life, before he was blinded but when he was in constant pain—you see how the words are written at an angle, as if the writer is lying down while he works."

Rapidly I translated in my head:

I, Galileo Galilei, do proclaim the following is a true account, and I give it for safekeeping of my own free will to John Milton, poet, an Englishman by birth but a kindred truth-seeker by mind. In the summer of my life, when I was a young man teaching at the University of Padua, I made a discovery that has plagued and uplifted my life ever since. While visiting friends outside the city, my two companions and I decided to escape the midday heat by taking a riposo in an underground room—

"An underground room?" I asked, looking up from the book. "Does he refer to a cellar? And what is 'riposo'? I don't know this word."

"'Riposo' is the Italian word for a midday nap," Antonio explained. He stood so close I could smell the charcoal on his neck, where he hadn't scrubbed hard enough. "These underground rooms are similar to cellars, and are common in country villas.

People often take *riposi* in them as a means of getting away from the heat. These rooms serve to—what is the word?—ventilate homes. They can be dangerous, though, for they can deliver noxious fumes."

Nodding, I returned to the book:

While visiting friends outside the city, my two companions and I decided to escape the midday heat by taking a riposo in an underground room. This particular room was cooled by means of a conduit that delivered wind from above a waterfall inside a nearby mountain cave.

Two hours after we went to sleep, my friends and I awoke in agony—our bodies were gripped with cramps, chills, and pounding headaches.

At once I decided to investigate this cave for myself—if I could identify the source of the danger, I might be able to figure out how to return us to full health. I set off in crushing pain, leaving my companions to recover.

Inside the cave I came across a luminescent pool of water. Lying in the middle of it was a rock, no bigger than the palm of my hand.

My thirst had grown so fierce I was willing to do anything to slake it. I drank from the pool. An examination of the cave told me there was nothing useful to be learned.

Within days, one of my friends was dead, the other clinging to life by a fraying thread. I alone appeared likely to survive, although cramps and chills still held me in their grasp.

The only reason I could determine was that I had drunk from the cave's pool—and they had not.

With utmost haste I returned to the villa. There the astonished owner answered my frantic questions. Several years ago a shower of stars had fallen to the earth. He and his neighbors had watched their silver trails streak across the sky, curving until they hit the ground and vanished. They must have landed approximately in the area where the cave stood.

I remembered the rock lying in the pool of glittering water—was it a piece of a star fallen from the heavens? Had it landed with such force that it had sheared through the ground, coming to a rest within the cave? Since ancient times, we have thought meteors result from atmospheric disturbances, like lightning. What if these harmless-looking bits of rock and metal actually come from the skies? And what if some of them possess medicinal or disease-causing properties?

I rode to the cave, filled a vial, and raced to Padua. One of my friends was already buried, but the second still lay in his home, taking his last breaths. Under cover of night, I crept into his house. He seemed as one dead to me: I felt no pulse in his wrists, heard no air rasp between his lips. Frantic, I pried his mouth open and poured the liquid down his throat.

He opened his eyes—

The page ended there in a jagged rip. I turned the paper over, but there was nothing written on the other side. "It can't end like this!"

"It didn't," Antonio said grimly. "Signor Galilei or your father wouldn't have torn the page. Which leaves . . ."

"The king," I whispered. Icy fingers trailed down my spine. "Why would he rip off the bottom of the paper? Does it contain information he wants to suppress? Or maybe he wanted to give it to someone who could make better sense of it than he could," I realized. "The king is an amateur natural philosopher; he has no real knowledge to fall back on."

Antonio took the book from me and set it on the table. "Who are these Royal Society men? Would the king have given the paper to them?"

"I don't know. And I still don't understand how this discovery could threaten kings."

Together we studied the page again. Our original theory that my father's secret revolved around the Stuart monarchy's claim to the throne had to be wrong—there was nothing in Galileo's writings hinting at kingly accession.

"Signor Galilei wrote that his friend appeared dead," Antonio said. "But the drink revived him—it brought him back to life."

"That's impossible," I said. "There's only one being in history who returned from the dead, and his rebirth signaled that he was divine. Christ himself."

My voice faded on the final word and all the air seemed to go out of the room. No. This couldn't happen. An ordinary person couldn't be pulled back from beyond the black edge of death. The ability to rise from the dead belonged to Christ alone—didn't it? I raised my gaze to meet Antonio's. He looked as shaken as I felt.

"No one is supposed to have the power to rise from the dead except for Jesus," he said hollowly. "According to the Bible, the only other person who did was Lazarus, and he was brought to life by Jesus's hand. Therefore, if this elixir can turn the dead into the living—"

"This could prove Jesus came back to life because of a medicinal cure," I gasped. "He, too, could have drunk from a pool permeated by a meteor's shower! Or there could be dozens of reasons he returned from the dead, all of them rooted in natural philosophy. He might . . . he might . . ."

"He might have been human," Antonio said in a low voice. "His divinity, his triumph over death, is the rock upon which all of Christianity is built. Crack that stone, and the entire building falls."

The room seemed to shrink, whitewashed plaster walls closing in on me until I could no longer breathe. My thoughts seemed to be made of ice: frozen, unmoving. All I could think was: *blasphemy, blasphemy, blasphemy.* I gripped the edge of the table, the wood pressing into my palms.

"We've been wrong about everything," Antonio whispered. "This treasure hunt isn't about politics. It's about religion."

"If this story gets out and others begin to question Christ's divinity, then the Christian faith is no more." A band had drawn itself around my chest, pulling tighter and tighter. Gray dots danced in front of my eyes. I forced myself to take a few deep breaths, feeling the air travel down my throat. *Concentrate*, I ordered myself. *Don't fall apart.*

"Why did your father believe this discovery could topple kings from their thrones?" Antonio frowned. "The Italian city-states have no kings, but we are ruled by dukes and the Papal States are overseen by the pope. I can understand how Signor Galilei's story could loosen the pope's grip on power, but the dukes shouldn't be affected."

"The root of kings' power supposedly comes from God himself," I explained. "It's a doctrine called 'the divine right of kings.' King Charles the Second believes in it, as did his father—that's why English kings engage in the Touching for the King's Evil, because they think they can heal the sick with their hands, just like Christ. Kings are seen as all-powerful and as Christ's ambassadors on earth."

"So an assault on religion is an assault on the king himself." Antonio looked grim. "I can see why every Christian monarch would do anything to suppress this discovery. If Christianity is disproved, countless governments will crumble. Signor Galilei's discovery won't just topple kings from thrones."

"It could lead the way for revolution!" My pulse pounded. "New governments could spring up—governments composed of ordinary citizens, just as my father has always wanted. Countries could be ruled by their people, like true democracies. And religion would have no place in government, as my father has advocated for decades. This could change the whole world!"

And it could transform my family's lives. Once again, my father could be an important, respected member of the government. No more living in fear, keeping his mouth shut, his ears attuned for the knock on the door that meant the king's men had come for him again. For the first time in years, we would be free. Joy flooded my chest.

But Antonio looked steadily at me. "Or, instead of revolution, there could be countless groups battling one another for supremacy. Like your royalists and parliamentarians twenty years ago. The world could descend into . . ."

He trailed off. But he didn't need to say the next words. I already understood.

We could have revolution and progress . . . or worldwide war.

Part

THE DIVIDED EMPIRE

So farwel Hope, and with Hope farwel Fear,
Farwel Remorse: all Good to me is lost;
Evil be Thou my Good; by thee at least
Divided Empire with Heav'ns King I hold
By Thee, and more than half perhaps will reigne;
As Man ere long, and this new World shall Know.
—John Milton, Paradise Lost, Book IV

Twenty

"YOU ARE SAYING EVERY CHRISTIAN NATION could plunge into anarchy?" I asked at last. "That's true, but eventually some sort of order is bound to—"

The ringing of footsteps in the corridor silenced me. I froze.

They came closer. The clatter of heels and the shuffle of leather. Both stopped directly outside the laboratory door. As I listened, I was able to separate the sounds into two distinct sets of footfalls.

Before I could even think, Antonio had grabbed my hands and dragged me to my knees. Together we crawled beneath the table. I had to bend nearly double to keep my head from rapping its underside. Our breath crashed in our ears; it sounded horribly loud. The black cloth draped over the table enclosed us in our own night.

The door groaned open. Two sets of footsteps entered the

room. They drew nearer, stopping next to the table. In the gap between the black cloth and the floor I could see scuffed brown leather riding boots and a pair of elegant heeled shoes tied with ribbons.

"My son returned last night." It was the king. A chill skittered down my spine. He was so close. All I had to do was reach out my hand and I could touch his shoe. His voice reminded me of snowflakes, cool and soft, melting on a river's surface. "What can you tell me about his movements?"

"The friend whose Yorkshire estate he was supposedly visiting was seen in London yesterday, shopping for clothes on Paternoster Row." I recognized the deep timbre of this man's voice. *Buckingham.* I had to bite my lip so I didn't make a sound.

"We have been friends all our lives," Buckingham went on, more quietly. "During your years of exile, I stayed by your side. No matter what happens, I'll remain loyal to you, Charles. You know you can trust me to tell you the truth, even when it is unwelcome. Your son must be watched carefully."

"I know it." The words sounded as though they had been torn from the king's throat. "But I can't bear to think Robert and I may have become enemies. He's my *son,* my oldest boy—"

"He's a liar," Buckingham growled. "He may be your eldest child by a number of minutes, but he can't be your heir and he will never belong to the house of Stuart. The most you could have hoped for from him was devotion. Now all you have left is deception. I say we lock him in the Tower until he tells us where he's been for the past week."

"Never. I can't—" The king faltered, then managed to say, "I can't imprison my son. Even when we know he has lied to me.

Bucks, for all we know he has spent the week chasing lightskirts and losing money at dice." There was a hopeful note in his tone.

"Maybe," Buckingham said gently. "I pray it's true. If you won't arrest him, then we'll need to make sure he's watched carefully at all times."

They suspected Robert! I pressed my hands to my chest, feeling the wild thumping of my heart through the fabric. In the darkness beneath the table, I saw the whites of Antonio's eyes widen.

"Very well," the king said so softly I barely heard him.

Buckingham barked out a laugh. "Let's adjourn for a drink. Send for some of your pretty girls to keep us company, won't you, Charles? I need someone to dull my mind and sharpen my senses."

The king's laugh sounded halfhearted. "Very well. Fetch me that jar first. Yes, the one with the purple liquid. I want one of my natural philosophers to inspect it."

There was the sliding sound of glass on wood. "Why?" Buckingham asked. "What does this liquid do?"

My heart beat faster. A liquid? Was it Galileo's elixir?

"So far, nothing at all." The king sounded irritated. "I placed a rat's carcass in it, just as I was instructed, but the animal hasn't regenerated. There isn't so much as a whisker moving on its body. I'm surrounded by charlatans, Bucks."

"Not all of them are." There was an edge to Buckingham's voice I couldn't understand.

"No, not all of them." The king sighed. "Why do the cleverest of my men have to die?"

"You don't know they're dead," Buckingham said quickly.

"They had better be. Only their deaths could excuse their lateness."

What were they talking about? My eyes met Antonio's, and he shook his head a fraction, as confused as I.

The men's footsteps crossed the room. As the door shut behind them, I let out a breath, but it didn't ease the burning in my chest. The burning that nothing, I feared, would ever lessen.

For the door hadn't merely closed on a duke and the king, but on a duke and my father's version of a modern-day Satan—a man who was hunting the very substance that could destroy our faith forever . . . and the world as we knew it.

Antonio and I remained under the table for several breathless minutes, listening for footsteps in the corridor. I hugged my knees to my chest, needing something to hold on to so I didn't fly apart. My mind moved as ceaselessly as a river's current. Galileo's elixir could cheat death. It was an abomination—wasn't it?

In the warm, sheltered darkness, Antonio shifted beside me, his arm bumping mine. "I don't hear anything. I think we should go now."

Without a word, I slid out from under the table. Together we slipped from the room. The corridor was empty, and we walked without speaking, keeping our heads down. I prayed no passing courtiers would call out to us in greeting.

When we had finally gone through the gates into the bustling city streets, we melted into the jumble of people: farmers walking their cattle to market, housewives and servants carrying baskets of vegetables and fish, nobles rolling past in carriages. The sight should have seemed familiar, but it felt strange, as though I were caught in a dream, walking through an altered landscape. I kept my gaze on the ground, tracing the lines of mortar between the cracked stones.

Antonio's hand fastened around my wrist. Before I could react, he pulled me into an alley. Here the walls sagged toward each other so closely they blocked out the sunlight, and all I could see were the whites of Antonio's eyes as they focused on my face. My hands felt icy in his warm ones.

"You look like your heart is breaking," he said.

"Because it is." My voice sounded half strangled. "If anyone can come back to life by drinking this elixir, then our religion is discredited forever. Anyone can drink this liquid, becoming a god or an imposter depending on your definition."

Antonio's hands tightened on mine. "We don't know if Christ drank a similar substance. There's no proof that he was human. All Signor Galilei's discovery does is call his divinity into question—and, truly, does it matter how he was brought back to life? Shouldn't we care more about how he lived than about how he died?"

I stared at him.

"Jesus's teachings upended all the values of the world," Antonio said gently. "He taught others about love and compassion and mercy. He believed the meek, not the greedy, would be raised high. He shared his table with the lowliest members of society— prostitutes and tax collectors and lepers. Aren't his lessons more important than the manner in which he might have been resurrected?"

This was heresy. His words should have been knives, cutting my ears. But they were as soft as velvet.

Because maybe he was right.

I gave him a small smile. Together we walked out of the alley into the sunlight, following the curving streets to Piccadilly, and I let my thoughts unfurl in my mind, promising myself I wouldn't be afraid of them anymore, no matter where they took me.

Twenty-One

IT WAS NIGHT; THE SUN HAD BEEN CHASED FROM the sky, leaving behind a sheet of black. Antonio, Robert, Lady Katherine, and I sat in her library, surrounded by walls of books. Candles burned in iron candelabra, sending gold-flecked shadows across the room. A servant had drawn the heavy curtains, closing out the night, but I still felt it pressing against the glass, as though it were a weighted thing. The table we had gathered around was littered with glasses of cut crystal and a couple of bottles of claret. The liquid, bloodred and bitter, shone in the glasses.

I perched on an elaborately carved wooden chair. Antonio sat across from me, his head bowed, as if deep in thought. His hair fell forward, curtaining his face so I couldn't guess what he was thinking. Only his hands, white knuckled on his wineglass, betrayed his nerves.

When Robert had arrived after supper, we'd retired to the library to tell him what Antonio and I had uncovered. Now he sat motionless, tears gleaming in his eyes.

"So my father conspires against me?" he finally said. "Very well, then. From now on, we're enemies."

My heart ached for him. He must feel so alone. I leaned across the table, trying to catch Robert's eye, but he wouldn't look at me. "Do you think Galileo's discovery is the true reason he was brought before the Inquisitors in Rome?" I asked, hoping to distract him. "They claimed he was imprisoned because he wrote in the *Dialogue Concerning the Two Chief World Systems* that the earth revolves around the sun—but what if it was because the pope learned about Galileo's meteorite and wanted to silence him forever?"

Antonio shook his head. "It's possible. I'll doubt we'll ever know the full truth now."

Robert didn't seem to have heard me. He sighed, dropping his head into his hands. "I understand why my father wants to hide Galileo's elixir from the world. Part of me can't even blame him. For eleven miserable years he suffered in exile, and he'd be a fool to let anything loosen his grip on the crown. But Galileo's story needs to be told. The world deserves to hear it."

"Why?" Lady Katherine's eyes were wet. "What good could possibly come of sharing Galileo's heretical account with others? All you would accomplish is breaking thousands of hearts. Like mine," she added with a sob in her voice. "You're questioning the one true God, and you'll burn for it, Your Grace."

Robert jumped to his feet and paced in front of the fireplace. The flames had died out, leaving behind a pile of gray ashes.

"Don't you see, my lady? Galileo's discovery doesn't need to hurl us into despair; it can lift us to the highest heights. This could make us free in a way we never dreamed possible. No longer enslaved by our beliefs or to a tyrannical leader—we can be the agents of our destinies!"

My heart had surged into my throat, and I could barely breathe around it. Robert's idea was fantastic, impossible—wasn't it? All afternoon I had been reflecting on Galileo's discovery, poking at it as I would with a wound, my fingers soft and hesitant. I had been taught that every passage in the Bible contained incontrovertible truths. To think otherwise was sacrilege. Galileo's story could divide hearts and empires, bring governments crashing down and crack the Church in two. If Antonio and Robert were right and the answers to divine mysteries were rooted in natural philosophy, then every piece in our carefully constructed world would unravel, like threads in a tapestry, leaving a half-formed picture.

For the first time in history, we would be able to question our faith.

And if the king had his way, no one would ever know.

Tears flooded my eyes. Shakily I stood up, reaching behind me to grip the back of my chair for support. Robert, who had been in the middle of a sentence, fell silent. Everyone turned to look at me.

"You're right, Robert." My voice came out as a wobbly whisper. "The world deserves to know the truth. Even if it could rip apart governments and start wars." I took a deep breath, my voice strengthening. "People's freedom rests within their minds—my father taught me that. If our minds are in chains, then we are prisoners. So we *must* get the vial back and assemble my father's papers to share them with everyone."

Antonio half rose. "Elizabeth, if we do what you're suggesting, then your father—"

"Will die," I interrupted, clasping my hands, as if I could hold myself together and not fly apart with a touch. Antonio wavered behind a sheen of my tears, so all I could see was black hair raining down around a pale face. "I know. The king will have him executed. But this is what my father would want me to do. He's a lover of liberty above all else."

Through my tears I saw Antonio and Robert coming toward me, their faces concerned, and I knew if I didn't get out of that room I would pull apart like paper left out in the rain. I bunched up my skirts in my hands and ran.

Down the long, straight corridors, the candelabra flaring in the darkness, I raced heedlessly, losing all sense of direction, until I reached a set of doors leading to the back gardens. I pushed them open with the flat of my hand, bursting outside into the coolness of night.

The grass was a black carpet dappled with silver. I ran the stone paths, my shoes ringing on the pavers. The scent of roses hung heavy in the air, and the hedgerows were blurred shadows, closing me in a long tunnel.

When I reached a tree, I stopped, my chest heaving. I bent over, trying to catch my breath. For a long moment I stayed like that, my eyes tracing the stones in the path. *Don't think*, I ordered myself. Thoughts would only bring pain and doubt, and I couldn't afford either. Not if I wanted to remain strong enough to do what my father had intended—and let him die so Galileo's discovery could revolutionize the world.

But I still couldn't stop crying. From somewhere behind me I heard footsteps on the path, but I couldn't bring myself to care enough to turn around.

The footsteps stopped nearby. "Elizabeth." It was Antonio's voice.

"Go away," I muttered to the ground. "Can't you see I want to be left alone?"

In the quiet that followed, I could hear the buzzing of fireflies and the shallow rise and fall of Antonio's breath. He didn't move.

"Go away!" I shouted, finally straightening and turning to face him. My words died on my lips.

He was staring at me as if he had never seen me before. He stood so close I could smell the scents clinging to his skin, sandalwood and spiced wine, and I could feel the heat pumping off his body in waves. He said my name again, so gently I barely recognized the sound of it, and I knew then, with every particle of my being, what he was about to do, and I felt myself moving closer to him like a leaf swept by a river's current, propelled by a stronger force.

Antonio laid the flat of his hand on my cheek. His fingers felt warm and rough. Flickers of heat licked my skin where he touched me. I couldn't tear my eyes from his. He looked so serious.

"You want to do what you believe is right, even though you know it will bring you pain," he said huskily. "You're the bravest person I've ever met."

And then he smiled. Such a wide, open smile that something stirred in my chest, as if I were waking from slumber.

"This time when I touch you," he said, "you won't need to ask what I'm doing."

His hand guided my face closer to his. So close I could feel warmth emanating from his skin and hear the soft exhalation of his breath. My heart started to race, and my eyes drifted closed just as his lips brushed mine, as softly as air.

He deepened the kiss, his lips hot and insistent on mine, and everything within me turned to fire. *So* this *is what it feels like*, I thought as I kissed him back, winding my arms around him, tightening until I could feel the thundering of his heart through the layers of our clothes. Then and there I decided Galileo must have been right when he postulated that the earth moved, for I imagined the ground shifted under our feet like the surface of the sea, and it was only those opposing forces Antonio had mentioned that kept us firmly anchored to it. As the earth rotated on its axis, spinning us around in this seemingly endless journey, I kissed Antonio again and again until all I knew was the warm wine of his mouth and the blood roaring in my ears because I could not catch my breath.

Twenty-Two

WHEN WE FINALLY RETURNED TO THE LIBRARY, Lady Katherine had already gone to bed and Robert sat alone by the dark, cold fireplace, his chin resting on his clasped hands. One look at my flushed face must have told him everything, for he smiled slightly, saying, "I was wondering how long it would take the two of you to figure things out."

My cheeks warmed. Antonio only laughed and led me into the room, keeping our fingers intertwined. "Is Lady Katherine all right?"

Robert sighed. "She's upset about the elixir and what it could mean for our religion. I'm afraid her reaction is the one we should expect to receive from most people—that, or violence, frankly. Most Christians won't take kindly to the idea that their savior might have been as human as they are." He sent us a wary look. "How do *you* feel about Galileo's discovery?"

Antonio poured us glasses of claret, his expression thoughtful. "I don't think it matters how Christ returned from death. Whether he was resurrected because of his divine nature or because he had partaken of a medicinal substance, he was still a great teacher."

I took the glass Antonio handed me and settled on the red velvet divan, fussing with my skirts to give myself time to think about my answer. But my mind felt as disordered as raindrops in a storm, coming down in every direction. I had kissed Antonio. *Kissed* him. If Betty had known about it, she would have boxed my ears. But . . . I didn't feel sinful, I decided. I was the same person I had always been. Not rendered new and strange by the "impure" kisses Betty had warned me and my sisters about. Instead, I felt warm and happy. And older, as if I had stepped out of my family's circle.

"Elizabeth?" Robert prompted, making me start. "What do you think?"

"Oh. Er . . . a few weeks ago, I would have been horrified. But now, after everything we've been through, I believe there are dozens of hidden truths in this world waiting to be found. Besides, the nature of Christ's death doesn't detract from the majesty of his life. It doesn't diminish the lessons he taught, the lessons that revolutionized the values of his time and that continue to guide us today. Even if he was human—and Galileo's discovery doesn't confirm or refute it—even if he was human, we can still love and revere him."

"What Signor Galilei has done is give us a wondrous gift—the gift of thinking and questioning." Antonio sat down next to me. His leg brushed my voluminous skirts, and I fought a blush. Robert smiled behind his hand.

"Now that that's out of the way," he said, "I think we should investigate the Royal Society. It's likely my father has given Galileo's remaining papers—and the vial, if he has it—to natural philosophers within the group. After all, he is the Society's patron."

"Why would he do that?" I took a sip of claret. It tasted rich and bitter on my tongue, washing away the taste of Antonio. "If he wanted to suppress Galileo's discovery, he'd hardly tell more people about it."

"He probably wants to find the cave and needs their advice to locate it," Antonio said. "Either to destroy the meteor or to take it for himself. Imagine the kind of power your king would have if he possessed an elixir that could pull someone back from the brink of death."

Robert looked away, a muscle in his cheek twitching. "Anyone with that kind of power would be unstoppable." He waved a hand dismissively. "Let's not think about it now. You said my father mentioned 'his' natural philosophers to Buckingham. Did he say anything else?"

"Only that they'd better be dead," Antonio said, "for nothing else would excuse their lateness—"

He broke off. We stared at each other. I could practically feel lightning crackling in the air between us. *The men outside Oxford.*

"I slashed one of them," I said. "I doubt he's dead, but—"

"His injury could have slowed their progress to London," Antonio finished. He surged to his feet. "The king might not have the vial yet! We might be able to steal it back before it ever falls into his hands."

Robert jumped up, too. "We have to meet the Royal Society

221

men! We could find out from them which ones are my father's favorites—and which have recently disappeared."

He paced, deep in thought, his eyes darting around the room. "The Society typically holds its meetings on Mondays. It's now Tuesday, but I'm sure I can convince Robert Boyle to call an additional meeting for tomorrow night. Mr. Boyle is one of the Society's most prominent members," he explained when we looked at him blankly. "I should be able to ask him some veiled questions."

"Won't your father attend?" I asked.

Robert snorted. "He's the patron of many groups, and I've never known him to go to Society meetings. Oh, he remembers to send them venison every year on the anniversary of their founding, but that's the extent of his involvement. He's quite accomplished at making meaningless gestures." His laugh sounded hollow.

The sound made my heart ache. Poor Robert, illegitimate, unaccepted by his family, yet willing to put himself in danger simply because he wanted to do what he believed was right.

"Are foreigners permitted to attend meetings?" Antonio asked.

"The Society accepts men from all nations and classes," Robert said. "Its members believe in the pursuit of knowledge above everything else, and they won't even discuss religion or politics at meetings. So if you came, you'd be greeted with open arms—but you'd have to pretend to be someone other than an Italian, in case my father has confided in his philosopher friends. Can you pose as a Spaniard?"

"If I don't have to speak Spanish, I should be fine."

"I'm coming, too." I looked at Robert so he could see there

was no laughter in my face, only deadly seriousness.

But he merely nodded. Then he stopped walking and held out his hand across the table toward us. "This Royal Society meeting is the last road open to us. We *have* to find out if my father has gone to any of their natural philosophers for help. Only then can we track down the vial and the rest of the papers." The look he gave us was grave. "And then share Galileo's elixir with the world."

I laid my hand on top of Robert's. "I'm with you."

Antonio rested his hand on mine. "And I."

"Good." Robert's eyes flickered from mine to Antonio's. "I hardly need tell you that if we're unsuccessful, we'll probably pay with our lives."

Antonio and I looked at each other. In the candlelit gloom, his face was half in shadow, and I couldn't see his expression. But I felt his fingers tighten on mine and heard the iron of his voice as he replied, "I know. If it comes to that, I'm ready."

The next morning, a knock on my bedchamber door woke me. *Six days*, I thought automatically as my mind surged into wakefulness. That was all the time remaining before the next Hanging Day took place and the sand in my father's hourglass trickled out.

Even as I opened my eyes, the knowledge crashed down on me like a wave pinning me to the ocean floor: Hanging Day or not, Father would definitely die soon. And I would let it happen.

Don't think about it, I told myself fiercely as my throat tightened. Surely I was doing what Father and his two "traitor angel" colleagues wanted—exposing the discovery Galileo had made decades ago.

And they aren't traitors, I thought as I scrubbed my face with my hands, as if I could wash away this sick feeling clinging to me. They were explorers, readers, and questioners. Only someone who viewed life through a distorted lens would see them as betraying Jesus.

The knock sounded again. "Enter," I called, scrambling into a sitting position.

I had expected to see Thomasine carrying a tray of food, but instead Lady Katherine slipped inside. She held a bundle of sea-green garments in her arms.

"I beg your pardon, Miss Milton. I didn't intend to wake you." She held up the clothes. "These are my brother's. You're welcome to borrow them for tonight's meeting at the Royal Society. You can hardly wear the tattered clothes you were in when you first arrived at my door," she said when I started to protest. "Edward is sleeping off the effects of another . . . er . . . difficult night, and he won't notice if some of his garments disappear for a day or two."

I took the proffered clothes, running my hand along the satin sleeves. "Thank you, Lady Katherine. You've been generosity itself to all of us since we came."

"I enjoy the companionship. Ordinarily this house is so empty."

I set the clothes on the bed. "You must have been lonely, coming all this way from Ireland with only your brother for your chaperone. Do you like London, at least?"

Her hands fiddled with the silver-backed brushes lying on a table. "I've barely seen it—just bits through the carriage window on my way back and forth to Whitehall."

"Surely you jest!" When she shook her head, I cried, "You must explore it, then! It's the most wondrous city in the world—full of learned men and bookshops and people from every nation imaginable."

"It sounds like a fascinating city." She made a sour face. "As His Grace's intended, though, I'm forbidden to move about freely."

For a moment, I stared at her. It seemed wealth and privilege could build its own sort of cage.

"Don't you long to see London for yourself?"

She shrugged. "Yes, but by wedding His Grace I'll bring honor to my family. And surely you know how difficult life is for my people in Ireland."

I understood what she meant: during the last century, my country had fully conquered hers and had tried to force its residents to adopt our Protestant faith. Once Mr. Cromwell had assumed control, he ordered almost all lands owned by Irish Catholics seized and given over to English settlers.

Shame heated my face. The government my father supported had been responsible for massacres and mass misery in her homeland. "I'm sorry—"

"My family used to own an estate in the county of Wexford." Lady Katherine continued fiddling with the brushes, not looking at me. "Mr. Cromwell's soldiers stole it from us. They forced us to live in Connacht, with the other Irish Catholics.

"Four years ago, the king granted us new land. It isn't much, but it's enough to keep the despair out of my father's face." She turned toward me, her expression hard. "When the king summoned me to London, I knew it was to extend a conciliatory gesture toward my people. I'm willing to do anything to keep us safe—live in this house provided by the king, marry his son, anything at all."

She raised her chin, as if daring me to condemn her. For the first time, I realized there was something within her I hadn't noticed before—a length of steel.

I bowed my head to her. "You have my respect, Lady Katherine."

For a moment, she said nothing. Then: "I came to London prepared to be miserable for my people's sake." The smile she gave me seemed timid and unsure. "I didn't expect to fall in love with Robert."

I dropped her brother's clothes. "You are? I just assumed it was a political arrangement—"

"That's what I thought it would be!" Her smile widened as she plopped down next to me. "But he's so clever and brave and selfless. I fell in love with him as soon as I saw him. Anyway, tell me more about London," she said, settling on the sea of pillows. "I'd like to learn about my new home."

And so we sat on the bed while daylight stretched long fingers across the marble floor. I told her my father's stories, about the whale that swam up the Thames a few years ago and got stuck in the shallow water when the tide ebbed; people had thought it was a terrible monster and called it Leviathan. I told her about the Royal Menagerie at the Tower of London—a collection of wild animals whose roars and screams rent the air at night—and the polar bear the king of Norway had sent to London long ago, which had been allowed to roam along the banks of the Thames, swiping salmon out of the river with its paws. During my stories,

Thomasine entered with a tray and was entreated to remain. Soon we three found ourselves sitting together on the bed, eating cold game pie and laughing, and for that brief sunlit time, I could forget we were a presumed regicide's daughter, an aristocrat, and a servant, and imagine we were simply friends.

The Royal Society met in Gresham College, a mansion that had once belonged to a merchant, who had bequeathed the building as a seat of learning nearly one hundred years ago, Robert told us as our carriage rattled through the narrow streets that evening. I raised a gloved hand to draw back the curtain from the window. Candlelit lanterns hung outside the houses on Bishopsgate, barely breaking apart the blackness pressing down on the city.

"Remember to say as little as possible," Robert warned. "We don't want any of the Society men to guess who either of you is."

I nodded. We couldn't afford any mistakes. Our plan was simple: mingle with Royal Society members, learn which ones were the king's favorites, and, if they'd gone missing recently, hunt them down. With luck, they'd be the men who'd attacked us outside Oxford. We would break into their private laboratories—most Society men had them—and steal the vial back. Then we could tell the world about Galileo's discovery, just as Father would want—we'd simply be doing so sooner than he had expected.

Father. My hands gripped my knees, my fingernails digging through the satin into my skin. He would probably die before we could find him. Galileo's reputation as a heretic would be sealed for all time. But we would have accomplished their goal—their secret would be shouted from the rooftops. I swallowed against the emotion constricting my throat. And Father would be proud of me. It would have to be good enough.

"Elizabeth, you make such a pretty boy." Robert's voice sliced into my thoughts. "Try to hunch your shoulders more so no one notices your . . . um . . ."

I raised my eyebrows. "My what, Robert?" I asked sweetly.

Even in the dim carriage, I could see his face flush. "You know what I mean," he mumbled.

Antonio and I laughed. "*I* wish you wouldn't hunch, at least until we go inside," Antonio said, grinning.

"Bold talker." I nudged him in the side.

He leaned closer, murmuring in my ear, "You make me want to be bold. And Robert's right—you do make a pretty boy." His lips brushed my earlobe, sending shivers shooting down my spine. "But you make a truly beautiful girl."

Beautiful. Part of me wanted to snort in derision, but then I saw the gravity of his expression—he meant what he said. Everything within me softened, like butter left on a sunlit table. Unsure how to accept the compliment, I muttered a thank-you and glanced at my clothes. The breeches and doublet in green satin looked as though they had been tailored for me. I ran my hands down my arms, feeling the cold lengths of my knives through the fabric and glad for their comforting presence. Lady Katherine's brother's spare wig of rippling blond curls had transformed me into a stranger. In this disguise I planned to pose as one of Robert's boyhood friends, a nobleman from France whose inexact grasp of the English tongue would excuse my silence.

For his part, Antonio had dressed as he ordinarily did. He sat so close his knee brushed mine when he shifted on the seat, and

I had to fight a blush. It wouldn't do for this French boy to turn pink every time his Spanish friend looked at him.

The carriage jolted to a stop, rocking slightly as the driver leaped down from his perch outside. He opened the door for us. Robert, as was his due, stepped out first. I jumped to the pavement after him, then gazed up at the massive house looming in front of us.

Chattering gentlemen poured into the building, their satin and velvet clothes gleaming in the glow of the lanterns. Several of them bowed to Robert. He acknowledged them with a small smile and a wave of his hand.

Despite the danger we might be walking into, excitement ran a line of sweat down my spine. For years I had daydreamed of the opportunity to listen to these learned men discuss their theories and present their experiments. As I climbed the front steps, I had to wipe my damp palms on my breeches.

We followed the long line of men into a low-ceilinged room where rows of chairs had been set up. Something shaped like a box and concealed by a black cloth sat on the table at the front of the room. Beside it stood a slender, brown-haired fellow of middling age. He hurried to greet us, his slim face creasing into a smile.

"Your Grace." He bowed to Robert. "On behalf of the Royal Society, I welcome you to our humble quarters. We're gratified by your interest in our activities."

He spoke with a faint Irish accent, smiling at me and Antonio in turn. Robert clasped the man's hand and turned to us. "My friends, this gentleman is Mr. Robert Boyle, who, although he is far too modest to tell you, has one of the finest minds in

England, and whose knowledge of chemistry is without compare. This," he said, nodding at me, "is Baron Louis de Laval, a dear school friend of mine," then, nodding at Antonio, "and this is Senor Alroy de Vargas. He's a student of mathematics and is visiting from Spain."

Boyle shook our hands. "Baron de Laval, you are most welcome. Senor de Vargas, I daresay you will find our Society unlike what you are accustomed to in Spain—our organization is dedicated to disseminating our discoveries rather than keeping our advancements to ourselves."

Antonio's eyebrows rose. "An aim both honorable and revolutionary, Mr. Boyle. Most natural philosophers are lone geniuses who hoard their secrets. To gather in one place where you can share your knowledge and work out your theories . . ." He shook his head, looking troubled. His concern was one I shared: If the Society was composed of such generous men, how could the king's associates number among them?

Mr. Boyle ushered us into seats in the first row. Some forty men were in attendance, all gentlemen, to judge by their fine clothes. They sat quietly, their gazes fixed on Mr. Boyle. When one of them muttered to his companion, nearly everyone in the room glared at him and growled, "Hush!"

"Tonight we have assembled a special meeting in honor of the Duke of Lockton, who has kindly expressed interest in our proceedings," Mr. Boyle said. "As His Grace has told me of his admiration for the Italian natural philosopher Galileo Galilei, I have asked Mr. Hooke to present the experiments he conducted two summers ago concerning Galileo's theories on gravity. Mr. Hooke, you have the floor."

A short, pale man wearing a wig of brown curls scurried to the front of the room. He bobbed a perfunctory bow to Robert, then whipped away the black cloth to reveal a wooden box. With jerky movements, he removed objects from the box—a feather, a book, and a brass candlestick—and set them on the table.

"Two years ago, I devised a series of experiments to prove Mr. Galilei's suppositions about gravity were accurate," Mr. Hooke said. The room was so quiet, I could hear the rumble of carriages in the street. "Mr. Galilei assumed a constant force draws objects toward the earth, regardless of their mass. With that thought in mind, I went up to the tower of St. Paul's Cathedral, where I dropped a variety of items toward the ground, recording the speed at which they fell, the changes in air pressure, and a variety of other factors."

Cradling the objects in his arms, he clambered awkwardly onto the table. It groaned under his weight but held. "What I came to realize," he announced, "is that all bodies and motions in the world are subject to change."

All at once, he dropped the three items. Beside me, Antonio stiffened. I leaned forward in my chair, unable to tear my gaze from the white feather, its wispy edges brushing the book's spine as they lay on the floor next to each other. The candlestick glinted a foot away. The three weighed different amounts; they had landed at different times. I would have thought they would fall at the same rate of speed, since they had been dropped from the same elevation, but I understood what Mr. Hooke was saying: gravity varied depending on height and weight.

It was as though a candle had been lit in my mind, burning brightly in a corner that had been dark. *Nothing* was constant.

There were so many forces we had to take into account when considering how an object would react to external stimuli.

This world, this beautiful world, was filled with secrets we were only beginning to comprehend.

Which also meant there was so much we still didn't know about Galileo's discovery. I frowned. This liquid might not be as miraculous and beneficent as Galileo had believed. After all, it may have caused his and my father's blindness.

We did not know what we were dealing with. We only had guesses. Smoke that dissolved in our hands when we tried to catch it; suppositions and theories wrapped in darkness. I shivered. What would we unleash on the world when we shared Galileo's discovery? Perhaps we hadn't thought this through.

Someone started clapping. The sound pulled my mind into the room. Dozens of men had begun applauding and cheering.

"Huzzah!" the men shouted. "Brilliant!" "Excellent experiment, Mr. Hooke!"

He bowed, then scuttled to his seat. Mr. Boyle strode to the front of the room and launched into a discussion of a proposed treatment for eye ailments he had devised using dried dog excrement.

The men listened with rapt attention to Mr. Boyle. They looked ordinary in their long wigs and fine clothes. Any one of them could be in the king's employ, though, and I had no way of knowing. I ran my hands up and down my arms. Through the satin sleeves, I could feel the hardness of my knives. As long as I had them, I wasn't helpless.

When the meeting broke up, men milled about in clumps, chattering loudly. Robert, Antonio, and I stood together, forcing smiles at the fellows who hovered nearby, bowing and looking pointedly at Robert, no doubt hoping for a favorable comment from the king's son.

"We've learned *nothing*," Robert whispered to me and Antonio. "At least one of these men must be in collusion with my father, but I can't figure out how to ask—"

"Quiet," I muttered. Mr. Boyle was approaching us, his mild face wreathed in a smile. A short man of about thirty, with a fleshy face and a wig of dark brown curls, trailed in his wake.

"I hope you enjoyed your evening, Your Grace," Mr. Boyle said to Robert. "And both of your companions, as well. This is Mr. Samuel Pepys," he added, pronouncing the surname "Peeps" and gesturing at the small man at his side. "Mr. Pepys works for the Royal Navy."

"I am gratified to make your acquaintance, Your Grace," Mr. Pepys burbled, bending low in an overly dramatic bow. "I'm a loyal servant to His Majesty. At his request I stayed in London throughout the plague, to keep our naval operations running."

"My father and uncle have spoken to me about you." Robert gave the man a patient smile. "They were impressed by your selflessness in remaining in the city during such a dangerous time."

Mr. Pepys gasped. "Oh, thank you for your kind words, Your Grace!"

Robert's nod was a clear dismissal. As Mr. Pepys backed away, Robert glanced at Mr. Boyle. "My father often speaks of the high regard in which he holds your Society. There are a few men in particular he mentions frequently—special friends of his, I gather—but I can't recall their names. . . ."

Mr. Boyle easily picked up Robert's meaning. "Ah, Your

Grace must mean Sir Henry Vaughan and his two assistants. They often help His Majesty when he conducts private experiments in his laboratory at Whitehall."

Robert's eyes narrowed. "Indeed." The single word was loaded with so much venom that I touched his arm, a silent warning to be careful. Robert shook me off. "Where are Sir Vaughan and his assistants? I'd like to meet my father's favorites."

"Hmm." Mr. Boyle scanned the crowd. "I regret to say I don't see them. Rather unfortunate. They'll be disappointed at having missed the event—they're keen adherents of Mr. Galilei and would have enjoyed witnessing Mr. Hooke's demonstration."

"Adherents of Galileo's," Robert repeated slowly. "I think I have become one myself tonight." He shot me and Antonio a guarded look. "Perhaps we should call upon these gentlemen. We can tell them how informative we found the meeting." He turned to Mr. Boyle. "Where do they live?"

"Sir Vaughan has a house on the Strand, and his assistants reside with him. But you might not find Sir Vaughan at home. I believe he's out of town."

Robert paused in the act of pulling on his gloves. "Where is he?"

"I don't know," Mr. Boyle replied. "I last saw him a week ago—he didn't attend this past Monday's meeting, either."

A week. It was just enough time for Sir Vaughan and his assistants to have heard about an Italian searching for my father in London and to have made the journey to Chalfont. They could have arrived after my family had been rounded up. Like Robert, they could have forced my location out of Francis Sutton.

They might be the three who had attacked us in the fields

outside Oxford and wrested the vial from Robert's grasp. If they hadn't yet returned to London, it was possible they were still making their way to the capital, slowed by the injuries I had inflicted on one of them.

There might be time to steal the vial back from them—and retrieve the torn piece of Galileo's story, if the king had given it to them as Robert suspected.

These were big leaps in thinking to make, but they were all we had. My eyes met Robert's. It was time to go before we asked too many questions and raised suspicions. He nodded in immediate comprehension and looked at Mr. Boyle. "Thank you for a pleasant evening. My friends and I must take our leave."

"Wait, Your Grace," Mr. Boyle cried as we started to walk away. He hurried after us, stopping and bowing low when Robert swung around to look at him. "If you wish to meet Sir Vaughan, you might see him tomorrow night at the ball."

"What ball?" Robert asked. A few feet away, Mr. Pepys was still making his groveling way from us. He bumped into a chair and burst into a flurry of apologies to the elderly man sitting in it. Robert glanced at him and shook his head, looking irritated. No doubt he was accustomed to having his presence turn grown men into fawning, anxious sycophants.

"The ball at the Duke of Buckingham's estate," Mr. Boyle said. "Sir Vaughan is a dear friend of the duke's. May I be bold enough to ask if you plan to attend, Your Grace? It should be one of the great social events of the summer."

Robert smiled thinly. "Mr. Boyle, I wouldn't miss it for the world."

Twenty-Three

IN THE END, ROBERT RETURNED TO WHITEHALL IN Mr. Pepys's rented hackney coach, rolling his eyes at us through the window opening as Mr. Pepys bubbled with excitement beside him. They pulled away from the pavement, iron wheels rattling on the pavers. Antonio and I stood on Gresham College's front steps, watching the carriages inch forward to pick up their passengers and rumble off into the night. In the dim light of the lanterns, the conveyances gleamed, all painted black wood and nail-studded leather.

Lady Katherine's carriage lurched to a stop in front of the college; I recognized it by the coat of arms painted in gold on the door—a snarling lion intersected by a *D*, for "Daly." The footman jumped down from his bench, opening the door for us with a flourish. I stepped into the shadowy interior. The carriage rocked as Antonio settled beside me on the padded seat.

The horses started forward, the familiar *clip-clop* of their hooves floating to our ears.

In the glow of the passing lanterns, Antonio's jaw looked hard. "I don't like the idea of you attending this ball at Buckingham's home. It sounds far too dangerous."

I bristled. "But it's fine for you and Robert to go?" I rolled up my sleeve, exposing the silver gleam of my knife. "Don't tell me the two of you would be safe because you're men. I think we both know I can handle myself."

His gaze fell to my bare forearm. "You're right," he said quietly. "I do know that. But I still hate the thought of you in danger."

Something delicious and warm spread through my chest like mulled wine, fragrant with spices and heated over a fire. I rested my hand on the curve of his cheek, feeling the roughness along his jaw where he hadn't shaved closely enough. "What will you do when this is all over?"

"I haven't let myself think that far ahead." The carriage jolted over the uneven paving stones, and my hand fell from his face. "When I first arrived in your country, all I wanted was to return to Florence. But now . . ." He glanced at me, his eyes guarded. "We don't know what will become of any of us. It seems pointless to plan when we might not have very long to live."

I thought of Father, vanishing somewhere in London six years ago when the king had made his triumphant return. Yes, he had run and hidden, much to the merriment of his political enemies. And yet he hadn't fled to a foreign land, as so many others had. He had stayed in his beloved England—daring to believe he might have a future.

"Hell is the absence of hope," I said softly. "And I refuse to live that way. Of course we might die . . . but we might also survive. And we could work—" I could barely get the words out, nerves wrapping their tentacles around my throat "We could work side by side in a laboratory." *Please, please don't let him laugh.*

He didn't. Instead he looked swiftly at me, his eyes searching. "There is nothing I would like more than that. You're right—we can't give up, not when there's so much to fight for." He stared out the window, lost in thought. "We've been forgetting your father's poem. Except for him, you're the only person who's read *Paradise Lost* in its entirety. You said yourself he wrote the story with us as the characters. Perhaps he's left a message for you secreted within its lines—something the king and his men would never be able to figure out. Maybe it's time for us to look at it again."

Sitting cross-legged on Antonio's bed, still dressed in the clothes we had worn to the Royal Society, we talked late into the night. I had removed my wig, letting my hair tumble loose down my back. A servant had left a bottle of wine, and Antonio poured us glasses and set them on the table, their scarlet liquid glowing in the candlelight.

"I've already written out the first seven books, as best as I can remember them," I told him. We spoke in whispers, our ears attuned for creaking floorboards in the corridor. The estate was grave-quiet except for the occasional breeze that rattled the windows in their frames. "He's left no special messages for me in them, I'm certain of it."

"Then tell me about the eighth book," Antonio said.

I described the events to him: Eve and Adam separate while

going about their daily chores in the Garden of Eden. Meanwhile, Satan possesses a snake by crawling through its mouth. Then, as one, the Serpent and Satan slither toward Eve. Satan knows precisely how to tempt her: he promises she will become as wise as Adam if she eats an apple from the forbidden Tree of Knowledge. She can't resist.

"When Adam discovers Eve's transgression," I said, "he bites into an apple, too. Not because he wants to grow smarter but because he knows Eve will be banished from Eden for her misdeed. He loves her so dearly, he can't bear to be parted from her. Then they begin to argue with each other. After they fight, God visits them. He punishes them, expelling them from Paradise forever."

Antonio frowned. "The natural philosophical ideas your father expresses in his poem are faulty and antiquated. He presents the earth as hanging from a golden chain—which is what people used to believe kept our planet from hurtling through the cosmos. Is that what he truly thought?"

I shrugged. "He rarely speaks of philosophical matters, at least with me. His interest has always lain in stories. One of his favorite activities is devising literary tricks. The poem even begins with one. The first scene takes place in Pandemonium, where Satan and his warrior angels have been expelled after battling God and his army in Heaven. The word 'pandemonium' is Greek for 'all the demons,'" I explained in response to Antonio's uncomprehending look. "My father's fond of playing games with words. Even the poem's locations are meaningful. It takes place primarily in Eden, and makes no mention of London or any other places in England. My father alludes to some cities in the Italian city-states, however, and Hell is clearly meant to be Rome: glittering, sumptuous, but, beneath the lavish surface, broken and corrupt. My father described Rome to me in similar terms many times. He visited it during his grand tour of Europe, and he said he found Rome both beautiful and fallen."

"Could he be hinting that additional clues are hidden in Rome or Tuscany?" Antonio asked. "Perhaps he concealed a map of the meteor cave somewhere."

"I don't see how. My father never returned to the city-states, and he began hiding the clues here about twenty years ago, during the civil war. If there are more treasures or clues hidden in Tuscany or Rome, then they must have put there by someone else, possibly Galileo or your master."

Antonio groaned, flopping onto his back. "We're no nearer to the answers than when we began talking tonight!"

Exhaustion had crept into the spaces between my bones, until all of my body ached from it. I rested on my back, too, staring at the shadows from the candle flames dancing on the ceiling.

"Our traitor angels may have been too clever," I said. "What use is there in hiding messages when no one can decipher them? Trying to do so is like walking in the dark with your eyes closed, doubly blinded."

Antonio rolled onto his side. "I know."

For a long moment, we were quiet. I listened to the whisper of air between his lips, a sound as reassuring as clockwork. My father had six more days until the air stopped passing his lips and died in his chest. How could I live with myself if I didn't save him? But how could I live with myself if I did and let Galileo's secret fade into nothingness?

There were no good choices. Only terrible options. And I knew which one my father wanted me to choose.

Blinking hard, I stared at the golden lines on the ceiling. I wouldn't cry for Father. He deserved my strength, not the poor gift of my tears.

With the tip of his finger, Antonio tapped one of the buttons on my doublet. At the pressure of his hand, the button pushed down into the silk of my shirt, spreading its cold circle of brass through the fabric into my skin. The intimacy of the gesture stopped my breath.

"Did you know, when I met you," he said, "I didn't want to like you at all."

Rolling my eyes, I pillowed my hands behind my head. My knives pressed into my forearms, the metal warmed by the heat of my skin and as familiar as a well-worn glove. "Thank you very much."

His teeth flashed white in the darkness. "You despised me at first. I believe I heard you telling Anne in a rather loud voice that I was—what was it?—handsome and therefore insufferable, as most good-looking fellows are." He sent me a wicked grin. "At least you thought I was handsome."

"Yes, as handsome as you are modest," I threw back at him, and he laughed again. He rested his hand on my hip, tugging until I rolled onto my side so we were face to face. The laugh froze on my lips. I gazed at him. The lean face I already knew so well, so much darker than mine. The black hair that tumbled to his shoulders, so unlike the wigs donned by most men in my country. The lips that spoke Italian, the hands that were running up and down my arm, sending delicious sparks of pleasure racing through my body. The doublet that concealed his beating heart. I rested my hand on his chest, feeling the steady thump through the fabric.

"When I touch you here," I said, "then I am touching you everywhere. For your heart pumps blood to the rest of your body, and your blood carries the sensation of my touch."

He grinned. "Pretty words," he teased. "Do they work on all the boys in London?"

"I don't care about them. All I want to know is if they work on you."

He leaned forward, inch by agonizing inch, until his lips were so close they brushed mine. And then he was kissing me, so hard and so fast that he stopped thoughts from running through my head. So warm and insistent he transformed the strains of candlelight shining through my eyelids to black. He stole all light and worry; he took away everything surrounding us until there was only the heat of his mouth and the golden fire in my chest, turning me molten from the inside out.

Twenty-Four

IT MIGHT HAVE BEEN MINUTES OR HOURS LATER when I reluctantly slipped from Antonio's embrace. My lips were so swollen from his kisses that my voice sounded shaky even to my ears. "I must go."

He lay on the coverlet, smiling up at me. The top three buttons of his shirt were undone, exposing the brown birthmark below his collarbone. Somehow the sight seemed even more intimate than the sensation of his lips on mine—this was one of the secrets of his body that probably only those closest to him, his brothers and parents, had seen. I might be the first person in over ten years to have laid eyes on that swath of skin. We were beginning to know each other in ways I could never have imagined. It was as though the world were slowly unfolding all around me, and it was far bigger than I had guessed.

I expected him to entreat me to stay. But he merely lifted my hand to his lips and kissed it. "I'll escort you to your room," he said.

"Truly?" I couldn't keep the surprise from my tone. "You don't beg for more kisses?"

He shot me a startled look. "What pleasure is there in kisses that aren't mutually given?"

And just like that, I was lost.

In the corridor, we walked in companionable silence, our hands linked. At my door, he kissed me one last time. "Good night," he said. Smiling, I ducked into my room. And even though I didn't look at my reflection in the glass, I knew my eyes must be shining in the dark.

"You are," Lady Katherine said, "quite possibly the worst dancer I have ever seen."

Groaning, I flung myself on the divan. "I know. I'm hopeless."

"You aren't trying hard enough." Lady Katherine stood in the middle of the library, her hands on her hips, regarding me with exasperation. It was the following afternoon, and we had spent part of the day closeted in this room while she had attempted to teach me dances. In the dimly lit Royal Society meeting room I had passed as a boy, but in Buckingham's ballroom, which would be illuminated by countless candles, it would be obvious I was a girl. Therefore I would pose as one of Lady Katherine's friends. A decent solution, except for one problem: I did not know how to dance at all. The intricate steps of the galliard were manageable, although I found myself automatically slipping into the man's role, which was much livelier than the woman's.

"How can you have made it to sixteen without learning how to dance?" Lady Katherine demanded.

"It was forbidden in my home."

"Oh. Puritans." She looked at me pityingly. "Does your kind truly believe entertainment is inherently sinful?"

I remembered looking at myself in the glass at the inn in Oxford. How good it had felt to study the landscape of my face. And my body may have felt graceless when I danced, but it had felt free and strange, too. Not wrong. Not wicked, but right and true. "I don't. Not anymore."

"I pity the feet of the men at tonight's ball, for surely they'll ache after dancing with you." Lady Katherine's lips twitched. I grinned at her. She had teased me—now I knew we were friends.

If anyone had told me a fortnight ago I would become friends with an Irish aristocrat so beautiful that candles seemed to burn brighter when she entered a room, I would have laughed in his face and called him a blockhead. It was as though in my old life the earth had stood still while the other planets had circled us, and in this new life the world had begun revolving, spinning me around and around until the ground tilted under my feet and I had to walk with my arms out flung for balance. Yet I would not trade this delicious dizziness for the comfortable smallness of my old life.

Except for Father. The loss of him was an ax, cleaving my life in two, turning all my days into a series of befores and afters.

My smile died on my lips. Somehow I murmured my excuses to Lady Katherine and hurried along the corridors to my bedchamber.

Don't think about him, I ordered myself. My actions were just, and I was doing what he wanted. If tonight we met the men who had stolen the vial from us and took it back, we could share Galileo's story with every European nation. We could trace the path of his life and find the cave that had brought him so much sorrow and joy. Citizens would be free to question their beliefs; they could explore the tenuous connections between religion and natural philosophy without fear of imprisonment or execution. The world would be changed forever.

And Father would be proud of me. Somewhere, he would be an eternal soul watching me—and he would know what I had done. I managed to smile, even though it felt as though my heart had been wrenched from my chest.

In my chamber, a scarlet gown had been left lying on the bed. The full skirts spread out like a bell over the white coverlet. Ribbons and intricate stitch work in paler shades of red covered the bodice. As though moving of its own will, my hand reached out to stroke the satin sleeves. They felt as smooth as water.

"Lady Katherine knows your people don't wear color," Thomasine said behind me. "But she said any ball guest who sees you in this gown will never guess you could be Mr. Milton's daughter."

"It's beautiful. But I can't borrow something so fine."

"Lady Katherine wanted you to have it, miss. She said the color would go well with your dark hair."

I smiled, knowing I would have to trust Lady Katherine's judgment, for I had no eye for frippery and finery. "Then I'll wear it, and be grateful."

"Very good, miss. We must get to work, or you won't be ready in time."

Although the word "work" made me laugh, I soon realized Thomasine had spoken in earnest: preparing oneself for a ball was serious work indeed. First servants had to haul ewers of water to fill the copper tub; then I had to scrub my hair and every inch of my body with a cake of soap. Clad in a fresh shift, I had to sit motionless while Thomasine heated curling tongs in the fire before winding strands of my hair around them, and then I had to try not to panic and shout that I smelled burning hair even though my nose had caught no whiff of any such thing.

I was brought a tray ("It's customary to eat before a ball, so you can refuse any refreshments served there and impress others with your ladylike appetite," Thomasine had explained, much to my amusement), and I sat at the writing table, dining on pheasant and potatoes and wondering why anyone would praise a girl for not eating enough food to feed a bird's belly. Aristocrats were people I would likely never understand, I decided as I pushed back from the table. But then I thought of Lady Katherine's averted eyes when she had talked about her family's ancestral castle in Ireland. Robert lying wounded in the tall grass. The Duke of Monmouth kissing my hand. Mr. Boyle speaking excitedly about his experiments. And I could not hate them.

I didn't even want to. Not anymore.

Thomasine helped me step into my skirts. With quick hands, she fastened their ties around my waist.

"Close your eyes, miss," she ordered.

Something as soft as feathers dusted my cheeks. Thomasine's finger traced the outline of my lips, her touch whisper-light. Then she pronounced me done, and I opened my eyes.

The sight of cosmetics on my skin was so startling I couldn't speak. My face had been powdered cloud-white, my lips painted cherry red. The shade of the gown was as rich and vivid as the sun in the final throes of daylight, blazing red and bright. In the glass, I could see gold thread must have been worked through the bodice as well, for bits glinted and caught the light. Rubies set in a gold chain gleamed around my neck. The front of my hair had been drawn into a bun, the rest left to fall down my back in loose waves.

"Lady Katherine was correct," I said. "No one would take me for John Milton's daughter in this costume. But the sleeves . . ." I frowned at them. They ended at my elbows, exposing my forearms. "I can't wear my knives."

"This length is the fashion," Thomasine said. "If you wear longer sleeves, everyone will look at you." She closed the hinged wooden boxes of powder and cerise. "His Grace and Mr. Viviani will be wearing their swords, though, miss, so you'll have protection."

I looked at her narrowly. "If you know we have need of protection, then Lady Katherine must speak frankly to you."

"She does," Thomasine said simply. "She's a rare jewel, and I hope His Grace knows how fortunate he is."

Before I could reply, the crunch of carriage wheels on stone pavers sounded through the window. Robert must have arrived. It was time.

Now that the moment had come, nerves swirled in my stomach like bats' wings, strong and impossible to ignore. I pressed a hand to my belly, willing it to settle.

After thanking Thomasine, I hurried from the room. As I strode down the corridor, I heard Lady Katherine's voice in the hall and rushed toward it.

When I blinked, Father's image loomed against my lids: narrow-shouldered, auburn-haired, sitting on the steps of our

London row house, his hands strumming the strings of his mandolin, an object of ridicule in his Puritan clothes. I could feel his hand digging into my shoulder for balance as we walked the streets, me describing the sights to him in a whisper. He had given me a thousand memories: the intoxicating scents of paper and ink, the wooden hilt of a dagger in my hand, the crackle of coals in a brazier while he dictated to me on winter mornings. Impatient and cantankerous and exacting, gentle and brilliant. Irreplaceable.

Lady Katherine's voice grew louder. "What do you think, Signor Viviani?"

"Signor Galilei's discovery is a powerful tool against the Church," Antonio said. "My master has spent years trying to repair Signor Galilei's reputation, to no avail. If I brought it to the officials in Rome and promised to keep it quiet in return for Signor Galilei's pardon, I'm certain they would agree."

I stopped in my tracks. What was Antonio saying?

"And I would like to find the cave and explore it for myself," he added, sounding excited.

"Hush," Lady Katherine said quickly. "I think I heard footsteps."

A hot lance seemed to press against my chest, burning the breath out of me.

My ears must be mistaken. Antonio would never go behind my back to seize control of Galileo's vial. Not my Antonio, who had shown me the stars and who laughed constantly and who had held me in his arms while he kissed the thoughts right out of my head. I could still see him standing next to me in the moonlight, his eyes intent on mine as he said I was the bravest person he had ever met. He wouldn't lie to me. I was wrong. I *had* to be.

For a long moment, I remained standing in the middle of the corridor. I heard a clock marking time from another room, a relentless *tick-tick*. Along the walls, candles flared in their iron brackets, splashing pockets of light across the stones. Everything looked too clear, too sharp, each detail imprinting itself on my mind.

I understood. Antonio wanted to possess the vial so he could salvage Galileo's reputation and find the meteor pool for himself. The only way to gain control of the vial had been to tell Robert and me what we'd wanted to hear . . . and trick us into believing he was on each of our sides.

Originally he had suggested deceiving Robert. But he hadn't stopped there. He was also planning to deceive *me*.

Twenty-Five

I TOOK A STEP FORWARD, THE CARPET RUNNER whispering under my feet. Memories rushed through my head. Antonio's hands on mine, guiding his telescope toward the sky. Another step. Lying beside each other in a field, my telling him he could call me Elizabeth. Another step, faster. Kissing in the garden, his breath crashing in my ears until all sound had faded away and there was only Antonio left.

I started to run.

The stone walls and iron candelabra flashed past. My breath hitched in my chest as though I had been racing for miles. Ahead, the hall entrance was a black rectangle, its edges colored gold by the candlelight. I slowed my pace to a moderate walk, pressing my hands to my thudding heart, as if I could ease its frantic beating by touch alone. My dry eyes burned.

Don't you dare cry, I told myself fiercely. Later I could fall apart, when there was no one to see.

I braced my hand on the wall, the stone scratching my palm. The pain was welcome; it was something to feel beyond this widening hole in my chest. *Think*, I ordered myself. What could I possibly do to beat Antonio at his own game of deception and manipulation?

He mustn't suspect I was onto him. I had to smile and flirt and dance. The whole time, I would be looking around the ballroom, seeking Sir Vaughan and his men. If they were the men who had attacked us outside Oxford, then I would recognize at least one of them—the man whose side I had cut with my sword. No amount of time could obscure his face; I would remember it, and the fury in his eyes, for the rest of my life.

The instant I saw him, I'd make my way to him. If Fortune's wheel turned in my favor, he wouldn't recognize me in my elaborate dress, and I would laugh and encourage him until he was more than willing to leave the ballroom with me—whereupon I would overpower him somehow, steal his sword, attack him with my fists, anything, and then take the vial. I would run from Buckingham's estate before anyone noticed. Later I would send a message to Robert, and together we would finish the work my father had begun decades ago. And the world would know the truth. It would be my final, best gift to Father.

I let my hand fall from the stone. My palm was lined with scratches. A distant part of my mind registered the stings of pain; they felt remote, as though they were happening to me in a dream. With an effort, I set my shoulders, imagining my spine was a ribbon of steel. I could do this. I *would* do this. I stepped into the hall.

Antonio and Lady Katherine stood in the middle of the room. They were dressed in luxurious clothes: Lady Katherine in pink satin, Antonio in black. They were still talking, but I couldn't hear them above the buzzing in my ears. Lady Katherine glanced in my direction. I felt my lips pulling into something that felt like the semblance of a smile. She smiled in return, beckoning for me to join them.

My heels echoed on the marble floor as I crossed the room. Antonio grinned at me. He leaned forward, touching his lips gently to my cheek. It took all of my willpower not to shudder.

"You look like a queen," he murmured in my ear. The tips of his hair, soft as feathers, brushed against my bare neck.

I studied the interlocking black and white marble squares in the floor. "Thank you."

"Are you well?" he asked. "You seem upset."

Somehow I found the strength to lift my head. Antonio was watching me closely, his eyebrows lifted.

My throat was so dry I had to swallow twice before I could reply. "I'm just worried about tonight." That, at least, wasn't a lie.

His face relaxed. He lifted a hand to brush a stray curl from my cheek, the red stone in his ring glinting. "It will be fine."

I looked away. "Isn't it time yet to leave?"

"Yes, but you're not riding with us," Robert said, entering the hall from another entrance. He was dressed in yellow satin, as usual. "Lady Katherine sent a courier to me at Whitehall this afternoon, with a message that you had found her dancing lessons difficult. If one of my guests is a young lady who clearly doesn't know how to dance . . . well, people will wonder about your pedigree. Some of my friends will escort you instead. They're waiting for you outside. You'll pose as one of their cousins. Don't worry—my friends are loyal to me, and I've given them strict instructions to look after you and do anything you tell them."

I barely heard him above the blood roaring in my ears. Somehow I managed to murmur, "Thank you. I will see you at the ball."

The boys kissed my hand. A servant flung open the doors for me, revealing the full darkness of the night. I strode down the steps into the courtyard, where a carriage waited, its black wood shining in the torchlight. All of it—the horses shifting slightly, their harnesses jingling; the long avenue of trees stretching from the courtyard to the front gate; the groomsmen standing at attention, dressed in silver and green livery—looked unreal, as though I were watching a dream unfold.

The groom opened the carriage door, extending a gloved hand to help me inside. Half bent over, I paused in the door frame. Five men sat on the padded seats. They reminded me of Robert: their clothes were as fine and bright as his, their postures erect and alert. Like him, they sported long, curly wigs and wore swords at their waists. One of them looked older than the rest, his forehead lined, his jaw sagging. He looked up at me.

"Miss Milton, please join us," he said. His voice sounded heavy, as if weighted with years of ale and food—a rich man's voice. He reached out his hand, guiding me onto the seat beside him. My voluminous skirts spilled over his lap, and I apologized, trying to bunch the fabric in my hands.

"It's a small price to pay for viewing such a vision of loveliness," he said.

I smiled faintly. *Pretty words.* Just like the lines Antonio had teased me about last night. Everything he had ever said to me was fading into smoke: flimsy, insubstantial, untouchable. Had he meant any of it? What an idiot I was! I'd been dreaming of a future with him—he would teach me all he knew about the skies, and together we would design experiments. Laughing while we peered through telescopes, grinning at each other when our theories were proved correct, kissing each other breathless in the laboratory we shared.

Without him, there would be no laboratory, no experiments, no lessons with me as the eager pupil. No one else would accept me into the men's world of natural philosophy. I was alone again. I'd have to hide my true self under tasks like embroidery and cooking, and pray for a husband whose company I tolerated— that was the best I could hope for. My future was an unvarying gray road, all the color sucked from it.

My hands fisted in my skirts; through the thick fabric my fingernails dug into my palms. Dimly, I wondered if my scratched palm was leaving a bloody smear on the gown, but I couldn't bring myself to care.

"The ride should be quick," the rich man said. "Buckingham lives in a grand estate on the Strand. I'm Sir Richard Gauden," he added, and I murmured I was pleased to make his acquaintance.

The carriage started with a lurch. Dully, I listened to the city rising up all around us: dogs barking in alleys, wooden shop signs creaking in the breeze, the high-pitched chattering of doxies on street corners as they waited for their customers. Somewhere church bells rang the hour, but I didn't bother counting their chimes: it was enough to know the hour was growing late and night lay as thickly on the city as on my heart.

Antonio's image rose in my mind: his hair tousled, him

flashing me a grin as he asked where my sense of adventure was. I pressed my knuckles against my lips so I wouldn't shame myself by crying. If only I could escape from the thoughts in my head, retreat into the dark where there was nothing except silence and peace.

But that was impossible. I remembered Satan's words in *Paradise Lost* as though they had been engraved on my heart, so many times had I listened as my father had tinkered with them: *Which way I flie is Hell; my self am Hell; / And in the lowest deep a lower deep / Still threatening to devour me opens wide* . . . For the first time, I understood what Father had meant—regardless of how fast you run, how far you go, you cannot get away from yourself.

You carry Hell with you all the time.

The carriage jerked to a halt. Gauden swung the door open and leaped down to the pavement. From within the carriage I watched him stride under a stone archway. Beyond it stood a mansion, its windows blazing with golden light. Up and down the Strand, men and ladies in brightly colored clothes were pouring out of carriages and strolling toward Buckingham's estate, their chattering voices floating on the breeze to reach me.

"Come with us," one of Robert's friends said to me. He was fair-haired and smelled of spirits.

We scrambled outside. The Strand was lined with enormous homes, their windows gold with candlelight, an extravagance whose like I hadn't seen before. Carriages clogged the avenue. The far-off hum of violins laced the air.

"Hurry," said the fair-haired fellow, looping his arm around mine. He snapped his fingers and the three remaining men melted from the shadows cast by the carriage, framing us on either side. They walked at such a quick pace I had to break into a half jog to keep up with them. The mansion loomed ahead of us, a big block of pale stone. Its doors sprang open at our approach.

As I was ushered into a hall, the mixture of voices bounced off the ceiling, creating such a cacophony of sound I couldn't hear my own thoughts. A long line snaked out of the room, heading to what I assumed was the ballroom. We joined the queue, my companion acknowledging others' nods of recognition and introducing me as his cousin, Miss Knightley, visiting from Bath. I forced smiles at the finely dressed gentlemen and ladies, hoping I wouldn't have to speak. I should have warned my companion I couldn't mimic non-London accents if my life depended on it.

The ballroom was a massive, high-ceilinged space lit by hundreds of candles flickering in wall brackets and in gold candelabra that had been scattered on tables. Men and women swirled across a checkerboard floor of white and black marble. They moved in a complicated routine Lady Katherine hadn't taught me: the ladies and fellows facing one another in lines, then moving closer in a series of quick, mincing steps. In the far corner a twenty-man orchestra played, filling the air with the sweetness of strings and horns.

Near the orchestra stood the king. Even from a distance of some fifty feet, he caught my eyes. Tonight he wore a jet-black wig and a doublet and breeches of dark blue satin. A heavy gold chain encrusted with diamonds and emeralds encircled his neck. Every head in the room kept turning toward him. Whispers rippled among the elderly ladies standing along the walls: "There he is, the king!" "At such proximity, he looks even more of a giant, doesn't he?"

"We should dance," my companion said.

Panic swamped my chest. "I can't. I don't know—"

He interrupted me with a loud sigh. "His Grace warned us you're a Puritan. May I fetch myself a drink or is that against your kind's rules?"

"Do as you wish," I snapped. "I make no demands on your behavior."

"Thank God for that." He ambled off, leaving me alone.

I made my way to the edge of the room, where elderly ladies and wallflowers gossiped among themselves. Next to me stretched a long table groaning under platters of food: oysters in the shell, slivers of cheese, small berry tarts, and fruits—strawberries and peaches and ball-like things I had never seen before, but which I heard someone call "oranges." At another time, my mouth would have watered to taste one. Now my stomach cramped with anxiety.

Through the crush of dancing bodies, I glimpsed Antonio. My heart contracted painfully in my chest. He was standing on the opposite side of the room, his head swiveling as he scanned the dancers. *He must be looking for me.* Lady Katherine stood by his side, holding a fan in front of her face. Above its scalloped lace edge, her eyes looked sharp and alert. Where was Robert? Shouldn't he be accompanying his betrothed?

Frowning, I surveyed the room. Everywhere there were dancing bodies, a riot of color. At the ballroom entrance, I caught sight of a figure dressed in yellow, topped with a head of light brown curls. I recognized the muscular line of his shoulders. Robert. It had to be him.

An arm wrapped itself around my waist. Quickly I looked

down. The arm encircling me was clad in black satin, the fingers were long and tapered. *Antonio.*

I twisted around in his grasp so we were facing each other. "What are you doing?"

He looked surprised. "Trying to dance with you. Isn't that what you English do at balls?"

"I don't want to dance."

"We have to if we want to blend in and get closer to the king," he whispered.

I'd sooner die than help him. I took a step backward. "Dance with Lady Katherine."

He smiled at me. "We might never have another chance to dance with each other at a ball." His hands gripped my waist and he lifted me high in the air as easily as if I were a bag of feathers. I looked around frantically. All the other male dancers were raising their female partners, too.

He set me on my feet again. Now we *had* to dance or everyone would wonder why we left the floor in the middle of the routine. I watched the others for guidance, my heart racing.

The partners were executing a series of complicated steps around each other. I slid a few steps to the right while Antonio did so in the opposite direction. When we came together again, he gripped my waist, the heat of his hands burning through my dress. Part of me wanted to push him away, but another part wanted to stay in his arms and hear him say it had all been a terrible misunderstanding.

As we spun around in a circle, I caught sight of Robert. He was walking through the ballroom entrance, away from us. Where was he going? He shouldn't be alone—he might need help.

"You look beautiful, Elizabeth," Antonio murmured, his breath warm on my neck. "I can't stop thinking about you."

Liar. The muscles in my stomach were knotted so tightly I feared I would be sick. I ducked my head, letting my side curls fall forward to obscure my face. "Excuse me," I muttered. "I'm not accustomed to dancing. My head feels light."

He led me to the edge of the room. "Are you well?" His eyes, dark and concerned, traced my face. "You look pale."

I forced a smile. I had to get away from him and follow Robert. "Could you get me a glass of wine? Perhaps that will help my headache."

"Of course." He hurried away, presumably to find a servant.

This was my chance. I crept along the room's perimeter, past the clumps of wallflowers and elderly guests. I held a handkerchief to my face, hoping anyone who saw me would think I was faint and heading outside for a breath of fresh air.

When I reached the hall, Robert was vanishing through a side door. Two elegantly dressed footmen rushed forward, offering me assistance, but I waved them off and scurried after Robert.

I stepped into a long passageway lit with flickering torches. Robert was walking a few yards ahead of me, his steps purposeful, his hand resting on the hilt of his sword. My heartbeat quickened.

He darted through an opening along the passage. Throwing caution aside, I grasped my skirts in my hands and crept after him, tiptoeing to soften the sound of my shoes. Behind me, heels clicked on the floor. I whirled around to see Lady Katherine scurrying down the corridor toward me, her face tight and frightened.

"Lady Katherine!" I whispered in surprise. "What are you doing?"

"Following you." She nodded at the entrance through which Robert had disappeared. "I saw you and His Grace race out of the ballroom, and I was worried you were in danger—"

"Where's Antonio?" I snapped, peering along the shadowy corridor. No one.

"Still in the ballroom. He had just left my side when I saw you leave, so I didn't have a chance to speak to him before I came after you." Lady Katherine looked surprised; doubtless she couldn't understand the vehemence in my tone.

I remembered how she had listened without comment when Antonio told her how he wanted to find the cave himself. Her silence hadn't proved her complicity—but it also didn't mean she was trustworthy. It would be easy to overpower her, though, if need be.

"Very well," I said. "Follow me and be quiet. I think Robert must be looking for the natural philosophers—in which case, he might be in trouble and need our help."

Nodding, she stayed at my heels as I approached the entrance Robert had passed through. I found myself at the archway of an enormous room. Candelabra dotted the walls, white candles gleaming in the holders. Between the candelabra hung gilt-framed paintings. Half pillars had been set up across the floor, each topped with a piece of sculpture that looked to be either ancient Greek or Roman.

Three men stood among the sculptures. None looked in our direction; we must have moved quietly enough. Two of them were middle-aged, the last looked only a few years older than me. They didn't wear fine clothes and heeled shoes like the other male guests, but instead were dressed in plain, dirt-spattered garments and riding boots. They were staring at Robert with a mix of surprise and fear. The glow from the candles softened the lines of their faces, but I knew them all the same: these were the men who had attacked us outside Oxford.

"What are you doing here?" the youngest of them growled at Robert. I recognized his wild eyes—he was the man I had cut with my sword.

"I think we all know the answer to that question." Robert sounded calm, but at his side his left hand contracted into a fist. "You took something from me that I badly want back."

"You're too late," said the tallest man. Dirt and exhaustion had left a gray film on his face. "We've already spoken to the Duke of Buckingham. He and the king are preparing to meet us here in the Great Chamber momentarily."

"My friends will arrive before them," Robert said. Antonio and me, and the men who had ridden here with me, that must be whom he meant. But did any of those men know where he had gone? Or was he merely bluffing, trying to gain more time for others to notice his disappearance and look for him? "Sir Vaughan, you have two choices," Robert continued in a hard voice, "either hand over the vial and live, or refuse and die."

I stepped forward to go to his aid, the heel of my shoe clacking on the marble floor. The youngest man glanced at me, his eyes narrowing. "*You*," he growled. He turned to his companions. "That's the regicide poet's daughter."

Robert spun around. "Elizabeth," he whispered. His gaze shifted to Lady Katherine behind me, the color draining from his face, leaving it deathly white. "My lady! If you two value your lives, you'll return to the ballroom at once!"

"I'm staying," I shot back.

"Me, too," Lady Katherine said, her voice shaking.

"She can't be the regicide's daughter!" One of the older men gazed at me. "Clearly this is a noblewoman."

"Don't be fooled by her appearance." The young man studied me, his expression rigid. "I'll never forget her face. I had been hoping we would meet again, Miss Milton." He tapped his ribs, where I had slashed him. "You slowed down our journey to London considerably, as I was forced to spend a few days recuperating in an inn. If it weren't for you, we would have returned and given the king what is rightly his several days ago." He drew his sword. "You have much to answer for."

Automatically I clapped my hands to my arms, seeking the cool metal of my knives. All I encountered was bare flesh.

Twenty-Six

THE YOUNG MAN RAISED HIS SWORD. BEHIND HIM, his companions watched without expression. My eyes darted around the room, searching for a possible weapon. Framed paintings, heavy drapes, white marble busts, and candles in their holders—a motley assortment, but they presented distinct possibilities.

"Come now, she's only a girl," Robert said. He looked at me and Lady Katherine and mouthed, *Run!*

We didn't move. Through the brown wool doublet of the young man I had stabbed I could see the outline of something long and cylindrical. *The vial.* It had to be. As long as it was in this room, I wasn't going anywhere else.

I turned my head a few degrees to the left, catching the shimmer of candlelight on the walls. An iron bracket was only a dozen feet away from me; an instant's work, and it would be in my hand, a serviceable weapon.

"Your friends seem to have abandoned you, Your Grace," said the tallest man in a heavy Yorkshire accent; he was the one Robert had called "Sir Vaughan." His sword rang against his scabbard as he pulled it free.

The young man moved toward me, holding his sword outstretched so its tip grazed my bust. Through the layers of my clothes I could feel the point of the sword, icy cold and sharp. One thrust of his wrist and I was dead. I couldn't rip my eyes from his—they were as angry as I remembered, dark brown, the fragile skin beneath them smudged with fatigue.

"I will enjoy this," he said. "I hope you suffer as much pain as you put me through."

"Don't hurt her!" Robert shouted. Lady Katherine screamed my name.

Footsteps thundered from the corridor. The three men looked toward the entryway. This was my chance. I jumped backward. With a guttural cry of rage, the young man slashed the empty air where I had stood seconds ago. He advanced on me, cutting wildly at nothing. I stumbled back again to avoid the arc of his blade. From the edge of my vision, I caught the pale gleam of a life-sized carved marble head. Only a foot away.

I seized it. The bust hadn't been affixed to its display pillar, and it lifted easily in my hands. The accursed thing was so heavy I stumbled backward a few paces, my arms buckling under its weight. The young man came closer, his teeth bared in a snarl. Without another thought I flung the bust directly at his stomach as hard as I could.

The bust glanced off his belly to land on the floor, breaking in two with a resounding crack. He let out a harsh cry. Behind him, men raced into the room, their swords already in their hands. They were Robert's friends who had ridden here with me—he must have alerted them before leaving the ballroom. Robert shouted something I couldn't make out, and the new-comers flung themselves at Sir Vaughan and his men. The air filled with the sound of steel hitting steel and muffled grunts.

The young man sank to his knees, clutching his belly and gasping for breath. *The vial!* I had to get it before he fell on his stomach and crushed it!

I shoved him onto his back just as someone else landed on the ground at my feet. It was the fair-haired boy who had escorted me into Buckingham's home. He had collapsed face-first, his wig pillowing out on either side to hide his face. Blood seeped from beneath his body, in a widening arc of dark red.

Something hot and sick swooped in my stomach. I looked away. Sir Vaughan's young man lay on his back, whimpering. His hands rubbed his belly; his eyes bulged. Around his neck was looped a white string; it disappeared beneath his clothes. I grabbed the string, giving it a hard yank. Its knotted ends broke, the string slackening in my hands. I pulled on it, drawing some-thing from beneath his shirt. It was a leather pouch, no bigger than my hand, and the color of dried mud. I closed my fingers around it. Inside was an object that felt hard and roundish—the vial.

He made a wild grab for it. I pushed him aside with my free hand, then jumped to my feet. Lady Katherine stood beneath the archway, her hands knotted in her skirts. In the center of the room, Sir Vaughan and his remaining assistant stood back to back, their swords flashing silver. Robert and his friends had surrounded them. As the men parried and thrust, they shuffled up and down the aisle created by the rows of pillars, their shouts and the clash of their blades so loud it was a wonder the houseful of ballroom guests hadn't come running yet.

Robert had a cut on his cheek. Above the wine-dark line, his eyes were narrowed and fierce. As I watched, he plunged his sword into Sir Vaughan's stomach.

Sir Vaughan fell to the floor. A dark hole had appeared in his doublet. Blood began pouring from it, black against the brown wool. He scrabbled at his belly, trying to hold the severed flesh together. "My God," he gasped out.

My hands started shaking. Dazed, I staggered backward a few steps. Robert crouched beside Sir Vaughan and grabbed the man by the front of his doublet. "Where is it?" he demanded. "Give it to me!"

"I have it!" I shouted. "We have to get away from here!"

I turned and fled. *Get out, get out, get out*, each beat of my heart screamed. I barreled past Lady Katherine through the chamber entrance. "Come with me!" I shouted at her.

The corridor was empty. No, I couldn't return in the direction from which I had come—the king and Buckingham might be walking along that portion of the passageway even now, believing they were heading to their meeting with Sir Vaughan and his assistants.

I ran in the opposite direction, my cursed skirts wrapping around my legs and nearly pitching me headlong onto the floor. I kicked myself loose and kept going.

Somewhere behind me, someone was shouting my name—it might have been Robert. Up ahead, a door sharpened into focus;

an oblong of varnished wood, it stood at the end of the passageway. I flung it open. Cool night air wafted over my face. I had reached a garden, its manicured hedges and grass shining with moonlight.

I raced down the steps. I must have come through a side door, for I didn't recognize my surroundings. The hedges rose all around me, forbidding and dark, walls within which I might easily lose my way. Overhead, stars pricked the black veil of the sky, casting a pale sheen of silver over the grass that I ran across. I kept the leather pouch clutched to my chest, my grip tight as a vise.

Footsteps thudded in the grass behind me. I glanced over my shoulder. Robert. He was running hard, his hand clapped to his sheathed sword to keep it from banging into his legs. The moonlight had drained all color from his face, except for his dark eyes and the cut beneath, which was still dripping.

"Elizabeth!" he yelled. "Get to the street—I have a carriage waiting!"

I reached the Strand. Skidding to a halt on the pavement, I cast a desperate look up and down the street. It was lined with carriages, probably those belonging to the ball guests. A handful of groomsmen stood several feet away, smoking and talking in low voices. Where was Robert's? I took a step forward just as a hand clamped onto my wrist. I twisted around to stare into Robert's face.

"Are you hurt?" He lifted a hand to touch my cheek, the gesture so gentle and so unexpected that I started in surprise. "Come into the carriage with me—we have to get away before my father figures out what has happened."

"Where's Lady Katherine?"

"I told her to return to the ballroom. Hopefully no one noticed her absence, and she can pretend ignorance once those men are discovered in Buckingham's Great Chamber."

The front doors of Buckingham's mansion opened. A couple of footmen stepped outside, their heads turning as if they were looking for someone. Buckingham appeared behind them. He was yelling something unintelligible and gesturing wildly. We had to leave at once.

"Let's go," I said.

Robert grabbed my arm, directing me toward a nearby carriage. Its doors were emblazoned in gold paint with a coat of arms: a lion and a unicorn, like the king's, but linking these two animals in flowery script was a massive *L*, for "Lockton." It must be Robert's.

The groomsman stiffened to attention and opened the carriage door. Robert scrambled inside first, then turned to help me up. Together we sank onto the cushioned seat just as figures appeared on the pavement outside: it was the remaining four of Robert's friends. Without a word, they clambered in after us. Robert thumped the roof of the carriage.

"Go!" he shouted.

The carriage rumbled forward. For a moment, the six of us said nothing, filling the carriage with only the sound of our ragged breathing. We were crammed so tightly into the small space that I could barely move. I kept my hands wrapped around the leather pouch in my lap.

Gauden sat opposite me. He glanced at my bundle, his eyes narrowed. "Don't open it," he said sharply.

"Surely we can look at the substance we've sacrificed so much to obtain," said the dark-haired fellow sitting next to me. On my other side, Robert sighed and shook his head.

Sir Gauden scowled. "The only people known to have looked at its contents were Mr. Galilei and Mr. Milton, and they both went blind. It may be a coincidence . . . but it may not."

Something about his words pushed a gear within my mind. Frowning, I looked out the window, watching the darkened streets roll past. Gauden was correct, of course; my father and Galileo had lost their sight, and at this juncture we could only guess at the cause of their ailment. Robert had warned me of the same thing when we found the vial in the Physic Garden.

But that didn't make sense. In my mind, I could see Robert standing in the spare room at the Bodleian Library, his arms crossed over his chest, listening as Antonio and I discussed my father's sonnet about a young shepherdess tending a non-native plant. He had interrupted when Antonio brought up Galileo's knowledge of astronomy. *Who's Signor Galilei?* he had asked. Before we could offer an explanation, he'd continued, *You needn't seek any heavenly ground in Oxford. The only special land around here is the Physic Garden.*

Yet only a couple of hours later, after we had dug up my father's box, he warned us not to open the vial. *Mr. Milton complained of a headache after viewing its contents, and we mustn't forget both he and Galileo went blind.*

It was impossible for him to have known about Galileo's blindness. Robert, Antonio, and I had spent the afternoon at the inn, closeted in our own chambers, until Antonio brought me supper. Antonio hadn't had the opportunity to tell Robert about Galileo, and I knew I hadn't.

The only way Robert could have known about Galileo's blindness was if he had already studied the man.

Which meant Robert had lied to us.

I sucked in a breath. There could have been no rational reason for Robert to feign ignorance about Galileo . . . unless there was something *else* he was hiding from me. Something that would come to light if I discovered he was knowledgeable about Galileo. Something he wanted so badly to hide that he had told a seemingly inconsequential lie.

My eyes darted around the carriage. Robert and his four friends sat in silence. One of them wiped blood off his sword on the leg of his breeches; another had produced a flask and was handing it around. Robert sat so close the bones of his shoulder ground into mine. He stared at the pouch on my lap. Passing lantern light illuminated his eyes, turning them into blank, gold discs. Smiling, he looked at me.

"We should reach Lady Katherine's home soon. With luck, she and Antonio have already left the ball and will meet us there. Then we can figure out our next step."

My voice sounded hoarse when I replied. "Yes. A good plan."

The carriage continued rattling through the streets. My mind was spinning. I gazed out the window at the timber-framed houses winding past. What could Robert be concealing from me?

Memories streamed through my head. Robert finding me in the woods, explaining he had learned our route from Francis Sutton. Robert pretending he hadn't heard of Galileo. In the Physic Garden, Robert rushing off to ask the Oxford tutor which apple trees were not indigenous to England. I could still hear the tutor's loud voice; could still hear his Yorkshire accent. . . .

And then I knew. There had been one tutor and two students. Three men in total, one of whom had spoken with a Yorkshire accent—just like Sir Vaughan.

Vaughan and his men had not only attacked us in the fields outside Oxford, they had been in the Physic Garden earlier that night, too. And Robert had gone to them. He had spoken to them on the pretext of seeking their counsel on non-native apple trees. He had talked with them at close quarters; he must have seen their faces clearly, both in the garden and later in the fields, for the night had been bright with moonlight.

Yet Robert had never shared this detail with Antonio and me. And he had feigned ignorance about Galileo.

He was a liar.

I looked down at my hands cupping the leather pouch. Instinctively they tightened, showing the delicate blue tracery of veins under my skin. Beside me, Robert shifted slightly. His long legs, encased in yellow satin breeches and white stockings, pressed against my skirts. He was so close to me. On my other side, the dark-haired boy stretched out his legs, the tip of his scabbard scraping on the carriage floor. Across from me, the three other men passed a flask, talking in low voices about how furious Buckingham would be when he found the dead bodies in the Great Chamber, their blood splattered on his precious statues.

Nausea roiled my stomach. So they had killed Sir Vaughan and his assistants. I could hope for no mercy from them. Probably the only reason I was still alive was that I hadn't yet given them a reason to kill me.

So little made sense. Why hadn't Robert told us that the "tutor" and "students" in the Physic Garden and the men who attacked us had been the same people? By concealing this truth, what had he gained? I felt as though I held one half of a picture; the rest had been ripped away.

"Miss Milton," Gauden said, "you look unwell. Have you fallen ill?"

"I—some fresh air. Stop the carriage, please." I prayed they didn't notice my voice was shaking.

"We can't stop here," Robert objected. "Breathe deeply, and you should feel better."

The men stilled. As one, they fastened their eyes—narrowed, suspicious—on me. Had they guessed I had figured out that Robert was up to—what, exactly? The lie he had told me might have seemed meaningless, but a small lie usually concealed a greater one.

"Very well," I heard myself saying. "Thank you, Robert."

Get out, said a voice in my head. Slowly I craned my neck to peer out the window again. Our carriage was moving at a steady clip, but not so fast that I couldn't jump to the pavement. Around me, the men were talking and laughing, but their voices had retreated to tinny echoes, as if I stood at the opposite end of a long tunnel. My breath crashed in my ears. *Get out*, said the voice again. Motionless, I watched the street trundling past, thinking. These wealthy men probably didn't know these streets as well as I did; their money had likely kept them pampered in their homes and their carriages. If I was quick enough, I might be able to get away from them.

No more time to think—I had to act now. I might not have another chance.

I jumped to my feet. As Robert shouted "Elizabeth!" I scrambled over the men's legs to get at the carriage door. Someone grabbed me around the waist from behind; I kicked at him, my heel connecting with his leg. He released me with a muffled curse.

I wrenched the carriage door open. Wind flung my hair over my face, so all I could see through the waving strands were the cobblestones rushing away beneath us. Taking a quick breath, I squinted at the stones bleeding together and threw myself at them.

The ground surged up to meet me. I landed hard. The instant my feet hit the ground, I was racing forward, making for the swinging beams of lantern light up ahead. Behind me the carriage driver yelled "Whoa!" and the horses' harnesses jingled as they were pulled. I risked a glance over my shoulder. The carriage was rocking to a stop. Already Robert and his companions were pouring out of it.

I whipped my head around, concentrating on the road ahead. In the distance, a line of lanterns hanging from the fronts of houses shone brightly. A large black gap showed between two of the houses. An alley. With luck, it would twist and turn before spilling into another lane so I could lose my pursuers. I ran faster.

My heel caught in a groove between the cobblestones. With a sharp cry, I pitched forward onto my hands and knees. My palms were on fire. At once I scrambled up, hissing in pain. I started to run, but an arm wrapped around my waist. Even as I struggled in my captor's grip, a part of my mind registered the fact that it was too late: the men—breathing hard, their swords raised—had surrounded me.

With my free hand I clawed at the man's arm around my waist. His grip was like iron; I couldn't budge him at all. I twisted and kicked, straining to break free.

Two of the men stepped back. Robert slithered through the

space between them. His eyes were hard. With two strides he reached me, and he grabbed my chin in his gloved hands, turning my face this way and that.

"Why did you run?" he growled.

I said nothing. Blood roared in my ears, so loudly that Robert's voice sounded tinny and far off, as if he were calling to me from the end of the street. I took a deep breath, the air burning as it traveled down my throat. *Be calm*, I ordered myself, but my hand holding the pouch to my chest shook badly, the vial knocking against my sternum.

"Very well, stay silent, it doesn't matter what you have to say." Robert snapped his fingers at the other men. "You know what to do to her."

As one, the men moved closer, their circle tightening around me. Frantically I looked up and down the street for a night watchman on his rounds, someone, anyone, but the place seemed deserted, the windows on all the houses shuttered and dark. I opened my mouth to scream for help just as Gauden rushed toward me in such a fast blur of movement that I had only enough time to throw up my free hand for protection before his fist connected with my jaw and the world exploded in a shower of stars that quickly faded into silver pinpricks before vanishing altogether in a pool of black.

Twenty-Seven

I WOKE IN DARKNESS. MY CHEEK WAS PRESSED against something cold and hard, my body shaking with a rhythmic rocking, as though I lay on the bottom of a boat. But I didn't hear the sound of water slapping the gunwales, nor smell the Thames, salt mixed with mud. Where *was* I?

My eyes opened wider. All that greeted me was a uniform blackness. Dear God, what had happened to me—had I finally inherited Father's blindness? Terror stole my voice, and all I could let out was a muffled moan.

Under my cheek, the stiff surface seemed to rise slightly, pushing against my face for the space of a heartbeat, settling down, and then starting the process again. Below me, I heard the unmistakable sound of iron wheels rattling on pavers. I was lying on the floor of a carriage, I realized. It was the unevenly laid paving stones that were jolting me.

For a long moment, I lay motionless. Unending blackness

pressed heavily on my eyes. Why couldn't I see? Had Sir Gauden's fist knocked my eyes loose in their sockets?

Please, God, anything but that. If I couldn't see, I was powerless. I blinked hard several times, my eyelashes brushing against a soft obstruction of some sort. Scarcely daring to breathe, I turned my attention inward, focusing on my body. There was something wrapped around my head. A blindfold? Yes, that was it; now that I lay quietly I could feel the edges of the fabric cutting into my cheeks. I hadn't lost my vision. I swallowed a sob, hating myself for the way relief flowed through my limbs, making me weak all over.

Clearly Robert and his friends didn't want me to know where they were taking me. Very well, then. I would have to use my remaining senses to figure out what was happening.

Gently I flexed my hands. Something rough and scratchy had immobilized my wrists, and I could rotate them only a few degrees before any further movement was impeded. Ropes. Robert and his companions had tied me up.

I lay still, listening with every fiber of my being. The groan of a wooden seat, perhaps responding to someone shifting his position. A throat being cleared.

I wasn't alone.

The thought made the pain in my jaw explode with white-hot intensity. I couldn't hold back a gasp.

"Ah, you're awake." It was Sir Gauden. "Good. I was afraid you would be knocked out for hours, which would be exceedingly tiresome as we have many matters to discuss with you."

"Where's Robert?" I muttered, waves of agony pulsing in my jaw.

"Robert?" A foot nudged me in the side. "If you mean the

Duke of Lockton, then I wonder at your audacity in calling him by his Christian name. His Grace thanks you for the vial, by the way, and he's waiting for you to provide him with the location of Galileo's cave."

The cave? Why did they care where it was? My stomach tightened. Robert must want to find it in order to destroy it—or to bottle the liquid for himself. But why did he and his men think I knew where to find it?

"Galileo's cave?" My words came out as slurred as a drunkard's; my lips felt swollen and thick. Curse Sir Gauden and his fist. I ran a considering tongue along my teeth. Thankfully, none of them felt loose.

Sir Gauden barked out a laugh. "Your father hid clues in *Paradise Lost*, didn't he? So perhaps he hid the exact location of the cave in his poem. As he is unfortunately secreted away at His Majesty's pleasure, that leaves you as the sole person capable of figuring out where the cave can be found."

So this was the reason I was alive: I was still valuable to them.

My throat was so dry I couldn't swallow. "Please," I whispered, "I know nothing—"

Hands seized the bodice of my gown and hauled me to a sitting position. Sir Gauden's breath was hot on my face. "You had better hope that's a lie," he said. "Or I can promise that you don't have much time left for this world. His Grace wants to find the cave before he takes the crown."

The words hit me as hard as a fist in the face. This was what Robert had wanted all along—to be king. His illegitimacy would keep him forever trapped in his position as the Duke of Lockton . . . unless he had a powerful weapon in his arsenal.

"Is he planning on blackmailing the king—exchanging the vial and the cave's location for the throne?" As soon as I had spoken I knew I had to be wrong, for Sir Gauden released his hold on me and started to laugh. I sagged against the wedge of something hard—the edge of the carriage's cushioned seat, I guessed. Someone's leg brushed my shoulder; I was surrounded by these men.

"What nonsense," Gauden chuckled. "No, His Grace will prove to his people that *he* is the rightful king. He'll stand on the steps of St. Paul's and, as crowds gather to watch, he will die."

"*What?*" I cried.

"His other dearest friends and I have been given the honor of killing him," Sir Gauden continued as if I hadn't spoken. "Four of them will pierce his hands and his feet. I will stab him in the side."

Icy awareness trickled into my mind. "You are going to reenact the death of Christ," I breathed.

"His death *and* his resurrection," Gauden corrected. "His Grace will die in full view of dozens of people in the street. Three days later, while his body is lying in state in Westminster Abbey, we'll pour the contents of the vial down his throat. And he will live again."

"That's wicked!" I cried. "You're making a mockery of our faith—all for the sake of a crown!"

Gauden went on as if I hadn't spoken. "Can you imagine what the populace will do? They will think he's the Second Coming, the King of Kings, returned to save us all! They'll demand that he assume the throne. His Grace will be the greatest and most powerful king in the world."

A sick feeling cramped my stomach. In my mind, I saw Robert in the Bodleian Library, his eyes intent on mine. *I consider the English to be my people, and I would battle my father to protect them*, he had said.

It had been the truth. I merely hadn't understood the true meaning behind his words.

Angry tears burned my eyes, wetting the blindfold and making the fabric stick to my skin. "How could he do this to us—"

"His Grace said to explain everything to you," Sir Gauden interrupted. "I daresay he thinks an enlightened prisoner is more likely to be forthcoming than an ignorant one, and His Grace is right in all things. What do you wish to know?"

"Does the king know what Robert—His Grace, I mean—is plotting?"

I could hear the smile in Gauden's voice. "The king is a fool. When Mr. Wren found Mr. Galilei's story hidden in St. Paul's a fortnight ago, he immediately presented it to the king. The king didn't comprehend the true significance of the account—he stupidly believed Mr. Milton was involved in a nefarious plot involving Italians and decided to dispatch a spy to watch Mr. Milton's London home. It wasn't long before a Florentine appeared at the house, seeking Mr. Milton's company, and word was brought to all of us at court."

A Florentine—*Antonio*. The space within the left side of my rib cage tightened. No, I mustn't think of him or I would break.

"The king sent his most trusted friends to Chalfont St. Giles, to arrest your father and learn precisely what sort of treasonous activities he was plotting with foreigners," Sir Gauden continued. "I need hardly tell you that the Italian city-states pose a terrible danger to our country—these Catholic nations have grown populous and powerful, and England is still weakened by her years of civil war and warring governments."

"My father is a loyal Englishman! He would never concoct a treasonous scheme."

I tensed, waiting for the slap that must surely come. Instead the men muttered angrily. "Mr. Milton is no patriot." "He advocated the beheading of our beloved King Charles the First!"

"Tut, tut, let's not argue about the past." Sir Gauden sounded amused. "If a king-killer's daughter wants to pretend her father is a good man, there's little we can say to convince her otherwise. At any rate, Miss Milton, His Grace was sitting with the king when Mr. Wren brought them word of the strange discovery in St. Paul's. His Grace at once realized the true significance of a liquid that can revive the dead. He summoned men he thought were his friends—Sir Vaughan and his assistants—and together they sped to Chalfont St. Giles."

He paused for breath. "Do you remember how Galileo's account of the cave was ripped? His Grace saw it before the king tore it up. There was a notation at the end, made by your father some twenty years ago. He was afraid future generations might not figure out that he planned to immortalize Galileo's story in a poem he would create someday, and so he was writing his intentions there. He wanted to call the poem *Paradise Lost* and turn himself, Galileo, and Galileo's apprentice, Vincenzo Viviani, into three of the angel characters."

So that was why my attacker outside Oxford had called the three of them "traitor angels"! He'd already known about my father's intention to weave himself and the two Italian natural philosophers into the story. As a man immovably loyal to the king, of course he would have seen my father and his colleagues as false, or traitor, angels, who were trying to discredit the Son of God—and destroy the divine right of kings.

"From there," Gauden said, "I imagine you can figure out the rest."

I nodded. Robert and his companions had arrived in Chalfont St. Giles soon after Antonio and I had departed. They had forced or connived our location out of Francis Sutton, who must have drawn them a replica of the map he had made for me, so Robert could race after us, finding us before we reached Oxford. Meanwhile, his companions had ridden ahead using another route. They had known to wait for us at the Bodleian, for I had asked Francis a number of questions about the library, and it must have been obvious to them where we were headed. Parts of the story Robert had told us had been true, slender strands he interwove with falsehoods until they formed a rich tapestry.

But then his plans had unraveled.

"Robert's friends betrayed him," I said.

"All along, they were loyal to the king!" There was no trace of amusement in Gauden's voice now, only rage. "They tricked His Grace—overtaking all of you outside the city and stealing the vial from him. But it was God's will that you reached London first," he went on in a changed tone. "His Grace was able to question Royal Society members about those turncoats without letting you and the Florentine catch on to his true intentions. Yes, he made it all seem very natural, didn't he?" he asked when I winced. "His Grace is quite clever. He knows that a much larger supply of the elixir lies within the cave outside Padua.

And you'll help him find it, Miss Milton."

He rested his gloved hand on the curve where my neck met my shoulder, and he squeezed slightly. "Sir Vaughan and his men were killed before they could give their report to the king. His Grace's plan is still a secret from his father . . . but the king must suspect they have become enemies. Even if he can't prove it yet, he must be watching His Grace closely."

My hands twisted in the ropes; I was yearning to break free. If only I could tear off this cursed blindfold, I wouldn't feel so helpless. The darkness pressed down on me, as warm and dry as kindling. I tilted my head back, seeking a sliver of space between the blindfold and my cheek, just a narrow opening through which I could see. But there was nothing.

"Why are you helping His Grace?" I asked. "Can't you see what he's doing is wrong?"

Sir Gauden must have brought his face close to mine, for I felt the whisper of his stubble on my cheek. "After King Charles the First was beheaded, I had to flee to Europe like most of the nobility," he snarled. "For a decade, I lived in horrific poverty, never knowing where the money for my next meal would come from, having to depend on others' charity to survive. And through it all, I remained loyal to Charles the Second. I believed he was our rightful ruler, and I was ready to suffer for his sake.

"And what do you think happened when we returned at last to our beloved country? Did the king reward me for my years of devotion? Did he annihilate the men who had caused us such torment? No! Oh, some were put to death, of course, but others he allowed to escape England, and still more, like your father, he permitted to live. He said he couldn't pardon them but he was *tired of death*." Gauden spat the words out. "Ever since then, I've known he wasn't fit to rule. We need a king who isn't afraid to be ruthless when he needs to be, a king whose claim to the throne is beyond question so another civil war can never happen again." He paused. "His Grace is that king."

"What you want isn't a king but a tyrant!"

"You will remember every line of *Paradise Lost*," Sir Gauden said as if I hadn't spoken. He squeezed my neck harder. Gray spots began dancing in the blackness before my eyes. "Every word, every image, Miss Milton. You *will* figure out what your father hid in his poem."

"No," I said through gritted teeth.

He slapped me. Fire arced through my cheek, so hot and so sudden that I couldn't breathe.

"And what do you say now?" Sir Gauden's voice was whisper soft.

I clenched my still-throbbing jaw. "No."

And then they were on me, all of them, dragging me down onto the carriage floor and grabbing my arms and legs so I couldn't fight. A couple of them sat on me; they were so heavy I felt as though I were oozing into the floor.

"You are alone," Sir Gauden growled. "Don't you understand you have been abandoned by everyone? The Florentine that His Grace told us made your eyes shine, is he anywhere to be found? No. He's at the ball, dancing with beautiful girls—proper girls who don't wear boys' clothes or hunger for philosophic knowledge. You must have been a figure of fun to him, Miss Milton."

My tears trickled under the blindfold, winding down my face to drip off my chin. "Stop it," I whispered.

"Did you truly believe he cared for you?" He laughed. "My

poor, misguided Miss Milton. Your Florentine was after Galileo's elixir, just like the rest of us. The only difference is he had the forethought to romance you in hopes of gaining your assistance."

All the fight went out of me. He was right. Antonio had shown his true self in the hall tonight, when he talked to Lady Katherine about using Galileo's discovery for his own purposes.

In the end, he had manipulated me as skillfully as Robert had.

I let out a low cry. Even to my ears, I sounded like a wounded animal. I lay still, listening to the carriage wheels rumble over the road, carrying me closer to whichever place Robert had decreed I should be taken.

No one spoke. We rolled through the streets, finally stopping when I heard water lapping on a shore. I was hauled to my feet and half carried, half led out of the carriage. The men held me tightly by the elbows. I heard them breathing around me, as though they had hemmed me in on all sides.

Beneath my feet, the ground felt marshy. The stink of dirty water assailed my nose. Except for the whisper of wind skimming over water, the night was quiet.

The men holding me dragged me forward. I sagged in their grip, letting them lead me across the soft ground. My legs bumped into something hard. Then I was lifted by several arms and set on my feet on a gently swaying surface. More hands grabbed me, yanking me down onto a seat. We began to move, rocking slightly. The lonely sound of water hitting the sides of a boat reached my ears. I was being rowed somewhere.

Ahead of us sounded the creaking groan of waterlogged wood and iron. A portcullis gate, I guessed, but I couldn't bring myself to care; all of my thoughts seemed sluggish, as though they had to travel a long distance before unfurling in my mind. As the boat skimmed onward, water droplets hit my face—dripping off the portcullis spikes as they rose above us, perhaps.

The boat glided to a stop. For a moment, I remained in place, rocking, while I heard shuffling around me. Then arms were lifting me onto solid ground. From far off, a low, throaty cry rent the night air. I stiffened. It had sounded like a wild animal. Where in Heaven's name had I been taken?

The men seized my arms again and marched me forward, our silence broken only by their panting as they broke into an almost-run. I had to run, too, or risk falling.

They rushed me across paved ground, then through a door and up some steps. The stairwell was so narrow my shoulders brushed its sides, and my captors released me so we could climb single file. I had to lift each foot carefully, seeking the flat smoothness of a step.

Abruptly the man in front of me stopped climbing, and I bumped into him. He grunted. A key rattled in a lock. The man behind me prodded my back, urging me upward. I climbed another few steps before hands gripped my shoulders and threw me to the floor. The side of my body hit stone, the impact knocking the breath from me. I rolled onto my back.

The door whined shut. I lay motionless, listening. Were they gone?

No, I heard them breathing. Short, quick inhalations through their noses, as though they were angry or exhausted. Probably they were both. So they hadn't closed the door in their leave-taking, but had shut it in order to prevent the sounds of our struggles from being overheard.

Someone moved, the heel of his boot rasping on the floor.

"Shall I remove Miss Milton's blindfold?"

"Not yet," said Sir Gauden. "I need her to suffer a little longer."

The iciness of the floor seeped through my sleeves and I couldn't prevent a shiver. I was lying on top of my hands, my clenched fists grinding into the small of my waist. Through my satin sleeves I could sense the shapes of the stones in the floor; they were evenly cut. A finely constructed floor; we were in no hovel, then, or back room of a disreputable inn. Wherever Robert had ordered me taken, the accommodations were impressive. If the floors were stone, then most likely the walls were, too. A clever place to hide me. The stones would muffle my screams.

I had to bite my lip so I wouldn't cry out.

"A few hours of darkness," Sir Gauden said softly, "and you'll be ready to do anything we want in return for restoring your sight." The warm leather of his gloved hand touched my cheek, as gentle as a caress. "Reflect upon your father's poem. I'm certain you have all the information you need. You only need to put the various pieces together."

"I will never tell you anything," I said.

"You'll change your mind." His hand smoothed the blindfold more securely over my eyes. At my temple, his fingers paused, as if he were considering whether or not to untie the black strip of fabric.

I held my breath. *Please*, I begged silently, *take it off.*

He let go of my face. "We'll return in the morning." His boots creaked as he stood up. "Perhaps after a night of absolute darkness, Miss Milton's memory will have improved."

"I don't know where the cave is!" I shouted. The men murmured among themselves; their boots rang on the floor and a door opened and closed. A key scraped in the lock. They were gone.

Awkwardly I rolled onto my side. My hands tingled at the sudden relief from their imprisonment between my back and the floor. I staggered to my feet. Although I picked at the ropes around my wrists, they remained taut, their rough edges digging into my skin.

Giving up, I left my hands fastened behind my back and took a cautious step forward, then another.

Nothing. The men didn't charge into the room, shouting at me to lie down. Nearby, I heard water lapping the shore and the distant roar of an animal. It sounded like a lion. It reminded me of the other times I had heard lions growling in their cages here in London and—

All at once, I realized what those sounds signified.

No.

Moving backward, I skimmed the emptiness with my hands, searching for a clue to tell me more about this room. My fingers brushed the cool stones of the wall, their surface damp with condensation. Inching sideways, I followed the curved walls with my hands until there was no longer any doubt in my mind.

I knew where I was.

Although my mind screamed I must be mistaken, I knew, deep down, that I was not. This room could be in no other place. Its shape, the stone walls and floor, the nearby shushing of the Thames, the boat ride across a moat, and the wild cries of the animals in the Royal Menagerie told me the truth.

I had been locked in the Tower of London.

Part

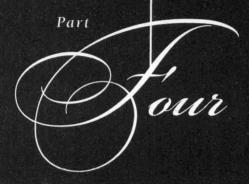

THE JOINING

Between us two let there be peace, both joyning,
As joyn'd in injuries, one enmitie
Against a Foe by doom express assign'd us,
That cruel Serpent . . .
—John Milton, Paradise Lost, Book IX

Twenty-Eight

MY LEGS BUCKLED. I LET MYSELF SINK TO THE
floor, where the chill of the stones pushed through my dress. But
I barely noticed the cold; my mind already felt disconnected from
my body, as if I had stepped out of it.

Somehow Robert had arranged to have me housed here in
secret. One of the jailers must number among his many friends.
Otherwise I couldn't fathom how he had managed to have me
kept here, for this place was reserved for our city's wealthiest or
most notorious prisoners. The king and Buckingham wouldn't
dream of seeking me in the Tower. Robert and his men could do
whatever they wished with me, and no one else would be the wiser.

I wouldn't be treated like other prisoners. I would have no
trial, no public execution. In five days, I wouldn't be crammed
into a cart with the other condemned—possibly with my father.
I had failed him. If only I could magically send my thoughts into

his mind, so wherever he was in London, he could hear me and know how bitterly sorry I was.

Fresh tears pressed against my blindfold, but I blinked them away. They wouldn't help me at all. Father and I were as good as dead.

Five days. That was all the time he had left before they strung him from the executioner's tree on Tyburn Hill. Five days until the rough fibers of the rope scratched his neck. Until the rope tightened and tightened, turning his mind dark.

And I had merely days, maybe hours, of torture before I cracked. They had plenty of ways to break a person; Father had told me of them, after he was released from prison six years ago. *They might slit your nose, Elizabeth*, he had said to me as I knelt at his feet, so grateful to have him with us again that I gladly listened to his horrific tales although they would give me nightmares for weeks afterward. *If the jailers are angry with you, they may crop your ears down to bloody stumps. Or brand your face with letters. There was a man in the cell next to mine who was marked SL.* He hadn't told me what the letters stood for, and I hadn't needed to ask—they must have meant "seditious libeler," one of the many terms that had been thrown at my father, too.

I would hold out for as long as I could, but at some point I would come apart and confess I would never be able to figure out the additional clues my father may have concealed in *Paradise Lost*. My final moments should be quick, at least, for once it was clear I was useless to my captors, I imagined, they would wish to get rid of me at once. A dagger through my heart or a snap of my neck, and that would be the end of it. I would be buried in a pauper's grave or dumped in the river.

The jest, however, would be at Robert and his friends' expense. You can't kill someone who is already dead, and Antonio had broken my heart tonight.

Dawn had lightened the inside of my blindfold from black to gray before I heard footsteps again. A whisper of leather on stone, so faint I feared I had imagined the noise and my mind was already playing games with me. For a moment, I lay on the pallet that I had stumbled into during my blind wanderings about the room last night. If I moved, the straw in the mattress would rustle, muting the person's footfalls.

They were a light shuffle. Not my captors, then, who had walked with a heavy tread. Maybe they had dispatched someone else to deal with me. Someone stronger and carrying the instruments of torture Father had warned me of—thumbscrews to break my fingers, a butcher's knife to slice off my ears or nose.

Shuddering, I muffled my mouth against my shoulder, forcing the whimpers back inside where they couldn't shame me. I jerked my hands in their bindings, but the ropes only dug deeper into the bloody grooves I had already worn into my flesh. Biting my lip against the red-hot ache, I didn't make a sound. I wouldn't give my new assailant the satisfaction of my pain.

The footsteps passed my door. They faded into the distance, and I heard another door open and close. Slowly I let out the breath I had kept inside. Father would be so ashamed of me—my nerves were stretched so taut the slightest sound might snap them.

All night I had staggered around this room, seeking a way out. The walls were solid stone, broken only by a slit of a window, too narrow for me to fit more than my hand through. The door was locked. No matter how many times I had thrown my body against it, it hadn't budged in its frame.

At last I had turned my attention to the floor. With my arms bound behind me, inspecting it had been a difficult task, and I was forced to sit cross-legged and stretch my arms back as far as they would reach, my fingers running over the chunks of stone. No loose pieces, not even a missing line of mortar. This room was a securely locked box. The only way I was leaving this place was with Robert's permission—or as a corpse.

Rolling onto my side, I closed my eyes, begging for the sleep that would not come. Every time my body started to relax, Antonio's image loomed against my lids and I jerked to wakefulness. His face was like a knife in my ribs, and every time I saw him, the knife twisted more until it took all of my strength not to cry out. How could have I been so stupid? Of course he wouldn't want me—the Puritan girl who tried to inhabit men's spheres of sword fighting and knowledge. If only we'd never met! Then I wouldn't have imagined a future alongside him, full of useful work and shared companionship. Thanks to him, my world had expanded, and now it had to contract again to its former size, leaving me alone, shaking, in the middle of it.

Sometime later—I wasn't sure of the time, for it seemed to pass with agonizing slowness, and I couldn't say whether minutes or hours had gone by—footsteps sounded again in the distance. Closer. Closer still. Motionless I waited, every muscle in my body tensed. Had Robert's friends returned at last?

The creak of the prison door was like a shard of ice impaling my heart. I bolted upright on the mattress. "Who's there?" I called.

Boots clicked on the floor, coming nearer. Beneath the blind-fold, my eyes squeezed shut. *Escape into your memories*, I ordered myself. Anne. I would fill my mind with her. Again I saw her, perched on a kitchen stool, flashing me a wide grin. I could see her lips moving, I could almost hear the high treble of her voice: *E-E-Eliz—so strong—*

Hands gripped my shoulders and flung me to the floor. With my hands bound behind me, I was powerless to break my fall and I slammed onto my stomach. Gasping, I lay still, trying to force Anne's image into my head. Her face evaporated like mist.

A hand caressed my hair. "You're a pretty maiden." It was Sir Gauden. "A pity. I would have preferred an ugly girl, for then I shouldn't have minded making a ruin of your face."

I clenched my jaw, preparing to hold in my screams. The beating would start soon. It *must*. Why did he wait? If only he would begin, then this horrible anticipation would be over—

He yanked me into a sitting position, then grabbed my hair, snapping my head back and bringing his lips to my ear. My mind snatched hold of details that couldn't possibly help me: the silk of his sleeve brushing my face; the scent of cold game pie and oysters on his breath; the chill of his rings when he splayed his fingers over my cheek, keeping me immobile so I had no choice but to listen to him.

"Unfortunately for me, His Grace prefers to use other meth-ods," he said. "He wants you to write out the final three books in *Paradise Lost*."

Why had we returned to Father's poem? There must be some-thing we had all missed—but what?

"He has already read the first seven books," Gauden

continued. "Come now, Miss Milton, don't act surprised!" He sounded annoyed when I started. "Did you truly imagine His Grace wouldn't take the first opportunity to read the pages you were copying? He told me he looked through them at night while the Florentine and you slept during your journey from Oxford to London."

But I . . . I had thought he'd been weak and feverish from his injuries. He had played me as masterfully as a musician plays upon an instrument.

I made a sound low in my throat but couldn't say a word.

Sir Gauden toyed with the knot at the back of my blindfold. "All it will take for me to remove this is your promise to write out your father's last three books."

"No!"

For a moment, he was silent. "You'll change your mind," he murmured. Then he let go of me. I heard his boots ringing on the stone floor as he walked away. The door opened and shut. A key turned in the lock. I was alone.

So they wouldn't hurt me, at least not yet. Robert had something else planned for me—something he must think would work better than whips or knives. I shuddered. *Don't think*, I told myself. All I could do was live through the next moment.

I scooted backward on the floor until the tips of my fingers found the hard surface of the wall. Bracing my back against the stones, I took a fortifying breath. What if Robert was correct and the cave's location *was* hidden in the final books of *Paradise Lost*?

Quickly, I considered the last three books. The Serpent in the Garden. Eve's temptation and fall from grace. Adam's decision to taste the apple, too, so he would never be parted from Eve.

Their reckoning before God. And, at the last, their expulsion from Paradise.

Nothing. The only "real" places I could think of in *Paradise Lost* were Rome, symbolized by the lethally beautiful Hell, and various biblical locations my father alluded to, like Mount Sion. No Padua, no mention of Tuscany except for the Tuscan Artist. Robert had to be wrong.

And . . . tucking clues into the ending didn't sound like something Father would do. He was a great believer in the power of the first line, and he had often advised me that the beginning of a poem was its most important part. What if the clues were concealed in the opening lines instead? So seamlessly woven into the first stanzas that I had skipped over them countless times? That would be far more like Father.

I stared into the blindfold, imagining it as a blank canvas for Father's words. The first lines unfurled across it, red letters of fire on black: *Of Mans First Disobedience, and the Fruit / Of that Forbidden Tree, whose mortal tast / Brought Death into the World . . .*

Something about the words gave me pause. I repeated them in my head, turning them over and over until they were old ribbons, rubbed smooth by my mind. In the first lines, my father is telling readers what the subject of his epic will be—namely, man's "first disobedience," his decision to thwart God's wishes and eat an apple from the Tree of Knowledge in the Garden of Eden. Therefore, if the entire poem is about "disobedience," the word itself must possess special significance.

It had to be a clue! Father was exacting with his diction, and if he wanted to draw attention to the word "disobedience," he must have had a reason. My pulse pounded in my temples. I closed my eyes, waiting for the wave of dizziness to pass.

Think. I knew of my father's habit for playing with words' multiple meanings. He had often told me the Hebrew name for Eve was related to the verb "to live." Therefore Eve, who had brought death into the world by eating the forbidden apple, was conversely considered the mother of all living things. Life couldn't exist without death—two opposites joined together to form a whole. It was exactly the sort of literary trick that Father loved.

I ran "disobedience" through my mind, then chopped it apart as Father had taught me, dividing it into separate sections. The prefix "dis" was Latin, and it meant "apart" or "asunder." Thanks to Father's lessons, I also knew it referred to the Roman underworld, known as Dis. The ancient Romans hadn't believed in Heaven; they had thought all departed souls resided in the underworld, a dark, hellish place. The god who ruled over it was known in Latin as Dis Pater, but he had other names, too—

Suddenly everything flew together, like fireflies in the night converging simultaneously in a single spot, creating a blinding ball of light.

Another name for the god of Hell was Hades.

And the name of my weapons instructor, the same man who had been one of Father's students many years ago after he had returned from the Italian city-states, was Mr. Hade.

I let out an inarticulate cry. *This must be the answer!* Father had hidden something valuable—something crucial about Galileo's discovery—in Mr. Hade's home. In his letter to Vincenzo Viviani, he had written that only educated people who *also* knew the intimate details of his life would be able to decipher his clues.

I stood, my legs threatening to buckle from exhaustion. But my mind was finally, blessedly clear.

How simple and yet fiendishly clever of Father! Robert would never think of this, and I would die before I told him. Let him think the clues were in the last three books: I would even agree to copy them out, earning my family more time to realize I was never coming home and to escape from London. My father's secret would stay safe, for Robert knew nothing of my old instructor.

But . . . that was wrong.

I sank to my knees. *Oh, dear God!* Robert *did* know about Mr. Hade. I had told him myself when we rode across London Bridge. Side by side with him, the two of us on our steeds, I had nudged him and pointed to where Mr. Hade's house stood on the bridge, explaining it was the home of the man who had trained me. And I had said Mr. Hade's name. I had *said* it.

So there was a chance Robert could assemble Father's clues after all.

I staggered to my feet. The hours without food and drink must have been taking their toll; the stones in the floor heaved under my feet. No matter. Gritting my teeth, I walked gingerly, my feet searching for something I could use to untie my bonds. Maybe I had missed an object or means of escape when I searched this room last night. Somehow I had to get out of this prison and journey to Mr. Hade's house. And I might not have much time.

But the day passed, and then the night, and I could find no way out. There was nothing in the room to help me escape: a straw pallet, a bucket to serve as a privy, and the window. I had pressed my face to the latter, breathing in the hot air and wondering which of the prison's many buildings I was standing in.

From the courtyard below, I had heard men talking, probably the countless fellows who worked in the Royal Mint or in the Ordinance and Records offices. They had been too far off for me to separate their murmurs into distinct words. None of them would help me if I screamed, I had known; they must be accustomed to the convicts' pitiful wails.

During the night, lions growled in their cages and the Thames washed the shore, a ceaseless shushing of water. In the morning, I lay weakly on my pallet, thinking. Today was the first of September. Three more days until Father's execution. And only God knew how many days remained until my death. Already I had been without food or water for a day and a half.

Specters rushed through my head, wispy things made of darkness and veils, nightmares of the dying or the mad. My throat was aflame. One drink. One sip of cool water was all I needed to banish the ghosts in my thoughts. If only I could break through this terrible fog and think.

Sometime later, after I used the bucket, my legs shook so badly on my walk to my pallet that I was forced to sit. I rested my forehead on the floor. My breaths felt like broken glass, cutting the inside of my throat as they went down.

So this was how Robert planned on breaking me: through neglect. No water or food, no visits, nothing but the sweat-dampened blindfold and my feverish thoughts for company. A clever plan; he was letting me break myself.

I must build up the walls in my mind, if I hoped to prevent Robert from climbing inside. The final three books of *Paradise Lost*—I would go through those again, so I could figure out how to weave a new story within their lines when Robert ordered me to write them out and hopelessly confuse him.

After consuming the apple, Adam and Eve begin fighting—vicious sniping at each other that used to thicken my throat when I wrote down Father's lines. In Book Nine, an angel comes to Eden to expel them. Adam refuses to admit they've eaten from the Forbidden Tree, but Eve readily confesses and entreats Adam to reconcile with her, saying, *Between us two let there be peace, both joyning / As joyn'd in injuries . . .*

The world seemed to stop rotating on its axis. I sat up so fast my head swam.

I had been entirely wrong about my father's version of Eve. While Adam can't face their sins and tries to lie to an angel, *Eve* is the one who is strong enough to accept their misdeeds. She stops Adam from fighting; she's the voice of reason and peace.

At last I understood what my father was truly saying about Eve—and, by extension, me. We weren't empty-headed decorations, content to bow to men's supposedly superior intellect. No, my father had presented us as the only people willing to accept our fallen behavior and capable of bringing about a reconciliation.

In the end, my father had made me the most powerful character of all.

Something golden and warm unfolded inside my chest. I *was* strong. And I would prove it to Robert. If Antonio somehow managed to hear of what happened to me in this prison, he would know, too. They wouldn't break me. Nothing would. And when I died—for die I would, from starvation or beatings—I would do so with my head held high and defiant curses on my lips.

For the first time, I fully understood why my father had

been willing to keep silent and die. There were some things that mattered more than any of us—liberty, faith, natural philosophy, and, above all, truth. I would die for them, too. Leaving my sisters and stepmother alone, with no one to care for them. A sob rose in my chest, but I swallowed it down. They'd find a way, somehow.

I forgive you, Father, I thought, wishing he could somehow hear my thoughts. *I know why you did this. Some things are worth dying for. I'm proud of you, Father, and I love you. I only pray you know it. And maybe soon we'll be together again behind the closed door of death.*

The rattle of metal made me freeze in place on the floor. Someone had come.

Twenty-Nine

THE CELL DOOR GROANED AS IT OPENED.

"Elizabeth."

The single word was enough. It was Robert. I recognized his crisp upper-class accent, the deep timbre of his voice.

Don't react to him, I ordered myself. I lay unmoving, a crumpled heap of scarlet skirts.

Robert sighed. His footsteps crossed the floor, stopping somewhere close to me.

His hands rested on the back of my head. "Oh, Elizabeth," he said again, sounding sad. "Why couldn't you have made this easier on both of us?"

He picked at the blindfold's knot, the half-moon of his fingernails scraping my skull in his haste. After a moment's struggle, the black cloth fluttered away, leaving me to blink, dazed, in the sliver of moonlight struggling through the window.

The room was cloaked in the darkness of night: stone walls and a floor, a straw pallet, the privy bucket, all blurred shadows. And Robert's face, inches from mine. For the space of several heartbeats, we stared at each other. Tears glittered in his eyes, catching glimmers of light from the candle in his hand so his eyes looked as though they had been speckled with dots of gold.

"I didn't want to have you brought here," he said. "I'm afraid, however, that you left me with no choice when you ran away. What was it that made you suspect, I wonder?"

His tone was conversational as he got to his feet. His free hand rested on the sword hanging from his waist, his touch light, as if he didn't anticipate having to use the weapon. He stood with his head cocked, waiting for my response. Tears continued to spill from his eyes, but his face might have been chiseled from stone. "Come, Elizabeth, tell me."

I licked my cracked lips. "It was your comments about Galileo. In the Bodleian you pretended you didn't know who he was, but later, in the Physic Garden, you knew he had been blind."

"Ah." He nodded, his expression impassive. "Very clever. I realized my mistake as soon as I had spoken. At the time, I was relieved when neither you nor the Florentine seemed to notice."

Despite myself, I had to know: "What have you done to him?"

"Still pining for the foreigner even now, when surely you must hate him?" Robert sighed. "You disappoint me. I thought you were stronger than that."

He glanced at a man who was sidling through the cell door behind him—a middle-aged man I didn't recognize, dressed plainly in brown and carrying a tray. "Set that on the floor and leave us."

"Very good, Your Grace." The man deposited the tray and departed, closing the door behind him. A pewter tankard and a plate of bread and cheese sat on the tray. My stomach contracted. *Please, Lord, let the food be for me! I would do almost anything for it.*

"Yes," Robert said, watching me closely, "you're hungry and thirsty, aren't you? I bet you can almost taste the water. Think of how cool and refreshing it will feel, sliding down your throat."

"Curse you," I whispered.

Robert managed a small smile. "I already have been cursed, for all of my life. That will soon change." His face hardened. "Take a sip, Elizabeth."

As he set the candle in its holder on the floor and picked up the tankard, I tried to make sense of what he had said a moment ago. *Surely you must hate him.* How had he known I was angry at Antonio? I hadn't confided in him, and he hadn't been in the hall when Antonio talked about pardoning Galileo.

"Easy, now." Robert put the tankard to my lips. I gulped greedily. The water coursed down my throat, putting out the fires burning in the soft tissue.

When the tankard was empty, Robert set it down, its metallic clank filling the quiet in the cell. Still crouching on the floor, he wrapped his arms around me, his scent of rose water wafting into my nostrils. What was he doing—embracing me? The ropes jerked against my wrists. Robert sat back on his haunches, holding up a knife and the severed pieces of rope.

He smiled at me. "Do you see how much I trust you? We can be friends, just as we were meant to be. Both of us the children of great men, rejected by our fathers for reasons that weren't of our own making. You because of your gender, me because of my birth. They thought we would never belong. But you and I will prove them wrong, won't we?"

He cupped my chin in his hands. The handle of his knife pressed into my jaw, its jewels sharp and cold. I fought a shiver. His hands slipped from my face. "You're weak; I can feel you shaking. Here, eat." He dragged the tray across the floor toward me, the pewter rasping on the stone.

I let out a cry that sounded like an animal's and shoveled bread and cheese into my mouth. The bites of bread stuck in my still-dry throat, and I had to swallow hard to get them down. When every crumb was gone, I sat back, shuddering. Robert knelt beside me, resting a gentle hand on my shoulder.

"Do you know why I usually wear yellow?" He didn't wait for my response. "It's to honor my mother. She often told me about her childhood in Wales and how she loved to walk its fields of wild yellow gorse. I wear it to remind my father that my mother lived, and that he wrongs her memory and my brother, James, and me by forgetting her."

Tears continued trailing down his face. "Let's work together. Once I'm on the throne, I can have you made a member of the Royal Society. You'll take your rightful place among the greatest minds in London. Your father will be released from captivity." He brought his lips to my cheek, so close I could feel them move as he whispered, "We can start a new world."

"No," I choked out. How could I convince him to abandon his plans? Perhaps if I appealed to his concern for his own neck, he would listen to me. "Think of what you're doing! If you drink the elixir and manage to cheat death, the life you live might come at too high a cost. You might become blind, like my father and Galileo. Or suffer ill health for the rest of your life, as Galileo did."

Our cheeks were pressed so tightly together I felt his tears, icy cold, on my skin. "Don't pretend you care about me," he muttered. "No one does."

"I do care!" I tried to pull back in his embrace, but his arms were iron hard, holding me in place. "I care," I repeated, quietly this time. "Please, don't go through with your plan. You aren't beyond redemption yet. But if you drink the elixir in order to rise again, you won't only destroy your soul—you'll throw all Christian nations into chaos."

His breath shuddered, quick and uneven, in my ear. "Their citizens will see me as the new light of the world. Their savior."

"But you'll destroy the Christian faith!" I cried. "Don't you understand? Yes, the elixir calls Jesus's resurrection into question, but exploiting the substance for your own purposes will slowly ruin our religion. The story behind your rebirth will get out; no secret of this magnitude can remain hidden for long, and some of your men won't be able to keep their boasts to themselves. Eventually, people will learn the truth. They'll turn on you, Robert. And they'll begin to doubt their Christian faith. You know how inextricably linked so many European rulers are with the Church. Poison our religious beliefs, and governments will fall. One by one, nations will descend into anarchy."

There was a long pause. Through our clothes, I felt the pressure of Robert's heartbeat against my collarbone—a wild, irregular thudding.

"No," he said at last. "I've worked too hard to stop now."

Something in the calmness of his tone made me pull away from him. His grip was loose now, his hands slipping from my shoulders. He had such a beautiful face, heart shaped and rosy skinned. And horribly blank, as though all emotion had been sucked away, leaving him hollow inside. Handsome, though, the sort of face you expected to see in paintings or read about in love poems. In appearance, he and his brother, James, must have taken after their mother—all they seemed to have inherited from their father was his height.

His father's height . . . The words bumped around in my head like berries in a bucket. And then I knew.

I scrabbled backward, crablike. "*You* are my father's Satan," I breathed, unable to tear my gaze away from his still-damp eyes. "Not the king! My father must have used the gossip about you for inspiration, never dreaming how right he was to choose you as the model for his devil. You must have suspected what he did—that's why you convinced Antonio and me that the devil in *Paradise Lost* represented your father!"

Robert's eyebrows rose. "Your days without food or drink must have deprived of your wits. Didn't we already discuss the similarities between your father's devil and my father? Of course my father represents Satan—his name even falls into your father's stupid alliterative naming scheme!"

"So does yours!" I shot back. "Didn't you know Satan has many names? The Devil, Beelzebub, the Serpent, the Devourer. And Lucifer—the angel in the Bible who is cast out of Heaven. '*How art thou fallen from Heaven, O Lucifer, Son of the Morning!*'" I quoted from the Book of Isaiah. "My father presents his version of Satan as this Lucifer, Heaven's greatest angel, the star who burns the brightest. Haven't you heard of Lucifer before, Duke of *Lockton*?"

For a breathless moment, he stared at me, his eyes as hard as stones. Then he jumped to his feet, grabbed the candle off the floor, and threw it directly at my face.

Instinctively I ducked. The candle landed behind me, its flame reflecting on the stones, sending golden glimmers dancing across their pale surfaces. I bent down and blew it out. The cell plunged into a darkness so heavy the only things I could discern were the whites of Robert's eyes—eyes wide and focused on me.

"Very well." His voice was eerily calm. "I gave you a chance. If you insist on our being enemies, then enemies is what we'll be. I don't need your help anyway."

"Wait! What do you mean?"

His smile was quick, his teeth a slash in the darkness. "Come with me. There is someone who I think you'd like to see again."

My father. Somehow Robert must have found him and broken him out of the king's custody.

I glared at Robert. He would never tell me where he had taken my father; I could see his resolve in the blank calmness in his eyes.

There was no choice at all: I must go with him wherever he led.

"If you harm a hair on his head," I ground out, "then nothing can save you. I'll hunt you to the ends of the earth."

He raised his eyebrows. "Such theatrics from a Puritan! You surprise me, Elizabeth." He opened the door, his face hardening. "Come."

All I managed was a curt nod. Robert ushered me out the

door into a yawning blackness. Without any torches to light our way, we were forced to move by feel, trailing our hands on the walls as we descended the narrow stairs. From behind me I heard a clink as Robert placed his ringed hand on the hilt of his sword. He was ready for me.

Somehow I had to prepare myself for him, too. Because I couldn't let him win—even if stopping him meant my life.

Thirty

ROBERT LED ME ACROSS THE TOWER COURTYARD, holding me lightly by the wrist. All around us rose the prison's massive outer walls, blocking out the sounds of the city. Night had swathed the network of buildings so they resembled hulking shadows. Somewhere, lions roared, their throaty rumbles cutting through the quiet.

The sound of lapping water twined with the lions' cries. Robert yanked on my wrist, forcing me to halt. At our feet gleamed the murky water of the moat, lines of moonlight rippling across the surface. A boat bobbed below us, its side bumping against the landing with a wooden *thunk*. Sitting within it, watching us, were four men: indistinct outlines of long, curling hair and broad-brimmed hats. All but one wore a sword at his waist. Was the unarmed man Father? *Please let it be him!* I squinted, but the night was too dark; I could make out the dejected slump of the man's shoulders and the plume on his hat, nothing more.

Robert elbowed me. "Get in."

Hands reached up, grasping my arms and pulling me into the boat. I sank onto a seat and twisted around to look at the weaponless man sitting behind me. As he lifted his head, the boat was pushed away from the landing. Two of the men dipped oars into the water, propelling us forward. The unarmed man's eyes met mine.

All the air vanished from my chest. This wasn't Father—Father's eyes never would have been able to find another's. This man was sighted, and his eyes were wide and frightened. Had Robert lied to me? Had he lured me out of my cell with an elaborate ruse?

I spun on my seat, seeking Robert. He sat in the stern, expressionless, as the boat glided across the water. Ahead of us loomed the portcullis gate, its interlocking black bars dividing the night beyond it into small pieces, like panes of glass. It groaned as it was pulled up. When we passed beneath it, water dripped off its spikes, hitting my face and shoulders.

"You said you were taking me to my father!" I shouted at Robert.

He shrugged. "If you made an illogical leap in your thinking, I'm hardly to be blamed for it."

What did he mean? Who was this man?

Behind us, the portcullis gate rattled as it was lowered. Fog crawled across the water's surface, obscuring the Tower complex until it had vanished behind a curtain of mist. The men stopped rowing. We drifted across the water, like a rudderless ship at sea. My hands curled into fists in my lap. What was Robert planning now?

"We're ready," said one of the rowers. I recognized his voice; he was one of Robert's friends from the ball at Buckingham's mansion.

A scuffle broke out behind me. As I turned around, I saw that one of the men had wrapped his arm around the unarmed man's neck. The second man so confined gasped for breath, his hands scrabbling in vain at the other's arm.

"Mr. Pepys," Robert said, "you'll answer my questions or my friend will squeeze the life out of you."

Pepys! The funny little gentleman from the Royal Society meeting—I remembered him bowing to Robert, burbling about his service in the Royal Navy. What the devil was he doing here?

"Please," Mr. Pepys wheezed, "I know nothing!"

"Why must everyone lie to me?" Robert snapped. "Only a man immovably loyal to my father would have remained in London during the plague outbreak, and only a man who suspected there was something suspicious about Sir Vaughan and his assistants' absence from the Royal Society meeting would have jumped and nearly fallen over a chair when their names were mentioned. Yes, I saw your reaction when I brought them up," he said when Mr. Pepys winced. "Clearly my father has taken you into his confidence. Did you run to him after the Royal Society meeting and tattle on me, I wonder?"

"I told him you had attended the meeting, that's all," Mr. Pepys whispered. "We knew there could be a reasonable explanation for your actions. Maybe you had become interested in natural philosophy—"

"Stop your rambling," Robert interrupted. "Now tell me where my father has hidden Mr. Milton or die."

"No! Don't tell him anything!" I shouted.

Something poked me in my side. I looked down and saw it was the tip of a dagger, its point disappearing into the heavy folds of my scarlet gown. The man holding it gave me a thin smile. My mouth went dry.

No one said a word; the only sounds were Mr. Pepys rasping for air and water slapping the sides of the boat. My eyes roved across the men's faces, searching for an instant of inattention in which I could seize one of their weapons. But Robert and Sir Gauden sat with their hands resting on their weapons. The two rowers rested their paddles on the gunwales, leaving one hand free to clasp their swords at their waists. What could I possibly do?

Mr. Pepys's eyes bulged, his head jerking like that of a puppet on a string. Robert snapped his fingers and the man released Mr. Pepys, who sagged forward, coughing hard.

"Mr. Thomas Farriner's bakeshop," Mr. Pepys gasped. "It was my idea to keep him there. The king wanted him housed at the Duke of Buckingham's home, but I thought it was too obvious a choice. I know Mr. Farriner well—he supplies the Royal Navy with biscuits." He raised streaming eyes to Robert. "The king loves you! I beg Your Grace, don't go through with whatever it is you're planning and break his heart!"

Robert looked away, the muscles in his neck working as he swallowed. "He has already broken mine by refusing to recognize me as his heir. I'm only taking what rightfully belongs to me," he answered. "Row!" he snapped at the men. At once they dipped their oars into the water.

So Father was definitely still alive. My heart swelled, pressing against the cage of my ribs.

I waited for Robert to ask Mr. Pepys where Thomas Farriner's bakeshop was located—heaven knew there must be dozens of bakeshops in London. But Robert said nothing more. Perhaps the name Farriner was known to him.

My hands fisted in my skirts. Even if I managed to get away from these men, I couldn't find Mr. Farriner's bakeshop and my father before they did.

I would have to stay with them.

Through the thinning mist, the shore came into focus: a shallow, muddy ditch and, beyond that, a road and the humped shapes of hovels. We must have rowed to the street lining the western side of the moat, known as Tower Ditch. The area was the sort of maze inhabited by the wretchedly poor: crooked lanes, twisting alleys, and passageways that seemed to double back on themselves.

"Return Mr. Pepys to his house." Robert pointed past the rowers. "He lives in Seething Lane, in the grouping of buildings reserved for Royal Navy officials."

Our boat felt as though it were being pulled across the water by invisible hands, so steady and smooth was our progress. I watched the lip of the ditch rear up in the darkness until our boat bumped into it. Sir Gauden leaped onto the shore, then leaned down, extending his hand for me to take.

"Come, Miss Milton," he said. "Aren't you eager to see your father again?"

Glaring at him, I took his hand and jumped to the shore. The marshy land sucked at my shoes when I landed. From far away, footsteps rang out on cobblestones.

"Hurry, we have a carriage waiting." Sir Gauden tugged my arm.

I looked over my shoulder. The rest of the men had clambered ashore. The two rowers were walking away, gripping Mr. Pepys between them by the arms. That left only me, Gauden, and Robert. Two against one wasn't insurmountable—provided I could lay my hands on a weapon.

My legs felt like blocks of wood as I pushed them forward. One step. Another. The soggy ground hardened into oyster shells and rocks embedded in mud, a poor man's road. A black carriage waited a few yards away; I recognized it as Robert's from its coat of arms.

Inside the carriage everything was made of shadows: Sir Gauden lounging on the padded seat; the leather curtains covering the windows, leaving only a sliver of moonlight showing around the edges. As I sat down, Robert jumped in after me. He settled next to me so closely that every breath I took tasted of his rosewater cologne. My stomach heaved.

The carriage rolled forward. Robert stretched out a ringed hand to raise the curtain. Outside, no lanterns had been lit; the street was left black. The tumbledown houses passed in a blur. Somewhere church bells rang the hour, a solemn single note reverberating in the warm air. It was the first hour of the Lord's morning. Farther off I could hear the roar of the river's receding tide, then the groan of the massive waterwheels beneath London Bridge. All else was quiet: the tippling houses and gaming rooms had already been closed.

The carriage lurched to a stop. Before it had even finished rocking, Robert and Sir Gauden had pulled the door open and leaped to the street. I jumped down after them.

I found myself standing in the middle of a narrow lane lined with wooden houses. Most of them were only a room or two wide but towered five or six stories high in a series of additions, the jetties projecting out so far they nearly touched those of the houses opposite. They blacked out the stars, leaving the lane in complete darkness save for a couple of candles sputtering in windows.

That illumination was all the light I needed as I scanned the buildings, seeking a sign with a painted loaf of bread that would tell me we had found Mr. Farriner's bakeshop. I saw a cradle for a basket maker, a unicorn's horn for an apothecary, and a coffin for a carpenter. No bread, but I did recognize my surroundings, for I had walked this neighborhood with my father many times: we stood in Pudding Lane.

Somewhere in the distance sounded the rattle of carriage wheels on paving stones. I ignored the noise, continuing to peer at the houses. Across the lane a weathered sign hanging from the first story of a ramshackle wooden structure creaked in the breeze. A loaf of bread was painted across its surface.

This must be it.

I dashed across the lane. I pulled at the heavy wooden door, but it didn't budge. It was locked. Even as I yanked again on the handle, Sir Gauden pushed me aside.

"Get away!" I cried, but he ignored me.

He hacked at the lock with his knife. Robert was watching him closely. His trembling hand gripped my shoulder. "I visited this place once," he said without looking at me. "Mr. Farriner hadn't been paid in a timely manner, and my uncle thought if my brother and I called upon him, the gesture might engender his goodwill—and keep our ships supplied with Mr. Farriner's biscuits." His laugh sounded bitter. "I daresay my uncle forgot the errand or he would have convinced my father to have yours kept elsewhere. But James and I aren't important enough for our deeds to be repeated to our father. For once, it seems to have worked in my favor."

The scream of wood and iron giving way tore through the air. The bakehouse's door hung drunkenly in its frame, the wood surrounding the lock gouged and splintered. With a bow, Sir Gauden stepped back.

"Good work." Robert's face had tightened into a grim mask. He strode through the doorway with me dogging his heels. Whatever I did, I couldn't let him get to my father first.

Inside, the darkness was as impenetrable as stone. I had to move slowly, bracing a hand on the wall for guidance. We had to be in a hall, for I sensed no furniture. My fingers drifted across a series of pegs, accidentally knocking a cap to the floor.

I had to slip away from Robert and Sir Gauden. The bake-shop itself should be in a separate structure from the home, likely in a backyard. If I had understood Mr. Pepys correctly, then that must be where my father was being held.

We shuffled across the room, keeping to the walls. The room remained black, and no creaks sounded from the stair-case. No one was coming, then. So much the better. I could find a way to fight Robert and Gauden without the fear of any-one interrupting us.

My hip brushed something hard—a table, I guessed, for it continued for a few feet as I squeezed my body past it. Ahead of me, Robert fumbled with something. Metal rattled. He opened a door and disappeared beyond it.

I darted after him and found myself outside. Here the

starlight tumbled down unobstructed, showing me a small yard lined with stacks of brushwood. A few paces away stood what must be the bakehouse—a little wooden building, its windows black with night.

I broke into a run. Robert raced alongside me. We reached the door at the same instant and I flung my arm out, catching him square in the chest. He fell back a step, gasping in surprise. I threw the door open and dashed inside, shouting, "Father! It's me!"

In the bakehouse something gray coated everything in sight: the floor, the tables, the frame of the single window. Squinting in the sudden wash of darkness, I peered around the place, seeking the shadow that might be my father.

Someone grabbed me from behind. I fought him, kicking and hitting, my heel connecting with his shin. He staggered, then fell hard, taking me down with him. We collapsed in a tangle of limbs.

It was Sir Gauden; I recognized the scent of his cologne. His elbow jabbed my eye. For an instant, all I could see were starbursts of color, forming and reforming in front of me. Half-blinded, I scrambled onto my hands and knees. Gauden kicked me in the ribs. Pain exploded in my side. I grabbed his ankle, jerking as hard as I could. He stumbled a little, then slithered from my grasp. Gritting my teeth, I clutched at the nearest table, using it to pull myself up. Dimly I sensed him rushing past me, deeper into the interior of the bakehouse.

A scraping sound reached my ears. I spun around. Robert had followed me inside, too, and was thrusting something into an oven. It was a large brick opening set directly into the wall. Its bottom was littered with twigs and ashes. Among them a single spark glowed orange-red.

Robert pulled out the item he had pushed into the oven, and I saw what it was: a paper twist, its edges flickering yellow with flame. He must have grabbed it from the basket of kindling and twists on the ground by the door. Quickly, he used the paper to light a candle sitting on a table. Its illumination threw lines of gold onto his face. In the moment since I had last seen him in the yard, he must have lost his wig. Without his familiar tumble of brown curls he looked like a new person: older, thinner, his shorn head shining white. His expression was impassive as he placed the candle inside a lantern, then closed the glass door and set the lantern on a table.

In its flickering glow I could see the bakehouse more clearly. It was one small room, its walls blackened with soot, its floor and three trestle tables coated with a film of flour as gray as long-dried ash. Several barrels stood stacked against the far wall. A pallet lay on the floor behind the tables. Sitting motionless upon it was my father.

He looked exhausted. Wrinkles scored his cheeks and forehead more deeply than when I had seen him last. Flour dusted his black clothes, like snow on tar. His hair hung about his face in uncombed knots.

"Father!" My harsh cry seemed to burst directly from my throat. I rushed toward him.

Sir Gauden emerged from the shadows behind my father. Before I could shout a warning, he had dropped to his knees and laid the flat of his blade against my father's throat. I skidded to a halt.

"Elizabeth!" my father called out. "Is that you?"

When he spoke, the skin of his throat rippled, nicked by the edge of the sword. A few drops of blood welled up, then slid across the gleaming blade like balls of red glass.

"Don't hurt him!" I shouted. "Please!"

"Oh, I don't want to hurt *him*," Robert said.

Something in his tone turned the blood in my veins to ice. Slowly I turned to look at him. He stood between the tables, toying with the latch on the lantern's glass door. "I want," he said softly, "to hurt *you*."

I gasped as I realized what he meant. He hadn't been able to break me when he had deprived me of food and drink—so he would break my father instead. He would torture me until my father shattered and confessed he had hidden something in Mr. Hade's home.

"Father," I shouted, "no matter what they do to me, you must stay silent! Do you understand?"

"Elizabeth!" my father rasped out. "Get out of here—they'll try to kill you!"

"I won't leave you!" I yelled.

The door crashed open behind me. I whirled around. Standing in the doorway, his chest straining with labored breaths, was Antonio. On either side of him stood Lady Katherine and Thomasine, daggers glinting in their hands.

Thirty-One

THE ROOM FROZE. I COULDN'T TEAR MY EYES FROM Antonio. He looked terrible. The color had drained from his face, leaving it bone white. His hair fell to his shoulders in a wild tangle. A bruise stretched sickly yellow fingers along the length of his jaw. He was still dressed in the clothes he had been wearing when I last saw him; now the black satin breeches were wrinkled, and dirt streaked the front of his intricately stitched doublet. He held a sword at the ready.

When our eyes locked, he let out a shuddering breath. "Elizabeth!"

"Get out." My voice was so rough I didn't recognize it as my own.

Bewilderment flickered across his face. "What—"

"Silence!" Robert thundered.

In the lantern light, Antonio looked pale and exhausted.

His eyes, though, were unblinking as they focused on Robert. "*You*," he growled with such venom that the hairs on the back of my neck rose. "I could rip you limb from limb for what you did to Elizabeth."

"Your betrayal was far worse." Robert smiled slightly when Antonio started.

"What are you talking about?"

"His Grace tricked me!" Lady Katherine cried. "I swear to you, Miss Milton, I didn't understand what I was doing! His Grace told me to ask Mr. Viviani what he would do with Galileo's vial if your father hadn't been imprisoned. His Grace was waiting in the next room, and he coughed when he heard you coming, which was the signal for me to pose the question to Mr. Viviani."

Antonio's words, uttered before we left for the ball, rushed back to me: *Signor Galilei's discovery is a powerful tool against the Church. . . . If I brought it to the officials in Rome and promised to keep it quiet in return for Signor Galilei's pardon, I'm certain they would agree.*

He had said "if." It could have been idle chatter. Not a plan to steal the vial in an attempt to salvage Galileo's reputation. Just a response to Lady Katherine's hypothetical question. Even now I could hear her asking, *If Miss Milton's father hadn't been captured, I wonder what we could have done with Galileo's secret. What do you think, Mr. Viviani?*

Antonio had responded precisely in the manner I would have expected from him—indeed, precisely as Robert had hoped. And his words had pulled us apart, making it easier for Robert to manipulate us.

Not once had Antonio suggested stealing the vial.

"Then it was all a trick!" I breathed. "Antonio didn't betray me."

Robert blinked, a slow shuttering of his lids over eyes as cool as glass. He didn't speak. I whirled around. Antonio hadn't moved from the door. The hand holding his sword had begun to tremble, but whether from emotion or fatigue I couldn't tell. His voice cracked when he said my name. "Elizabeth, I promise I wouldn't deceive you—"

"He's telling the truth," Lady Katherine interrupted, throwing a scornful look at Robert. "His Grace returned from the ball full of stories. He said you and he had been separated in Buckingham's garden. Mr. Viviani didn't believe him and attacked His Grace."

"You need to shut your mouth," Robert growled. He rushed toward them, but Antonio jumped in front of Lady Katherine, sweeping his blade. Robert leaped back. His face darkened.

"You might manage to slay me before I draw my weapon," Robert spat. "But you'll never get out of London alive. Once my men know I'm missing or dead, they'll move Heaven and Hell to avenge me. You're already as good as dead, Florentine."

"Then I'll die fighting," Antonio said.

Pride fired in my heart—a hot conflagration that pushed against my ribs, eager to escape. My Antonio, with his dear, tired face. His broad shoulders that sagged with exhaustion, his voice that cracked with strain. And yet he stayed. A hundred times he could have returned to Florence, but he hadn't. I had vanished, and he had remained. For my sake. I knew it by the way his eyes flickered over to mine, tracing my face as if he wanted to remember it forever.

"And I'll fight beside you," I said to him.

Antonio gave me a relieved smile. He'd just started to speak when my father called from the back of the bakehouse, "Take heed, daughter! I hear someone moving!"

Robert was edging toward the back of the building, away from me and Antonio. He scowled at Sir Gauden. "Keep Milton quiet, can't you!"

My father was still sitting on the pallet, his neck bared for Gauden's blade. A shallow red line marred the skin of his throat. My eyes flew to Robert. "Don't move," I said.

"Your father's the only person I see in mortal danger," he growled. "You'd be wise not to anger me."

"Kill him and you've lost the chance to learn the secret of *Paradise Lost*."

Annoyance flitted across Robert's face. Instead of responding, he glanced at Lady Katherine. "Indulge my curiosity, my lady. How did you know to come here tonight? I myself was unaware of Mr. Milton's hiding place until a short while ago."

The dagger in her hand shook so badly it had become a silver blur, glinting against the pale pink of her gown. "For the last two nights, Mr. Viviani has haunted Whitehall's gates in the hope you would leave and lead us to Miss Milton. Tonight, when he saw you and a group of your courtiers riding out, he followed at a distance. As soon as he saw you rowing across the Tower moat, he raced to me and Thomasine. We sped to the Tower in my carriage, reaching it just as all of you entered your coach. I am gladder than words can express that we returned in time to see Miss Milton, but"—she hesitated, her lips compressing into a line, as if she were trying to hold in her tears—"but I wish with every particle of my being that we had been wrong about who had imprisoned her."

Something warm spread from my chest down my arms and legs, pooling in the spaces between my bones until all of my body felt alive and thrumming from it. My friends hadn't abandoned me. Every moment I had spent in a cell, they had been seeking me. Not once had I been alone. *Not once.*

"I've grown weary of all of your voices." Robert, his eyes flat, glanced at Sir Gauden. "Mr. Milton, you have until the count of ten to tell me about the secret in your poem or I will throw my dagger into your daughter's chest." He paused. "I have excellent aim."

"I beg of you, don't!" my father cried. Gauden yanked his hair, forcing his head back. He pressed the point of his sword into my father's throat, digging so hard a small red circle welled up.

"Say nothing, Father!" I yelled.

I raced around the table toward Robert. His eyes widened with surprise, and he fumbled with the sword at his waist. Before he had unsheathed it, I cracked him across the face as hard as I could. He let out a startled cry and staggered a few steps away, cupping his nose. Lines of blood snaked between his fingers; in the dimness, they looked black.

"I'm safe!" I started to shout to Father just as Robert yelled, "Kill her! I want her dead!"

"No!" Father screamed. "The secret is hidden in Mr. Hade's home! It's a map—a map of the exact location of the cave outside Padua where Galileo found the sunken meteor!"

The room seemed to hold its breath. Robert's hands fell from his nose. Blood continued to gush from it, and when he spoke, blood dripped off his mouth. "Ah, Elizabeth's old weapons instructor who lives on London Bridge. Very clever." He glanced at Sir Gauden. "Now kill him."

"No!" I screamed. Dimly I heard Antonio shout something. From the corner of my eye, I saw him racing toward my father and Sir Gauden. Twenty paces distant. He would never reach them in time; already Gauden was bringing the sword down in a silver arc. Ten paces away. I whirled around and shouted at Lady Katherine, "Throw me your dagger! Now!"

Her mouth dropped open in surprise, but she obeyed, flinging the dagger at me. I caught it by the handle and spun around. The sword was descending toward my father's neck; he was struggling in Gauden's grasp, his face white with terror. I didn't hesitate. I threw the dagger as hard as I could at Sir Gauden.

It embedded itself in his upper arm. Only the silver hilt, studded with jewels, showed. Gauden's eyes bulged; his mouth gaped like that of a fish. He clapped a hand to his arm, trying to pull the dagger out, and let his sword fall to the dirt floor with a soft thump.

Antonio reached them. He pulled his arm back, winding up for a blow, then plowed his fist into Gauden's eye. Gauden crumpled at once. As he fell, he collapsed against my father, knocking him to the floor.

"Father! Are you all right?" I dropped to my knees, scrabbling at Sir Gauden's body.

Antonio helped me tug Gauden's limp form off my father's body. We dumped Gauden unceremoniously on the floor, where he lay motionless, still unconscious. As my father struggled to sit up, I wrapped my arm around his waist, steadying him. His familiar scent of tobacco and wool, now mixed with flour and grease, wafted over me, and a lump rose in my throat.

"Father," I managed to say, but couldn't push any more words out of my mouth.

"Where's the Duke of Lockton?" he gasped. "Don't let him get away!"

I looked over my shoulder. Robert had hurried to the bakehouse door, but Lady Katherine and Thomasine stood in front of him, blocking his way out. From the back, the line of his shoulders looked rod straight.

"Don't cross me," he said through clenched teeth.

"Please don't go." Tears shone in Lady Katherine's eyes. "I love you, Your Grace. Robert. Don't retrieve this map, I beg of you."

He shifted slightly, so I could see his profile. Blood now coated his mouth; his lips looked as though they had been painted red. "Get out of my way!" He grabbed Lady Katherine's arm, trying to yank her aside, but she stood firm.

"No!" she shouted. "I won't let you go so that you can ruin your soul!"

Metal rang out as Robert drew his sword. Even as I relinquished my grip on my father and started to rise, Robert thrust his weapon forward in one smooth movement. The sword buried itself up to the hilt in Lady Katherine's stomach. She looked down, vague surprise registering on her face.

"What . . . ?" she whispered.

Time seemed to stop. Unable to understand what had just happened, I stared at Lady Katherine. Her face had gone white, and worry creased the ordinarily smooth skin of her forehead. She lifted a trembling hand to her cheek, pushing away a stray curl, as if she needed to see better in order to comprehend what had occurred.

Robert pulled out the sword. Its blade was stained scarlet, glimmers of silver showing in a couple of places that hadn't been slicked with Lady Katherine's blood. It clattered onto the ground, flinging droplets of blood in every direction. Robert let out a shaky breath.

Lady Katherine sagged against the wall. Her mouth opened and closed, but nothing came out. A red hole had appeared in the pink silk of her bodice; even as I watched, it widened, spreading out on either side of her navel, like a nightmarish version of an embrace. Slowly she slid to the ground, leaving a long, dark smear on the flour-streaked wooden slats. Her body began to shake, her feet drumming a rapid tattoo on the dirt.

Robert stared down at her, his chest rising and falling with heavy breaths. His eyes were dark and grim; his mouth was set in a thin line.

Beside him, Lady Katherine's head lolled on her neck. Thomasine threw herself onto her knees beside her mistress's body, sobbing and chafing Lady Katherine's hands. Robert backed away, his eyes panicked, his lower lip trembling. I felt rather than saw Antonio stand next to me, for I couldn't look at him; all I could see was Lady Katherine's mouth continuing to open and close without making a sound.

I let myself sink down next to her. Her lips were still moving. She was saying something, a whisper so faint I had to rest my ear against her mouth to hear it.

"Robert?" she murmured, sounding confused. I jerked my head around. Robert was lurking in the shadows at the far side of the room, near my father. His head was bowed.

"Where's the vial?" I shouted.

Robert looked at me, his eyes glazed with shock. "The vial?"

"Yes, the vial, curse you! Lady Katherine is dying, and its contents will save her!" When he did nothing, I yelled, "Don't you care about your betrothed?"

His face changed then—a tightening of the muscles along his jaw, perhaps, something so subtle I couldn't tell exactly how the transformation had taken place. But he had become calm. With the heel of his hand, he wiped at the blood on his mouth, leaving dark streaks fanning out from either side of his lips.

"Yes," he said quietly. "I care for her." He paused. "But I care about myself more." He ran a careful hand down the front of his doublet, smoothing it. Bloody lines from the tips of his fingers now marred the satin, scarlet-black on yellow. Through the fabric I could see the vial's slender outline; he was carrying it close to his heart, as Sir Vaughan's assistant had.

Antonio took a step toward him. "Give it to us!"

"No," Lady Katherine murmured. "I don't want it."

Pink bubbles dribbled out of her mouth and down her chin. Her insides must be awash in blood, with nowhere for the welling substance to go but out.

"Help her!" I shouted at Robert. "Give us the vial or we'll take it by force!"

"You heard my lady," he said. He looked at me then, his eyes hooded by the faint candlelight. "She doesn't want it."

Antonio's hand brushed mine. "Elizabeth, he's right. We can't treat Lady Katherine against her will."

I jerked away from him. "She's ill—she doesn't know what she's saying!"

"Elizabeth." There was an immeasurable sadness in Antonio's face. "She knows."

Blinking hard, I rested my hand on Lady Katherine's cheek, praying my touch gave her comfort.

"The Lord is my shepherd," Thomasine said through her tears. With a lurch of my heart, I realized she was giving Lady Katherine her last rites. Beneath my cheek, Lady Katherine's cheek went slack. I waited for it to rise with another breath.

There was none.

A ragged cry hurled itself up my throat. I jumped to my feet, seeking Robert in the shadows. Near the far wall lay Gauden, still motionless, and close to him crouched my father, his head swiveling as he tried to make sense of the sounds within the bakehouse.

Robert had moved. Now he stood between the trestle tables, his head hanging, his shorn skull shining white in the dimness. His hands gripped the lantern's handle.

At my side, Antonio raised his sword. "It's over, Robert. You have no friends left. Surrender or I'll be forced to hurt you."

Robert's eyes flashed onto mine. A new emotion rippled across his face; he looked just as he had before he'd thrown the candle at me in my cell—silent and seething. In that horrible instant, I realized what he was planning to do.

"Don't!" I screamed, but it was already too late: Robert had thrown the lantern at the piles of kindling lining the wall behind my father. It shattered with a tinkling of glass, followed a heartbeat later by the *whoosh* of a fire flaring to life.

Thirty-Two

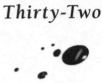

FLAMES RACED ALONG THE WOODPILES. EVEN AS I dashed toward my father, the entire back wall was vanishing behind a sheet of glowing red. He was crawling on his hands and knees, shouting my name, sounding panicked.

I reached him at the same instant Antonio did. Together we hooked our arms under his armpits and hauled him to his feet. Around us the bakehouse was turning to flame, its grease- and soot-caked walls disappearing into red waves. Smoke had transformed the air into a thick black mist. Another few moments and we might not be able to find the door.

With the crackling of flames filling our ears, we half dragged, half carried my father across the room. A few feet from the door, Thomasine cradled Lady Katherine's body in her lap, sobbing.

"We have to get out of here!" I shouted. Thomasine shook her head, tightening her arms around Lady Katherine's shoulders.

"She's gone," I said, more gently. "We can't help her anymore. All we can do is save ourselves."

Tears shone in Thomasine's eyes. Nodding hard, she eased Lady Katherine from her lap and rested her lifeless form on the ground. Then she scrambled to her feet and pushed the door open. The fire roared forward, eager to race through the doorway.

We dashed into the yard. Except for the stacks of kindling, it was empty. There was no sign of Robert.

I clutched blindly at Antonio's arm. "Robert escaped! I wasn't paying attention—all I could think of was helping my father!"

"It's too late to worry about Robert." Antonio thrust my father at me, then slammed the bakehouse door shut. "Get into the street. Raise the alarm."

Wind whipped my hair over my face, so I saw him through a brown screen. "But . . . aren't you coming with us?"

"There are people in there." He nodded at the wooden house on the other side of the yard. "They will be burned to death in their beds if I don't wake them."

"I'm coming with you." I guided my father between the piles of kindling, the two of us moving so fast it felt as though we were flying across the grass. Thomasine hurried ahead of us, flinging open the house door and darting inside.

"Go!" Antonio called out to me. "You must get far away from here."

Heat licked up my back, so intense it felt as though my bones were fusing together. I risked a glance back. The bakehouse had disappeared completely behind a wall of wavering flames. Lady Katherine's and Sir Gauden's bodies must already have been consumed. Most of the yard behind us was red with fire.

We kept running, my father stumbling on the uneven ground and nearly pitching forward onto his face. I yanked him up. We continued in an awkward jog that didn't feel nearly fast enough. Father's arm was heavy on my shoulders, and he panted from exertion. We half fell into the house. Antonio shoved the door closed behind us. With my arm still wrapped around my father, I led him down a narrow passageway, following the gleam of Thomasine's fair hair. Smoke curled along the ceiling and closed off my throat. The walls and floors were disappearing before my eyes, replaced by roiling black smoke. I whipped out my free arm, frantic to touch something that would tell me where we were.

My hand hit emptiness. No wall. Perhaps we had reached a room. Father and I staggered on, Antonio's hand resting on the small of my back, urging me forward. Together we stumbled into a room that must have been the kitchen—I thought I saw the outline of a long table and the dark hole of a hearth. The walls were already aflame. Including the far wall, which we needed to pass through to reach the lane. We were trapped.

Father erupted into a coughing fit. He hunched over, bracing his hands on his knees, his body shaking from coughing. "Leave me, daughter," he sputtered. "I'm an old man, I have lived long enough."

"I'm not leaving you." Again I scanned the room, fighting the hopelessness cresting within me. The walls were collapsing in flames. The bricks beneath my feet were so hot I feared my shoes would start smoking.

"There!" Thomasine pointed. Flames had leaped across an empty space in the opposite wall, leaving behind a black rectangle. A staircase. "We can jump out a second-story window!"

There was no time to think. Antonio and I nodded, and she raced ahead of us. He and I grabbed my father's arms and followed on her heels. The stairwell was too narrow for the three of us to navigate together, so Antonio flung my father over his shoulder like a sack of grain and began climbing. His legs shook from the effort.

Up and up we went until we reached a corridor filled with smoke. Three filmy white shapes hurtled toward us—as they neared, they sharpened into two middle-aged men and a girl my age, all dressed in long nightgowns and nightcaps. The girl's face was badly burned, her cheeks scored bright red.

"Who the devil are you?" one of the men shouted. He was thickset, and his nightcap had slipped to reveal his shaven skull. This must be the baker, Mr. Farriner. He glanced at my father, his mouth dropping open in surprise. "Mr. Milton! How did you get out of the bakehouse?"

"We were passing by and saw fire," I yelled, ignoring the question directed at my father. "The ground floor is an inferno. Is there any other way out of here?"

Farriner nodded, gesturing for us to follow him. We took to the stairs again, Antonio still carrying my father and now bringing up the rear. His ragged breathing mingled with the crackling flames, creating such a wall of sound I could hear nothing else. The steps narrowed as they curled around and around; we must be nearing the garret. The walls had grown hot to the touch, and I kept my arms at my sides. Every breath I inhaled burned my chest. Tears poured out of my eyes so thickly that the door at the top of the stairs wavered in and out of focus.

Farriner opened the door. We stumbled in after him. Once

Antonio and my father had come inside, Farriner slammed the door shut. In here the smoke had grown so heavy I couldn't see my own hands as they stretched in front of me, seeking the rippling sensation of glass under my fingers; glass in a window we could break and escape through—

Someone seized my hands and dragged me to the floor. Antonio. The whites of his eyes were shockingly bright in his face; the rest of his skin was black with soot, making him almost unrecognizable.

"Stay low, where the smoke is lightest!" he shouted.

He began worming his way across the floor on his belly, keeping one hand clamped on my father's wrist so he knew to follow him. They crawled side by side, vanishing from my sight into the smoke. He was saving my father. He hadn't abandoned him, even though it would have been easier.

Blinking to keep the tears at bay, I slithered after them. Through my dress I could feel the bare wooden floorboards buckling with heat. Beneath the roar of the flames, I heard the wrenching sound of a casement being forced open. My fingertips brushed the back of someone's shoe; I recognized the battered leather of Antonio's boot. He was standing. I scrambled up.

Next to us, Farriner jerked a window back and forth in its frame until the wood gave way. The window fell, sliding across the tiled roof to break on the pavement below.

Farriner wriggled through the opening. For an instant he sat hunched on the sill; then he crawled onto the roof, a ghostly figure wavering behind plumes of smoke. He braced his foot against the roof's gutter, twisting around and reaching out to the burned girl, who stood at the window. "Hannah! Come!"

She climbed on the sill, then hesitated, her form washed black by smoke. Finally she took Farriner's hand and scrambled across the roof after him.

The other man, a servant by the look of his much-mended nightgown, slowly climbed out after them. It took all of my strength not to push him out of the way and clamber out myself. I looked at the garret door. Flames curled over its edges. It couldn't be long before they spread to the walls.

A skinny, gray-haired woman appeared—the maidservant who must live in the garret, I guessed. She moved toward the window, then stopped, shaking her head.

"I can't!" she cried. "It's too high!"

"Go!" Antonio yelled. I gripped Father's hand. It was almost our turn through the window—just another moment more . . .

The servant backed away from the window, her face frozen in terror. Giving up, Antonio nudged Thomasine toward the window, then nodded at me, his meaning obvious: I would be next.

I had to shout in Father's ear to be heard above the flames: "I'll climb out of the window first. Then Antonio will guide you through. We'll have to crawl across the roof to reach the house next door. I will guide you the entire way. You *must* trust me, do you understand?"

He nodded. His face was tight with concentration, his head cocked; he must have been listening to the flames, trying to judge how far away they were from us.

Thomasine scrambled through the opening, pausing in a crouch on the sill as the others had, searching for a secure roof tile to hold on to. Then she climbed onto the roof and vanished from sight.

My turn. Antonio gestured me forward, and I released Father's hand. I clambered onto the sill, peering out to see the others crawling like beetles across the slanted roof. They were heading toward the garret of the next house. It hadn't caught fire yet and stood like a black sentinel. Below, the lane looked far away, a distance of at least forty feet. It was empty. The fire alarm mustn't have started, for I didn't hear church bells ringing.

All this I took in at a glance. My hands felt the roof tiles. One of them didn't shift under my touch. I clung to it as I leaned forward, preparing to slither onto the roof.

I slid off the sill. On my hands and knees, I crawled a few feet. The rough tiles dug into my palms, but I was glad for their uneven surface; if they had been smooth, I might have skidded right off the roof into certain death. I braced myself on my knees, then looked back at the window. Through the opening, I could barely see Antonio and Father, their forms half hidden by swirling smoke. I reached toward them.

"Father!" I screamed. "Take my hand!"

He nodded without hesitation and let Antonio help him onto the sill. Gripping the broken frame with one hand, he stretched out the other, skimming the air wildly in search of mine.

My hand closed around his. "Come toward the sound of my voice!"

Father crawled nearer, staying on his knees, one hand touching the tiles for guidance, the other clasped in mine. His face gleamed with perspiration. Behind him Antonio appeared in the opening.

When Father reached me, I yelled in his ear, "I must let go of your hand! We have to crawl to the garret of the next house. I'll put your hand on my ankle, so you know which direction to go."

"No," he said at once. "That's too dangerous. If I fall, I'll take you with me."

"It's the only way!" I shouted. His mouth opened, probably to argue, but I clamped his hand around my ankle and started crawling. Ahead, the others were banging on the window of the garret in the neighboring house. A face appeared behind the glass, and the casement was thrown open.

The tiles cut my hands, a dozen stings making me grit my teeth. Father and I inched forward. At last the garret window yawned wide before us. Arms reached through it to grasp my father under the armpits and pull him inside. I clambered onto the ledge, then looked back.

Antonio was crawling a few feet behind me. At some point he had lost his hat, and his hair hung over his face, obscuring it from my view. The elderly maidservant was nowhere to be seen. A thick column of smoke poured through the window we had crept through.

Hands grabbed my arms, yanking me into the garret. I landed hard on my feet, the impact sending vibrations up my legs. A handful of people pressed against me—Farriner and his manservant, the burned girl, and another man, presumably the house's owner. Father and Thomasine stood a few feet away, coughing and wiping their sweaty brows with the backs of their hands.

"Who are you?" the others demanded. "What happened?"

Ignoring them, I whirled to watch as Antonio climbed through the window and jumped to the floor. He straightened, and then he opened his mouth, but all that streamed forth was a series of wracking coughs. His doublet was ripped in several places, revealing the silk shirt he wore under it, once snowy white, now a faded gray. A welt had already risen on the back of his hand. A line seeping blood marred the smooth skin of his cheek.

He had never looked better to me.

I opened my mouth to thank him for helping my father, but my throat was sealed with smoke. Hacking, I staggered to him, grabbing his hand and interlacing our filthy, bloodstained fingers. He gave me a small smile, then looked away as he started coughing harder, his entire body shaking.

"We have to get out of here!" Farriner shouted. "The fire could jump to this house at any moment."

My father shook his head. Understanding, I dropped Antonio's hand and seized my father's. He wouldn't agree to leave unless he knew I was with him. I tried to speak again, to reassure him of my presence, but all I could manage was a series of violent coughs. In desperation, I ran my father's hand over my face. At once his worried expression smoothed into a smile. He had recognized me.

As one, our group raced from the garret. In full blackness we hurtled down the stairs, tripping over uneven steps, trying to keep inside us the screams that wanted to burst out. We bolted into the lane, where lanterns and candles were flaring into life and people leaned out of windows, shouting, "What's happening?" The bells of nearby St. Margaret's had started ringing, the signal a fire had broken out.

Flames had burst through the roof of Farriner's house. Even as we looked, the single shower of sparks widened into a swath of fire that raced across the roof in all directions. The roof tiles turned black, and I realized what was happening—the roof was coming apart, the tiles falling inside into the attic. A black hole started to spread across the roof. With a massive roar, the remaining tiles disappeared, leaving a dark space rimmed with red to show where the roof had been.

Far above our heads, embers carried by the breeze spun across the lane to land on the roofs of the houses opposite. Men and women, most still dressed in their nightgowns, poured into the lane. Some carried buckets of water. "To Butchers' Hall!" they yelled. "There should be fire squirts stored there!"

It was a hopeless proposition; the brass fire squirts contained a gallon at the most and shot only a skinny stream of water. This fire was already leaping to more houses, fed by their wooden frames and the wind. I feared there was little we could do to halt its progress; the city hadn't had rain in nearly a year and most of the houses in this area were hovels, constructed so shabbily their jetties nearly touched, giving the fire an easy route to take.

The city was a tinderbox. But we had other nightmares to confront.

I glanced at Antonio. "We have to go after Robert! He might already be at London Bridge."

He nodded, his grim face colored red by the flames. I whirled on Thomasine. "Please take my father home," I begged her. "It's a small row house on Artillery Walk, not far from Bunhill Fields. Can you guide him there?"

"Yes," she promised at once.

I stepped toward Father, intending to kiss him farewell on the cheek in our usual manner, but he reached out, his hands cutting through the air until they found me. He drew me close, holding me in the cradle of his arms so my head fit in the hollow of his neck. The protective embrace clogged my throat with tears; I couldn't recall feeling sheltered by him before.

"You've done well." It was the highest praise I had ever received from him. "You must end this, daughter. Do whatever you have to."

"I will," I vowed.

Then I grabbed Antonio's hand. Together we plunged into the crowded lane, which was slowly turning red from the glow of the flames. For once I didn't look back at my father to see whether or not he wore an expression of approval.

I did not look back at all.

Thirty-Three

PUDDING LANE HAD GROWN THICK WITH SMOKE, slowing our progress. Men, women, and children poured out of their houses, their arms laden with possessions—clothing, bowls, wooden chests. They streamed along the lane, no doubt planning on storing their valuables at St. Margaret's, the only stone building for blocks.

Our pace was practically a crawl. More and more people charged up the lane, their faces white with horror. We squeezed between them. My breath was coming in quick wheezes, strangled by the growing smoke.

A chain of people had formed up and down the lane. They passed leather buckets, bowls, and chamber pots brimming with water in a desperate attempt to douse the flames. Firelight bathed their faces red, turning them into the figures of nightmares. Frantically I spun around, trying to figure out exactly where we were.

From far off, beneath the veil of screams and crackling flames, I caught the rumble of waterwheels.

"This way!" I shouted at Antonio, pointing south, in the direction of the bridge.

We tried to run, but we were moving against the tide of people rushing up the lane, and we could barely take a step. A man in a white nightgown and cap pushed me out of the way, and I fell to my knees. I cried out in frustration. We would never reach the bridge in time to stop Robert.

"Go!" I rasped at Antonio.

He grabbed my hand, hauling me to my feet. "Come on!" he panted.

Trying to reach Fish Street Hill, we weaved through the tangle of shouting men and women. Each step I took, my mind screamed, *Faster!* Fire had spread outward from Farriner's house, turning the buildings on either side into glowing red walls and transforming the air into a miasma of choking smoke and glittering embers. Men swung axes at the cobblestones, trying to reach the elm pipes beneath that carried water throughout the city. The roar of flames and the groan of breaking timbers filled the air, and somewhere, far off, I thought I heard horses neighing in terror.

We shoved through another clump of people and popped like corks into the suddenly empty air leading to Fish Street Hill. Fire had already spread here, too: twin lines of flames coursed down the sides of the street. More people were running, some holding their possessions, frantic to save whatever they could, others throwing buckets of water at the inferno. Antonio and I took to the middle of the street, running as hard as we could. I skirted a sobbing little girl clutching at her mother's nightgown. I looked away, my heart twisting. All around us our city was disintegrating, and I couldn't stop to help anyone.

Fish Street Hill spilled directly into London Bridge. As we ran, I peered ahead. The bridge's hulking shape loomed like a dragon in the night, a massive pathway rising from twenty stone arches spanning the Thames. The stone keep of Bridge Gate, topped with the severed heads of traitors and criminals, should have been a black, tangled mass at night, but I could see it as clearly as if it were bathed in daylight: the sun-whitened skulls on pikes, their gaping eye sockets, picked clean by the ravens from the Tower.

The flames' reflection had painted the sky red, turning night into day. Beneath its hellish dome, I could see the stately homes lining the bridge past Bridge Gate; their gilded facades flashed gold from the light of the fires. The houses, though, still seemed quiet; I didn't hear anyone's voice.

We raced onto the bridge. Beneath the walkway, I could feel the enormous waterwheels churning, sending vibrations up my legs. We dashed through the stone keep. Ahead stood the houses. Here the roadway narrowed to some twenty feet, and the houses rose four, five, or six stories high, jutting out over the river on either side of the bridge and supported by a network of timbers. Some of the finer homes spanned the bridge from one side to the other, and the roadway continued beneath them, forming black tunnels.

People had begun trickling out of their homes to stare, slack jawed, at the carpet of flames spreading across the cityscape behind us. I glanced back. The once-dark riverbanks were turning orange.

My stomach clenched. This fire was spreading faster than I could have ever dreamed.

I whipped my head around to face front. We had reached the first span of houses. There was another grouping of houses farther on, the gap between the two sets of homes spanning six bridge arches. A handful of people had begun running toward the opposite bank, which was still dark, and others were darting inside their homes, presumably to gather their valuables. None of them were paying attention to me or Antonio.

Mr. Hade's house was the last on the right. "That one!" I shouted, pointing to a five-story wooden house with an elaborately carved facade. Its ground-floor windows were black, but a yellow glow bobbed in an upper window. The light of a candle held in Robert's hand, perhaps? Or was Mr. Hade still at home?

The door gaped open, and we dashed inside. The darkness was so complete we couldn't see where we were going. I bumped into a table, knocking something to the floor—several somethings, for they landed on the floor with soft thumps, and I belatedly remembered the ground floor contained a shop.

"Mr. Hade!" I yelled. "It's Elizabeth Milton! Are you here?"

Please let him be gone from here, safe somewhere else.

No response. Only the groaning of the waterwheels under the bridge and the cascade of running feet outside. Through the windows, I could see men and women racing past, making for the southern end of the bridge. *Oh, God.* We had to hurry. The fire could jump onto the bridge itself at any time. The flames would easily eat the wooden walkway and houses.

"He must have gone already," Antonio said. "Come, Robert must be upstairs." He handed me a knife. "You'll want this."

It was one of my knives, the plain, wooden-handled weapons I had strapped to my forearms for years. My hand closed around the hilt; it felt as familiar and comforting as a well-worn garment. "Thank you."

Together we fumbled through the darkened room, trailing our hands across the walls until we found the opening for the stairs. We pounded up them, stopping at every landing to listen for someone rifling through Mr. Hade's belongings. At the third floor, Antonio stiffened. "Do you hear that? It sounds like what I heard when I took a boat across the Channel—like the roar of the ocean hitting the shore."

This was a sound I didn't know. But I heard something— an overwhelming rumble, the river tide magnified a thousand times. "That's impossible. . . ."

I shoved open the window on the stairway landing and ducked my head out. What I saw nearly stopped the beating of my heart. The fire had reached the bridge. Flames had already engulfed the gate tower; it was a hulking black shadow surrounded by plumes of flickering red and orange. Even as I watched, flames were racing along the walkway and sides of the bridge—heading directly toward us.

I jerked back from the window. "The bridge is on fire!"

Before Antonio could reply, the screech of wood giving way reached our ears. *Robert.* He was upstairs somewhere, searching.

Antonio and I looked at each other. I saw understanding in his face. We couldn't take the chance Robert would find Galileo's map and survive this inferno. We had to go on.

"Are you ready?" Antonio asked, pulling his sword free.

My hands tightened on the knife. "Yes."

As one we rushed up the stairs. The door of the first room on the left was open, and candlelight glimmered from within. Together we burst in.

Robert stood over a large writing table. He looked up, his eyes wild. He had set a candlestick on the table; in its weak light, his face was pale, his skull ghostly white. Blood still smeared his chin and nostrils.

When he saw us, his lips firmed. Without a word, he returned to his task, sliding the point of a knife into the lock on the top drawer.

"Robert, stop!" I cried. "The bridge is on fire. We have to get away from here!"

He didn't bother looking at me. The lines of his shoulders were tight as he bent over the table, muttering to himself, "It *must* be in here; there's no other place left to search."

"It's over!" Antonio shouted. "Come with us."

He gripped Robert's arm, trying to pull him away from the table, but Robert shoved him off and cracked him across the mouth. Antonio staggered backward. I grabbed him by the shoulders, steadying him.

"You want to distract me and take the map for yourselves!" Robert's eyes glittered with tears. "It's *mine*. I need it!"

He returned to the drawer. I ran to the window and peered out. I could see the fire had consumed the first group of houses on the opposite side of the bridge, leaving blackened shells in its wake. Some of the houses' jetties tumbled into the river, hitting the water with such force that splashes rose over the side of the bridge—iridescent showers gleaming with reflected light. Steam puffed up in large clouds from the surface of the Thames.

A few men and women had clambered out of their windows onto the timbers projecting over the river, the wind whipping their nightgowns about their legs and sending blazing embers dancing through the air.

I leaned out the window, craning my neck to see if the fire had reached the houses on our side of the bridge. Flames had turned some of them into glowing red boxes. Smoke pressed against my eyes, filling them with stinging tears. The horrifying sight—the flames, the white-gowned men and women crouched on the timbers, the steam rising from the water—blurred before me. I jerked my head around to shout a warning into the room, but I saw Antonio had joined me; he was peering through the glass, his face hard.

"There's no time to search for the map," I said quickly. "If we stay, we die."

He nodded. "Can you swim?"

This was hardly the question I had expected. "No. But why—"

"I can." He shucked off his shoes, then his doublet, as I stared at him. "Take off your clothes!" he ordered. "They'll weigh you down in the water."

At once I understood. There was no time to run for the southern side of the bridge.

We were going to jump.

Fear made my fingers clumsy, and I struggled with the laces at my waist, finally untying them and letting my heavy skirts fall to the floor. I kicked off my mules. Clad in only my bodice and shift, I ran to Robert, dropping my knife to the floor. Despite everything, I wasn't willing to use it on him.

"Elizabeth!" Antonio shouted. "We have to jump *now*!"

I looked at Robert, his face deathly pale, blood-darkened in spots. He was paying no attention to me; he was intent on the lock. There was nothing there of the boy I had thought was my friend. And yet I still hated myself for what I was about to do.

I plowed my fist into Robert's cheek with all of my strength. A terrible crack sounded, perhaps from his cheekbone shattering.

He gasped, sinking to his knees. Before he could react, I plunged my hands under the collar of his doublet. My fingers trailed over the smooth hardness of his muscled chest. There it was. The vial. I could feel it, its slender, rounded shape, warmed by the heat of his flesh. I grabbed it, the string of the necklace yanking loose.

"No!" Robert shouted.

He staggered to his feet, lunging at me. I raced across the room, holding the vial tightly to my chest. Antonio crouched on the windowsill, which overlooked the river. He was waving me on, yelling something I couldn't make out above the crackle of the flames. Smoke drifted through the open doorway from the stairs, harbinger of the horrors to come.

I scrambled onto the windowsill. The black water below looked hundreds of feet away. My stomach plummeted. How could I jump into that water when I didn't know how to swim?

"You must trust me," Antonio said, as if he had somehow sensed my thoughts.

Swiftly I looked at him: his familiar face, rendered strange by smoke and soot. "I trust you," I said.

He held out his hand. I clasped it in my free one, keeping the other pressed to my chest, clutching the vial. I glanced over my shoulder. Flames were racing across the floor, throwing nightmarish red wavering lines on the ceiling. Robert was stumbling toward us, pressing a dirt- and blood-stained hand to the cheek I had punched. He was halfway across the room, just a few paces away. His boots had begun to smoke, gray tendrils drifting up. He looked down, his eyes widening in horror.

"Help me!" He looked at me pleadingly. He took a step and the floor groaned under his weight. "Elizabeth! The floor's collapsing!"

"Run to us! We can jump together!"

His eyes looked like enormous dark pools. He didn't move. "I'm too heavy—the wood will break under me!"

I couldn't just watch him die. I started to slide off the sill. Antonio jerked me back, close to him.

"Don't!" he yelled in my ear.

"Help me!" Robert shouted again. Flames were shooting across the floor in a carpet of glowing red.

Robert's face was a mask of terror. He raced toward us, a flickering figure of yellow behind the screen of smoke. He reached out his hand toward me. We were so close—our fingers almost brushed. "Please—" he started to say, but what he would have said next I would never know. With a horrible groaning of wood, the floor collapsed.

One instant Robert stood a few feet away from us; the next he was gone, with only the echo of his scream to tell us he had ever been there.

Thirty-Four

"ROBERT!" I SHOUTED.

The space where the floor had been was a black hole rimmed with red. Everything was gone—a couple of chairs, the desk where Robert had thought the map had been concealed, everything vanished. Smoke had begun filling the air, turning it gray and opaque.

"We can't wait any longer!" Antonio yelled.

I nodded. Robert was gone. No one could survive such a fall, let alone a fall into an inferno. He was dead, and as my fingers tightened on the vial, I knew I wouldn't bring him back.

"Now!" I shouted, and we leaped into the darkness.

We hit the water with a resounding splash. Immediately my body plunged into shocking coldness. I opened my eyes and saw I was cutting through the dark river water like a knife, plummeting toward the bottom. Antonio was gone; I couldn't sense his grip on my wrist.

My arms flailed uselessly, churning the brackish water until all I saw beyond them were white bubbles and blackness. Air pressed against the spokes of my rib cage, pushing, pushing until I could bear it no longer and opened my mouth for a hopeless breath. Dank river water streamed down my throat. I started to choke, gasping.

An arm wrapped around my waist. Antonio. I recognized the white of his shirt, the black of his breeches, but I couldn't see his face; my head was tucked into the hollow of his neck. Blindly I twined my arms around his chest, my hands meeting on his back and the vial gripped tightly in my right hand. Antonio kicked hard once, twice, and we glided up.

My head broke the surface. I sucked in a mouthful of hot, smoky air. It burned my throat as it went down. Overhead the sky was a flickering, faded red, obscured by a drifting screen of smoke. The surface of the water was flecked with orange and scarlet, the reflection of the flames. Charred timbers and burned furniture floated all around us, bobbing gently on the current.

Antonio treaded water next to me, keeping an arm braced under my armpits. The Thames had washed the soot from his face, leaving it pale gray. The cut on his cheek had stopped bleeding; it looked like a thin black line. He was breathing hard.

"Wrap your arms around my neck," he panted. "I'll swim us to safety."

I clung to him as he kicked and paddled. With each stroke he took, the enormous underworkings of London Bridge drew nearer: stone pilings, vaulted archways, and, far to the left and the right, the massive circular shadows of the waterwheels. One of them had caught fire and come loose from its moorings; it drifted away on its side, a burning circle on the dark water.

We reached the stone pilings. There we huddled with a dozen others. Soon enough, watermen would rescue us, they told me and Antonio. We nodded dully. My soaked shift clung to my skin, and I shivered despite the smoky heat pressing in on us from all sides. From our vantage point under the bridge, we couldn't see the city, but the illumination of the reflected flames had turned an enormous swath of the Thames red, showing us the far-reaching path the fire had already taken. Smoke curled and twisted across the water's surface. The distant rumble of flames was so loud I had to place my lips on Antonio's ear.

"You could have returned to Florence after I was imprisoned," I said. "You could have left my father in Mr. Farriner's house." Emotion choked my voice, so the next words came out sounding half strangled. "But you stayed. You carried him."

He looked at me, his eyes startled. "Of course. I never would have left him—"

"But you could have," I interrupted. "You had the choice. You might have died for our sakes, Antonio."

He rested his hand on my cheek. His fingers were cold and wet, but they warmed me all the same. "Elizabeth, don't you know by now I would give up anything for you? Even my life."

Tears gathered in my eyes. I turned, letting his hand fall from my face. I gazed across the ruby-spattered water to where the white dome of St. Paul's gleamed in the reddish darkness, rising high above the city. Around us, the others muttered among themselves, some sighing, others sobbing.

"I shouldn't have doubted you," I said.

"How could you not?" he asked. "Robert was a skilled manipulator. It's a miracle we even managed to become friends, with him as our constant companion."

"Maybe there are miracles in this world." I twisted from my crouched position on the stone piling so I could look Antonio in the face. He was watching me, his expression calm. "No matter what Galileo's discovery truly means, I still believe in them. You're the miracle of my life, Antonio."

He grinned. "And you're mine." He leaned closer, his lips brushing mine. I could feel his touch in the base of my spine, as though every particle of my body was attuned to his mouth or his hands. This boy would be a challenge, I knew; there would be nothing easy or straightforward about our relationship.

Then again, we Miltons were accustomed to hardship. I wouldn't wish for soft hands adorned with rings when I could have callused hands gripped around a telescope.

Antonio moved closer, bringing his lips to my ear. "I think we need to arrange an audience with the king. We can persuade him that the vial was lost in the fire. As long as he thinks it's been destroyed, he might be willing to let your father remain free."

I watched the smoke curling over the surface of the Thames, thinking. *Father, free.* He could walk the streets of his beloved London once more without fearing that the king's men would drag him off to prison. He might even be able to have his work published again.

And Londoners—all of the Christian nations—could continue to believe in the miracle of Christ's resurrection. Governments wouldn't fall. There would be no revolution. No separation of church and state. Until the day when, maybe, the two might split apart.

For now, the world wasn't ready.

I glanced at Antonio. "It will mean keeping Galileo's discovery a secret."

His jaw was clenched. "I know. His reputation will remain in tatters. But he is dead, and my allegiance will always be to the living."

I shook my head. "You aren't fooling me. I know you're doing this for my sake, not my father's." I rested my forehead on his, feeling the warmth of his skin flow into mine. I could almost pretend our thoughts pushed through the layers of bone and muscle and blood separating us, and we could speak without saying a word. *I love you*, I thought. *I love you, Antonio Galletti, the boy who exists beneath the fine clothes and elevated status, the vineyard worker's son. And someday I will be brave enough to tell you.*

Aloud, I said, "Thank you."

He nodded. I doubted he could bring himself to speak. But I knew how much his decision cost him, and I would be grateful to him for the rest of my life.

And so we sat together on the pilings, Antonio and I, the vial cold in my grip, and watched the sky darken to bloodred as we waited for the boatmen to come.

The sun had become a gold coin in the sky glinting through the drifting layers of smoke by the time three watermen rowed their wherries under the bridge to rescue us. We had agreed we had to go to Mr. Pepys first, to rescue him from the two of Robert's friends who had escorted him from the Tower moat.

We found him in a garden behind the cluster of buildings where Royal Navy officers were housed near Tower Hill—burying, of all things, a giant wheel of Parmesan cheese, apparently to keep it safe from the encroaching fire. His assailants had argued over what to do with him and had slain each other in a fight. Once we had told him that the Duke of Lockton had set the fire and perished in the blaze, we begged him to take us to the king, and he agreed immediately.

Since we were half dressed, Mr. Pepys gave me his wife's blue gown to wear and lent Antonio a black velvet doublet, which was so small that he looked as though he were a man trying to fit into a child's clothes; but wearing them was preferable to calling upon the king in our undergarments.

We took a wherry to Whitehall. As the boat skimmed across the water, fire tore west along the northern bank, following us. For the first time in hours, I allowed myself to think of my family. They were out there somewhere, behind those walls of smoke and flame. I prayed with all of my strength they were safe and the fire hadn't reached our neighborhood.

Slowly the fire's roar receded. As we alighted on the palace boat-stairs, I looked at the thick plumes of smoke rising from the ruined city behind us. Then, my heart clutching in my chest, I followed Mr. Pepys and Antonio onto Whitehall's grounds.

For a long time, we waited in the king's closet in the chapel, while a group of courtiers bickered over whether or not the fire was dangerous enough to warrant disturbing the king. At last we were escorted up the Privy Stairs and through a long gallery whose walls were crowded with paintings and tapestries. Mr. Pepys explained that the king would receive us while lounging in bed, in the French fashion, and that the king, having spent so many of his formative years on the Continent, must be excused for his decidedly un-English manners.

We were brought through a seemingly endless series of chambers, ending at the Royal Bedchamber. I paused on the threshold. This moment might determine the course of the rest of my life. I couldn't afford to make a mistake. Taking a deep breath, I strode into the room. Inside my bodice, the vial, cool and smooth, lay against my bare flesh.

The room was bursting with so many people I wondered the walls didn't bow outward from the pressure: a group of nobles played cards at a table laden with goblets of wine and gold coins; a handful of men in much-mended clothes stood near the door, clutching vials of cloudy-looking liquid—peddlers of medicinal potions, I supposed, for the king's interest in such matters was well known; and a brown-haired man of about thirty, attired in fine clothes, looked out a window, keeping himself aloof from the chamber's other inhabitants. A box containing a recent litter of spaniel puppies sat on the floor. The king himself lay on an enormous bed with velvet hangings. He looked sleepy, and his long black wig sat slightly askew on his head.

"Ah, Mr. Pepys!" he exclaimed. "What can you be doing out so early on the Lord's morning?"

Mr. Pepys bowed so low his nose nearly scraped the floor. Antonio and I hastily followed his example.

"I don't come on pleasant business, Your Majesty," Mr. Pepys said. "A dreadful fire is ravaging the city, and I"—he hesitated, his voice dipping—"I convey news of your son I don't think you would wish anyone else to hear."

The king sat bolt upright, the sheets puddling in his lap to reveal his plain white nightgown. He snapped his fingers. "Leave us," he commanded to the room at large.

At once the nobles and potion makers shuffled out of the room, leaving only the man at the window and a second at the table remaining. The latter stood, his dark eyes sweeping over us, and I froze in midbow. It was the Duke of Buckingham.

He gazed at me, recognition dawning on his face. "The girl who played servant," he muttered to himself.

The king leaned forward. "Mr. Pepys, what tidings do you have of my son?"

Mr. Pepys gestured at me and Antonio. "Your Majesty, I present to you Miss Elizabeth Milton and Mr. Antonio Viviani of Florence. They are far better suited to tell you the story than I am."

The king's eyes widened. "So this is the poet's daughter and the Florentine mathematician? Very well, Miss Milton and Mr. Viviani—tell me about my son. The *truth*," he added. "I will know if you're foolish enough to lie to me."

Haltingly we explained the horrific events of the last several hours, omitting the part about my hitting Robert and taking the vial from him. As far as the king would know, the vial had perished with his son.

After we had finished, silence descended on the room for a long moment. Then the king dropped his head into his hands. "*Robert*," he moaned.

"You always spoiled the boy." The man at the window turned. I recognized his long, lean face surrounded by waves of brown curls: it was the king's younger brother and legal heir, James, the Duke of York. "I warned you no good would come of giving him a title and an endless stream of gifts without the anchor of responsibility and royal duty." He crossed the room, stopping by the bed to place a hand on the king's shoulder. "But you don't deserve this pain, Charles."

"He conspired against me." The king's voice trembled. "I wondered, of course I wondered, but I couldn't bring myself to believe he would try to overthrow me and seize the crown for himself—and in such a horrific way."

He lifted his head to reveal red-rimmed eyes. "How can I tell Lord Daly that his daughter died at my son's hand?"

"You can't," Buckingham said at once. He sent me and Antonio a wary look. "The only people who know what happened in Mr. Farriner's bakehouse are either dead or in this room. As a blind man, Mr. Milton can't claim to have witnessed anything."

The hairs on the back of my neck rose. Buckingham was right, since we hadn't mentioned Thomasine. As far as they knew, Antonio and I alone were aware of who had plunged the sword into Lady Katherine's stomach. Had our knowledge signed our death warrant?

"Your Majesty," Antonio said, "the bakehouse was dark and there was much confusion when we found Mr. Milton." He paused, his meaning clear. "It's difficult to say precisely what happened in that room."

Buckingham sent him a considering look. "I'm glad to see our foreign guest has a cool head on his shoulders." He turned to the king. "The solution is simple: the Duke of Lockton, while out carousing with friends, caught sight of the fire spreading across the bridge. He went into one of the houses to warn the occupants, whereupon he was overcome by the flames.

"This is the story we must tell if we don't want London to

descend into anarchy. Think of it, Charles," he urged when the king sat motionless, tears shining in his eyes. "If the populace knew your son was responsible for setting the blaze that has destroyed their homes, cost them the lives of their loved ones, there would be a mass riot. You will end either on the scaffold as your father did or exiled in Europe again. And I tremble for the future of our country—England isn't strong enough to weather having another king deposed."

"Yes," the king said slowly. "If the truth is told, our country will come apart again, as it did in my father's time."

I took a steadying breath. This was my chance to bargain for Father's life. I would never have another opportunity. "My father is scheduled for execution, Your Majesty. But we . . . we are prepared to keep our silence in return for his life."

The king regarded me without expression. "I have no desire to find the cave and trumpet news of a discovery that could only plunge countless countries into mass riots. The vial has been destroyed in the fire; let that be the end of it."

I swayed on my feet. This was it, the oath I had needed to hear. He was going to let Father live. "I will never speak of the vial again, Your Majesty," I promised.

There was one thing that still needed to be said, though, the one thing that might make my father's past sufferings bearable. Fear was a piece of broken glass in my throat, cutting every time I tried to speak, but I pushed the words out all the same.

"Your Majesty, my father's poem was destroyed by the Duke of Buckingham. As the vial and the map are now gone, you can have no further objections to *Paradise Lost*—it has become simply a poem. I'm certain my father could dictate it to me again.

If Your Majesty could . . . that is . . . if you could ensure it's approved by the government censors so it can be published, my father . . ." I paused for a steadying breath as my voice wobbled out of control, "I think my father could be happy. He has had little joy in his life, Your Majesty."

"My years of exile have taught me we must find joy whenever we can," the king replied. "*Paradise Lost* will be published; you have my word."

Tears spilled down my cheeks. "Thank you, Your Majesty."

"And all else shall be forgotten," the king ordered.

Antonio and I bowed our heads in submission. "The world isn't ready for the truth, Your Majesty," Antonio said quietly. "It may never be."

"We are done." The king clapped his hands. "Bucks, be so good as to fetch the nearest clerk. I need to issue orders about the best ways to contain the fire. Mr. Pepys, you'll deliver my orders to the Lord Mayor. James," he added, glancing at his brother, "we'll take a barge so we can view the fire from the river."

It was clear we had been dismissed. Mr. Pepys remained in the Royal Bedchamber for instructions as Antonio and I backed out of the room, careful to keep our fronts to the king. Once we had wended our way through the series of chambers to the gallery, we took to our heels, hurrying to the Privy Stairs that took us outside, where the air was slowly turning bitter with smoke. And yet, in a way, the air tasted like freedom, too.

Thirty-Five

WE WALKED TO MY FAMILY'S HOUSE IN EXHAUSTED silence. The fires hadn't reached this far north yet, although I heard the distant rumble of flames. The house looked deserted, the steps empty, the shutters flung open wide without the usual accompaniment of chattering voices from inside. Perhaps my family was hiding out in Moorfields until the fires were extinguished.

We had barely taken two steps into the hall, though, when my sisters surrounded us, half laughing, half crying.

"That's enough." Father's voice cut through my sisters' sobs.

He stood in the door frame leading to the parlor, dressed in the same flour-smudged black clothes in which I had seen him last, his face still smeared with soot. Despite his gruff tone, I smiled: he hadn't even been able to bring himself to wash, not while he waited for news of me. He had been worried.

"Come now," he continued scolding my sisters. "Elizabeth

and Signor Viviani must be dropping on their feet. Mary and Deborah, fetch them food and drink; let us have them fed and rested in case we need to flee our house in advance of the flames." He shuffled into the parlor, calling over his shoulder, "I want to speak with you, daughter, before the king sends his men for me again."

Antonio and I looked at each other. "He doesn't know yet he'll be safe for the rest of his life," he said.

I took Antonio's hand, leading him into the parlor. "Then let's tell him the welcome news together."

My father wept when he learned that *Paradise Lost* would be published. Antonio and I didn't tell my father every part of the story. The vial, still nestled in my bodice, remained ours alone. After the meal, we were sent to separate bedchambers, with the assurance that we would be roused if the fire grew close to our neighborhood.

Alone in the bedchamber I used to share with Anne, I stripped off my borrowed clothes. Even under the sheets, I clutched the vial, unwilling to let go of it for an instant. Every time I closed my eyes, images pressed against my lids—remnants of the last twelve hours. Lady Katherine, her mouth opening soundlessly as she stared at the sword protruding from her stomach. Robert staggering across the burning room toward us, smoke drifting from his boots. The black-and-red water rising to meet us as we hurtled through the air.

Again and again my eyes flew open, needing the comfort of the plain whitewashed ceiling. At last, though, fatigue dragged me down a dark well of oblivion, and I fell with relief.

※

The fires raged for days. At night the sky was red from flames that chased away the stars and blackness until there was no distinction between light and dark. By daybreak on Thursday, more than four days after the fire had begun, all of the flames had finally been put out. My family's home had been spared, although the fire had once come so close we'd thought we would have to camp out in Moorfields as hundreds already had done.

After a somber morning meal, my father asked me to come into his sitting room.

"Now we can resume our work," Father said. "Elizabeth, you still have the final three books to copy, I believe, as yesterday Lady Katherine's servant brought over the pages you've already written out. As soon as you have finished them, you will read the entire poem to me, so I may revise as I see fit. As for Signor Viviani, I'm most grateful to him and his master for their gracious assistance, but as you must understand, there's no need for his continued presence. Galileo's discovery has been lost to posterity, and the need for you and Signor Viviani to keep it safe is gone. He may return to Florence when he wishes, although he is, naturally, free to stay as our guest if he requires more time to recover from the physical hardships he has undergone."

He sat back in his chair, steepling his fingers. Shocked into silence, I stared at him for a long moment. It was evident from my father's calm expression that he believed what he had said: in his mind, nothing had changed, despite everything we had experienced. He expected the past to fly away like the bits of ash on the breeze outside.

But I wasn't that breeze anymore, blowing in whichever

direction my father commanded.

My dry eyes burned. "Father, I can't suffocate my true self or deny it any longer. I love natural philosophy—I need it as I need air to breathe. I'll write out the final books of *Paradise Lost* for you. And then I'll continue Galileo's investigations into the workings of the stars and the motions of the planets—"

"The young man," Father interrupted, an angry red suffusing his face. "You believe you've fallen in love with him. That explains your sudden inclination for astronomy."

I stood up, my chair scraping on the floorboards. At the sound, my father's head snapped in my direction, and I could almost believe he saw the determination on my face as I said, "I've loved the skies for as long as I can remember."

"What sort of nonsense is this?" Father demanded.

"I want to be a natural philosopher," I continued, my insides quaking as though I was about to be sick. But I didn't stop talking. "You have told me that liberty exists in our minds. Well, I choose to be free, and nothing you say will dissuade me."

Father's face crumpled and he dropped his head into his hands. "Then you've chosen a hard life, and I'm sorry for it. You will either have to live as a man or resign yourself to a lifetime of ridicule and scorn. Maybe it's my fault. If I hadn't brought you into men's matters . . ." He dragged in a shaky breath. "It's too late now. Fetch me the family Bible."

Wondering what he could possibly want with it, I retrieved it from the bookcase and set it on the writing table.

"Open it to the page of your birth," he said.

I flipped through the book until I found the proper page. There, in his cramped handwriting, my father had recorded the details of my entry into the world: *A daughter, Elizabeth, born this twenty-eighth day of March in the year of our Lord 1650.* The neighboring sheets contained other births and deaths—the arrivals of my siblings, the passing of my mother, my brother, and my first stepmother, followed by her and Father's baby daughter. All these beginnings and endings, small words that said so little but meant so much.

"The king has revised history," Father said, "by claiming the fire started from a stray ember in a baker's oven. The Duke of Lockton will be hailed as a hero until he's finally forgotten under the weight of the years. My internment will never be known. All traces of Galileo's discovery have been wiped clean. Now it's your turn to decide if you want to rewrite your life."

He hesitated. "You are my beloved child. But I must think of the good of the entire family. If you insist on pursuing your love for natural philosophy, then you'll expose the rest of us to scandal and condemnation. It will be difficult, if not impossible, for your sisters to find suitable husbands or employment. So if you must follow the longing of your mind, you can be a Milton no longer." He tapped the tabletop with his finger. "Choose—rip out your page or remain with me."

Tears filled my eyes. I knew what this meant. Once I tore out the page chronicling my birth, I would be erased from my family—forever. Elizabeth Milton would cease to exist. And who else I would grow into, I couldn't guess.

But I knew what I had to do.

Moving like a girl trapped in a dream, I felt my hand reach out for the Bible. I grabbed a corner of my birth page and pulled. I balled up the page in my hand, my heart beating fast.

Father let out a muffled sob, then gestured for me to bend down. I leaned close to him, letting his hands roam over my face. He moved slowly, as if he needed extra time to cast my features in stone in his mind. This time, I touched his face, too; the sharp planes of his cheeks, the wrinkle-grooved forehead. At last he sighed, as if satisfied, and his hands dropped to his lap.

"My head aches, and I must rest," he said. "We shall continue our work tomorrow. Once we're done with *Paradise Lost*, you may be on your way."

"Very well." My voice sounded strange to my ears—rusty, as if I hadn't used it in a long time. "But I must tell you, when the time comes for me to depart, I'll ask Anne if she wishes to leave with me."

Tears glimmered in his milky eyes. "I've always been glad for the friendship between the two of you." His voice cracked. "Good-bye, my Elizabeth."

I opened my mouth, but could not speak. I kissed his hand— the dear, age-spotted hand I loved so much, which had once been able to wield its own quill and which now must depend on others for almost everything. Quickly I slipped from the room and found Antonio standing in the hall.

"I heard everything," he said. "I'm sorry."

I moved into the circle of his arms, breathing in the mingled scents of smoke and sandalwood. "I'm no longer his daughter," I whispered to his shirtfront.

"Your father has set you free," he said softly, "as my parents did me, years ago. I promise, someday you'll be the stronger for it."

Numbly I stepped out of his arms. A part of me already knew

he spoke the truth. Perhaps someday the rest of me would, too. I swallowed down the lump in my throat, saying, "I think it's time."

He didn't need to ask what I meant. The fate of the vial had lain heavily on our minds for days, and the object itself had not once left my grasp. Even now, it was nestled in the pocket sewn into my underskirt—a steady presence that bumped against my leg when I moved.

"Let's walk and discuss this," Antonio said. "We can't take a chance of anyone overhearing."

Outside, the deserted street was half hidden by a lingering veil of smoke. We walked slowly, hand in hand, heading south into the heart of London. Everywhere I looked, I saw a dead city: houses with a single wall standing and all their windows blown out, holes where homes had once stood, clumps of melted metal and glass, the carcasses of dogs and cats who hadn't run away fast enough. It was almost impossible to guess where we were, for most of the city's landmarks had burned to the ground. I felt as though we were walking through a desert where everything looked the same, like leagues upon leagues of sand stretching to the horizon.

We had to clamber over piles of rubble. In some spots, the cobblestones were still hot, pressing heat through the soles of my shoes, and I had to bite back a cry of pain. We kept walking, Antonio and I, into that vast ruin of a city. The streets were mostly empty, except for a few people poking through twisted huddles of junk: cracked stones, burned timber, pieces of shattered glass glittering among them like diamonds. Most Londoners must still be camped out in the fields on the city's outskirts.

I pulled the vial from my pocket. Gleaming silver, it lay in my hand.

For a long moment, neither of us spoke. Then Antonio said in a ragged voice, "Signor Galilei's good name was ruined when the Church found him guilty of heresy because of his discoveries about the motions of celestial bodies. If the truth about the vial was known, then people would question the stories in the Bible—and the Bible's claims that the earth stands still. People could reexamine Signor Galilei's theories from a natural philosophical standpoint, not a religious one. His reputation could be restored."

I touched his shoulder gently. "Yes. But we can't trust people with the vial. The Church and governments will want it suppressed. Some people will be desperate to possess it for their own purposes. Others will have their hearts broken when they learn of its existence and doubt their faith." I took a deep breath. "It has to be destroyed."

Antonio bowed his head. "I know," he whispered. Then louder, "Maybe someday Signor Galilei's reputation will be salvaged by other means. Or the world will become tolerant enough or advanced enough that we can share this story with it."

"We haven't lost," I said. "We saved my father's life and his masterpiece—and now we both see the world with new eyes. That matters, Antonio. And we should write about Galileo's discovery, preserving it for future generations. The story isn't gone. But the day hasn't yet come when we can tell it to others."

Antonio looked up, his eyes strained. "You get rid of the vial. I—I can't."

Clutching the vial, I walked across the broken cobblestones.

Through the parting veil of smoke, the ruins of St. Paul's reared up. Many of the stones in the walls had shattered, leaving gaping holes through which the interior could be seen, a twisted mass of burned wood and melted metal. The stained glass rose window was gone—turned to liquid by the fire's heat, I guessed. The portico was in pieces, the big blocks of stone split asunder.

The cathedral's lead roof had melted, sending rivulets running down the sides of the building, leaving long, dark tracks in their wake. The masonry in the roof had crumbled entirely and fallen through the marble floor, exposing the crypt underneath; I could see the wreckage through the enormous holes in the walls. Flames were still flickering in the crypt—fed by the piles upon piles of papers and books and pamphlets stored there, I realized, remembering that one of our neighbors had said the city's printers and booksellers had placed their wares in the crypt, reasoning it was the safest place for them as the fire approached.

My throat closed. All those books—gone forever. The largest church in my country, a wreck of broken stone and twisted metal.

"My city's gone," I whispered. "This is a dead place now."

"No." Antonio took my face in his hands, tilting my chin so I had no choice but to look into his fierce eyes. "London will rise once more, and she'll be stronger than ever before. She will be reborn, a phoenix from the ashes. She can never be destroyed."

"You're right," I said, partly because I believed him, partly because I needed to. "London still lives."

I walked to the nearest hole in the wall. Dozens of feet below, flames danced in the crypt, a bowl of flickering red and orange. For a moment I stared at the flames, letting my mind empty.

Then I dropped the vial into the fire. It fell through the air, a slender arc of silver, before vanishing altogether.

It was a good place for the vial: in the darkness and the flames, surrounded by stone. I found it comforting to think of my countrymen someday sitting in pews in a rebuilt church, heads bowed in prayer, while the vial's melted remains lay below them. This was a union of faith and natural philosophy, these two subjects that seemed so incompatible. But perhaps they weren't, if we only knew how to open our eyes wider.

Antonio laid his arm across my shoulders, drawing me near to him. Linked by his touch, we crossed the ruined churchyard.

"At night, when I try to sleep," I said in a low voice, "I see Lady Katherine in my mind. She was such a kindhearted person, the first thoroughly decent aristocrat I ever met . . . and Robert killed her as though she were *nothing*."

"Perhaps to him she was," Antonio said.

"She will matter to me for the rest of my life," I said. "It's comforting to believe her soul is out there somewhere. In the heavens in the sky, maybe, or woven into the firmament of this earth for all time."

Only a few weeks ago, my comments would have terrified me. Now they no longer felt blasphemous, but good and right.

Antonio halted our progress, nodding at the sky. It was colored gray by the dome of smoke that continued to hover over the city. "The sun has risen again. The earth has continued to rotate on its axis. We're still spinning through the galaxy."

"The world hasn't stopped." I managed to smile.

"And we're alive and we're here together." His eyes were intent on mine. "I must know—what do you wish to do now that you're free? Whatever road you take, do you plan to travel it alone?"

My heart began pounding. I understood what he was asking me. "Whoever decides to walk with me must understand I've chosen a hard path."

He didn't drop his gaze. "I've never wanted an easy life, either. You might like Florence. It's a beautiful, learned city. My master is receptive to new ideas, whether they are philosophical or social. And if others can't accept you, we'll move on to the next place."

Would we be forced to wander as Adam and Eve had? Or would we someday be able to find a home? I looked at Antonio, and gladness welled in my heart until I imagined it would burst out of my chest. Whether we wandered or not, it didn't matter, for we would be together and studying the subjects that gave our lives meaning. "Antwerp grants freedom to all of its citizens," I said. "That might be a good city for us to try."

"We have a half-dozen languages between us and no Flemish," he said. "Oh, well. I've always liked a challenge."

I grinned at him. "And you still haven't shown me sunspots."

He threw his head back and laughed. "An oversight I will correct at the first opportunity."

Smiling, I stood on tiptoe to press my lips to his. We kissed again and again in the abandoned churchyard, while overhead the smoke hung like clouds. But when I closed my eyes and let darkness press against my lids, I could almost imagine Antonio and I stood beneath a sky full of stars.

Author's Note

Although *Traitor Angels* is a work of fiction, many of the characters and events in this book are factual. Please note that this section contains several spoilers, so read no further if you haven't finished the book!

Elizabeth, Antonio, Robert, Lady Katherine, Thomasine, Francis, Luce, Mr. Hade, and all of Robert's associates are fictional characters. Although everyone else was a real person and this story is woven around several real events, *Traitor Angels* is very much a work of fiction.

Today John Milton is generally regarded as one of the most influential political writers in English history. He was born in London in 1608 and attended the University of Cambridge, where he earned both bachelor's and master's degrees. In 1638, like many members of the gentleman class, he embarked on a "grand tour" of Europe. While in Florence, he managed to procure a meeting with Galileo Galilei, who had been sentenced to house arrest for life by the Italian Inquisitors. To this day, no one knows what the two men discussed. It's clear, however, that Milton admired Galileo, because he later commemorated the scientist in *Paradise Lost* and in his famous anticensorship tract, *Areopagitica*.

The popular image of Milton is that of a dour-faced Puritan, but in reality he was a complicated man who was far ahead of his time. He smoked and drank; when he was sighted, he carried a sword; and, unlike many Puritans, he didn't think entertainment was inherently sinful but considered it an essential part of life. He really did believe that religion had no place in government. The revolutionary ideas he expresses in this book are based on his writings.

By 1666, when *Traitor Angels* takes place, Milton was a political outcast. A staunch antimonarchist, he had served as Oliver Cromwell's Latin Secretary when England operated as a commonwealth and a protectorate. During this time, Milton went completely blind, a condition that provided plenty of fodder for his numerous political enemies throughout Europe. He became known as "the notorious Milton" and was castigated for his political ideals and his four divorce tracts.

When the government collapsed and Parliament invited Charles II to return to England in 1660, Milton's life hung in the balance. He placed his three daughters, Anne, Mary, and Deborah, in the care of their maternal grandmother and went into hiding.

Some members of Parliament wanted Milton to be hanged as a traitor, but he was spared—no one now knows why, though many suspect that the intervention of influential friends, including the poet Andrew Marvell, kept Milton alive. After he came out of hiding, he was arrested and briefly imprisoned. Upon his release, he moved to new lodgings with his daughters. Three years later, he married his third wife, the much younger Elizabeth "Betty" Minshull.

When the plague struck London in 1665, Milton's family fled to a nearby village, Chalfont St. Giles. It's unknown when they returned to London; many scholars guess it was sometime in February–March 1666. Since the exact date is unclear, I decided to let the Miltons remain in Chalfont for a few months longer.

During this time, Milton was completing the work that would become his most famous: the epic poem *Paradise Lost*. The version of *Paradise Lost* that appears in *Traitor Angels* is the original ten-book 1667 edition. A later edition, published in 1674 and divided into twelve books, is the one commonly studied today. The poem itself is generally considered a masterpiece, both for its beautiful language and for its portrayal of Satan as a charismatic, brave, but ultimately evil character. Intriguingly, the poem's only contemporary personage is Galileo, whom Milton refers to as "the Tuscan Artist." In this book, when Milton dictates the "Tuscan Artist" section to Elizabeth, she forms her own interpretation of the passage. Although *Paradise Lost* is rich in allegories, there's no indication that Milton hid a secret scientific message within its lines. The poem that directs Elizabeth, Antonio, and Robert to St. Paul's is not Milton's; I wrote it myself.

Milton dictated all of *Paradise Lost*—some say to his nephews and family friends; others say to his daughters Mary and Deborah. The two women were uncommonly well educated for females of their time. Both could read and write, and some historians believe they also knew foreign languages. (Milton himself was fluent in Latin, Greek, Italian, and Hebrew.) There's conflicting evidence, however, that says Milton only taught them how to write foreign words phonetically, so he could dictate to them without their having any idea what he was saying. I decided to adhere to this latter theory, as I believe it's in keeping with Milton's character. The classroom lessons Milton teaches Elizabeth are based on the instruction he provided for his male students when he was a young teacher.

Anne, his eldest daughter, was illiterate. Although her exact medical condition has never been identified, we know she was lame, had a severe speech impediment, and apparently was mentally disabled.

Sometime during 1669–1670, Milton's three daughters left home to become apprentices in the lace-making industry. Deborah didn't last long in the profession; she became a lady's companion in Ireland. She later married a weaver and had a daughter named Elizabeth. Mary remained single, while Anne married a master builder and died young, in childbirth. As for Betty Minshull Milton, she eventually sold off many of her late husband's copyrights and died in 1727.

Charles II probably lived a life filled with more highs and lows than any other English monarch. As a teenager, he fought in the Civil War but was eventually ordered to leave England by his father, who feared that the tide of the war was turning against them and was concerned for his eldest son's safety. Charles then spent over a decade in exile in Europe. At nineteen, he had a child, his first, with his mistress Lucy Barlow, who was also known as

Lucy Walter. Although rumors of their marriage dogged Charles II for years, there's no proof the two were ever wed. Lucy died in Paris in 1658. Their son, James, adopted a guardian's surname. After his father was crowned, this James Crofts was made the Duke of Monmouth. He later married a Scottish noblewoman and took on her surname, becoming James Scott.

Charles II really was fascinated by "natural philosophy"—the seventeenth-century term for science. He maintained a private laboratory at his palace and carried out numerous experiments. After he died in 1685, his younger brother, James, the Duke of York, became king. Monmouth, who had been trying to prove his parents had been married and he was his father's legitimate heir, openly opposed his uncle's ascension to the throne. He staged an unsuccessful rebellion and was beheaded for treason less than six months after his father's death. Per the etiquette of the time, Monmouth tipped his executioner six guineas before baring his neck for the blade. Aspects of Monmouth's personality, and of Satan himself in *Paradise Lost*, inspired me to create Robert, who burns to rule just as fiercely as they did.

George Villiers, the second Duke of Buckingham, was raised alongside the young man who would become King Charles II after his father, the best friend—and, some say, the lover—of Charles I was assassinated. Buckingham fought on the royalist side during the Civil War and lived in exile in Europe with the future king for several years. After the Restoration, he was involved with a number of political intrigues, and was imprisoned in the Tower for various charges on a few occasions. He really did bring in a supposed unicorn's horn to a Royal Society meeting. He died in 1687.

Samuel Pepys, who after this story's timeframe became the secretary of naval affairs, is one of the most famous diarists of all time. His journal offers a fascinating glimpse into seventeenth-century life in London. A member of the Royal Society, he was also instrumental in carrying out naval reforms. At the king's request, he stayed in London throughout the plague. When the Great Fire of 1666 occurred, he personally brought news of the blaze to the king. He really did bury a wheel of Parmesan cheese in his garden to keep it safe from the encroaching fire. He died in 1703.

The Royal Society, a pioneering scientific organization, was founded in 1660. Its original patron was Charles II. The Royal Society was the first of its kind; previously, scientists had jealously guarded their own discoveries. This group, however, encouraged the open sharing of ideas. The members met weekly to discuss scientific advances and their own individual experiments. Any mention of religion or politics was forbidden. The Royal Society still exists today.

Robert Hooke, who demonstrates his experiments on Galileo's theory of gravity in this book, was the Royal Society's curator. In real life, during the summer of 1664 he dropped objects from the roof of St. Paul's Cathedral to test Galileo's postulations. He was a gifted engineer and originated the physics principle known as Hooke's law, which states that when expanding or compressing a spring a certain distance, the force needed is proportional to distance.

Robert Boyle, who shows Elizabeth, Antonio, and Robert around the Royal Society meeting room, is considered the father of modern chemistry. He conducted a series of experiments with air pumps Hooke constructed that led to the creation of Boyle's law—namely, that the volume of a confined gas varies inversely with the pressure applied to it.

Galileo Galilei is often called the father of modern science. His work in astronomy, physics, and science methodology and his trial before the Italian Inquisition have become legendary. While a young mathematics professor at the University of Padua, he really did take a *riposo* in an underground room with two of his friends. This room, as was common with country villas during this time, was ventilated and cooled by a conduit that supplied wind from a waterfall in a nearby mountain cave. When the three men woke from their nap two hours later, they experienced cramps, chills, intense headaches, hearing loss, and muscle lethargy. Within days, both of Galileo's friends died. Although Galileo survived, his health was affected for the remainder of his life.

During Galileo's time, people believed that meteors, or falling stars, were atmospheric disturbances, similar to lightning. Apart from his discovery of the meteorite, Galileo's inventions and scientific theories presented in this book are real.

Vincenzo Viviani was a brilliant mathematician who became Galileo's assistant and secretary in 1639 when he was seventeen. He lived with Galileo until the latter's death. Later he became the court mathematician to the Grand Duke of Tuscany, Ferdinand II, and was one of the first members of the duke's experimental academy, the Accademia del Cimento. He tirelessly tried to repair Galileo's reputation and convince the Catholic Church to pardon the scientist but was unsuccessful. He died childless in 1703 at the age of eighty-one and was buried with his beloved teacher, in accordance with his wishes.

Antonio's telescope is based on one Galileo himself built and gave to Cosimo II de' Medici, the Grand Duke of Tuscany from 1609 to 1621.

The Great Fire of London began in the early hours of Sunday, September 2, 1666. Although no one knows exactly what caused the blaze, it's commonly believed that a stray ember from baker Thomas Farriner's ovens started it. Farriner provided biscuits for the Royal Navy, and therefore he really did know Samuel Pepys.

London, which hadn't had rain for nearly a year, was a powder keg waiting to explode. When the fire overtook London Bridge, a number of its residents escaped by jumping into the Thames, just as Elizabeth and Antonio do.

When the fire was finally extinguished by Thursday morning, the city was a ruin—a hundred thousand people were left homeless and four-fifths of all of the property in London had been destroyed. The country's largest church, St. Paul's, was decimated. Christopher Wren, who served on the real-life commission to renovate the church, became extensively involved in rebuilding the city, and designed another St. Paul's, which still stands today.

Like London, Milton's and Galileo's reputations have undergone a rebirth of sorts, too. Milton, the one-time "notorious" political pariah who died in genteel poverty, is now widely considered one of the most important writers in English history. Galileo's name was blackened for centuries. It wasn't until 1992, after a thirteen-year-long investigation into the Italian Inquisition's case against Galileo, that Pope John Paul II formally acknowledged that the Church had erred in condemning Galileo for asserting the earth revolves around the sun. Although the Church has reversed its standing in Galileo's case, struggles such as those Galileo encountered hundreds of years ago in attempting to reconcile science and religion continue to confront all of us to this very day.

Selected Bibliography

Ackroyd, Peter. *London: The Biography*. New York: Nan A. Talese / Doubleday, 2001.

Beer, Anna. *Milton: Poet, Pamphleteer, and Patriot*. New York: Bloomsbury Press, 2008.

Bevan, Bryan. *James, Duke of Monmouth*. London: Robert Hale, 1973.

Black, Christopher F. *The Italian Inquisition*. New Haven: Yale University Press, 2009.

The Bodleian Library in the Seventeenth Century: Guide to an Exhibition Held During the Festival of Britain, 1951. Oxford: Bodleian Library, 1951.

Boschiero, Luciano. "Post-Galilean Thought and Experiment in Seventeenth-Century Italy: The Life and Work of Vincenzo Viviani." *History of Science* 43, no. 1 (March 2005): 77–100.

Bryson, Bill, ed. *Seeing Further: The Story of Science, Discovery and the Genius of the Royal Society*. New York: William Morrow, 2010.

Dolnick, Edward. *The Clockwork Universe: Isaac Newton, the Royal Society, and the Birth of the Modern World*. New York: HarperCollins, 2011.

Evelyn, John. *The Diary of John Evelyn*. Edited by John Bowle. Oxford: Oxford University Press, 1983.

Fraser, Antonia. *Royal Charles: Charles II and the Restoration*. New York: Alfred A. Knopf, 1979.

Gribbin, John. *The Fellowship: Gilbert, Bacon, Harvey, Wren, Newton, and the Story of a Scientific Revolution*. Woodstock, NY: Overlook Press, 2007.

Hanson, Neil. *The Great Fire of London: In That Apocalyptic Year, 1666*. Hoboken, NJ: John Wiley & Sons, 2002.

Heilbron, J. L. *Galileo*. Oxford: Oxford University Press, 2010.

Hill, Christopher. *Milton and the English Revolution*. New York: Viking Press, 1978.

Hollis, Leo. *London Rising: The Men Who Made Modern London*. New York: Walker, 2008.

Jones, Nigel H. *Tower: An Epic History of the Tower of London*. London: Hutchison, 2011; New York: St. Martin's Press, 2012.

Lewalski, Barbara K. *The Life of John Milton: A Critical Biography*. Malden, MA: Blackwell, 2000.

Milton, John. *Areopagitica*. 1644. In Milton, *The Riverside Milton*, 997–1024.

———. "Doctrine and Discipline of Divorce." 1644. In Milton, *The Riverside Milton*, 930–976.

———. *Eikonoklastes*. 1650. In Milton, *The Riverside Milton*, 1078–1095.

———. "Of True Religion." 1673. In Milton, *The Riverside Milton*, 1151–1155.

———. *Paradise Lost: A Poem Written in Ten Books*. Transcribed and edited by John T. Shawcross and Michael Lieb. Pittsburgh, PA: Duquesne University Press, 2007.

———. "The Readie and Easie Way to Establish a Free Commonwealth." 1660. In Milton, *The Riverside Milton*, 1136–1149.

———. "The Reason of Church-Government Urg'd Against Prelaty." 1642. In Milton, *The Riverside Milton*, 903–925.

———. *The Riverside Milton*. Edited by Roy Flannagan. Boston: Houghton Mifflin, 1998.

———. "The Second Defense of the English People." 1654. In Milton, *The Riverside Milton*, 1097–1118.

Ogg, David. *England in the Reign of Charles II*. Oxford: Oxford University Press, 1934, 1955, 1956.

Ollard, Richard. *The Image of the King: Charles I and Charles II*. New York: Atheneum, 1979.

Parkes, Joan. *Travel in England in the Seventeenth Century*. London: Oxford University Press, 1925.

Pepys, Samuel. *The Diary of Samuel Pepys*. Vol. 6, *1665*, and Vol. 7, *1666*. Edited by Robert Latham and William Matthews. Berkeley: University of California Press, 1970.

Picard, Liza. *Restoration London: From Poverty to Pets, from Medicine to Magic, from Slang to Sex, from Wallpaper to Women's Rights*. New York: Weidenfeld & Nicolson, 1997.

Porter, Stephen. *Pepys's London: Everyday Life in London 1650–1703*. Gloucestershire: Amberley, 2011.

Sobel, Dava. *Galileo's Daughter: A Historical Memoir of Science, Faith, and Love*. New York: Walker, 1999.

Sprat, Thomas. *History of the Royal Society*. Edited with critical apparatus by Jackson I. Cope and Harold Whitmore Jones. St. Louis: Washington University Press, 1958, 1966.

Tames, Richard. *A Traveller's History of Oxford*. New York: Interlink Books, 2003.

Thurley, Simon. *Whitehall Palace: An Architectural History of the Royal Apartments, 1240–1698*. New Haven: Yale University Press in association with Historical Royal Palaces, 1999.

Tinniswood, Adrian. *By Permission of Heaven: The Story of the Great Fire of London*. London: Pimlico/Random House, 2004.

Wilson, Derek. *The Tower: The Tumultuous History of the Tower of London from 1078*. New York: Charles Scribner's Sons, 1979.

Wootton, David. *Galileo: Watcher of the Skies*. New Haven: Yale University Press, 2010.

Acknowledgments

So many people to thank! As always, I'm grateful to my editor, Kristin Daly Rens, who is as brilliant as she is kind and whose editorial letters I simultaneously look forward to and dread because she catches every single misstep. Kristin, thank you for making me work so hard. *Ich bin fest davon überzeugt das wir dazu bestimmt waren zusammen Zuarbeiten. Das wir beide Deutschland und Paradise Lost lieben war lediglich das Tüpfelchen auf dem i.* Thanks for letting me indulge my Miltonic urges and name a character in your honor. For those wondering, Kristin and Lady Katherine share surnames, fabulous hair, and steel spines, but the similarities end there.

Many thanks to everyone at Balzer + Bray/HarperCollins, including Alessandra Balzer, Donna Bray, Nellie Kurtzman, Jenna Lisanti, and Megan Barlog in marketing, and designer Michelle Taormina for a gorgeous design and a book jacket that

I cannot stop calling "my preeeeeecious." Big thanks to Caroline Sun in publicity for promoting my books, making sure my events go smoothly, and trading recipes and pictures of our little ones. Smash cakes for the win! I'm grateful to copy editor Bethany Reis for all of her hard work and to copy editor Janet Fletcher, who probably needed a glass of wine after the amount of fact checking she had to do. Special effects artist Sean Freeman created a cover that made me gasp the first time I saw it. And a special thanks to Kelsey Murphy, who read early drafts of *Traitor Angels* and helped me figure out how to make *Paradise Lost* more accessible for readers who are unfamiliar with the poem.

I'm grateful to everyone at Adams Literary, including Josh Adams and Samantha Bagood, and especially my agent, Tracey Adams. There's no one else I'd rather have in my corner than you, Tracey. Thanks for always looking out for me—and for letting me name a character after you!

I could not have written *Traitor Angels* without the assistance of several experts. Hugh Jenkins, professor of English at Union College, sparked my fascination with *Paradise Lost* when I took his seminar course on John Milton during my senior year. When I began researching this novel, Hugh's advice on Milton, seventeenth-century British literature, and resources was invaluable. Hugh, thanks for letting me pick your brain and for (patiently) answering my many questions. I'll always cherish the memory of coteaching a class with you on *Paradise Lost*'s Book Ten when I returned to campus to serve as the spring term's Alumna Writer.

Cristina Della Coletta, dean of the Division of Arts and Humanities at the University of California, San Diego, graciously translated John Milton's Italian sonnet for me and provided valuable insight into Milton's grasp of the Italian language. Greg Peck, assistant professor of horticulture at Virginia Polytechnic Institute and State University, advised me on botany, especially apple trees. My cousin, John Lewis, PhD, spoke to me at length about seventeenth-century Protestantism, helped me wrap my mind around Puritanism, and translated passages into biblical and modern Hebrew for me. My brother, Paul Blankman, helped me track down historically accurate terms (Paul, I still owe you for "sumpters").

My mother, Lynn Brostrom Blankman, has been my first reader since I started writing stories at age four. Mom, thanks for saying all the things I didn't want to hear but needed to. And for going over and over the historical timeline with me ("One more time, Anne, when did Milton meet Galileo?"). My agency sister, Sara B. Larson, is always ready to read a manuscript and isn't afraid to tell me the truth, in her sweet, tactful way ("Anne, this is just my opinion and feel free to take it or leave it, but this part doesn't really make sense. . . ."). You were spot-on, every time. Lynne Matson, owner of a phone with the most unintentionally funny autocorrect in the world, read an early draft and offered excellent advice.

My father, Peter Blankman, spoke candidly to me about his experiences with severe vision loss. Dad, you probably won't believe this, but some of my favorite childhood memories include reading books to you and taking you for walks around our neighborhood. I'll always be grateful to you for being so tough.

My husband and best friend, Mike Cizenski, talked with me for hours about the Royal Society, Galileo, and seventeenth-century science. Mike, I hope I made your electrical engineer's heart proud. My daughter, Kirsten, was only four when I began working on this book, but her fascination with the night sky convinced me to turn Elizabeth from a poet into a budding scientist. Special thanks to Mike and Kirsten for following me all over England while I researched this book. To my in-laws, Richard and Julie Cizenski, who took care of Kirsten so I could go on a book tour and who always cheer me on.

The relationship between my lifelong friend Alissa Murray Orzea and her late brother, Scott Murray, inspired the dynamic between Elizabeth and Anne Milton. Alissa, whenever I feel weak, I think of Scott's determination to lead an independent life near his beloved Disney World and I immediately feel stronger. I'm honored to have grown up alongside him.

Thanks to my coworkers at the York County Virginia Public Library System, especially Pat Riter, who remains the ILL goddess. To the booksellers, teachers, librarians, and readers—you are wonderful. As a librarian myself, I know how hard librarians work to put books into patrons' hands, and I'm deeply grateful for all you do. Thanks also to Becca Fowler, who designed beautiful *Traitor Angels* tote bags. To the bloggers, especially Hannah McBride of the Irish Banana, who put together an amazing blog tour; Patri and Anasheh of the Fantastic Flying Book Club; Jess of Read My Breath Away; and Danielle of Love at the First Page. A special thanks to the wonderful Sasha Alsberg, who hosted the reveal for the *Traitor Angels* book trailer. I'm grateful to many booksellers, especially Ward Tefft of Chop Suey Books in Richmond, Virginia; Janet Hutchison of the Open Door Bookstore in Schenectady, New York; and Rachel Strolle of Anderson's

Bookshop in Napier, Illinois. Many thanks also to librarian Serena Butch, who helped me find books to read when I was a little kid, served as my mentor when I was in library school, and has hosted me several times at her library over the past few years. Thanks, Serena, for showing me that books are magic.

And thanks to the men behind this book's title. I have loved John Milton's poetry ever since I began reading it as a college student. As the daughter of a man who has dealt with significant eye trauma, I can understand a little of what Milton's battle with blindness must have been like—and his determination to continue writing despite it fills me with awe. To Galileo Galilei, whose deposition before the Italian Inquisition breaks my heart every time I read it and who kept inventing and experimenting long after he lost his sight. And to Vincenzo Viviani, whose steadfast dedication to his mentor and unsuccessful attempts to clear his name brought me to tears. You three men have haunted me, and I'm grateful to you for teaching me to view the world through a new lens.